Crimes of a Guilty Land

—⚬⚬⚬—

Brooke Stewart

ISBN: 1481890999

ISBN-13: 9781481890991

LCCN: 2013900666

Createspace Independent Publishing Platform

North Charleston, South Carolina

This book is dedicated to the memory
of my dear friend Fred Gilbert

Author's Notes

───❧───

I am most indebted to my wife Maggie for putting up with the hours of research and writing.

And I am also indebted to my good friend Harry Anderson who encouraged me and even prodded me to complete this novel. He read the first manuscripts and provided very helpful advice.

I am not a historian and this book is not intended to provide a history lesson. This is a work of fiction in which the characters and events are set in specific periods of American history.

Consequently the reader will encounter some factual characters. I believe that their names will serve to identify them, as most of them are well known. The actions surrounding these people are for the most part based on historic events.

The Roger Hart and Simon Gladstone fictional characters were inspired by two people who lived in the nineteenth century.

For Roger Hart I drew just a little on the life of Alexander Morrell. Morrell was a nineteenth century New England Baptist minister who was at the forefront of the move towards the education of the children of slaves and freed slaves. He and other New England Baptists opened a school in Harpers Ferry West Virginia, and that school became Storer College.

The character of Simon Gladstone has some of the characteristics of John Colby - a nineteenth century New England evangelist.

Apart from that, all of the characters are imaginary.

The novel follows a retired teacher by the name of Brownie, as he tries to write down his life story. He moves back and fro from his time back to various important events that helped to shape his life. Consequently the reader will need to keep on his or her toes, so to speak, to keep up with him.

My hope is that the reader will not only enjoy that experience, but might just share Brownie's dream at the end.

Brooke Stewart January 2013

Prologue
Narragansett Bay, Rhode Island, August 1825

The young boy skipped along the sandy shore, just above the water level. The tide had reached its lowest level for the day and was just beginning to turn. He was fascinated by the way he left tracks in the sand and every few skips he stopped and looked down to see an impression of his feet form under his weight. Looking back at his tracks he was impressed to see that each step further back was less evident than the proceeding one as the water seeped back in. Just a few yards back along the way, the tracks disappeared completely and it was as if he had never been there. As if no one had ever been there. For a while he stood still and slowly counted to twenty before stepping back to watch the most recent tracks beginning to fill as the water seeped up through the sand. Before that happened however, the turning tide swept in over his feet and obliterated all of the tracks. The water was warm and he knelt down and ran his hands through the water. Putting his hand to his mouth, he tasted its saltiness.

Roger Hart felt, quite simply, the happiest he had ever felt. At the age of twelve, this was his first trip to the seaside and everything was so different to his home just fifty or so miles to the north in Glocester. There, all he knew were open fields alternating with forest groves and streams, and one small village after another. Roger had heard about the shore many times but could never have imagined the beauty of the place. Even the air had saltiness about it, while the breeze coming off the bay was cool and refreshing. Back at the farm any movement of the air was usually hot and humid at this time of year.

His mother had often told him about her sister's house down on the shore, and how wonderful a place it was to visit in the mid-summer heat, but these few days had turned out to be more than he had even dared to dream about.

The boy resumed his skipping and running, this time through the water. A flock of black and white sea gulls circled overhead and cried out as they alternately soared above the waves and then came down to catch a small fish swimming too near to the surface. Feeling a little tired from his running, Roger walked back out of the water and sat down on the dry sand. It was warm, and he lay back and closed his eyes and listened to the gulls. A cloud that had for just a few moments shut out the sun passed by and allowed the full warmth to reach Roger again and his pleasure was once again complete. There was no one else on the beach and he felt as if this was his own property - that it had been put there for his pleasure and for his alone.

"No, no, stop won't you! Just get off of me."

The shout was jarring and broke into Roger's daydreams. He was not alone after all. Sitting up he looked all around but could see no one. Another cry came from behind him and he realized that it was coming from some dunes at the edge of the beach and some thirty yards from the water's edge. The cry scared him more than a little.

But the curiosity of youth overcame his fear and he stood up and ran to the dunes. Hearing another cry from a dune to his left, he approached it as quietly as he could, and knelt down to look into it. A young man and woman were lying in the sand. The woman was on her back and the man was lying on top of her, struggling to hold her down. As she beat his back with her clenched fists and cried for him to stop, so he pushed her shoulders all the more into the sand. Soon she was screaming again for him to let her go.

Roger had never experienced anything like the anger and fear that was coming from this young woman. Instinct told him to run off as fast as he could, but instead, his curiosity held him still, crouching in the thick grass that grew around the dune.

The couple continued to struggle and the more she tried to free herself, the more aggressive the man became, until he suddenly slapped her hard across the face and placed his hand over her mouth.

"Shut up, will you!"

Roger now had no idea what to do. The pleasure of the beach was completely gone and he felt scared for the woman and for himself. His mouth had gone dry and his legs seemed to be tied together and he wished that he had not walked so far from his Aunt's house. Deciding that the best action really was to quietly move away, he forced his legs to move. But what happened next caused him to freeze again.

The woman had thrown her arms back on to the sand and there she had found a good size rock. With the strength of someone fearing for her life, she had brought the rock down on the back of the man's head. Blood began to run down his neck and on to the shoulders of her unbuttoned white blouse.

In a rage of anger the man began to beat the woman across the head. Throwing any fear to the sea breeze, Roger took off across the sand as fast as he could. And in his fury, the man remained unaware that anyone had witnessed the events of that morning.

Running through the dry powdery sand above the high tide level was tiring, but Roger gave little thought to that until the ache in his legs forced him to slow down and look back. There was no sign of anyone back in the dunes. No one was chasing after him. Only the seagulls kept up their noise and continued to soar and dive looking for food. Had he imagined it all? No, there was little chance of that. It had been all too real. Perhaps the man's head wound had not been as bad as Roger had thought though, and maybe the man and woman had just got up and walked away. And as much as he hoped that that was the case, something told him otherwise.

A hundred yards or so before his Aunt's house, Roger crossed over the shore road and gathered his thoughts. The house was a simple saltbox with weathered shingles on the walls and the roof. Whereas the Glocester farmhouse was built on a thick stone foundation, this little house stood on large square stones with gaps between them. His Aunt had explained to an incredulous Roger that sometimes during a storm, the sea would come right up over the beach, across the road, and wash under the house. Two days ago that had worried him a little, but now his mind was racing with other fears.

His mother was standing at the door, with her arms crossed and staring at Roger as he approached. He knew that she was angry and that she was worried because he had been away from the house for too long. Would she understand what he had seen? And for that matter, what had he seen and just what was it that the man and the woman were doing in that dune? Whatever it was, he knew that it was not right. It would probably add to his mother's anger and get him into even more trouble.

And so he decided to not tell her about what he had seen, and the first of many lies was told. He'd had a wonderful morning and had just not thought about time and how far he had walked, and how he had had the beach to himself. But his tale was not convincing and he knew it. There is a look that mothers can give that tells all, including doubts as to honesty.

The next morning was taken up with breakfast and then packing their few possessions and in preparing to say their goodbyes. The journey down from Glocester had been an adventure for young Roger and he was expecting the return to be just as exciting. Just like the previous days, this day was warm and sunny and he sat down on a bench near the back porch to soak in the sun and wait for the trap that would provide the first leg of the journey.

"What? Dead you say!"

For the second time in as many days, a loud voice broke through his daydreams. This time it was his aunt's voice.

"I am afraid so. Her body was found last evening in one of the dunes way up the beach. She had been beaten to death and it seems that she and a man had been..."

Roger had come around the side of the house and joined his mother and aunt. The young man who had ridden out of town and up to the house suddenly looked embarrassed as he faced the two women and young boy.

"...well, you know what I mean. Her brother went looking for her when she didn't come home for supper, and he found her body. And then it seems that young Jimmy Penny has disappeared. He was last seen yesterday morning. It's no secret that he was keen on Nancy and I am of the opinion that he got carried away and when she resisted him, he lost control and killed her. So now he's gone and done a bunk and run-off. Anyway that's how I see it."

Roger felt his legs turn soft and his head begin to spin. His mouth was dryer than he had ever known. His worst thoughts were coming around and he felt fear and he felt guilt. The woman was dead.

"The question now is whether either of you two good ladies saw anything of Nancy or Jimmy yesterday? Your house would be the nearest this side of the dunes and no one saw them from the other side. Did you hear anything at all? And how about you boy, did you see or hear anything"

Both of the women told as to how they had not seen or heard the couple, and how they had been wrapped up in their time together since that was a rarity these days. The boy had gone for a long walk but had not said anything about seeing anything unusual.

"Is that right boy? You walked along that beach and saw and heard nothing?"

Roger tried to say that that was true but the dryness of his mouth made his words unintelligible.

"What? Don't mumble boy. If you saw anything just tell us, you won't be in any trouble at all."

Somehow Roger got the words out, saying that he had not seen anything. Although this man had said that he would not be in trouble, Roger now had a great fear of this man Jimmy who had acted so violently and, for that matter, also of his mother if she found out that he had lied. And then there was his father when they got home. Roger worried what would he do.

"Well, it's all very strange if you ask me. We found two sets of tracks coming from the road into the dune, and that would be Jimmy and Nancy. Then there are tracks going off through the sand to the east and up to the road, and we think that was Jimmy leaving the scene. But the strange thing is that obviously Nancy never left the dune, but there are other tracks around that finally go west and up to the road. Either there was a third person involved or just maybe those tracks were from sometime earlier. The sand is pretty fine up there and it blows around and it gets hard to tell. Tell me boy, you sure you never saw nothing?"

Roger shook his head and looked away, afraid that the truth was somehow printed on his face. Before the man could ask another question, Roger's mother took the boy by the hand into the house.

"I think that that is enough for my son sir. I am sure that this Penny man will turn up."

Roger knew that more questions would be coming from his mother and that this was not the end of things. But somehow he maintained his story as those questions came, and in the coming days also repeated it more than a few times to his father.

Two days after the return home, Roger had been cleaning up in the dairy shed and was about to come into the kitchen to wash up when he heard his parents arguing. This was a rarity as neither of his parents usually raised their voices at each other. Taking a quick look through the window, Roger saw his mother sitting at the table with her head in her hands and obviously crying. His father was standing over the stove waving his arms in anger.

"I tell you that the boy knows more than he is saying and he is turning out a pack of lies. My mind spins when I think about what he may have seen going on in that sand dune. And then the murder, did he see that too? I say yes he did and now he is too scared to tell us. I tell you mother, he better tell it to us clean and he better tell us right now."

But mother held on to her hopes and stood up for Roger and said as how the boy was just scared and was surely telling the truth. And probably the more he was questioned, the more scared he became and so the more he fumbled around and looked like he was telling fibs.

"Fibs, woman? Fibs? I am talking bare faced lies here not fibs."

And with those words, he had taken his wife's shoulders in both hands shaking her as though trying to loosen up her reasoning. Roger had never seen his father either act or heard him speak like this before. And to make it worse, somehow all of this was his fault.

Without thinking, Roger yelled out at the top of his voice for his father to stop, and then he ran as fast as he could across the farmyard and down the lane towards the village. As much as he wanted to tell his mother all that he had seen, there was now the added shame of admitting all of the lies and then the consequent punishment. But there was also a growing fear of this man Jimmy Penny then coming after him. Lord knew what he might do to Roger after what he had done to that poor woman.

The next morning, father apologized to both Roger and his mother, and he tried to explain how he thought that Roger knew more than he was saying and that the way things were going, he might just get them all into a pack of trouble. Mother did her best to smooth things over and to get back to normal. The days went by until word came from his aunt that Jimmy

Penny had been found in Providence and had confessed to the murder. When questioned as to whether anyone else had been mixed up in the matter, Penny acknowledged that he and Nancy had been alone and no one else had been involved and that he had not even seen anyone else. Apparently he had told everyone that now he was full of remorse and how he would curse that day for the rest of his life, adding that he supposed that would not be long now.

The opinion around the farm was that, that was now the end of the matter, and that it should not be brought up again. Mother told herself and the family that the boy had obviously been telling the truth. Father said that he could accept that now, but gave Roger a look that clearly told that he still held doubts. Life around the farm returned to near normal for all of them. Except that Roger could not put some scenes out of his mind.

Roger had seen the violence and passion of Penny take hold over his actions. He had seen and heard the fear in Nancy. He had seen the blows and the blood. And he had seen the total loss of control as Penny had begun to beat the girl. But somehow worse than all of that, was that his father had acted in a way that also scared Roger - it was just too close to the way that Penny had acted.

Roger had heard his father shouting and had seen his father shaking his mother by the shoulders and he had seen his mother crying. And that was all Roger's fault.

Over the coming years the nightmares took on different forms. Sometimes it was his mother and father in the dune and sometimes it was Penny and his mother in the farmhouse. Even when he reached an age where he worked out what had been going on in that sand dune Roger could not escape the fear and the guilt.

Through his school years and into his calling as a Baptist Minister, that day on the beach haunted him. What had begun as an idyllic morning on the beach would haunt him for the rest of his life, bringing periods of depression and insecurity.

And yet, over the years, Roger Hart managed to touch many people at a deep level. I certainly know that he touched me.

1.

December 8th 1941,
Dartford, West Virginia

———⚮———

Yesterday I celebrated my seventy-fifth birthday.

It was not really much of a celebration because no one visits me anymore. I suppose that is one of the consequences of outliving friends and family. My Grandma Annie, who was very special to me, died when she was seventy-five. So this year's celebration for me on reaching the same age was a little sobering. My dear wife and my boy died a few years ago, and my grandson Adam lives down in Atlanta somewhere. He is a good boy but I don't see much of him.

But I did celebrate yesterday, and I enjoyed some cake that I bought for the occasion. I also remembered that some time ago I had put away some special coffee, and so I brewed some of that to go along with the cake. My goodness, but I had a good time with that little meal and I played all of my Louis Armstrong records on my trusty old phonograph. I was careful not to play them too loud of course, because the walls of my room are rather thin. I reckon that it was a pretty good celebration after all.

Sitting back all alone and with my eyes closed, listening to the musical stories coming from Armstrong's horn, caused me to think back and to realize that I may not have much time left to tell my story - that is the story behind my name. And I do believe that it is a story that is worth telling.

I had quite a nasty experience a few nights ago. I can tell you that experience shook me, and I have been thinking as to how things are today compared to how they were before I was born. I am afraid that not much has changed.

My name is Brownie, and people sometimes ask me why I have such a name. It's a fair question as I have never met another man with this name, but it is also a question that cannot be easily answered.

Some people, who do not know me well, assume that my surname is Brown and that I picked up a kind of nickname. Others assume that my name is related to the color of my skin. Neither is true. The fact of the matter is that my name is closely tied with what was probably the worst struggle in American history. And in spite of having lived through the Great War and being faced now with another one in Europe, I do believe that statement to be correct.

The Great War came to an end as did the terrible depression that followed it. People eventually moved on after those crises. But the struggle that my family lived through has never fully come to a close.

Europe is at war again and I have seen the photographs and the movie news of men in black uniforms and brown uniforms jack-booting in parade after parade. I have heard their leaders shouting and just about screaming at the tops of their voices about something or another. The aggressive bullies and bigots of the world are at work again and lovely innocent people are being killed or forced to run for their lives just because of their religion or the color of their skin or where they came from or whatever else simply does not sit well with these dictators. And every photograph and every news reel and every radio broadcast of those happenings bring back memories of how bad things were for me and my family.

And then just a few days ago, like I already mentioned, I had that bad experience. It did not just remind me of those past days but in a very real and even physical way, it took me back there. That is one of the reasons I have for trying to think back now and write my story. It was a bad thing that just happened and when my mind is settled I will try to write about that.

But first I want to try to put down my story. As hard as that might turn out to be!

All of my working life I have been a teacher and I have always enjoyed writing. I still have my trusty old Underwood typewriter that has been with me since forever it seems! When I was eighteen and nineteen I used to keep journals. They will certainly help in putting this in some order. Then when I was in my early twenties I felt the inclination to write down some things that I had heard about my family and the years before I was born. All of those books and notes are spread out around me now, but still I realize that I am also going to have to exercise my memory quite a lot. Am I up to that I wonder? I will soon find out!

Anyway, with this new determination to write my story, I find myself thinking back and wondering where to begin. I remember a day back in 1876 when I first started to ask the questions about my family. 1876! Is it really that far back? It all seems like yesterday but that is where I must begin.

2.

December 7th 1876,
Westhill, New Jersey

———⁂———

Y ou never quite know what to expect from the December
weather in New Jersey. In the northwest end of the state,
snow is always a possibility; a heavy wet snow that can make
any form of travel a nightmare. Towards the coast continual
rain is not unusual. Geographically and weather wise, the town
of Westhill falls somewhere in between, which is to say that a
nasty damp cold is often the winter norm.

I remember that cold, and how it could find its way
through every gap and hole of a house and penetrate every
part of a person's body. A cold that could only be warded
off by standing in front of a strong blazing fire with arms
outstretched and eyes fixed upon the flames – and even then
the cold could bite you in the backside.

I knew that I had been out in this cold for too long, and
that thought scared me a little. For a ten-year old, the walk
from my Grandmother's place to the graveyard just outside of
Westhill took a good thirty minutes, and the rain had started

twenty minutes into the walk. My clothes had absorbed all of the rain that they could hold in the first few minutes. By the time I reached the graveyard I recall being literally soaked to the skin. My head was cold and my feet hurt. But those regular visits to my mother's grave were very special to me. And today was my birthday and I wanted to spend some of it with Momma.

Of all times of the year, the springtime was always my favorite time. It still is. Although I had never known my mother, I felt sure that she also must have just loved the springtime. Oh yes, I had no doubt that she loved the bird songs, and the light breeze that carried all kinds of smells, and the greenness that always made its way back after a long winter along with the promise of a summer soon to come.

As I straightened some flowers that I had brought with me, I thought about how my Grandma Annie always loved to talk about how my Momma Beth was just full of life and how it seemed that she was always looking forward to something or another.

Because of the way Grandma spoke, I thought about how much Momma must have looked forward to summer, especially on a wet and cold winter day like this. But Momma had died years ago, and questions about that had begun to bother me more and more frequently.

I already knew that Momma had died on the very day that I was born. Grandma Annie had told me that some years earlier, and just recently I had begun to think about what that meant. The knowledge that on the very day that I started out in life, Momma lost her life just did not sit right with me. There was something wrong with that. And maybe, just maybe, what was wrong had something to do with me. And I did not care for that thought at all.

Of course Grandma had assured me many times that it was no fault of mine or of God or anyone else.

"Sometimes these things just happen, and you give it no matter. You understand?" Grandma had told me that many times.

I always told her that I understood, but of course I didn't. How could I at that age? And so on those visits to Momma's grave, some days I tried to think about it and other days I tried not to think about it. Sometimes one thought won out and sometimes the other. On that day in 1876 I thought about it. And I thought about Willard.

Oh let me tell you that Grandma loved to tell me stories about my mother and one suppertime the previous year, she had started to mention that man's name.

"...it was one of them West Virginia July days that seem to just come out of nowhere. One day it's winter and next day it's spring and before you know it, summer is 'on you. Just like that. The trees were full of leaves and there was such a scent of summer flowers comin' up from the meadow. That mornin' after chores, your Momma ran out into the orchard and just soaked up the sunshine.

Her brother Elijah had put up a swing on one of the old apple trees and your Momma sat up on it and instead of swingin' back and fro, she twisted it and twisted until the ropes was all coiled up. Then she just leaned back and spun around and around. When she came to a stop she jumped down and was so dizzy that she fell over. We laughed and we laughed.

And then she began to dance. She held her frock out to the sides and just spun around and around and around. I couldn't hear no music but your Momma sure did. Somewhere inside her head some music played and played and she danced."

Grandma had paused just then, and she had looked at me with such a faraway look that I recall turning my head to see what might have been behind me and that had her attention so. There was nothing there of course. Grandma was looking straight at me, but she was seeing somewhere far off in another time and place. It was such a happy look as Grandma enjoyed her memory.

"Your Momma was so happy those days until that Willard!"

Grandma had stopped abruptly at the very end of the last syllable of the name. I heard her teeth come together on the last letter and it was almost as though she had bitten off a piece of hard candy - sour candy at that. I had never heard that name mentioned before and for that matter, I could not recall ever hearing that tone in my grandmother's voice before.

My curiosity was aroused and over the next few days I asked many times about this man Willard. But after a while, I stopped pestering Grandma with questions about him because she had made it clear that there was no more to be said and that I just had to let it go. But on that day at Momma's grave, I began to wonder again. If my mother's death was not my fault, or God's fault, could it be that Willard had something to do with it? Whoever Willard was that is.

Like I said, I was painfully cold and so I stood up and looked across the deserted graveyard and decided to start off for home. Elm trees that provided wonderful shade in the summer months stood tall and bare, and they wore a sad shade of gray that matched both the location that afternoon and my own feelings. I just missed ever knowing my Momma, and I do think that it was at that very moment that I decided to do something to find out more about her.

The heavy pouring rain had stopped, but the misty rain continued and it was as cold as ever. A squally wind that felt as though it had just come off the Jersey shore cut across the field and alternately forced the mist away and then died down allowing the mist to regain itself and close in on me again. It was time to begin the long walk home. I said goodbye to Momma and straightened the little wooden cross that Grandma had helped me make some years ago. There was no name. Nearly all of the graves each side of Momma's had no markers at all.

"Most people don't care so much about us," Grandma had said once when I had asked her about that, "we black people lives and we dies and that's that. But it used to be so much worse years ago. You just be thankful for that my boy"

The heavy rain had begun again as I started up the long hill towards the big house where my grandmother worked, and my spirits rose at the thought of her drying me out in front of the stove and giving me some of her hot cocoa. Grandma was a good lady and everybody knew that - and that thought made me feel good. The front windows and door were lit with the warm glow of oil lamps, but I knew better than to go in that way. Breaking into a run, I was soon up the side alley and around the back yard and bursting in through the back door.

Grandma often told me about how I used to enter the house when I was young. She loved to tell how she would be working away in the kitchen and suddenly the back door would open with a crash as I unlatched it and threw it back without a second thought. For a ten year old I apparently had quite a voice and in Grandma's opinion I could have been quite a good preacher-man if I had so chosen. I used to be so embarrassed to hear her telling people that. On that wet and cold afternoon I suppose that I must have behaved just like that, probably shouting over the crash of the door in that loud voice of mine.

"I'm home Grandma and I'm wet and I'm cold, but I'm home!"

As Grandma came to the door, I do remember feeling better already.

I had forgotten that the house had a visitor. Grandma quickly admonished me.

"Hush, hush boy and kindly have some respect here. Don't you know a man is dying in the front room? Let's get you out of these clothes before you just go and beat him to it!"

Grandma silenced me as she helped me undress in front of the old stove and as she wrapped me in a warm fleecy towel. Oh I remember now, how after that I began to feel so much better.

After the much-anticipated hot cocoa and quite a few cookies, and after a long and thoughtful stare into the stove, I did feel a whole lot better.

Thinking about my decision to learn more about my mother, I sat myself up at the kitchen table to watch Grandma lay up a tray of scrambled eggs and warm milk. The questions had been skirted many times and I wondered how to ask again but Grandma beat me to it as she topped off the milk.

"No matter what time of day it is, this is one of the Reverends favorites. I hope he can eat this. He was sore sick enough when he arrived from Rhode Island two weeks ago and then he got himself soaked to the skin visitin' that church over the other side of town to preach. A man his age - and a boy your age for that matter – should know better! I don't rightly know how sick he is. The family is sure worried and don't seem to think that he's for our company for much longer. As for me Brownie, I am not so sure, and so I am goin' to do my best to build him up again. Fact is that if he does go and die, well this whole family is goin' to miss him and so will I!"

I recall thinking on that for a few moments, but my only conclusion was that Reverend Hart would probably be buried in a different graveyard than Momma and that he would most likely have a grand looking marble marker. Grandma had said many times how it was different for the white folk, but how things used to be a whole lot worse for us.

Let me tell you right now that I loved Reverend Hart. At the kitchen table watching Grandma, I thought about all the times that the Reverend had told me about those old days when things really were worse. Like all good preachers, the Reverend knew how to tell a story – especially a true one. Grandma was right that everyone would miss the Reverend.

When I looked up, I caught Grandma's stare. I could always tell when she was reading my thoughts. Sometimes that made me blush, but not this time.

"Come on child. Help me take this in to the Reverend and maybe you can sit awhile. You know how he likes to talk with you. Fact of the matter is that I do believe that you seem to cheer him some."

The front parlor had an unusual smell to it that day. Normally in the winter, I always associated the parlor with the smell of wax polish and of wood-smoke from the open fire. Sometimes there would be the added smell of cigar smoke, depending on just who was home at the time. But on that day there was a strange smell that I could only think of as something to do with medicine. It was as though the horse liniment that Grandma rubbed into her aching elbows, and the cough syrup she sometimes poured down my throat, and the carbolic soap she scrubbed the kitchen table with were all mixed together. The family had been saying that they just did not know what to give the Reverend, and so perhaps they were giving him all they had. That would certainly have explained the smell.

As we entered the room, Reverend Hart was laying on his back on the small bed that had been set up in the parlor. He was quite still, with his eyes closed, and I tried to shut out the immediate and unpleasant thought that had come to mind. I stepped back and watched Grandma lay down the tray, and gently shake her patient.

"Come on now Reverend, come on now, time to eat somethin' as best you can. How are you feelin' now after your nap?"

The Reverend stirred and took in the familiar prospect of the smiling face that showed a genuine concern. Not a polite 'how are you feeling?' casual remark of many visitors, but the honest to goodness concern of a real friend. Managing to sit up as Grandma packed the pillows behind him, he pushed away the tray of food. And then seeing me, he pulled it back, and looking first at Grandma and then at me, he managed a smile and remarked that maybe he would try to eat some of it. And he thanked her very much.

Grandma left us together, telling her patient that she thought he might enjoy talking to Brownie but that he should not tire himself, and telling me to be quiet and respectful. Grandma always felt better when she could lay down clear instructions to all concerned. As the door closed behind Grandma, Hart looked at me with a wry smile.

"Well boy, don't look at me like that! I am not dead yet no matter what people may be telling you. Sometimes I feel as strong as ever but then mind you, I confess sometimes to feeling tired to a degree and thinking that the good Lord may well be making final preparations for me. But don't look so mournful boy. I still have my wits about me and I can still hold a conversation."

The words were spoken kindly. He had known me since the day I was born and I could remember him as far back as I could remember anything. On his visits to the house he always had time for me. I loved talking with Reverend Hart.

I later learned that although Roger Hart had been loved by a number of congregations during his career as pastor, he had always had a problem opening himself up to people. As much as he wanted to be close and personal, it seemed that some barrier would always come up in front of him. Many people put it down to a natural reserve. Some of his colleagues thought it perhaps an indication of some insecurity on his part. But I had learned that it was nothing new to him, and that it had plagued him since his childhood. I realize now that the ones he felt most comfortable with were the children. And I knew that I was a favorite.

"Best tuck into those eggs now Brownie, before your grandmother comes back. I know you love 'em. Grandma will let us think that she believes that I ate them and she will tell me how well I did. But we both know that she will know that it was you who ate them. There's some logic in that somewhere I suppose!"

I had to explain that Grandma had just taken care of me and that I was full of cookies and cocoa. It was then that I saw the opportunity to ask about my mother and so I told the Reverend about my day in the rain.

I knew that Reverend Hart was quite familiar with the graveyard and he told me how well I described the place. I also knew that my questions would have to wait a few more minutes because I had set in motion a number of memories for the Reverend and I remembered Grandma telling me to be respectful. So I sat back and listened.

"You know my boy, you are good at telling this, and I can picture that place just outside of the town limits. That field has boasted some fine old elm trees and a dry-stone wall for many a year. A good friend of my son-in-law's uncle deeded the land over for the use as a cemetery for the colored folk. That was years before most people gave such matters a thought. I have conducted a few funerals there myself. It seems like folk were always asking for my services when I was visiting here.

Oh, those funerals Brownie. They were so different from the Rhode Island ones that I had officiated. Where the New Englanders for the most part kept their grief and feelings bottled up inside and worried what folk might be thinking of them, these folk wept and cried and sang and laughed. Sometimes all at once it seemed.

My goodness Brownie, I can remember back about ten years – just before you were born in fact, and the occasion when I conducted my first funeral over there. It was for a colored person who had been a friend of the family. It had been at the very burial ground where you were today and quite close to where your mother is buried. Just on the south side of the hill, a place had been prepared and I met the group of mourners there. After some prayers the box had been lowered into the ground. I read from the Psalms and the Gospel, said some more prayers and spoke about how much the man would be missed. And I meant that. He was a dear man.

But then at the last amen, and without any warning, a young man began to sing in a deep bass voice.

'Amazing grace, how sweet the sound...'

It was not a wet day like today, but a warm sunny autumn day and I recall how still and quiet everything had been, and how the words of the hymn had seemed to hang there in the air so beautifully, as one by one the others joined in.

'...that saved a wretch like me, I once was lost...'

I smiled at how some of the folk had begun to clap to the rhythm of the hymn and begun to sway, first this way and then that. I had no trouble picking up their rhythm and in no time everyone had joined in, and the song rang out across the valley as the congregation made their way down the side of the hill, with me following along behind and joining in every word as best I could. O happy day."

I remember how the Reverend finally stopped speaking and I could see that he was enjoying his thoughts and the memory of that day. He did not hear my question when I asked about Willard. And so we were both quiet again for just a moment or two until he became aware that neither of us was speaking and that I was looking him straight in the eye, as though waiting for an answer.

"What did you say boy?" He asked me, realizing that a question had indeed been asked.

"Who is Willard?" I quietly repeated, trying to use a tone of voice that expected, and in a sense almost demanded an answer while still being mindful of Grandmas order to be respectful.

The question had clearly not been expected. At least it had not been expected just then and so there was no immediate answer. Reverend Hart lay back and thought about it for a few minutes before speaking.

"Brownie, I know that the name has come up at other times over the last year, and that on each occasion the issue had been duly put away for another time. You see your Grandma Annie does not like to speak about him. But maybe this is the time. Certainly you deserve to know about Willard, and most likely only Grandma Annie and I can tell you all about him. Maybe your uncle Elijah can add some information too.

Brownie, first you need to know that your family and I have been kind of woven together for many, many years now. It's like our lives were wrapped together. I just kept running into your Grandma and your mother and her folk, over and over again."

I could see that the Reverend was trying to collect his thoughts and I remember feeling just a little guilty about putting him on the spot when perhaps he did only have a few weeks or a few days to live. But if that was the case, maybe this was the only time to get at the whole story.

I did not pester him for the answers but sat quietly as he closed his eyes and thought. Finally he opened his eyes and sat up a little more and gave a sigh. It was as though he was putting any remaining doubts aside.

"Tell me boy, do you know why they called you Brownie?"

"No sir, I guess because of the color of my skin – anyways, that's what I have always thought."

To be honest, up until that day I had never thought about my name and in any case it was Willard that had my interest. The Reverend was quiet again and was looking at me, and I later realized that his mind was racing back over the many years trying to get the story into some kind of sequence that a boy of my age could understand.

"No Brownie, that's not why you have that name, you were named after a certain man. Some folk hated him and still do, and others admired him. Your grandmother for the most part admired him. His name was John Brown and you need to know about him if you are to ever understand Willard. I may be a little tired, but I remember those days like yesterday. I need to tell you about what happened at Harpers Ferry all those years ago. Both your Grandma's family and my family lived there at the same time you know. No you did not know did you?

But where do I start? I know that some people out there call you names and I know that your Grandma Annie has told you some things about slavery. But that was all before you were born and I suppose it doesn't mean a lot to you. But Brownie, I was in the thick of it all and so were your Grandma and her family.

I am feeling pretty good right now, so let me tell you first about my early days in Rhode Island because that will lead into how it was that I came to be mixed up with the likes of John Brown. Sit back my boy and don't be afraid to drink that milk if you fancy it."

But the milk and the scrambled eggs and toast were quite cold by then, as both the Reverend and I were absorbed in the story and in each other. And I must note at this point that I am grateful for the notes that I made many years ago when I was about seventeen. Grandma had helped me with writing them one day when we were talking about all of this.

Anyway, Reverend Hart settled back down again and began to spin me the story.

"I grew up on a farm in the north west part of Rhode Island. I had two older brothers and they just loved the farm and all the work with the crops and the animals. It was hard work then, but they just lived for it.

I was different. Oh don't get me wrong now, I liked the farm – especially in the summer months when it was warm and we could take time off in the woods or on the lake. But something happened to me when I was about your age Brownie and it seemed to set me off from the others. It doesn't matter what happened but let's just say that I did not feel at home any more.

I know that when other boys call you nasty names, it makes your hair stand up a bit. I understand. Grandma Annie tells me about when you come in sometimes all confused and moody.

You see, that's how I felt for too much of the time. You and I have more in common than you might think Brownie."

The Reverend was famous for his winks and he had winked at me then as he shifted his position a little, as he would do many times. I realized later that he was trying to push details of memories away while bringing up just enough to help me understand.

"I concentrated on my school work and, even if I say so myself, I did pretty well at it. I also used to enjoy going to the meeting house where the Baptist Church worshipped. I got to know the minister quite well. So when I was eighteen years old I went off to Bible College and studied there and after a few years I became a Baptist minister myself. I married Mrs. Hart and soon we had our daughter Jenny. She of course is the lady who your Grandma now works for.

Working with people helped me a lot Brownie, and I am sure that God called me out for that job. And you see that's what started me along the line of mission service and brought me to meeting your Grandma and her family."

At that moment, the parlor door swung open and Grandma and the Reverend's daughter Jenny came into the room. Much to my annoyance I was promptly ushered out by Grandma while the daughter chastised her father for tiring himself with chatter.

I remember hearing him begin to protest that he was not tired, and how he tried to explain that he felt fine. Then he suddenly let it all go as though acknowledging that there would be time to tell the story, and that it would be good for him to take some time to put it all in order. He agreed that it was time for a rest.

And I realize that now is a time for me to take a rest from this account. In the morning I need to read my records again to try to keep all of this in some kind of order.

3.

December 9th 1941,
Dartford, West Virginia

———— ✺ ————

We are at war with Japan!

I have been reading all of the reports about the attack on our ships in Pearl Harbor. Our president called the 7th a date that will live in infamy and he is right about that. Another bunch of bullies have misled their people and plunged us into another war. I wonder if we will now enter the war in Europe and end up fighting there and in the Pacific at the same time. Now how will we manage that I wonder?

Well, I am very thankful for the notes Grandma Annie helped me write all those years ago. Grandma never did learn to write that well, but she could certainly pull a story from her memory. I remember having to tell her to slow down a few times as I tried to catch it all and write down my notes. I spent some pleasant hours this morning re-reading those old notes and working out some sequence for all that the Reverend Hart had told to Grandma and to me.

But this morning I also read in the newspaper some more reports about how some folk are saying that now it is time to straighten out a few things about our country. In particular they are calling for the need to push for an end to segregation in the schools. How many times have I heard that? More times than I care to think about I must admit. But it is something that is very dear to me, and it was the issue that just a few days ago, caused me to start thinking about my life, and then started me down this path of writing my story.

One of Grandma's favorite sayings used to be that things were not as bad for us as they used to be. This morning she would be sad to read that there is still so much difficulty for us.

But for now I want to return to 1876 and to Reverend Hart's beginning of the real details of my story. The other stuff can come later.

4.

December 8th 1876,
Westhill, New Jersey

———— ✖✖✖ ————

The next morning I was allowed to sit with the Reverend again on the condition that I was not to tire him unduly. I did not dare ask what that meant, but Grandma stressed that she would be dropping in every now and again to make sure that I was obeying her.

The Reverend began by telling me that yesterday when we all left him, he had settled back to sleep, adding that he was more than a little grateful for the interruption in as much as he needed some time to think back and get things in order for me. He told me how he was determined now to spend the next few days telling everything to me, adding that I deserved to know the truth.

As for me, I was just hungry for whatever he had to say.

"Well now Brownie, as tired as I was yesterday, it took me quite a long time to fall asleep because my thoughts carried me back over the years and to what had made me first become involved in anti-slavery actions and mission work. Oh yes my boy, I was involved alright as you will discover!"

The Reverend went on to tell me how last evening he had let his mind go back to 1853 and his first call to a church. It was to a small Baptist church in his old home town in Glocester, up in Rhode Island. But before that call, he told me how he had been assigned to help out in a larger church in Providence, Rhode Island, and that was where his involvement with missions and anti-slavery had all begun.

That morning I was on the edge of my chair as he settled back in his bed, and I leaned forward to catch every word as he went back to 1853.

5.

1853,

Rhode Island

———oᴔᴕᴕ———

"**B**rownie, I must say that I did not take to Providence right away. I suppose that it was a pretty town and it was nicely set on some rivers. But I couldn't get over how cramped and overcrowded some parts of it were compared to my home in the country. Providence, like many of the surrounding towns had a port and quite a lot of industry like metal and wood and stone working and the like.

Close by was a place called Pawtucket and it was on both sides of another pretty big river. It kind of sat between Rhode Island and Massachusetts. In fact it became a part of Rhode Island just a few years ago. Back in '53 there was a lot of industry along the river and it seemed that just about everybody made a living based on the production of all kinds of cloth – textiles that is. I learned that years ago a man by the name of Samuel Slater had come over from England with considerable knowledge of the English textile industry. Working largely from memory he had constructed America's first water powered textile mill that really worked. He built it along the river side and by the time I arrived, scores of textile mills and factories had been set up along the river banks in Pawtucket and up-stream.

Slater and the other textile men quickly became very wealthy; in fact some became very wealthy indeed!

Many of the mill workers on the other hand led a miserable life. As the mills grew, more and more people were needed to work them, and of course they needed somewhere to live. A lot of homes were built around the mills and into the towns.

Some of those were nice little cottages and some were what are called tenements. A tenement in that area Brownie was usually a wooden two or three level building where a family had just a couple of rooms to live in. They were built all the way down into Providence where I was working. There was not much sanitation or much of any kind of health care. Lots of families lived together in those buildings. There is a passage in the Bible that talks about feeding the poor and clothing the naked and that was always with me as I paid my visits to the people living around the church where I was an assistant. I found that so many of them had a miserable life. On the other hand many more would tell me how glad they were that they had come to America. They came from many different parts of Europe.

Alcohol was cheap and plentiful and it seemed to me that too many people did not care much for each other. On many occasions I would meet a lady who had been beaten by her drunken husband and I would find myself remembering something that happened to me as a boy. It did not take very much to remind me of my boyhood."

I remember the Reverend stopping there and looking at me as though he regretted mentioning his youth just then. It would be years before I found out why that was and exactly what he meant. After a while he shrugged his shoulders and went on with his story.

"Anyway my boy, that is something that Grandma Annie can explain when you are older.

It was through that Providence experience that I realized that a city pastorate would not be good for me and for that matter it would not be good for any city congregation that I might be asked to lead. Somehow it seemed that I needed the openness and the rural freedom of fields and farms in order to be of help to others.

Now, when I say that conditions were bad for the people, of course there were some exceptions. Some mill owners were very good to their workers. And a man by the name of John Davidson was one of those exceptions, and I struck up a good friendship with him.

Davidson had built up both a sound business and a good reputation. His fair dealings with his workforce, who were largely immigrants, contributed to his reputation.

During my rounds of the parishioners I would sometimes go over to Pawtucket and drop in on Davidson for coffee and talk. Our conversations ran the usual course of local politics, the state of the mill business, and of church affairs. One morning we had been discussing the anti-slavery work - we called it the abolitionist movement Brownie, and I mentioned my own feelings about the need to end slavery. I always thought that slavery was wrong and I need you to really understand that my boy.

Now, I am going to tell you a bit of an adventure story Brownie. It's a true story, so listen up now.

It seemed to me that talk was easy and I remember asking Davidson one morning if he thought that anything could really be done towards ending slavery.

'Well, we Northerners can be pretty high handed about the whole matter its true. But it was pretty widespread up here once and we put an end to it.'

I could tell that Davidson had no doubts about his conviction, as he went on.

'You know Roger that I just heard from some friends out near the Connecticut line, that back in your home of Glocester the last slave was set free somewhere around 1806. Now that's a long time ago and the rest of this state phased it out by about 1840. We did it. So it took another thirty four years, but we did it and the rest of the country can if we just make a start.'

It all just sounded too simple to me Brownie and so I argued that the huge culture of slavery in the south could not be compared to what had been the custom in New England. And it was that exchange that led the two of us to open up to each other and to honestly share our thoughts about slavery.

We discovered that we both held the same deep abolitionist feelings.

After that morning, this topic became a mainstay of our conversations, and eventually led Davidson to trust me enough to talk about his activities in arranging for the safe passage of runaway slaves into Canada.

It was during one of our morning chats at Davidson's place that I mentioned that I had received a call to serve the small Baptist church in Henryville in Glocester and that I was inclined to accept the call.

I explained to him that I just didn't seem called to the city, and I that I was of the opinion that I could do much more good out in the country. Both Mrs. Hart and I were in agreement on that. I also told him that I had heard that there were a lot of folk out there, and close by in eastern Connecticut, that took ending slavery very seriously. I was thinking that I could join them in that work. But I had to add that of course the move meant that we would not be seeing so much of each other.

Davidson was quiet for a minute or so, and then he turned to me with an expression of trust.

'Come outside Roger, I want to show you something.'

We walked out of the house and across to the mill and I remarked that the river was very high after the heavy rains of the previous week.

Those mills were pretty complicated Brownie with dams causing the river water to change levels and to being forced to run through the mill workings. We were standing at the point where the water run-off channel that powered the mill wheel, drained and re-entered the river, and again I was surprised at how high the water level was. Davidson agreed.

'Yes Roger, the rain was very heavy all week. There is a dam just upstream that provides the water drop to power this mill, but the entire river water level came up higher than I have ever seen. We shut off the sluice gate and stopped the mill for a couple of days. I have never seen the water level so high. In fact, that's what I want to show you my friend.'

Davidson led me across a small bridge and into the first working level of the mill, and then down three flights of wet and very slippery stone steps and into the wheel-chamber. My goodness Brownie but the noise was close to deafening as water cascaded over the wheel and then through a stone channel through an opening in the wall and into the run-off back to the river. Adding to the water noise was the wheel itself as it turned noisily and ran a series of gears and a heavy shaft mounted on bearings. This wooden shaft ran for a considerable distance under the mill and in turn drove a series of belts up through the floor and into the mill workings proper.

Davidson had to shout as explained that his old mill was probably the worst design along that stretch of river, but that she has stood him well for many a year now. He told me to be careful not to slip, and to follow him.

The stone floor was wet and very slippery and I did have to take great care as I followed Davidson to a large iron grating set in the floor. With the aid of a hefty crowbar that stood close at hand, Davidson lifted the grating and pushed it aside.

'Now, take a look down there Roger.'

I peered down into the near darkness of another channel that had been dug out and then lined with stone slabs. There appeared to be a couple of inches of water standing in the tunnel and I could hear the river maybe fifty feet or so further down the tunnel. It was a bit scary.

'When this mill was first built, the water flow was different and with heavy rain like last week, the wheel level would flood. So this drain was installed to help carry the floodwater away faster. Come on Roger let's go out into the quiet!'

The sunlight and the quietness were very welcome as we climbed the steps and walked to the river edge and sat down on a stone parapet.

Now Brownie, you need to know that over the years there was system developed to help run-away slaves from the south escape to the north. People called it the underground railway. It was a risky business and Davidson had told me earlier how he was involved with it. Now he wanted me to know more about just how much he was a part of that movement.

'Roger, you know all about my involvement with the so called underground railway, but I don't think that you know much of the detail. Most runaway slaves, who come this far to the east, come through either Westerly Rhode Island or New Bedford in Massachusetts. A network of experienced people who are determined to help, usually aid them out from there. But just a few come up the bay to Providence and sometimes up here to Pawtucket, and they are for the most part unorganized. Usually those who come this way have stowed onto a ship in Baltimore or some other southern port. They bury themselves among the cargo down below, and then somehow manage to slip off the ship in Providence. Sometimes they get apprehended and handed over to the authorities. Sometimes they escape, or maybe a captain kind of looks the other way and allows them to run off. Either way, once they are on their own, things become mighty tough for them.

Because of a government act, all of our northern states are required to aggressively search out those runaways and return them to their southern masters. Federal marshals have been ordered to hunt down fugitives and arrange for their return. In doing this, they are empowered to raise a posse and all citizens are required to help in the search. The marshal gains a reward when he abides by the law. Worst still for the fugitive though, is that any marshal who is discovered to have not pursued the slave, is open to disciplinary action including a $1000 fine. So the motives of both reward and avoiding penalties make the marshals very diligent at times. Once caught, there is usually no real trial to be heard or pleas to be made. Return is pretty well automatic. Roger, there have even been cases of free blacks being arrested and sent south. There seems to be no way around the brutality. We call the law the bloodhound law, since the marshals often hunt down the runaway with dogs. It can be terribly brutal.

A couple of us here do our best to help the runaways. That often means taking them in and putting them up for a few days. We provide them with some better clothes and some much needed food, and then arrange passage up-river and then to Quebec and hopefully to their freedom.

Roger, I can tell you that they are often in a really bad state. They are frequently hungry, poorly clothed, and as often as not thoroughly depressed and scared. So I reckon that you see how it is that we just have to help. But they are not the only ones who are scared. My family becomes pretty scared too when we have runaways here, because we face a fine of $1000 and the order to pay the slave's owner another $1000. It's all pretty stressful. You have a spare $1000? No I thought not, so you see what I mean – it's a lot of money. And on top of that there is the risk of up to six months in prison.'

I can remember now Brownie how at that point Davidson had paused and looked hard at me as if wondering whether to continue.

'Let me tell you what happened last week Roger.

Late one evening there was a rapping on the door at the rear of the house and I found a man by the name of Nichols whom I knew a little from trading in Providence. He was agitated and very nervous, and quickly came into the kitchen, looking all around to see who might be there. Seeing only me, he started to talk.

'I'll come straight to the point Davidson. I know that you have helped fugitives before and I need your help now. I have also helped out in the past but the family who took care of all of the details is out of town. Three fugitive men stowed onto the ship Glory, hiding among the cotton shipped up from Baltimore. They had a terrible voyage up the coast and are pretty well knocked around. Anyway, they managed to slip off the ship in Providence and quickly mixed in with some of my black workers so as not to stand out. But I guess that one of the seamen saw them and reported them to the marshal. I got them in my cellar now, but that's likely to be searched any time soon. I need them out and fast. I want your help.'

Well Roger, what could I do but agree. I needed some supplies anyway and so I agreed to buy those from Nichols, and I sent a wagon down to his place for loading. It was beginning to get dark when it arrived so we had some help there. As the supplies were loaded, the three men took part in the work and managed to stay in the back of the wagon when it was fully loaded.

Once back here, I had them put in the basement of the house to rest up, and a couple of my people got them food and some fresh clothes for the trip to Canada. I sent my man Flannigan up the river to find out what they could do there about a passage.

The risk was that someone watching Nichol's place might see the connection and come up here poking around.

So I put my foreman in charge with instructions that at the first sign of agents or anyone else calling, the three slaves were to be taken out the back and over to the mill, and put down into that drain that I showed you. And they were told that if they saw or heard the iron grill being lifted again, they were to scurry down that drain and into the river and to try to hide in the bank. They would have to fend for themselves. It would be cold, but if they kept their wits, we would be able to pick 'em out again later.

None of us slept well that night, and I took my turn watching.

Just as the sun was coming up I saw four men coming up to the house and they were obviously on the look. I shouted down to the foreman and then waited a while as their leader rapped at the door a few times. After a few knocks, I opened the front door and I brought them in to the house. I hoped that the slaves would be on the move below and I knew that I needed at least ten minutes to stall a search.

So, I listened as to how three fugitives has landed at the dock and had been seen going to Nichol's warehouse. How he had denied seeing them and how a search of his place had been fruitless. But, I was told that my wagon had been seen loading and as my abolitionist feelings were well known, a search here was in order. I stalled a bit by protesting and asking the ship's name and stuff like that, but pretty soon they split up and began to search.

Two of them went straight to the mill and I tried not to show any response to that.

I heard later that as they arrived on the first working level, my foreman was just coming up the steps from the workings below. They challenged him as to what he was doing up and about so early. But part of his job was to see that everything was operating and ready for the start of each workday, so he was pretty convincing about that explanation. Seems they were not convinced however and demanded that he show them down below.

It was wet and cold down there. The wheel was not yet running so it was much quieter than today. The foreman had dragged a crate over the drain grill and one of the two men sat down on it as they asked about the workings and fished around for possible hiding places. Imagine how the fugitives must have felt just below! I reckon that they would have heard all right.

The man sitting on the crate looked down at his boots and noticed a corner of the grill that was not covered. That got his interest. And so they quickly pushed the crate away and grabbing the crow bar - they began to pry up the grill covering.

The foreman protested loudly about damaging the drainage system, hoping and praying that the slaves would hear and follow their instructions.

As soon as the grill was up, one of the men quickly slipped down into the drain. Seeing no one in there, he crawled along to the outlet and looked out over the river, but still he saw no one.

Once up and outside the mill again, the man who had gone down the drain was cursing his luck as he was soaked through and getting pretty cold. He reckoned that anyone going out that way was better left to the river. He came back into the house while the others finished looking around.

After an hour of useless searching, the four of them gathered outside the house and with no apologies promised to be back later and issued all kind of threats against me and against the family. But without evidence, I knew that was all hot air. I just wanted them off my property and the three men fished out of the riverbank before they died. So I was most relieved when they got up onto their horses and turned towards the road.

Well, don't you know Roger, that just as they were starting off, Flannigan came riding hard down the drive!

'Whoa man, what's the hurry this time of day, late for work or something?'

I don't know if the agent was suspicious or just sarcastic but I tell you that my heart skipped a beat or two hoping that Flannigan would grasp the situation. I was also becoming more and more conscious of those poor men holed up somewhere in the river bank or worse still in the water.

Flannigan is pretty smart, and he immediately guessed what was up and started to tell how word had come to him about a problem with the mill and he wanted to help fix it before the start of work and what was that to them anyway? They bought the story and took off. And I gave up a simple prayer of thanks.

It turns out that while all of that was going on my foreman had already located two of the men. They had found a depression in the riverbank and although it was water logged, it provided screening against being seen. The third poor man was never found. I guess he was swept away.

Waiting until he could see the federal agents leave, the foreman had quickly brought the fugitives inside the house. They were now in a worse state than before they arrived here, soaked to the skin and damned cold. Excuse me Roger. I figured that they were probably wishing they had stayed back home. A bit like the people of Israel complaining to Moses that they should have stayed in Egypt!

An hour by the wood stove and another set of clothes and some more food helped turn them around. Flannigan had made arrangement and so all that remained for me was to get them on their way. And I can tell you that I did that as quickly as I could, getting them into a supply wagon that was going up to the north an hour or two later. I wished them well and they gave me their gratitude and we all agreed that we hoped to never see each again. And then they were gone.

Why do I tell you this? Because Roger I know of your feelings towards slavery; you feel the same as I do. It's a nasty business that has to be stopped and each of us has to do his part. Now you have been called to serve a church in Glocester, right on the Connecticut line and you have already heard how there are a number of folk out there who feel the same way as we do. I know a number of them personally and I have heard how they have started some kind of a mission society. They want to do something for the children of slaves down south.

If you are in agreement Roger, I will write you an introduction to them. Join them Roger! Join them and see what you can do to help. My God, these poor colored people need all the help we can give them!'

Well Brownie, I told Davidson how much I admired his courage, and that I had not realized how involved he was and what risks he took. I promised to look into the mission society once I was established out there.

And then lying on the bed here last night, I thought about all of that and I looked back at those years in Glocester. I remembered how much Mrs. Hart and I had enjoyed them.

We quickly settled into the routine of a being a country pastor and family. Three services were held each Sunday along with a midweek prayer service. I regularly visited all of my town and farm parishioners and came to know most of them very well. There was never a shortage of food as most days saw the arrival of eggs or fruit or vegetables from one source or another.

Over the next few years, an old curse of depression would come to me now and again, and that was usually after having to help a family through some tragedy like the death of a young child. But for the most part they were very agreeable years. When depression did come, my dear wife always stood by and helped me through as she had done many times before. Kind of like how your Grandma Annie takes care of you.

We all need someone like that Brownie.

It was during one of those difficult times, after the little boy of one of the church families drowned in a pond that she encouraged me to become more involved with the local mission society. I had made their acquaintance when we first arrived and I had given them Davidson's letter of introduction. The society had welcomed me very warmly and I began to attend their meetings now and again.

During my first meeting I had learned that they wanted to move past all of the talk and to do something. Their top priority became to help with the education of the children of slaves and freed people down south. I willingly pledged to work with them on this, and as a start I convinced my local church to set aside some money to contribute to the cause.

At Mrs. Hart's urging, I began to become more involved, and being something of a good speaker, even if I say so myself, I was charged with the task of promoting the work throughout the region. As a consequence, in addition to my church work, I travelled from meeting to meeting throughout the northern Rhode Island and eastern Connecticut mission societies, raising money and obtaining pledges for continued support.

At times Brownie, I must admit that I became a bit weary of the whole matter. But part of a call to be a pastor is a real love of people and, in any event, I was convinced that this movement was right. And so I kept going and eventually I took the leadership role in it.

And then, at an annual meeting of the regional society, they worked out an ambitious plan. There was a unanimous vote for me to travel to Virginia and to personally take the responsibility for recruiting local teachers and setting up a school out in one of the valleys in western Virginia. Although Mrs. Hart had gone along with the general idea of taking an active part, she was not happy at that sudden turn of events I can tell you.

It was not so much that she had second thoughts, oh no - she flat out wanted me to back out!

'Roger, we have heard such terrible accounts of how slaves are treated and how it is that no mercy is shown to those who try to run away. And it's against the law to teach them. Don't you think that some folk are going to be against you, and don't you see how they may get violent with a radical stranger like you from Rhode Island getting mixed up in the matter?'

We had been enjoying a late night snack of bread and cheese after the meeting when Mrs. Hart told me just how scared she was about me getting so involved. It was true that she had supported the work without much concern, and she had even travelled with me on some of the fund raising journeys. But just a month ago, as plans began to be set, she had caught the drift that the society was looking to me to be the field man, and that had led to those thoughts. She just did not like that idea and so she tried to find a way to convince me to refuse the responsibility. But that night I had accepted. She went on at me though!

'You know there's been trouble with one of the schools in South Carolina, and that one of our ministers had to come home last month from another region. Roger, I am just so worried about your safety.'

I confess Brownie that I was not without some concern myself, but I wanted more than anything else to calm my wife's fears. So I reminded her that we were talking about western Virginia and how slavery had never been as widespread there as it was further south. Most owners out there had only maybe five to ten slaves at the most. Some had twenty to thirty I suppose, but they were a real minority. And there was a genuine degree of tolerance and there were already a lot of freed slaves out that way. There were even unofficial schools in Richmond where for the most part, people tended to look the other way. They had black teachers and some white teachers and they were all taking risks. But as far as I knew no one took action against them.

I told Mrs. Hart that I thought that all would be well for our work, reminding her that if we were to add them all together, there were quite a lot of slaves working the towns and valley around Big Lick and Lynchburg. We just had to make a start."

The Reverend winked at me again as he added that he then gave Mrs. Hart a kiss and assured her that all would be well.

Of course he had to explain to his church elders that he planned to go to Virginia for up to two years to help establish a school. They reluctantly accepted the situation and announced that they would take on a young minister with the understanding that it was a temporary position. They gave Reverend Hart their blessing and wished him success.

I heard that Mr. Davidson was exhilarated when Hart visited him with the news. It was more than he had hoped for and he gave not only his encouragement but also a sum of money to help with the expenses.

The Reverend told me how excited he had begun to feel and he was starting to tell me about his journey south when his voice became softer and softer. Pretty soon I realized that he was fast asleep.

I slipped quietly out of the parlor.

6.

Dec 10th 1941,
Dartford, West Virginia

———⊙⊙⊙⊙———

L ooking over my notes from yesterday, I admit that I began to have some second thoughts about this journal. I have barely scratched the surface of what I want to say. I have written so much and yet there is so much still to be said. I confess that I am a little overwhelmed by the task and by being surrounded by my old notes.

As a teacher I have read and marked countless papers and examinations. The fatigues of writing and reading are familiar to me, but this morning I thought about whether this might just be too much.

I thought about just what it is that I am trying to say anyway. And then I wondered whether anyone else would ever have the slightest interest in my story. Most importantly, I questioned whether it has any relevance today.

But then I opened the morning paper and on page two there was a continuation of the story about ending segregation in schools.

I taught children for more than forty years. I taught children - and at first it did not matter if they were black or white or Cherokee or whatever. I just taught children. And I loved it.

And then people started to talk again about how the color of your skin made a difference and before long I was teaching black children. I still loved it, but it no longer felt right. Not after the struggle we had all been through.

It is as though we had learned nothing all those years ago. But now some people are again beginning to talk about the need to change how we treat each other. And all of a sudden I can once again hear Reverend Hart talking about this very same issue.

So I reckon that I will continue the journal and see where it leads me.

I now know where it all started, and I need to go back again to 1876 and how over the course of a few days I learned so much about my family, and about myself.

7.

December 9th 1876,
Westhill, New Jersey

—— ❧ ——

That morning, the Reverend had been allowed to sleep late and had to be awakened by Grandma with his coffee, toast and eggs. I recall how I crept behind her into the parlor.

"So how is you feelin' this morning Reverend? My word I think that you would have slept all day if I'd let you. Everybody is out now 'part from you and me and Brownie. He is itchin' to talk with you but I told him to bide his time. Miss Jenny looked in on you a couple of times in the night and she said that you was in a good deep sleep"

Hart concurred with that and added that in fact he was feeling remarkably good that morning. Grandma Annie was pleased to see how he sat up and ate most of the eggs and toast. He smiled as he finished his toast and looked over at me standing just inside the room.

"You know Annie, I think that talking with Brownie, and then thinking back on the years past, has made me feel a mite better. Last night, in my mind, I went over the early years leading up to how I first met you and your family. It's all so long ago and yet it seems like just yesterday. Do you remember the schoolhouse in Big Lick? Bring the boy over to me and sit yourself too, if you have time. I want to go over some more now with Brownie and about your part in all of this."

And so I was ushered into the parlor and told to sit next to the little make-shift bed. Grandma Annie took the opposite side and refilled the coffee cup.

"Let's see Brownie, I told you how I became a minister up in Rhode Island and how much I enjoyed that for a good few years and then in the new year of 1860 how I started on a big venture. My goodness, to be honest I do not think that I would have done it if I had known how it would all work out."

Hart glanced at me and saw the apprehension gather on my face.

"Of course I would have. If I hadn't - then I would never have met you boy would I?"

The words were spoken kindly. I loved him very much.

"But first I need to go back just a couple of months before my undertaking in Virginia and tell you about John Brown and Willard."

I recall nearly jumping out of my seat. Finally, this was what I had been waiting to hear.

The Reverend took my hand for just a moment, gave it a squeeze and then lay back in the bed. I was aching to hear the story and for her part, Grandma Annie was probably wondering about her part in it. That would all come out later.

Hart took some minutes to think awhile more, and I remember wondering if he was teasing me. Now I realize that he just did not know how to get those events into a sequence that I could understand. Eventually he sighed and looked up at me.

"Brownie this may get a bit complicated for you, but try to get some sense from it because it will tell you about Willard and how he came to be the way he was. It's another adventure story for sure boy, and maybe you can see it that way. This all happened just before I went to Virginia and then on to Harpers Ferry, but it is very important if you are to ever understand Willard Beauchamp.

I heard this account directly from Willard and his mother and then some others, and it's pretty well in agreement with reports I read in the papers."

I know that I probably began to wriggle a bit in anticipation, and Reverend Hart smiled at me as he began his narrative.

8.

October 15th 1859,
Harpers Ferry, Virginia

—⚬⚬⚬—

"**B**rownie, I am going to be talking about this town called Harpers Ferry in West Virginia, although back in 1859 Harpers Ferry was still a part of Virginia. And Virginia was very much a part of the South. Harpers Ferry is a place where two great rivers come together. After winding along the valley between two mountain ranges, the Shenandoah merges with the Potomac and together they continue on through Washington and then the Chesapeake Bay and into the Atlantic. In a sense, not only two great rivers converged there in 1859, but also the two cultures of the North and South. They came together and tried to make their presence felt downstream in the nation's capital. Recently though, it had become not so much a convergence as a clash of these two traditions.

Back in the mid-1700s, a man called Robert Harper used to operate a very successful ferry at this junction of the two rivers. In later years, Harper would love to tell how he had frequently ferried George Washington while Washington was surveying the area, and how Washington and his compatriots became customers again during the times around the war of our independence.

Much of the history of the nation had already been set on and around these waters but there was much more still to be played out there. Young Willard Beauchamp cared little for all of that. In fact he knew next to nothing of such matters. The ferry had long since given up to the railway systems and to the Chesapeake and Ohio Canal, and a small town had built up along the banks and up the hill from the river. Willard just did not care much about the history of the place. Harpers Ferry was simply home and the river was simply where he fished, especially under the bridge where sometimes he would just sit and watch the water run by him.

This was his birthday month; he was thirteen years old and serenely happy with a new fishing pole and line and all the stuff that he had always wanted for real fishing. Life could hardly get better as Willard settled back under the first span and waited for a fish to oblige him. But a voice broke into his thoughts.

'Are you crazy, or what?'

Willard jumped at the voice, thinking that he was about to get into trouble again for something he had not done, or at least had not done consciously. But looking around, he saw no one.

'How many times now have I told you that it's the craziest idea I have ever heard and that it cannot succeed?'

Now Willard realized that the voice, which sounded quite familiar, was coming from above. Carefully peeking around the edge of a beam he saw a small group of men leaning against the bridge wall.

'I know that. You have been going on about it so, but I tell you we have to take action and take it now!'

This man's voice had that certain tone which leaves no doubt as to the conviction of his remarks.

'We've wasted more than enough time and waited while politicians drag this thing out with their empty words, promised actions and wishful hopes of compromise. I tell you somebody has to take action and that we are the ones to do it, and that now is the time.'

There was a quiet lull among the men leaning on the bridge wall. They had heard this all before, and for the most part they agreed that John Brown was right. Willard inched closer to the wall.

'Yes, we all agree it is time for action, but I tell you that violence is not the way. I am convinced of that John. Let's allow this to play out during the elections next year.'

Willard had come close to losing his balance and was in danger of falling into the river as he realized that this dissenting voice was that of his father!

'No, the time for waiting is over.'

Here was that second and most strident voice again. Without seeing him, Willard immediately felt a little scared of this man.

'William here was down in Charleston last month at a slave auction, and he saw the brutality of it all. One family was split up with the father sold to a local plantation while the mother and three daughters went to a business on the docks. The young son, hardly more than six years old was sold to a blacksmith. The auctioneer was boasting about the high prices fetched and as to how everyone seemed happy with their transactions. But William saw the misery in the faces of those colored folk. Isn't that so William?'

As I heard about it Brownie, William confirmed all of that, and now this may be hard for you my boy, but it has to be said. William went on to tell about the unusually high number of slaves that changed hands that morning. A small group of them had tried to break out and run, but they were caught almost immediately. They were taken away and William told as how he heard later that one of them had been beaten right in front of the others to teach a lesson. The poor man died because of that beating and his owner was heard bitterly complaining how that had caused him to lose money.

'See! All of this goes against my understanding of God's teaching'

John Brown had broken in again.

'No man has the right to own another. Our southern system is wrong and now this nation extends all the way to the Pacific and here comes the talk of extending the slavery practice out west. This all goes against my feelings for what is right and what is wrong I tell you. This is not what this country is about. I am convinced it must end, and we must start working towards that now.'

John Brown's words again silenced the group for a few moments and Willard edged even closer to catch a glimpse of them, and his father. For some reason, he felt relieved to see his father was standing apart from the others. Although it was just a few feet, it came as a relief because to see any separation between his father and this John Brown was good. The men were deep in their thoughts, and it was Willard's father who broke the silence. Frank Beauchamp spoke with a voice that displayed both a well thought out response and a certain authority. Willard recognized it immediately, having been on the receiving end of that voice many times.

'John, you know that we are all in agreement with you except on the question of taking some kind of quasi-military action. You've said that you are committed to the cause of abolition and I know that to be true and that you are dedicated to it. But look what happened in Kansas. You took this kind of foolhardy action there and five men died. I know they were supporting slavery, but because of your actions they died, and many people now believe that you are guilty of murder.

Wherever you go, you have to watch your back all the time. A number of you are going under assumed names right here and now. You yourself John, you are living with this name of Isaac Smith for God's sake. Face it man, you lost a son in the struggles in Kansas. And now you have this wild idea of taking a US arsenal by force and taking all of the weapons and ammunitions, and setting up some kind of military camp in the mountains. John, it can't work and it will do the cause no good. Others have told you that attacking this Armory will be seen as attacking the federal government. Your friend Frederick Douglas warned you that such an attack would be like walking into a steel-trap and that you could never get out alive. The facts are that...'

'No!'

John Brown cut off his opposition with a rush of words. He had also thought this through many times.

'If we set up an armed camp with a good supply of weapons, hundreds of run-away slaves will come out there. We can train them and supply them with arms so that they can go out and help others escape and then be equipped. It will swell into a movement that will not be stopped until all recognize the evil of slavery and put an end to it. Politicians will be forced to get off their backsides and follow our lead. It's the only way now.'

A murmur of agreement went through the group and it was William who spoke next in a quiet voice that was clearly trying to bring reason to the argument.

'There are twenty or more of us ready to go this way Frank, with or without your support. Your local knowledge has helped us, and now we're all set up across the river in the Kennedy farm with arms and ammunition. It's been thought through and we are going to go with the plan. We may fail and we all know that. The odds are probably against us. But John is right that now is the time, and that action is the way. Both the northern states and the southern states want a way out of this mess. The North has the systems and the mills and factories; the South has cotton and the structure to produce it and ship it, both to the North and to Europe. Nobody wants war or a separation of the states. We all need each other. But right now we need a change and somebody needs to make a start, and as we see it, that start must be based on some kind of action.

Once we have a full-blown rebellion underway, the politicians will be forced into action and bring an end to the slavery issue. The new president, whoever he turns out to be, will have to agree on the rights of each state to make its own decisions about slavery. The South will then be free to continue its present culture until it can be changed – and believe me, it will quickly change. And there will be an agreement to prevent the spread of slavery out to the west. The important thing is that change will start. Can't you see this? If we succeed then the cause will move on and be settled. If we fail, well, we will have made a point and others will pick up on the need for progress. Believe me Frank, we know the risk, and the only question now is whether you are with us or not?'

Willard's eyes were fixed upon his father. He knew a little of what they were talking about, and he was captivated by the question. He wanted to know how his father would respond to such an argument. Frank Beauchamp took a step towards John Brown and answered the question.

'I cannot in all good faith and conscience support this wild step of violence John. May God watch out for all of you, especially if you fail in this action. But I will wait out the ways of politics and the negotiations that will surely come out of the elections. If I cannot stop you, then at least I wish you well. Good night friends.'

'You are a fool, Frank!'

John Brown came back with another outburst as Frank walked away.

'Your way will end in war more certainly than our way might. Blood is going to be shed and as I see it, the only question now is how much and when. It's a question of a little now or much more next year, and the next one after that.'

Frank continued to walk away and somehow Willard felt proud of his father at that moment.

John Brown and the rest of his group strode off to return to the farmhouse in Maryland. Frank walked off the bridge and sat on the bank of the river with his head in his hands. He could not remember when he had felt so disturbed and uncertain. And yet, somewhere inside, he felt the absolute certainty that Brown was wrong.

Still the shreds of uncertainty hung on and would not let go. He wondered if he was the one who was wrong about this. Frank was not particularly religious, but over the past months he had come to see that John certainly was, and that he not only had a strong faith in God, but also felt strongly that God was somehow in favor of these plans.

Frank had first met John Brown in Maryland when
Brown was setting up at the Kennedy farm under the name
of Isaac Smith. At that time he was giving the locals the
impression that he was investigating the potential for mining
opportunities. This had been his front for the scouting
activities in Maryland and across the river in Virginia at
Harpers Ferry.

As Frank made known his anti-slavery feelings, Brown
gradually come to trust him, and eventually to ask for his
support for the grand scheme to bring liberty to the slaves.

'When I was over in Kansas,' John had told him, 'I was
adamant about bringing about the abolition of slavery. But
everywhere I went these hecklers would yell at me that I
should know how the Bible tells slaves to obey and respect
their masters. And in any case, they said that most slaves
were happy with their situation – all the clothes and food and
security they ever needed.'

John had told as how, with almost fanatical zeal, these folk
had sometimes waved their Bibles and shouted him down. It
was during these times that he had decided take the initiative
and to start some action.

And so Frank wondered whether he was now failing John
and the others. All of this weighed heavily on his mind that
late afternoon, as the sun began to set and the river just ran on
towards the bay.

Frank had not heard the boy approaching. Willard quietly
sat down next to his father and put his arm around the big
waist, or at least as far as it would reach, and he squeezed it.

'Papa, I am proud of you!'

They sat in silence for just a moment or two. Both were
surprised; Willard that he had spoken up and so made a

certainty of the fact that he would have to admit to eaves-dropping, and Frank at the unexpected words from his son.

'Willard, what are you talking about? And where did you spring from?'

'Papa, I'm sorry that I listened in, and I don't rightly know what you and those men were talking about, but I think you said it right, whatever it was. Are you or those men going to get into trouble?'

I do believe Brownie that Frank could never have explained why, but at that moment he knew that he had made the right decision. Looking at his son, he felt more of a pride than he ever felt about Willard, and any thoughts of scolding the boy for eavesdropping were quickly put aside.

'Willard, I wish you hadn't listened in, but thank you for your words. I know you don't understand, but I reckon that your instinct is the same as mine. We are right. Let's go home now. I have a lot of thinking to do. Later on I will tell you a little about what is happening to our country, and by the ways, no need to mention any of this to your mother just now.'

They strode up the hill and across the open ground, mostly keeping silence. Willard knew it was best to stay quiet for a while. The farm looked familiar and reassuring as they crested the brow of a small hill and sat down on a large flat rock and rested awhile. This was home, Hill Crest Farm.

Frank's father, James, had cleared the ground years ago. Working with neighbors, they had felled the trees that were of a manageable size. The larger ones they had just worked around, planning to clear them one day but somehow never getting to it. Now these old trees added some considerable character to the farm, and Frank would never cut them.

In the early years countless stones had been hauled away and the ground leveled somewhat. Planting had been done by hand with neighboring farmers coming over to help. After three years, James had almost come to the conclusion that this backbreaking work was not going to pay off. The land was just too difficult. But one autumn he had sat down on this same rock where Frank and Willard now sat, and he had looked over his land. An outline of fields was just about in place, and that past year a good amount of crops had been sold or stored. The house, although very basic, was comfortable and sitting alongside it was a substantial barn. Two horses were on order, to be picked up in a week or two. And at that moment James knew that he would not give up. This was his land and his son Frank would one day carry on the work. And his son, God willing, would go on after that. Hill Crest would be their home too.

Sitting on the old flat rock in the late afternoon sun, Frank looked at his son and realized again just how much Willard was like his mother. Not just in appearance, but perhaps even more so in temperament. They were both very sensitive and at the same time headstrong. And Frank loved them all the more for that. Looking down at the house, Frank saw his wife Betsy cross from the barn and go into the house. On her way across, she had looked up the hill to where father and son were sitting, and brushing the red hair away from her eyes she had waved to them. Frank loved Betsy as much then as when they had first married.

He could tell that the minutes at the bridge had clearly unnerved the boy. Willard was confused and more than a little frightened. Trying to ease the tension, Frank put his arm around his son and nodding towards Betsy he asked if he had ever told how he had met Betsy, adding that Willard's mother was pretty special.

Willard had heard the story many times, but he enjoyed the story and was content to let his father hold him and talk awhile.

And Brownie, I need you to know how Willard did come from a loving family. You may not like Willard after you learn some more, but he was from a good loving family and you need to know that. Anyway, back to the story.

Frank smiled and let his mind go back almost nineteen years, and then he began to tell the story again.

'My folk had been in various parts of Virginia for well over a hundred and fifty years, whereas your momma was a new immigrant. Her parents had brought her with them from Ireland when she was just ten years old. Her brother Michael was exactly a year older. Their family had settled near Norfolk, over on the coast, and made a good living there. Eventually Michael married and he and his wife set up house close by to his parents. It was in Norfolk that I met your Momma. Oh, I guess that we fell in love right away. That red hair of hers and all those freckles! And after nearly nineteen years of marriage, whenever we are together, I feel the same pleasure of simply being with her as I felt on that first day. Willard, I hope that you can one day feel like that about a woman.'

Willard knew how much his parents loved each other and hearing Frank speaking about it again gave him some reassurance and some of the confusion began to lift. Feeling his son relax a little, Frank went on.

'Well, I had been visiting family friends in Norfolk when we met at a general store. Your Grandmother had ordered some imported tweed that she needed to make an Irish shawl, and your Momma was visiting the store to pick up the material. She loved taking these store trips on her own. They gave her the chance to daydream a little, and you know how good that can feel Willard. And they also gave her the time to dawdle and look at the cloth and lace and the like that had come in from Liverpool, and sometimes even to buy a little. She was reaching out to pick up some fine checkered material, when she realized that a man was stretching out for the same bolt of cloth. That man was me.

'I am so sorry. I was just wanting to feel it and not so much to buy it.'

Your Momma stammered a little and her Irish lilt was something to hear Willard! It still is of course.

Well I told her that it was no problem. Even if I bought some, there would be plenty left for her. This stuff had just come in by ship and I was looking for a gift for my mother back at the farm. She never had any fine cloth to make clothes for herself. I thought that it would be nice. The farm and us boys kept her pretty busy.

You know that I am not much of a man of words Willard, and I was stuttering a bit myself and somehow found it difficult to stop talking.

In the end we both purchased a piece of the same cloth and your Momma let me carry the cloth and the tweed home for her. There was no weight in any of it but the walk was agreeable to both of us.

As you might have expected, her parents were pretty suspicious of me at first, but it seemed that they soon took to me and they invited me to stay for dinner. I visited twice more that week and told them all about the farm above Harpers Ferry and about the Shenandoah and Potomac rivers and the mountains. I think that your Momma fell in love with my talk of the mountains and the valley and the rivers as much as she did with me.

I went back to Norfolk twice more in the coming months. On the third visit, while we were sitting under an oak at the rear of the house, I asked her to marry me and to come to live at the farm. And then your Momma shook me something Willard I can tell you, because she didn't answer. She was so quiet and I decided to leave her be and let her follow her thoughts. It seemed ages before she answered.

'I'm not sure Frank. Maybe you are too much of a back-woods man for a town girl like me. I think that you probably need a farm girl for a wife.'

Willard, I was so shaken. I had had no doubts about your Momma's feelings for me and so I was just speechless. I sat staring at my boots and lost for words. And then she began to laugh and she kissed me and put me right.

'Don't be so glum Frank Beauchamp! As my husband, you'll have to learn and go along with my wicked Irish humor! Of course I would love to marry you! But first you need to talk with my father'

That was a relief Willard, I can tell you. But then there were indeed your Grandparents to ask. They had seemed happy enough since I think that they had taken quite a liking to me, but I could tell there was a problem. And I know that you have heard all of this before Willard, but you are getting to an age where you can understand more, so I will tell you something new about this. Something you have not heard before. And by the way, you get your stubbornness from your mother and I do believe that she got hers from her father!

The problem was that your Momma was a Catholic. And I was not!

I remember sitting out on a garden seat with your Grandpa. There was just the two of us and he finally came out with it.

'You are not a Catholic are you Frank, and I suppose you mountain men and families don't get to church very often do you?'

Willard, at first I was not sure whether he was showing the same sense of humor that his daughter had earlier, or if he was genuinely concerned. So there I was nervous again and not sure of what to say. Now here is some advice boy, when you are not sure of what to say just say the truth and out with it. You get that?

Anyway, I told him that first of all, we were not mountain men in Harpers Ferry, far from it. I told him again how the town is in the valley and the farm is just up the hill outside of town and that the mountains were way off. And I explained that we were a good sized town of mostly farm workers, traders, or armory people. We had just about every kind of store in town, although obviously not of the quality of Norfolk stores. We had banks, a hotel and a few taverns. For a moment Willard I wished that I had not mentioned the taverns, but Grandpa Sean made no comment, so I quickly went on to tell him that we had three churches, hoping that they would kind of balance out the taverns.

Anyway, your Grandpa was not happy.

'I confess that we have taken a liking to you Frank, but I am afraid that we could never allow Betsy to marry a man who is not a catholic. We had hoped that you might just stop coming over here and we did warn Betsy. It just can't be allowed and that has to be the end of it. I am really sorry.'

And with that he upped and walked away. I was so surprised by that turn of events that I just sat there on that garden bench. Then I decided to go and find your mother.

The back door to the house was closed but I just caught a glimpse of your mother at an upstairs window and I could see that she was crying. When she saw me looking up she stepped back and I lost sight of her. I suddenly became very angry and stormed up to the door. But then I stopped and turned away and walked towards the town. Here's another lesson Willard - that when you find yourself very angry and about to say or do something that you might later regret, stop and think it through. That's easy to say I know and it's hard to do, but it's still a good rule.

Anyway, I started to walk to where I was staying and then I turned off and decided to go and talk about things with your uncle Michael.

Now, you have had some pretty tough words from your mother when you did something wrong, but she had nothing on Michael! You have only met him the once but I can tell you that he can get pretty well wound up. But I figured that if I was going to hold my ground on all of this then I would start with him.

That was a mistake. He told me in no uncertain terms that he had seen this trouble coming and that he had warned your mother to stop seeing me.

'Father should have sent you packing after the first visit Frank! I told him that no good would come but he can be soft and he said as to how he thought that you would stay out west and not come back. I could see better than that because I know my sister and I could see where things were going from the start. So when you did came back, even though I warned them again, mother and father just let you go on and now it's come to this. You have hurt Betsy no end and I don't see how I will ever be able to forgive you for that.

You could see how we are for goodness sake. We are Catholics, living in a catholic neighborhood with catholic friends. You must have felt uncomfortable now and again. I remember a priest telling me as a boy that Protestants were going to hell and that even mixing with them would cause me to risk my eternity. You think I would allow my sister to take that risk? I am kicking myself for not pushing earlier on this.'

And with that Michael announced that he was going to see the family and advised me to be on my way home.

I never considered doing that because I was too much in love with your mother and so after a while I followed him, being determined to have a showdown.

When I arrived at the house I could hear Michaels voice loudly going on at his father. And then I saw your mother standing on the porch with a handkerchief to her face. She saw me and she turned and went into the house.

I stood there like an idiot wondering if she had also rejected me, until I realized how confused she must have been. Taking the bull by the horns, I walked into the house.

Michael and I began to speak at the same time with him going louder than me. But it was your grandpa who stopped us.

"Stop it now, both of you. I have heard your views on this Michael and I know what you mean. I myself have the greatest love and respect for my faith and my church. Along with my family they mean everything to me. I could never associate with another faith.

And you Frank Beauchamp probably have no idea of what some old time protestant folk around here have said to us and our like. All of us, especially it seems those of us who are more recent immigrants, have been called all kinds of names that I am not going to repeat here.

Michael, it is not the church that puts up these walls, it is people who either do not know better or should know better.

Old ideas, rooted in prejudice and bigotry, have no place in this house. May God forgive me Michael, but you sounded for a moment just like some of those who would put us out. I want no more of it. It is finished, all of you understand that.'

I just stood there Willard, not knowing what to say or do. Was that the final word for me to clear off or what? And then your mother came over and stood next to me and took my hand. I know that no one knew what to say just then. Michael walked to the window and stood with his back to us. Finally your grandpa spoke up.

'Frank, Betsy, I have no doubt that you love each other and I do believe that you have thought this through. Most likely the separation each time you went home Frank allowed you both to think about the future. Betsy, I have been turning this over and thinking about how much I love your mother. And I ask myself how can I stand in the way of you knowing that kind of love? I don't approve and that's just a fact. But you are not a child. Is there anything you can say Frank to make me feel better about this?'

And so it all came down to me! You know that I'm not a regular church man Willard, but I am god fearing. So I told your Grandpa that one of our churches was a Catholic church that was built just a few years ago because so many Catholics had moved to town. I told him that his daughter would surely be welcome there, and that if we had children, they could be raised catholic. That's why you and your Momma go there you know Willard.

Michael left the house but your mother squeezed my hand hard telling me to let him go. Grandpa Sean sat down next to your Grandma and they talked a little as your mother and I went into the kitchen.

Eventually I was asked to go back to where I was staying and that I should come back in the morning.

I learned later that Michael and his wife had come back that evening for supper and that the family had talked the matter over and over. Eventually it was agreed that if Betsy was determined, then a marriage would be allowed.

Anyway, the following morning your mother and I were given the blessing of your grandparents to go ahead if we were determined. We were told that the whole matter would be difficult and that the church would not recognize the marriage and that there could be no celebrating the mass for your mother. There would just be an exchange of vows and I would be expected to promise that any children would be raised in the Catholic faith. Well, I had already said that, so it really came down to your mother Willard.

To my everlasting relief, she agreed!

The marriage took place with the help of the friendly family priest and it was all arranged and handled quickly. Just a handful of us were present and I am glad to say that it included Michael and his wife. And then the next day we were off to the farm.

My family took to your Momma right away and we all quickly set to work in constructing a home for us across the far meadow.

Your brothers came along within a year of each other and as you know they both took after my side of the family with dark hair, and I never ceased to tease your Momma about that. You see she wanted a little girl just like her.

'Seems like God ran out of red hair and freckles' I would joke.

Of course your Momma had an answer for that and she shot right back at me how it was that God was just keeping the best for the last.'

Well, I began to think that perhaps God had run out of materials, as your Momma's hoped for daughter didn't come along. It was three years after Sean was born that you came along Willard, with this wild spread of red hair and too many freckles to count. You brought so much pleasure boy. And since you were so much like your Irish mother, we decided to balance things a bit and give you a good old Virginian Beauchamp family name – Willard.

Willard, you had never heard about the difficulty your Momma and I had getting married, but because you just overheard some very strong minded men over by the bridge, I thought it time. That kind of thing happens all too often. People, often with the best intentions mind you, get all fired up over something or another and they cause trouble. Look out for that my boy and try not to get caught up in stuff like that. Keep it simple and just try to respect others and their beliefs.'

With that advice Frank had tousled Willard's hair and laughed. The talking had eased Frank somewhat as well as Willard and they both felt better. Willard loved hearing his parents talk about each other. They sat a while longer looking over the farm until they became aware of Betsy calling from the porch.

Betsy looked across the yard as Frank and Willard approached. She never ceased to be amazed as to how different they looked, but how similar they were! Both of them open, honest, loving, and very, very stubborn when it suited them. And she loved them both for it.

Betsy immediately noticed that something was wrong with Frank. She had seen the signs developing earlier that week, but now she could see that he was deep in thought and it was obvious that those thoughts troubled him. But Frank would not talk of it.

'Later' he said softly as he kissed Betsy, 'later, and don't worry about it.'

Betsy worried about it."

9.

December 8th 1876,
Westhill, New Jersey

———— ❦ ————

The front parlor of the house in Westhill was near to silent as the Reverend broke off the narrative. Just the old clock in the corner ticking away marked the time.

After a minute or so, he asked me if I was getting tired. For himself, Reverend Hart said that he was not at all tired and was not even surprised at that. I think that he had known for some time that this story needed telling and he felt not only some relief now but also some excitement at reliving the events of so long ago. Grandma was enjoying this also and I believe that she must have been delighted to see me and the old man lost in each other.

Well, of course I acknowledged that I was feeling fine, and after standing and stretching, I sat down again clearly wanting to hear more.

"I needed you to know about Willard's background Brownie and how he was a part of such a loving family. He was not a bad person you can be sure of that no matter what you might hear. But I get ahead of myself. The next part of the story is not so nice Brownie, and it might be a shade hard for you to follow at your age, but I reckon you will get the gist. And that's important. You need to understand how things were back before the war.

The day after Willard overheard his father and John Brown talking on the bridge, was the day that their attack took place. My Lord, It all seems like yesterday to me.

You have never been to Harpers Ferry Brownie so you don't know how the town was laid out. There was a big warehouse full of guns and the like. It's called an arsenal. The US government arsenal was built on the Potomac River, near to the railway, because it was close Washington. A smaller armory had been built there many years earlier and in time it had become quite a complex. Initially planned as a storehouse, it had soon been expanded in order to contain a very large stockpile of weapons and ammunition. A factory was also set up to produce muskets. Sometime later a Mr. John Hall had been asked to build a shop to produce his rifles. In just a few years the Harpers Ferry Arsenal and Armory had become a war machine."

The clock in the corner kept ticking as Hart settled back and continued his narrative.

10.

October 16th 1859,
Harpers Ferry, Virginia

———

"Next to the main buildings and at the main armory gate was a heavily constructed chamber where the guard was located. This also served as firehouse with a fire engine and apparatus standing inside. The walls were thick and substantially built with brick and timber. On his first visit to the place, John Brown had been surprised to find that the place was not well guarded.

Over the past couple of months, from their temporary base at the Kennedy Farm in Maryland, John Brown and his men had conducted many visits to the town, and had made use of those trips to carefully put together a plan of attack.

The day began as many October days do along the Potomac. It was heavily overcast with a driving rain. By midday it had already been a long day of making final preparations. All afternoon they had checked and re-checked the plan and alternative fallback actions. They had drilled their signals again and again so that in the event of problems each one would at least have some idea of what was going on, and they had checked, rechecked and cleaned their weapons. Everything seemed good. It was as sound a military plan of action as could be expected.

Sometime late in the evening, the group crossed the Potomac into Virginia. It was a good night for this covert raid with heavy rain and the subsequent clouds providing cover. One group went immediately to the Baltimore and Ohio railway-bridge and kept lookout. The others went on to the Armory and split again, some to strategic positions in the town, and others around the Armory buildings themselves. By the early hours they were in position, and showing perhaps surprising military discipline, they were set up at their specific targets. At the predetermined time, the two men at the railway bridge cut the telegraph lines and took up position at the bridge. Others seized control of the Armory buildings and the rifle factory. John Brown and two of his sons entered the main gatehouse and firehouse building where they took control - easily overpowering the guard.

Everything had gone well and according to plan, but John knew that the difficult part was about to begin, as his group spread out into the town. Their intent was to take slave-holding citizens captive, and to release and arm their slaves. This was to be the real beginning of the movement towards freedom.

As twelve of the men began to spread out into the town and towards the surrounding farms, a Baltimore and Ohio train came down the tracks and was stopped. A station baggage man by the name of Hayward Shepherd came out to see what was happening, and he began to walk down the tracks to check things out. One of Brown's men ordered him to stop, but in the uncertainty of the moment, he turned and began running back. A single bullet stopped him and Shepherd later became the first fatality of the event. When he heard about it, Brown was very upset. You see the baggage man was in fact a freed slave.

Imagine that Brownie! There they were trying to do something good for slaves and they went and shot a man who had already been freed from slavery. Now we know that that was the first of just too many tragedies my boy. But let me get back to the story now.

The train was held by the men for some hours to prevent word of the raid from leaking out too soon. I can tell you that later Brown would regret not holding the train longer.

The gunshot that struck Shepherd startled Frank Beauchamp as he made his way up the short slope away from the river. It confirmed the reality that John Brown was intent on carrying out the plan and that it had in fact begun. Frank resolved all the more to try to stop this now. He heard more gunfire, this from the town, and for a moment thought how glad he was that his family were at the farmhouse and not in town. At the same time he hoped that these men would not reach the farms any time soon. If they did, Frank was not a slaveholder, and he knew their plans involved freeing slaves, and so again he felt some comfort. All the same, these men were not acting in a rational manner. These thoughts gave way to a sense of urgency that drove him on towards the Armory.

The rain had stopped by now and Frank could clearly see the Armory gatehouse. But seeing, often also means being seen, and this point was proven as a shot fired over his head.

'Stop where you are, whoever you are, and get down on the ground.'

It was Watson Brown, one of John's sons. Frank recognized his voice immediately.

'Calm down and let me in, it's Frank Beauchamp. I want to talk to your father.'

'Beauchamp, you're a dammed fool, get in here before you get shot and before you get in the way of my men.'

John Brown's words were surly and impatient. Clearly it was not Frank's safety that he had in mind, but rather the concern that nothing should interfere with the action that was now underway.

'If you have come to try and stop us, as I suspect you have, save your breath and get over in the corner. Things are about and that's that. If you have come to join us, you can just wait until we move on. Which is it?'

Frank stepped into the building, but did not move more than a few feet inside the room. He stopped when he saw the guard bound and unconscious on the floor in the corner and Brown's two sons with their guns - one pointed at him and the other out of the door. I suppose Brownie that at that moment he felt the senselessness of his mission and that he should have known that it was too late. Before Frank could say anything, Watson Brown sprang forward, and using the butt of his gun, struck him on the head and pushed him into the corner.

'Just stay back there and keep your mouth shut, we have work to do.'

Frank fell to the ground near to the guard, who stirred a little.

John Brown and his sons and Aaron Stevens, who was the planner for the group, were all engaged in talk at the open doorway. Depending on the success of this part of the mission, they had laid out three options for the next stage. If a good number of townsfolk were captured and brought in, and if the expected large number of slaves joined the rebellion, they would lock the captured town folk in the firehouse, and then with the freed slaves and captured weapons make their way back to the Kennedy farm, and re-group before moving into the mountains.

Or, if only a few slaves joined them, then they had the option to go to an old schoolhouse they had secretly taken a few miles from Harpers Ferry. They would hide out there and then come back into town and to the farms on a second raid before making the hasty return to Maryland. They had plans to take and store some guns there anyway.

A third option was to set up an armed base here in the Armory if the town successfully resisted this initial stage, and fight it out until more slaves joined them. With this option, they would keep a number of men outside to organize the slaves. Apart from his loathing of violence, it was the foolishness of this intended action that Frank had hoped to use to convince John Brown to stop.

'It is sheer stupidity, to hole yourselves up in a federal armory.' Frank had earlier emphasized, but to no purpose. John Brown had in effect pinned all of his hopes on the first outcome – a successful action and return to the Kennedy farm, and these men were now planning to implement that course of events.

A gradual uproar came across the yards, punctuated with occasional gunfire, and Brown stepped out of the firehouse to size up the situation. He felt a flush of satisfaction as he noted at least forty to fifty town people and Armory workers being ushered towards the firehouse.

'Over here boys, come on, get them over here in the yard now, quick as you can!'

Brown issued the orders and helped get the people grouped together just outside the firehouse. Brown looked around the yard.

'Where are the slaves?' He asked impatiently.

His men were hesitant in reply but eventually let on that they were back in town and at a couple of the farms. The men explained that mostly the slaves had just refused to come with them. Apparently they were all too upset and confused and scared.

'We didn't know what to do with them so we left them there. There are just a few that we brought up here now.

Anger swelled up inside John Brown. An anger fed partly by disbelief for the response of the slaves, but mostly by the realization that he had not allowed for this possibility. He came to a quick decision.

'Three of you watch these folk. Watch Frank Beauchamp too, that fool is in there with the guard. The rest of you come with me.

At the Armory gate Brown dispatched four men back into the town to round up some more slaves and incite others to turn on their owners.

The Reverend paused and cleared his throat a little. Grandma had left us earlier to do some kitchen work but just then she came back into the room and sat down next to me. I think that she had been listening from the door.

'Brownie, you just listen carefully to the Reverend now, I was probably wrong about that John Brown but it took me years to see that. I want you to get it right.'

I later learned that Grandma had heard all about this attack from other people who had been involved. In fact she filled in some of the details that I put into my notes years ago.

Reverend Hart closed his eyes and tried to get it all in order again. I inched forward so as to not miss a word.

11.

October 17th and 18th 1859, Harpers Ferry, Virginia

—❦—

"Sometime later the men returned to the Armory, but with no slaves. It was clear that most of the slaves had gone into hiding. I reckon Brownie that they were all confused and frightened. Some more of Brown's men had arrived after taking hostages from nearby communities. They had a few slaves who were given arms and told to follow orders.

By then word had spread around the town, and at first disbelief and then anger had taken over the townsfolk. Some the residents locked themselves indoors and tried to keep out of sight. Some others made a hasty escape to the neighboring farms or towns. But most of the men were determined to take action against their violent intruders.

Somebody knew about a supply of weapons outside of the Armory area and they quickly armed themselves from that supply. Running up to the Armory they began firing into Brown's group but of course they were met by strong resistance. One of the town men died and the rest pulled back to a safe distance. Firing went on from both sides but became erratic as no one really knew what to do.

Trying to make a quick change of plan, John Brown decided that he and the men had better make it back to the Kennedy place with whatever captured arms they could carry, and then work out another plan. Inside Brown cursed his misfortune, but aloud he blamed the ungrateful slaves.

'Well, they did not understand I guess, so now we've got to get out fast with the arms and, as it looks, with just a few slaves. There's no sense coming under more attack in this situation.'

Brown was already running through the Armory yard as he laid out the orders.

The men began to prepare to load a good supply of arms for hauling out, but they were interrupted when loud cries came up out of the town. Running to the edge of the Armory yard, Brown saw some militia and armed citizens coming towards the Armory. The townsfolk were screaming at the tops of their voices and it appeared to Brown that they were determined this time to invade the grounds.

What had incited the townspeople was the death of their mayor. He had been looking around an area just outside the gates and had been shot by one of Brown's men on guard there. Also word had quickly reached the surrounding towns and the response of militia and more armed citizens had been rapid. Brown cursed that the train had been allowed to continue. He knew that word from that quarter would also be out soon.

The citizens backed off as a troop of militia and guards from Charles Town spread out around the Armory, and gunfire broke out again. Five of Brown's men died instantly, and his son Oliver was mortally wounded. One of the town's men also died in that first volley of gun fire.

Brown quickly pulled his men back inside and began making off-the-cuff decisions. Ten of the most prominent of the captive citizens were ordered into the firehouse as hostages while others were herded together next door. Brown's son Watson, together with Aaron Stevens and a hostage, was sent out under a white flag of truce to buy some time. In the confusion the militia immediately opened fire, killing Watson Brown and injuring Stevens. The released hostage was not harmed. Also in this confusion, a few of Brown's men slipped out and somehow managed to escape the town. Brown positioned five armed men at windows and up on roof, at the tower. The big firehouse door was closed and locked, and the fire engine was pushed up against it as a further block. Brown looked out and saw that the released citizen had run to the leader of the troops, and he could tell from the pointing and actions that he was describing the incident and the situation inside the firehouse.

He was shocked to see the number of his attackers. Militia from other neighboring towns was now arriving, along with more armed citizens. He was surprised to see a number of slaves among them. Not armed of course. Shots were fired at the Armory and Brown ordered the fire to be returned.

'But only fire at white people' he ordered, 'don't forget why we are here.'

Of course that was small comfort for poor Shepherd, the colored man who had been killed at the railway. I often feel for him Brownie.

Rapid rifle fire was exchanged and two more citizens died. It was not clear whether the troops had suffered casualties. Brown gave the order to cease fire, and the attackers took the same action. Once again it became very quiet.

As the day went on, Brown could see more guards being positioned around the Armory and in strategic positions beyond. Clearly there was now no opportunity for escape. A net had been drawn around the Armory that would immediately capture any man trying to slip through. A deliberate military operation was being set up against him with precision and deliberation as even more troops arrived in the late afternoon. No attempt was made to contact him and no more shots were fired. It was all too organized for his stomach. He decided to wait out this preliminary action, as if there was any alternative.

The day dragged into evening, with no attack or contact. The hostages were off to one side so that a single armed man could watch them. Brown took a certain pride in his men as they began to sit out this apparent siege. There were no complaints or criticism or what-if questions. His thoughts went to Beauchamp, now sitting among the hostages, and he walked over to Frank.

'This is what you didn't understand Beauchamp. These men of mine believe in the cause, they knew the risk before we come up here and they accepted the possibility of failure. Now we have to wait it out and see what can be done.'

What Brown did not know, was that his attackers were undecided on what action to take.

As the evening wore on, the troopers and citizens from the surrounding area were joined by a detachment of United States marines under the control of Lieutenant Green. The marines had been dispatched by order of President Buchanan as soon as word of the attack had reached Washington. The marines were joined by Colonel Robert E. Lee and Lieutenant J. E. B. Stuart. Lee took control and on being told of the hostages, immediately made the decision to hold off any action until daybreak to avoid the risk of killing more citizens.

During the early hours of the morning, Lee spent some time alone weighing up the situation in the firehouse, at least as he understood things. It had been made very clear to him that Brown was fully committed to the headstrong idea of freeing slaves by means of an armed rebellion, and that there was little opportunity to talk him out of his wild scheme. Men had painfully pointed out that some of the most respected members of the community were being held hostage, including the great-grandnephew of George Washington. Brown considered him as being of great value as a hostage. Some, with obvious feelings of guilt, had told Lee that they had seen some of their family members or friends dragged away and held.

Lee thought on the quiet words of a man who had come to him just after midnight.

'Lee, if you can imagine it, some of his men are wilder than Brown himself. Before he'll give himself and his crazy idea up, all those town folk in there will be shot.' Mind my words. My son is in there and I need you to get in the back somehow and take care of him and the other prisoners, and only then go and get Brown.'

But Lee had carefully listened to descriptions of the building, and he had looked over their floor plans a number of times, and he knew that there was no way to get in without setting off deadly consequences. One option was a siege, but his military instinct gave him a conflicting direction - to just storm the main door and fight it out. There was just a chance that a quick surprise attack would immediately involve Brown and his men so intensely, that they would not have time to work on the hostages. On the other hand, one or two men might just open fire on the hostages.

Long before dawn, Lee had made his decisions and had given his orders to Stuart and Lieutenant Green.

'Under cover of darkness, line up three rows of marines across the yard. In the first line equip three men with hammers and axe ready to break the door. Behind those lines, have others man a heavy beam or something suitable as a battering ram. On the order, all men run forward. The door is to be attacked and weakened with hammer and axe, and then if necessary, let the men with the beam through the lines and bring the door down. No rifle fire is to be used, so we can try as best we can to avoid killing or injuring the hostages. The men are to breach the door as fast as possible, and with drawn bayonets take down the rebels. Every precaution is to be taken to avoid harm to hostage citizens.'

It was a risky plan for the hostages, and Lee knew that only too well. The time needed to gain access to the firehouse would allow sufficient time for Brown to turn on his prisoners. Another preliminary step was called for, which would at least demonstrate that all precautions had been taken.

'Stuart, before that action, I want to give Brown a way out. Under the cover of a flag, you will deliver a written ultimatum to Brown. You will make it clear that this is not a negotiation but an offer, and that no counter proposal will be listened to. Either he accepts my terms or we attack. You will signal his acceptance by waving the flag and returning to us, or signal his refusal by waving your hat and then I suggest running to the firehouse for cover, because with that signal the action will immediately begin. A fast response will then be the best defense for the prisoners.'

A long night for Brown and his men, and I suppose a longer night for the hostages, came to a close at dawn as bugle calls rang out from the perimeter of the troop formation. Brown rushed to the window pushing aside the guard who had been holding that watch. It was barely light, but as he stared out, Brown saw a man come out of the shadows and face the firehouse. The dawn began to come up quickly now, and behind the lone man, Brown could just make out the outline of officers and men in lines across the yard. He recognized these men as being marines, and he cursed again that word had gotten out so quickly. From the corner of his eye Brown saw one of his men standing at the next window raise his rifle, taking a direct line at the approaching man. Brown reacted immediately.

'No! Put your gun down for now, let's at least hear what they have to say.'

In his mind was another hopeless idea that the marines would accept the situation and negotiate some way out of this. In his heart, John Brown still believed that justice was on his side; that he was right, and that others would even yet see it his way.

Stuart raised the flag and began walking towards the firehouse door. He thought on Lee's words that he was under cover of the flag, but did not draw any comfort. Seeing the rifles at the windows and having heard about these wild men, he could not escape the thought that it was quite likely that he would die in the next few moments. But training brought discipline and discipline brought resolve, and Stuart walked closer to the door.

'Mr. Brown!'

Stuart's words were clear with no hint of any awareness of the danger that he faced.

'I have a written ultimatum from Colonel Lee. If you will peaceably surrender, give up your arms, release the prisoners and open the firehouse, Colonel Lee will take and hold you, and then await further orders from President Buchanan. If you refuse this ultimatum, you will receive an immediate forceful attack with no guarantee of safety for you or your men. How say you?'

Frank Beauchamp had been standing in the background with the other prisoners listening to the proposal. A murmur went through the group of citizens expressing a hope that Brown would accept Lee's offer. Brown looked back into the room and stared at his men for a moment, as though weighing up the options and inviting comment. A sense of dread slowly came over Frank Beauchamp, as he realized that these men knew that their struggle was lost. To them the choice was simple - either they would die this morning defending the cause, or they would surely die later at the hands of a hangman. And they knew it.

One of the men spoke up.

'I reckon we stand firm. There's no way out for us now, but yesterday we lit a fuse for the cause of freedom and today we best follow through. That way the word will get out and others will pick up on us.'

The others nodded and Brown turned back to the door.

Frank Beauchamp lunged forward at Brown.

'No, stop it now John while you still can! Later you will have the chance to tell people why you took this action and you will be able to...'

A shot came from one of Brown's men across the room, and it caught Frank squarely in the chest. He fell backwards and collapsed among the prisoners.

Brown quickly turned to the door and in spite of Stuart's insistence that the offer was an ultimatum, began to ramble over other alternative conditions. And then he just gave up the struggle.

'No sir! We stand for this cause and we will fight.'

The next events played out quickly. Stuart lowered the flag, waved his hat and ran to the fire house crouching under a window out of the immediate line of rifle fire. The first line of marines ran to the door allowing the three men to begin attacking it with hammers and axe. Rifle fire from Brown's men was wasted in the rapid action, with no immediate casualties among the marines. The door splintered but did not give way due to the heavy fire apparatus that had been secured behind it. The second line of marines charged, giving way at the last moment to allow the men bearing a heavy ladder to ram the door. Weakened by the hammers and axes, a portion of the door quickly gave way and entry to the firehouse was won.

Green, with raised sword, stepped into the firehouse and moved to the side of the fire apparatus. A young marine stepped in behind Green but was immediately struck and killed by a bullet from Brown's gun. The main line of men stepped over their fallen partner and using deadly precision with their bayonets and swords killed three more of the rebels in the first seconds of the fight.

For a few minutes total confusion overtook the firehouse. With the sun barely risen in the dawn sky, it was still quite dark inside. The prisoners screamed out; terrified at being fired upon by the rebels and at the same time afraid of being mistaken as rebels themselves as the marines struck out swiftly with bayonets and swords. The forced entry had happened so rapidly, and the marines were on top of the rebels so quickly, that Brown and his men found themselves unable to use their rifles at close quarter and so were reduced to using the rifles as clubs, or furiously trying to release and use pistols. Any discipline they once had was completely lost.

Green reached Brown, and with his sword struck Brown a terrible blow across the head and shoulder. Bleeding profusely, Brown collapsed to the floor. One of Brown's men raised his pistol at Green but before being able to fire, he was run through from behind by a marine's bayonet. Green lunged at Brown with the intent of finishing him off but the sword caught a buckle and bent double, sparing Brown his life.

Hearing the prisoners still calling out with fear for their lives, Green picked up a fallen weapon and ran across the room to check on their safety. As he reached the screaming prisoners, Frank Beauchamp tried to lift himself into a sitting position. From the corner of his eye, Green saw the movement in the dim light, and mistaking Beauchamp as a rebel, spun with bayonet raised and clearly with the intent to kill him.

'Not had enough man! Damn you then and take this.'

As the bayonet came down, Frank passed out again and fell back to the floor, causing the weapon to narrowly miss its target. Green raised his weapon a second time to finish the task, but paused as the Armory guard called out for him to stop.

'No, don't kill him. He is one of us and he tried all he could to stop them!'

By eight o'clock the attack was over. The hostages were checked for injury and finding that no harm had come to them, Lee thankfully released them to their families.

Apart from the injured men, ten of Brown's men had died, either during the early gunfire or by sword and bayonet during the attack. Two of his sons were among the dead. Five other men had escaped. Two of these were quickly caught and Greene immediately dispatched four parties of marines to scour the area and hunt down the others. Eight of the townsfolk had been killed or injured before Lee had taken control, and one marine and the one railroad man had died."

At that point, the Reverend paused again in the narrative. I thought for a moment that he was crying and I could tell that these were hurtful memories as he recalled first hearing about that morning with all of its confusion and the hatred and the killing. As gently as I could I took his hand and spoke to him.

'You can stop now Reverend if you likes.'

"No Brownie, thank you but there is just a little more before I stop for the day.

Brown and the other wounded survivors were laid outside the firehouse, to receive some medical aid in preparation to being escorted to Charles Town prison.

Aaron Stevens had taken multiple hits from a musket and was in great pain, while Lee's sword had come very close to being a fatal stroke for Brown. The marines carefully cleaned the shoulder wound and poured antiseptic over the exposed bone that had been almost split through. Wads of cloth and tourniquets were applied and after some time the bleeding stopped. Brown was in great pain as he lay on the ground outside the firehouse. Lee came over and walked towards him.

'Too many people have died or been hurt this morning Mr. Brown, and all for nothing.'

Lee stood over Brown and summed up the situation as he saw it.

'You and your group have attacked the Federal Government and have seized Federal property. You have caused the deaths of a number of good citizens and a United States Marine. And you have achieved nothing. I am to take you and your surviving members to Charles Town where you will be tried for treason, and I have no doubt that you will be found guilty and will be hanged by the neck. And again I will say that it was all for nothing.'

Having deliberately made his point three times, Lee had expected to receive a violent and bitter response from Brown. And so it was with surprise that he heard Brown eloquently and calmly explain that rather than being all for nothing, this action had just been the start of a greater undertaking.

Oh Brownie, over the coming weeks, Lee would not be the only one surprised by Brown's careful and calculated eloquence.

Two marines carried Frank Beauchamp out of the firehouse as soon as the fighting stopped, and took him to the nearest tavern, which had been set up as a makeshift hospital for the injured. The local doctor and a marine surgeon carefully opened the side of Frank's chest and removed the bullet that had been deflected by a rib and eventually lodged against a bone towards back of his torso. Mercifully, Frank was still unconscious and did not feel the pain of either the wound or the treatment.

The entry wound was very dirty and Frank had lost considerable blood and the doctors were not hopeful of a recovery. They cleaned everything as best they could, bound him up with clean cloths, and bandaged his head where he had taken a nasty blow from the rifle butt, and they had made him as comfortable as possible on a military cot.

Word of the raid on the Armory had come to the farm early that morning, and knowing that Frank had slipped out, and being somewhat aware of what had been on his mind these last few days, Betsy had immediately feared for the worst. Young Willard had then reluctantly told his mother about the discussions at the bridge and she just knew that Frank had gotten himself into a whole lot of trouble this time.

'Of all the most stubborn men, your father does take the prize and bless me if you are not coming along just as bad Willard Beauchamp. If there is trouble brewing somewhere, your father just has to push himself into it to try to straighten it out with nary a thought of him-self or sometimes even for us. Come on, all three of you, into town now, and let us hope to heaven that he is still alive. Dear God forgive me.'

And with that call to action, Betsy had harnessed the wagon, and with young Frank at the control they had quickly ridden the short distance down into Harpers Ferry. They arrived just as the final assault on the firehouse had been completed.

The town was in a chaotic state, with marines and militia seeming to be everywhere. While some men were behaving in an orderly manner, others were thoroughly disorderly. Betsy saw that the marines were clearly in charge of the event, and that they were for the most part respectful of the town folk. The militia from the neighboring towns, and some of the locals, were less considerate and many had clearly already had too much to drink. She saw a unit of marines escorting a small group of men towards an open wagon. These men were roped together, and she felt tight in her stomach as she realized that a number of them were badly wounded.

The marines were coming from the firehouse, which Betsy noticed was badly damaged. She quickly surmised that this had been the center of action that morning. Jumping from the wagon, she ran to the firehouse before anyone could stop her. At the gate, a marine blocked her entry and asked her name and business.

'Business! Business! What are you blathering about boy. I am looking for my husband.'

Peering over the marine's shoulder, Betsy was suddenly unable to continue her scolding, and she collapsed into the arms of Sean who had just caught up with her. The young marine, who was not much older than Sean, ran forward and helped lower Betsy to the ground.

Sean could now see the grounds around the firehouse, and he immediately saw what had caused his mother, who was normally the strongest in the family, to faint. Growing more apprehensive by the moment, he saw a group of bodies that had been roughly thrown together without covering. Off to one side was a solitary body draped with a flag. The marines were just beginning the process of moving the bodies out. It was impossible to identify if his father was one of the men in the pile, but Sean knew that it was that thought that had distressed his mother.

Looking back to the marine, Sean spoke up.

'My name is Sean Beauchamp and this is my mother. We are looking for my father, Frank Beauchamp.'

Sean paused and turned to the pile of bodies and he reluctantly nodded his head towards them.

'Do you know? Is he in there?'

'No sir.' seeing Betsy settled in her son's arms, the young marine had stood and regained his composure at the firehouse door.

'In fact I hear that he is a bit of a hero in town. Seems like he knew Brown and his men, and he tried to talk them out of this stupid action. But he got himself hit badly on the head and then later he was shot.'

The marine had heard that Green had almost killed Beauchamp, but he decided to hold that back from Sean.

'Your father is in that tavern across the way, but I warn you that he is in a bad state. I heard that the doc don't expect him to make it through the day. I am very sorry for your family sir.'

The marine had also heard that Beauchamp had known about the planned raid and had failed to notify the militia. If he survived his injuries, there was every chance that Frank would find himself on trial. He had decided to keep that to himself as well.

Sean explained the situation to Frank Jr. and Willard as they joined him, and then to Betsy as she slowly recovered consciousness. Grasping the knowledge that Frank was alive, she felt an even greater anxiety to see him. Losing no time in resuming her hasty search, she set out for the tavern. Willard was instructed to stay outside the tavern and to keep out of trouble.

'Out of the way, out of the way now! Don't be getting' in the way of me or my boys now! Where is that Frank Beauchamp who is so stubborn and thoughtless a man this day?'

Betsy had burst into the tavern room with the cheeks of her face afire, and a color to almost match her hair. Inside the tavern, both town people and military were tending to the wounded. Family members stood close by, and here and there bathed a feverish head, or just sat and held a hand. As Betsy had seen, the wounded rebels had already been patched up and taken outside for transporting to Charles Town. Until Betsy's arrival, there had been a quiet resolve to be about the work and to make the wounded citizens as comfortable as possible.

Taking in the situation, Betsy recognized Frank lying close to an open window. She strode across the room and quietly closed the window. She felt better now that she was at his side. Betsy was in control again as the three of them drew up chairs and sat at Frank's bed.

'Now, now Frank Beauchamp, we have to get you home where you belong my darling.'

Betsy gently wiped his brow, and spoke quietly. Unconscious and damp from a developing fever, Frank was restless and only occasionally spoke an unintelligible word or two. Betsy kissed him with a passion that surprised even the two older boys, who were used to seeing an open expression of the love shared by their parents.

'Now, now, I really thought I had lost you this time my love. But you are going to be all right.'

And with that, Betsy first offered a prayer, and then began to quietly sing an old Irish love song. She was definitely in control and all would be well, no matter what the doctor said. Inside the tavern, all was quiet again.

Willard stood outside the tavern, trying to see what was going on inside, but had difficulty making out any detail. Looking back at the firehouse and seeing the young marine still on guard, he made his way across.

'I bet my papa Frank Beauchamp put up a good fight against that John Brown. He's just about the bravest man I know, my papa. Were you inside here when the fighting took place?'

Not knowing if his father was going to live, Willard needed some details to try to make sense of it all.

'No son, I came in after the fighting was finished, but I heard that your papa really did try to stop this crazy man Brown.'

At that moment one of the mourners came out and passed the guard and Willard, and hearing the remark he stopped and stared at Willard.

'Willard Beauchamp, you don't need to be here. Where's your Momma? I can't understand why your father walked into this nest of killers, but I reckon he was on something of a mission to stop 'em. As I heard it, Brown turned vicious at your father and near killed him although he had no defense. My boy died out in the yard this morning and you and I will see Brown swing for what he's done!'"

The Reverend had stopped talking again and was lying still. The three of us were silent and I remember that I was trying to understand Willard. All those months I had wanted to know more about Willard and now I was hearing all kinds of detail and I needed to put it all into perspective.

I looked at Grandma and opened my mouth to speak, but she shook her head as if telling me to remain quiet and let the Reverend collect his thoughts. It was quite a while before he sat up a little and started to speak again.

"Oh my word Brownie, the bitterness and the grief of that poor man who had lost his son hit Willard hard, and he felt an awareness that was obviously new to him. If you are going to understand Willard, you need to understand this. It came on as deep loathing for John Brown and all he stood for and for all of the suffering he had caused. Looking back towards the tavern and realizing again that his father might already be dead, the loathing turned into a hatred that had a depth that should not be felt at any age and certainly not by a thirteen year old. Those innocent moments a couple of days ago under the bridge with his new fishing pole, now seemed an age ago. Everything had changed.

'I hate John Brown and his men and everything about them.'

The words were spoken quietly, but with such an intensity, that the young marine was shaken, and was about to make a remark, but Willard had angrily stepped away towards the tavern where he was met by Sean, just coming out through the open doorway.

'We're going back to the farm Willard. You can just step inside for a minute to see papa, but then get yourself to the wagon and be quick about it.'

It had been agreed that Sean and young Frank would take Willard back to the farm and that they would take care of things out there. The boys had already arranged that Betsy would stay with Frank at the tavern until the fever broke. Coming up to the bed, Willard now saw just how bad his father's condition was. But he made no show of it. His mother had never let him down, and when she told him that everything was going to be all right, he believed her.

Sometime the following afternoon, the fever did finally break somewhat, and Frank fell into a calm sleep for a couple of hours. Betsy changed his dressings whenever the doctor demanded. No one else was going to take care of such things now. The next day the doctor argued with Betsy that Frank should not be moved yet, but she was determined to take him home. And so the brothers carefully put Frank on the wagon and took him home to the farm.

Within a few hours, the fever returned and the wound looked worse than ever, no matter how much Betsy cleaned it. For two days Frank went in and out of a feverish sleep. Willard and the family took turns to sit with him. A representative of Lee came out to the farm and tried to talk with Frank about the days leading up to the raid. He never got past Betsy, and no action was ever taken against Frank.

Winter began to set in around Harpers Ferry, and Betsy tried to settle back something near to normal at the farm. But Frank remained very weak and remained in bed. He talked a little with the boys and tried to explain what had happened. The wound never did close up and heal, and the fever returned more than once.

One evening as the family was eating supper, Frank called out for Betsy. And then he died. Just like that with no warning and just the one word. Just her name and it was over.

Quite a crowd came out to the farm's graveyard on the morning that Frank was buried next to his mother and father. Folk said what a good man he had been and what a terrible thing this was to have happened.

Willard ignored them. He ignored his mother and brothers too. There were frequent visits to the river, not so much to fish as to try to understand what had begun there just a few weeks ago. But Willard could never make any sense of it. He came to hate John Brown and his men. He came to hate the marines, the town folk and the slaves who had not taken sides. My goodness Brownie, but in his young mind, they were all to blame for the misery that had come to his family.

I heard from young Frank that on one occasion, the priest had come up to the farm to speak with Betsy and to try to help her through her grief. According to Frank, the three of them sat together and he recalled that the man was very kind and helpful and he thought that his mother appreciated the visit. One suggestion was that she should visit her folk in Norfolk but that was quickly dismissed as out of the question.

As the priest was leaving it seems that Willard came out of his room. He had been listening to the conversation. He apparently then tore into the priest with a barrage of questions and sarcastic remarks and even turned on his mother for listening to the man. Frank told me how he was shocked at the boy's rudeness that was close to violence, and how he had to almost drag him from the room as his mother made apologies.

During visits into town, Willard generally would have nothing to do with anyone, preferring to be alone. On those visits he would sometimes hear about some of the talk coming out of Washington. Talk about the coming elections, and how many people to the north thought it was necessary for action to end slavery once and for all. But Willard had heard all of that before.

Instead of respecting the memory of his father and allowing himself to recover, it seems that Willard became harder and harder and more solitary than ever. He began to go off on his own for hours and hours, and during those times he began to think more and more about what John Brown had said that day up on the bridge, that whatever this was all about, it was not going to go away without more bloodshed, a lot more bloodshed.

12.

December 9th 1876,
Westhill, New Jersey

—◦◦◦—

We sat in silence again. A confused boy and an old preacher and a sobbing grandmother sat quietly for a few minutes.

And it was Grandma that broke the silence that time.

"So you see Brownie, now you have heard about two sides to this man Willard. The Reverend here had told you about the happy-go-lucky young boy and the hard and bitter young man he would become.

That was how John Brown got himself into mortal trouble. And that was how young Willard took it so badly. Remember now he was only a couple of years or so older than you are now. A thirteen-year old boy should not have had to work out such things for himself, but in her grief his mother Betsy, God bless her, couldn't talk about things. His brothers responded to their grief by keepin' the death of their father out of thought and talk. And the kind words that came from the town and the church people came through to Willard as just so much of a syrupy cover up.

I heard how he spent less time at school and more time on his own. Folk told me later that one mornin' he crossed the railroad bridge and visited the Kennedy farm to see where John Brown had put together his plan, but that made no sense. He used to stroll around the Armory and the railroad depot as though searchin' for an explanation but of course he couldn't find one. Mostly he came to spend his time in the woods or under the bridge, thinkin' back on the words that he had heard between his father and John Brown. And in those quiet hours I am afraid that his hatred for all those who had been involved hardened all the more and that was especially his hatred for slaves. You got to understand that Brownie. He came to hate colored folk like us."

The Reverend was exhausted, but I remember how he took up the account.

"That's how it was with John Brown and Willard. Anyway, that's the way I remember it and how I heard it and like I said, it's pretty close to reports I read in the papers."

I remember now that I was worried to see how the Reverend was worn out from telling the tale, but later I came to see that the telling all of that detail had been necessary. In fact, I firmly believe that if the truth were known, it was the detail that Reverend Hart loved most about the whole episode. Anyone could have told me about John Brown, but it was Willard's experience that counted the most, and I would soon learn how Roger Hart had heard about that directly.

But in order for me to even begin to understand things about our family, there was apparently one other detail that still had to be told to me. And the Reverend needed someone else to provide that account.

Grandma had been holding me closely for a while before standing up to send me off to the kitchen. She explained how she wanted to make the Reverend comfortable. I think that we both believed that he had already fallen asleep, and we were quietly leaving the room when he spoke.

"Annie, have the boy come back in a couple of days and I will tell him some more. But I need some rest and you need to tell him about your folk. You understand?"

With that remark, the Reverend had looked Grandma straight in the eye as he spoke again.

"You understand? I know it will hurt you but the boy needs to know. It must be told."

Grandma acknowledged that she would talk some more with me, and that later after he had napped some she would bring the Reverend some lunch.

I do believe that he was already asleep as the parlor door was gently closed and Grandma walked me back to the kitchen. You can perhaps imagine my feelings. All of the details of Willard that had been side stepped for months were now pouring out. And to add to that, here was some new background that only Grandma could tell. Oh yes, I was both confused and excited!

I remember stuttering a little as I tried to keep Grandma talking.

"Grandma, you mean that I was named after that man... that man John Brown? Because from what the Reverend just told me, I don't care for him one bit and that's the truth... I just don't care at all! And was he hanged? What could you see in him that was to admire so? And I still don't see where this Willard fits into our family."

Grandma sat down at the table across from me as she had so many times and she reached across the table to take my hands in hers.

"Brownie, Brownie, slow down now. Reverend Hart thinks that you need to know about all of this, and I suppose he is right. He is goin' to tell you some more when he is up to it, probably about how he and me first met up. But first I want to tell you somethin' about my family, no not just mine but somethin' about your family Brownie. I hope that this is not all too much for you.

When I was growin' up, I belonged to a family down in North Carolina, where I lived with my parents and my brother on a small plantation over in Wilkes County.

I was a slave. So was all my family.

Most people don't think of slavery out in the mountain area, but we had been there for years and years. We was treated not too bad when I was growin' up.

Anyway, I met and fell in love with another slave on the plantation and that was your Grand Pappy John, and we set up together. We had a son, your Uncle Elijah, and then your Momma Beth. The plantation was down in a valley, and we planted some cotton and other crops. Although life was hard, we were able to get by alright until the summer of 1853.

Everything went wrong that summer.

The owner of our plantation was a good-for-nothin' man who had taken over the business when his father died just a year earlier. He was not a match for his father and he was into drink and gamblin' and just cared nothin' for runnin' the plantation. All of his father's good hard work was squandered and by the middle of '53 he'd just lost everything. Bankers and people came in and sold off the land to a neighborin' plantation to the east of us and it was decided that between the two there were just too many slaves. It all came down to money then, not people. I guess it still does."

Grandma paused then, perhaps knowing that the next part of the story was going to be hard for me, and hard for her, but she knew that it had to be told.

"One day in August, a slave auction was held in Ashville. The sale had been advertised around for weeks with posters, and it was in all the papers.

Posters were put up all over tellin' how there was to be a sale of Negroes and then went on to tell how it was that some bargains were to be made that day. This was to be a big event as it was combined with a livestock auction of cattle and pigs and such. That's how it was back then. Some folk would come into town on such an occasion and make a day of it just to see what was goin' on."

Thankfully for these pages, I have a good memory. And I can hear Grandma's voice now as she told me about her family. Her voice had taken on a terrible tone of grief and remorse and I admit that I was a little scared. I had to lean forward to catch her words. I suppose that my young mind did eventually grasp the fact that she was struggling to say these things and struggling to drag moments from memories that over the years she had tried so hard to bury. And yet it was also clear that she had never forgotten a moment of those days. Nor could she ever forget.

After that day, neither would I ever forget.

"A couple of days before the auction, one of the bankers came to the plantation with a big cart and some hired help. They took ten of the slaves and put chains around their wrists and ankles and put them up in the wagon. I have thought so many times about the misery of that day Brownie, but forgive me boy, I could never bring myself to tell you about them until now.

In them ten slaves taken away, there was an older man and a young man. The older man was your great-grandfather and the young man was my brother. So you see Brownie, I lost my daddy and my brother that day.

My daddy was a big man and they wanted him 'cause he would fetch a good price from some railroad people. There was so much cryin' and shoutin' but we were all told to shut up or be punished. Just about all of the families on the two old plantations were broken up like that on that day.

A few days later, word came that Daddy and his son were sold to different owners and had been taken off to different parts. And then some weeks later we got news that Daddy had run-away with the idea of findin' his way back to us.

Brownie, he never got through. They caught him and the word was that he was killed during a fight, tryin' to get away again. I don't know as to whether that's true or not. I just know he was killed. And on top of that I never saw my brother again either. It just broke Momma's heart, and mine too.

Pretty soon after that, me and your grand pappy John, and Elijah and Beth too, was sold off to a man who owned the local store and livestock place. They kept my Momma on the plantation 'cus she was the cook. So she was left alone with nothin' and no one.

That's when I took on the great bitterness at slavery and all that went along with it. All of our lives, we had struggled with the indignities of it all and with the hard work, and we took the abuse, but so had our folk for a hundred years or more.

But when I lost my brother and my daddy that day, and then my Momma, may God forgive me Brownie, and I know that he has, I began to hate those people who ran things.

Now understand this Brownie – we would hear as to how people like Reverend Hart and his like up in New England and other places was already makin' all kinds of noise and makin' demands to stop slavery. We used to get scraps of news and we hoped and prayed that they would have their way.

And so, when I heard about that man John Brown, I just saw a good man who was tryin' to help us, and I thanked God and swore to never forget what he and his friends tried to do that day in Harpers Ferry. And that's why years later, I gave you his name.

Oh, I know some good innocent men died that day because of John Brown, but my daddy had died too, and I lost my only brother and my Momma. How could I ever forget them and all that had happened to us?"

Her last few words were almost unintelligible as Grandma's voice trailed off and as her tears came.

They were old tears and all too familiar to Grandma.

I had moved around to Grandmother's side of the table to sit next to her. Grandma softly stroked my head as I too cried in her lap.

"So yes, that's how you got your name, Brownie. I named you after John Brown. I know better now, but things were so bad in those days, just twenty three years ago. My Lord, is that all it is, twenty three years?"

For some minutes we just sat there, grandmother and grandson holding on to each other, gently rocking together and crying together. After a while I got up and went out to walk some. Grandma began to cut some vegetables. Things had to go on. They always had.

A few hours later, the Reverend was awake and Grandma took him in a light lunch.

I learned that he told her how he had enjoyed an hour or so sleep after his long story telling. But that sleep had come to a very abrupt end when he awoke with a start. The memories of the previous night when he had thought it all through, and then the telling of it all had come back. He said that he was beginning to think about how to tell the next part of the story to me. But that would have to wait. He was just too tired.

Grandma told him how she had told me her part of the story.

After eating a little of the lunch he lay back and let his mind run again over his own experiences in Harpers Ferry and along the Shenandoah Valley. He whispered to Grandma that I would need to know about what had brought him to Virginia and how he had met her and the family all those years ago, and how their paths had crossed so many times.

But that would have to wait he said, and Roger Hart slipped off into sleep again.

13.

December 11th 1876,
Westhill, New Jersey

———∞∞∞———

It was after ten in the morning and Grandma and Mary Hart
had taken care of the Reverend. To Grandma's pleasing, he had
once again eaten a little of the eggs and soft bacon and toast that
she had prepared for him. He had rested most of the previous
day and I had been told that he had enjoyed some restful sleep.
Mrs. Hart had seen the need for me to know the truth about my
family, and yesterday she had begun to encourage the Reverend.
It seems that she had noticed that he was quite excited about
going over the old stories and she could see that it was giving him
matters other than his illness to think about. That was good. And
so she asked me to join them in the parlor.

The Reverend smiled and lay back as the ladies left the
room. As Grandma picked up the tray, she had nodded and
reminded him that I now knew her earlier part in the story.

After a while, I poured the Reverend some hot coffee and
I sat down again at the bed. He took the coffee and pulled me
towards him and gave my hand that gentle reassuring squeeze.

He had known how all this talk could easily confuse me. But he had to finish it off now.

"Well my boy, it quite wore me out a couple of days ago with re-hashing all of that John Brown stuff, but you needed to know about it if you are to understand Willard and the rest of it."

Since hearing the story, I had been thinking a lot about Willard. I could begin to understand how Grandma felt about slavery and about John Brown, but I still could not figure out how Willard and I might be connected. I decided on taking a direct approach.

"Well now Reverend, are you going to tell me what happened to John Brown now? Did they hang him? Was he a hero as Grandma thought at first, or was he a criminal? 'Cuz I don't think I like him at all. And what on earth does all of this have to do with me anyway?"

"Slow down Brownie! Yes they held a trial for John Brown and his men and yes they were all hanged - although not all at once. Of course there was never any doubt as to how the trial would end but they had to go through with it. Later on I am going to have to tell you a little more about all of that, but for now let's leave John Brown. You know it's a funny thing but on the way to the place where the execution took place, Brown passed a note to one of the guards. It was all about what he believed in and what he had hoped to accomplish, and it ended with some words that I have never forgotten. He wrote that

'...the crimes of this guilty land will never be purged away but with blood.'"

The Reverend looked at me and sighed.

"Brownie, I know that your Grandma told you all about her folk. I expect that it near to broke her heart to go through it all again. But those things were not so unusual. It seemed as if they happened all the time in those days. That's why Grandma is always telling you how things used to be so much worse for your folk. She just can't forget it and she wants you to know something about it. It's a part of your history.

It was a guilty land. In a way I suppose John Brown was right about that Brownie. Maybe that's why so many folk like your Grandma took him up as a hero and why up in New England so many of my friends did the same and even saw him as a martyr. He wasn't a martyr though, now you make no mistake about that. He was a headstrong and violent man. And he was wrong, but my goodness, how much blood was wasted after all of that."

The Reverend's word's had taken a hard, and for him an unusually bitter turn. It was clear that he no more approved of Brown than he did of slavery. After a long pause, he added

"On the other hand, perhaps, just perhaps, he was not so wrong and not as bad as young Willard thought."

With the conversation brought back to Willard, Hart took my hand again and gave it a squeeze. I was beginning to learn that this was a kind of signal that he was about to say something important and that might be hard for me.

"Let me tell you now about how I recall meeting your Grandma and your Momma and Uncle Elijah for the first time and how I met Willard. It all started in Virginia.

I told you that I was a Baptist minister up in Rhode Island and how some of us were all wound up over slavery especially about the children on the plantations. We knew the system was wrong, and we just knew that it was so hard for the children, and we were set on trying to change everything. We thought as to how any real change would have to start with the children.

Some people, just like John Brown, were thinking of violence and forcing the issue that way. But we knew how that had ended for Brown and we had no intent of following that path. I told you already how our little group was of a mind to just start quietly among the communities by teaching the children of the slaves and of the free blacks. The other evening I told you how I had gotten myself mixed up in all of that and I guess that now I need to tell you about how it worked out, or more accurately, how it did not work out!

It was just a couple of months after the Harpers Ferry attack. My goodness Brownie, but it was a long journey from Providence, Rhode Island out to western Virginia and that's for sure."

14.

January 1860,
Big Lick, Virginia

——✳——

"I remember that for the last leg of the trip, I had boarded the train in Lynchburg. I think I was the only passenger in my car that day but the train was hauling a lot of freight. When the train came in I had noticed that the engine was named "Virginia" and I liked that.

Towards the end of the journey she was straining just a little on a short steep stretch of grade on the approach towards Big Lick. It was pulling a longer train than was usual. In addition to the couple of passenger cars, there were some full coal-haulers, some wagons loaded with crushed stone, and a chain of empty log beds that would be de-coupled at Big Lick. I knew that these would be loaded with logs at the depot and hauled down to Lynchburg on the train's return trip.

The Virginia and Tennessee Railroad line, joining Lynchburg to Bristol, had been completed about four years earlier, and although Big Lick was just a quarter of the distance down the line, the railway had already begun to transform the valley town. New roads were being developed or planned and the various businesses necessary for a town's expansion were starting up on a regular basis.

To the west of town, near a place called Salem, tobacco and corn farming had recently expanded. Just south of that area, iron and copper mining was providing good income to a small community.

Lynchburg, on the other hand, had been doing pretty well for many years. You see, the James River and a canal system helped to connect the town to Richmond and on down to the coast. Wheat, corn, and especially tobacco farming, was carried on down through the valley to the west of Lynchburg, and the town had grown up around those activities. Merchants built along the river wharfs and made a good living by bringing in supplies for the growers and then in season buying and carrying away the produce.

One of the results of the water and rail communications and the industrial and agricultural activity throughout the valley, was a period of great prosperity for the residents. Another consequence was an increase in the slave population. And it was this that caused me to be riding the train into Big Lick."

The Reverend paused to see if I was following along. I was. I had learned that sometimes some really important stuff came out of the Reverend's background talk. He took a big swallow of coffee before going on.

"The train began to pick up speed again as the track gradient eased. I thought to myself how different this country was to my native Rhode Island. Across the valley were the Blue Ridge Mountains and further away again the Alleghenies. To one side of the track was a great salt marsh and to the other a plain where some deer ran away from the smoky engine and headed anxiously into a wooded copse. The place got its name from the salt marsh as they say that animals used to come and lick the salt.

There had been a light snowfall earlier in the day, and some brightly colored bushes near the copse sat in brilliant contrast in the noon sun. Some of my friends in the ministry had told me about the beauty of western Virginia but I had not expected to be so completely taken-in by it all. I felt good at the thought that Mrs. Hart and Jenny would have no difficulty spending a few years there, and maybe, just maybe, settling there.

As the big steam engine slowed and eventually stopped with a great final escape of steam, I prepared to step off the train and on to the crude boarded platform that ran alongside the rails. Most of my effects, and there were not many of them, were in the freight car so I only had a small case to take with me. It had been arranged that a Reverend Gladstone would meet me at the station and I was anxious to meet him.

'Good day brother!'

The Rev. Simon Gladstone took my hand nearly crushing it in his grip.

'I have no doubt sir, that you are the Reverend Brother from Rhode Island and I bid you welcome to Big Lick!'

Well Brownie, he was a giant of a man. I wondered about the loudness of his voice, but then I realized that as I returned the greeting, I was speaking louder than was normal as though trying to keep up with him. And so, lowering my voice, I thanked him for his kindness in meeting me here. But Gladstone kept on talking - no, he kept on shouting!

'Yes sir, I spent most of my life out west in Ohio and the Indiana territory, always on the move in the service of the Lord among the pioneers out there with never a place to call home.

The birds and the fox had a place to rest their heads, but not me if I may paraphrase the good Lord. It was just the horse and me, trekking the plains and forests, accepting hospitality when offered and making our own when not. That's why I agreed to meet you and to help set you up on your own little missionary trip. I understand your call you see.'

Gladstone was a big man there's no doubt about that, and I had no trouble picturing him getting by in the wilderness and the forest. The loud voice was simply a part of the man himself. He stood at least six foot six inches and weighed a good 350 pounds. I thought how a loud voice was a good asset for an itinerant preacher anyway. We put my packages and stuff onto a small horse drawn cart, and we two reverends slowly made our way through town, getting to know each other. My goodness how he could talk!

'Why yes sir, I recall on one occasion being warned on no account to enter a small town that was known to be against any form of religion. So of course I went in and announced that a service would be held that very night at six o'clock. I walked the street singing some cheerful old hymns and inviting everyone to the meeting. People yelled at me and told me to clear off if I knew what was best for me. But that evening I set up at the corner of the main street and began to call these people to salvation. Roger, I have been called some pretty rich names in my work, but never so many and never as ripe as that evening! Still I read the Gospel and I preached and I prayed. And still they shouted me down. Finally three men approached me with rifles. They said they were loaded, and I could see they were aimed at me. That much was just too obvious!'

Gladstone gave me a quick look before continuing.

'What was I to do? I was hundreds of miles from home and determined to preach the good news. I thought about staring them down and taking my chance, but the thought of another place and another message in the coming days caused me to wave them off. I turned and began to walk out of that town, throwing out some final scripture words about shaking the dust of that town off my feet. Three shots came from behind me. Two kicked up the dust from my feet although I failed to see the irony of that just then. The third shot went clear over my head, and right now I still hear their laughter, and I sometimes I think that I still feel the draft of that shot!'

Again, Gladstone he gave me a sideways look and I wondered where he was going with this. He had a wonderful sense of drama – and that is another good thing for a preacher Brownie.

'That was the closest shave I ever had out there, second only perhaps to poisoning myself from a sulfur spring. You realize that some people around here might, and now excuse me for saying this Hart, but might just behave that way with you I suppose?'

Gladstone let that thought sit for a minute or two and then went on

'As you well know, I am with you in this mission and so are my people. But others round here will fight you. Talking about a need for black children to learn some education, and then talking of maybe opening a school for them one day is not going to sit right with some of the folk. You can be sure of that and I don't want to play down the risks you are taking, or for that matter that I am taking.'

So Brownie, now I knew where this was heading and I had to tell Gladstone that of course I knew the risks. But then I also thought back on all of those long contentious meetings I had suffered back in New England over the past years. The Mission

Society, or just the 'Society' as we called them, had spent close to a year planning for this one occasion involving me.

For a long time, the feeling with most people up north was that one way or another, slavery was going to be stopped. Yes Brownie we really did believe that. That was simply a given, and that now it was just a matter of time. But the Society saw beyond that, and questioned what would be done with the hundreds of thousands of freed slaves and as to how the local communities would adjust, and how would these suddenly freed slaves be taken up into the structure?

Our conclusion had been that education was a key to whatever would happen and so we decided on the need to start opening schools for the children of slaves immediately. A number had already been opened by then in the Carolinas. The mountain valleys of western Virginia and eastern Kentucky were next in line. At least that was the idea put out in my part of New England.

I hate to admit it now, but our enthusiasm behind the venture was such that two very significant problems had received short notice. The first was the inescapable fact that with very limited resources, the Society could only hope to open a few schools over the coming years. In fact it must be admitted that more than one skeptical participant at Society meetings had raised that issue. The rebuttal usually took the view that, while this was a valid point, at least this was a start and that some hundreds of slaves would begin to receive an education and that once under way, many other organizations would join in."

The Reverend stopped and gave me a good look.

"Brownie I am guessing that you won't see this just yet, but the Society leadership had no understanding as to how close their argument for education was to that of John Brown's for violence.

But back to Big Lick. The second problem was that what we were planning to implement was illegal! It was simply against the law.

Ever since people began to settle the colonies, some folk worked to organize the teaching of religion to everyone, including slaves when possible. White children also received other teaching, either at home or by attending a school. The slaves were not allowed to attend school but were usually allowed to continue with some bible teaching.

Over the years as the slaves continued to learn their scriptures, many of them were also taught how to read and some were lucky to also get some teaching in basic arithmetic and geography and the like. Someone in the slave community would often take the responsibility for that teaching. When they came together on a Sunday morning for worship, the slave children might get some teaching in those other subjects.

But the fact is Brownie, that in spite of good intentions very few slaves ever received anything like a real education. Now and again some parts of the church and some good folk tried to change things but they never got very far. Most people thought that if a slave could understand instructions and maybe parts of the Bible, then that was all that was needed. That sadly mistaken view of things changed abruptly in South Carolina in 1739."

I realize now that I must have started fidgeting a little. I enjoyed my Grandma's schooling and I was looking forward to going to school myself but back on that day I just wondered where the Reverends story was going.

"I know this is a bit of a history lesson again Brownie, but listen on now.

The first big change came about because of a nasty relationship between two European countries - Spain and Britain. It seems that they had been at each other for a hundred years or more. Every few years they went to war with each other and when that happened it sometimes made things tricky for their colonies over here, like in places like Georgia and the Carolinas and Florida.

And so in 1739 Florida, which was a Spanish colony, made an offer that any slave who ran off down there to Florida, would be declared to be free. I suppose that they hoped to just cause some mischief for the British in Georgia and the Carolinas.

Remember now what your Grandma told you about her family and slavery? Well, a hundred years earlier many slaves were desperate – especially those who were treated really badly, and so the idea of running away to Florida must have looked like their only chance for freedom.

Other things happened around the same time. Sometimes it would be a local issue like the one that affected your family years later. Other times it would be some heavy handed law or another. And one of those took place around that time.

That summer a lot of white people died of malaria and some slaves took the opportunity to try the run to Florida. Others just talked about it. Anyway, there was enough going on that some of the slave owners feared some kind of uprising. They started to restrict the little freedom that their slaves had. There was even a new law that every white man should carry a gun on Sundays.

Brownie, that is beyond my understanding, but then I was not there either.

I suppose that it was meant to be a form of protection since everyone was so worried and on edge, but some of the slaves probably just saw it as another thorn in their sides so to speak. All of a sudden it looked like their Sunday freedom was under attack.

Nobody knows now, but most people think that it was a mix of all those things that led to a very nasty slave uprising that year.

What we know is that some slaves in South Carolina upped and went on the run. They were from an area near Charleston and they had all met up very early one morning with the idea of making it to Florida. It was impossible Brownie, but desperate men will sometimes try anything.

They set off down a river side and pretty soon came up on a little village and they attacked a general store that sold guns. They killed the couple of men who ran the store and then ran off with a lot of the guns.

They felt pretty good about that I reckon and they proceeded to kill anyone that they met on their way. By all accounts Brownie, it was horrible. They killed men and women and children – anyone who seemed to be getting in their way. They set fire to homes and farm buildings and were determined to keep going. Sometimes they would order other slaves to join them and so the group got to be quite large, maybe close to a hundred of them. But they were soon in trouble.

One problem for them was that they had attracted so much attention that they were soon being chased. Perhaps if they had just kept on the run without all that killing they might have got away. The other problem was that they could not just keep running all day and night. They had to stop sooner or later to rest.

From what I read, they had covered less than twenty miles when they stopped to rest, and before they knew what was happening, their pursuers caught up and began firing into the group. Half of them were shot to death and the rest just took off in different direction. It had all come to nothing, except that the slave owners had something to really be afraid of now and so things became even worse for their slaves.

The owners called on the local governments to do something to protect them and their families. And so more new laws were added and it was one of those caused me and Reverend Gladstone and our people so much grief.

People had been quick to note that the uprising had been led by a slave who had been educated. That probably meant that he could read and write but they would have blown that out of all proportions as though he had been capable of working out detailed plans and the like. We do know that he was able to speak another language and so I suppose that he might have had some teaching. But when I think about how brutal and careless the run was, well I have my doubts.

The local law makers, however, saw a means to look very responsive and so they blamed the up-rising on the education that the man had received and they passed new laws. One of those was to put a stop to the teaching of slaves to read and they added a pretty stiff fine for anyone caught teaching them.

It seems that the fear of slave up-risings spread throughout the states and over the next few years similar laws were passed in all of the southern states. It was only after the civil war that those laws were cancelled.

Virginia joined in that movement and they passed a law to stop the teaching of slaves, free Negroes, or mulattoes to read or write. A mulatto, Brownie, is someone whose parents were black and white. Anyone going against that law could be fined a hundred dollars and the poor pupil would receive twenty lashes across the back. Yes Brownie, they were horrible times and there can be no doubt about that.

Anyway, In spite of all that, by the year that I went south, there were a number of schools in operation in Richmond and in the regions to the west that taught black children. The authorities seemed to turn a blind eye to these activities and maybe it was that fact that encouraged me and the others.

It remained a fact however, that the teaching of slaves in Virginia was against the law and I knew it. I knew that Gladstone was right in that we were following a risky venture. And that maybe I was risking my life."

The Reverend stopped speaking and watched me begin walking around the parlor again. I was confused and I had to ask him why he was telling me all of this.

'I know that was a horrible story Reverend. People getting murdered, people getting whipped and the like, and you might even have gotten killed yourself. But I have always been told to obey things and yet there you was breaking the law. I don't know what to make of any of this - and what has it to do with me and Willard anyway?'

I realized that Grandma had come into the parlor. She caught up with me and she put an arm around my shoulders.

'Come on now Brownie and sit down here again. How many times have I told you how things used to be so much worse for us black folk? That's what the Reverend is goin' on about now. You need to know that stuff. Anyway, I have the feelin' that you is going to hear about me anytime now - and that can't be so bad can it?'

I smiled back at Grandma and sat down again. Looking back now I remember how she could always calm things down and make me feel better. Once when I asked about how she could do that, she told me it was something she learned at 'Grandma School' and I guess that I believed her for a while.

I know that the Reverend had thought about how this was going to be hard for me, especially what was coming next, but I had to hear it all. And his coffee was cold too, but he went on anyway.

"I put all of those thoughts out of my mind and I reminded Gladstone that we had covered all of this when we contacted him and asked if he would act as my host and guide for the work there. I told him how we had thrashed it out in the correspondence when he had explained the risks and difficulties and that now we had to get going. So I told him that we need no more of this idle talk. I asked him if perhaps he was just trying to be the hardened backwoods man, and trying to scare me, the pale faced New Englander, just for the sake of it.

Well he could give as good as he got and he gave me an earful.

'To be frank and honest Hart, I must say that you are a pasty faced man. You have a hard and dismal appearance about you as well, and you look as though you find it hard to laugh. Not the best facial characteristics for a man trying to lead others to the joy of God. That's one reason why I felt the need to repeat the warning. I want to know if you are really up to this. Right now I have my doubts and that's a fact'"

Again the Reverend stopped speaking and lay back with his eyes closed. Obviously that memory was not good and still hurt him. Grandma later told me how the Reverend remembered how he had been shocked by the bluntness of Gladstone's comment and surprised that he himself had now mentioned it to me and Grandma. He had felt so hurt at the time, even though it was far from being something new. He told Grandma that many people had told him as much over the years. His congregation had come to love him though, and he knew that he had helped many a family through some hard times. But the Reverend knew it was true that his appearance gave a false impression. It was his continual problem he said, almost his cross to carry.

I would not know for a few years about the boyhood experience that had caused his problems. He had not spoken to anyone about it for years. And although he had told himself many times that shutting the memory out only added to the problem, he could not change himself. In spite of knowing better, he had become resigned to the state of sadness and the periodic bouts with depression. It usually took people awhile to discover the inner warmth and love that he felt for others, but given time, they always did.

All I can say is that I loved the Reverend Hart very much.

But I must get back to Big Lick.

We sat in silence for a few minutes. Grandma went to get fresh coffee and I leaned forward and took Hart's hand again as if to tell him that I knew that this was troubling him. He smiled.

"You are a good boy Brownie. Now where was I? Oh yes, Gladstone being the doomsday man. Well, I can tell you that I shot right back at him.

'Well, I hope that in the coming months you will come to know me better Gladstone. Make no mistake about this because I am as you put it, up to this - pasty face or not!'

We laughed and it was agreed that that was the end of any looking back. There was work to be done for sure.

A meeting cabin had been erected some years earlier on one of the tracks from Big Lick out into the valley. Easily reached from a number of communities, it was used maybe three times a year for community services, and once a year for a big revival meeting. Those occasions were special for many of the people living there and they looked forward to them with great anticipation. They typically lasted for three days, and they were not only an occasion to celebrate the faith, but also an opportunity for socializing with folk who otherwise would not have met together.

Two or three local ministers together with a visiting preacher from perhaps Richmond or Charlottesville would provide the leadership and the messages. They were sometimes designed to teach, other times to encourage and yet other times to be delivered with fire and urgency to wake up and recall the back-sliders. There was always a lot of music, mostly simple but stirring songs of faith. At the conclusion of the meeting, people would come forward to either confirm their faith or to acknowledge that they had just now seen the way. Pledges were signed to keep off of alcohol, and it was always a celebration when someone took the pledge for the first time. When some careless congregant came forward, either under the weight of his own conscience or of a neighbor's or spouse remarks, and took the pledge for a second or third time, the celebration although more restrained, was none-the-less genuine in the hope of success this time. Baptisms were held in the creek and sometimes ten or more would go down into the water with the preacher. And there was always a fine meal to end the proceedings.

The cabin was really no more than an enclosure with three log walls and a partial roof. Gladstone's congregation was planning to add more walls and complete the roof if the decision was made to go ahead and set up a school there.

A special service was held out at the cabin on the Sunday after my arrival, and I preached a sermon describing the New

England missionary work and my own plans for a school. I was quickly accepted into the local Baptist circle and many of the members were eager to help in my work. Miss Olivia Jackson and Miss Anne Walters, God bless them, agreed to help with the teaching when the time came. These ladies were daughters of a couple of local merchants.

I soon began to visit businesses and farms that held slaves, introducing myself and quietly feeling out the likely reaction to a school for blacks. As I had expected, the reception to the idea was mixed. A few of the valley folk responded positively, fully seeing the need for some move towards change. Others were hesitant and quietly explained that they understood my mission but did not want to be in the front of it all. I could see the suspicion and fear that they felt. But I was confident that they would join me in the effort once it was underway. A few however, I have to say were firmly set against me and the work. Some were downright belligerent in their resistance, even making threats against me and my coworkers. I confess that I felt a bit afraid for them Brownie.

The worst of those against me was Franklin Smith. Smith was the owner of a good size tobacco plantation, and with fifty slaves was by far the largest slaveholder in the area. He had come west, up the river from the Bertie, North Carolina region some twenty years ago. In Bertie, he and his father had run a small farm that his grandfather had started. They grew a small amount of cotton, enough to keep the family alive and well but not enough to get anywhere. It was hard work and as far as Franklin was concerned, it was not worth the effort. Consequently he did not put much effort into it.

When his parents died, Franklin sold the farm. There had been talk of the land getting tired, and that made him nervous. His neighbors were of the opinion that without his father, Franklin would let everything waste away anyway and that he would end up in the county poorhouse. He was not a popular man in Bertie. So it took little thought on his part to decide to sell up and move west.

He had heard from travelers that there was good land to be easily had out near the mountains, and that people pretty well kept themselves to themselves out there. He liked the sound of that. With one horse and the funds from the sale, Franklin had followed the Roanoke River to Big Lick. Out in the valley he had bought a tract of land and set up the beginnings of the plantation.

When I met him, twenty years later, he was doing well. The slave children in this place alone were more than my school could handle, but still I paid a visit. Gladstone had warned me that Smith would be against any attempt to educate the slave children, but I somehow felt a need to push the idea, perhaps just to see how far we could go with it. Maybe I was stupid and boneheaded Brownie.

The force of Smith's rejection shocked me. In fact the intensity of Smith's opposition startled me.

Excuse me Annie and Brownie but his language was heavy.

'Damn you, Yankee boy and all your likes! Here you come marching straight into our ways with your own weak-kneed thoughts. You come in preaching love and goodness and then try to take my own lawful property. Teaching the colored! That's not your plan at all; it's just a way to start up trouble. What's the point of filling their head's with knowledge they will never use? Where's the reason in taking them away from the field and shed each day? I'll tell you what, if people like you get away with this nonsense, it's all going to end with them growing up thinking they have rights that we all know they don't have!

And it's not, legal. You know that, I suppose?'

I was a little dazed, and I thought that he had finished because he had turned and started to walk away. But his final remark caught me completely off guard. I was thinking to myself that this man was a lost cause when he stopped and looked back.

'You damn people from up north don't know nothing about none of this. I would have thought all of that John Brown stuff last year would have warned you off. Your heads are filled with do-good nonsense that's just going to cause trouble for everyone – black and white. Well, the trouble just might start with you. Yes, with you, you yourself, reverend preacher. I reckon if you have any sense you'll get the hell out of here now before you come to a nasty end. You get that? Go home!'

Oh Brownie, he was a short stocky man with slightly bowed legs, a heavy face and incredibly yellow teeth. Forgive me but I thought how much he looked like an English bulldog, and wondered just for a moment whether Smith planned to literally chase me off of the land. I thought of Mrs. Hart and I was glad that she was not hearing those violent threats.

On the ride back to Gladstone's house, I thought more about the situation. Smith may have been the most violent opposition I had encountered, but he had not been the only one. Maybe this was a hopeless venture. Perhaps Richmond would have been a safer place to set up. Or perhaps I should have stayed home in Rhode Island. But then, a lot of people had put their trust in me to carry this out. And over the past days I had seen the children and I had felt their needs. So I decided that the best course for now was to keep the exchange with Smith from Gladstone and the others.

By the middle of February, the work at the meeting cabin had been completed. A fourth wall had been added and the roof extended over the whole structure. Two walls had been put up inside the cabin and a variety of tables, benches and chairs set up. Oil lamps had been set up so that some teaching could take place after dark during the short winter days, and two old woodstoves provided the heating. The men had cut up sufficient wood for weeks. The fact was that after the construction work, the men had enjoyed working together cutting and splitting and stacking the logs.

It was during that time that the first pupils had been nominated and arrangements for their schooling planned. Using the Society funds from me and donations from the local congregation, the misses Jackson and Walters had purchased slates, chalk and blackboards for the school. Twenty young children had been allowed to attend the first lessons, on the proviso that Gladstone and I and the teachers would pick them up and later in the day return them to their homes. Older children were to be allowed to attend later in the day after most of the days winter work had been completed.

That Sunday, Gladstone and I led a dedication service at the school. Thanks were given for all who had made this day possible, and God's blessing was sought for the teachers, the pupils and the future. The congregation sang out hymns at the top of their voices, and Gladstone loudly expressed prayers for the success of the mission.

My own prayer was a very quiet, and in many ways a very personal prayer, for protection for all involved with the endeavor.

It was a fine day, and that afternoon there was a grand social time with the sharing of much food brought by the congregation, some of it kept warm on or near the stoves but most of it enjoyed cold. The food was spread out in one of the rooms and the folk gathered in the clearing outside. I mingled with the people and, coming upon Miss Walters and her father, I was introduced to an old family friend from Harpers Ferry. Jason Clark explained that he had known the Walters for almost as long as he could remember. He always stayed with them when in this part of the world."

Grandma gave out a childish giggle.

"This is where I comes into the story Brownie!"

I gave Grandma a look that said for her to be quiet. Hart smiled and went on.

"Clark was the owner of a general store in Harpers Ferry and had been visiting Wilkes in North Carolina, negotiating to buy the contents of a large warehouse that had recently gone out of business.

'I plan on doubling the size of my place, and I was able to buy the whole lot down there in Wilkes; stock, furnishings and livestock. Included in the price were two slaves and their two children. I told them that I don't hold with slavery and that they were now free. If they wanted, they could come up with me and help run the Harpers place. Well, they jumped at that idea. That's them over there.'

I looked across the clearing and saw the family. I had seen them earlier that morning and had wondered who they were. And so Brownie, that was how I saw your Grandma Annie here for the first time.

Clark called over to them.

'John, Annie, come over and meet the man behind this school, and bring the children over too.'

And so like I said, I met Annie and her family for the first time. Grandpa John told as how they were all so grateful to Mr. Clark and as to how they had never dared to even dream about one day being free. After the sale of the business, they had helped sell the livestock and pack for the trip to Harpers. He explained that most of the stuff was on its way somewhere way behind them, and that they were as he put it, 'just tagging along with Mr. Clark.'"

Grandma could not resist breaking in.

"Your Uncle Elijah was only fourteen and he was full of excitement tellin' about the trip from Wilkes so far, and about how we were going on to Harpers Ferry. I remember how excited he was to tell Reverend Hart about what he had seen along the way so far. His sister, thirteen year old Beth, that's your Momma Brownie, was very shy and she didn't say a word."

The Reverend stopped talking for a few minutes while Grandma filled in some family talk for me. But I was impatient and eventually I urged him to continue the story.

"Alright, alright, by late afternoon most of the people had started on their way home, and come the end it was just me and Gladstone, the Walters, Jason Clark and Grandma's family doing the final clearing. The stoves were closed up and the lamps extinguished. The school was shut and all the remaining food stowed into the wagons. Clark's wagon went ahead, then Walter's wagon and me and Gladstone on horseback. We were so tired and very quiet and thinking about the pleasing day just finished. We were maybe ten minutes out, when young Beth, your Momma, cried out;

'Look, the sky is on fire!'

I hauled my horse around and saw the school ablaze. It was nearly dark and there was enough distance to understand why Beth thought it was the sky on fire. As Walter and Clark began to turn the wagons, Gladstone and I galloped back towards the school. By the time we reached it, the fire had consumed most of the old walls of the building. There was nothing we could do.

Just as the two wagons arrived, the roof fell in forcing the remaining wall to collapse outwards releasing a storm of sparks and smoke and debris. I was standing too close and was struck full in the face by the remains of a blazing plank that came bouncing out of the blaze. Grandpa John caught me just as I fell, and he pulled me back to safety.

Next thing I knew, Grandma here was cleaning my face with some water from the wagon and she was singing to me. When she saw me come around she started to speak.

'There, there, now Reverend you just take it easy now. You got a nasty gash and that knocked you out but you will be all right. I am just cleaning you up a little.'

You have always been so kind to me, Annie.

We looked at the charred remains, still alight here and there, and still smoking. The inner walls that were of new green wood still stood but at a crazy angle, while the two cast iron stoves looked as useless as they now were, standing in the rubble.

The women were in tears. Miss Walters was crying about having left one of the stoves open or the lamps burning. Gladstone had been walking around the remains of the school, and was now standing over me. I was propped up slightly with a couple of sacks. I knew what had happened. The fire had spread far too quickly Brownie to have been caused by a lamp or stove. I guessed that a couple of containers of oil had been splashed around and a number of fires started at the same time in order to have caused this damage so quickly. Someone had known what he was doing, and I figured that I knew who that person was. But to tell you the truth, I don't remember anything of the ride home that evening.

Some days after the fire and after I had pretty well recovered, Gladstone came over to me, and we talked about the future. I recall that I had needed those days not only to recover from the blow to the face but more so to my spirits. I have always thought of myself as a man of faith and a man who generally was able to see the positive side of anything. But this had shaken me, I can tell you Brownie."

He turned towards Grandma

"Annie, I became so depressed. Maybe you can remember that it came down hard on me. You've heard me speak a lot about Job in the Bible because I have studied him and other men and women who had suffered in the past. Thinking about them helped me recognize the self-pity I was feeling. But there was more to it than that. There was the feeling that I had let so many people down and how this would set the societies work back. And try as I did, I could not shake the bitter feeling towards the man that I suspected was behind the fire.

Gladstone as usual came straight to the point.

'You know, I am afraid that no one here has the strength to start again.'

I realized that Gladstone was talking and explaining how distraught the people were, and before he had finished I knew that it was over as far as the valley school was concerned.

But mostly I just wanted to hold Mrs. Hart again, to feel that we were both safe and together again. I missed her so much and I wanted to hold on to her and to tell her that she had been right after all.

I wanted to face the society members and explain how the people here had tried so hard but how the opposition was so much stronger than any of us had expected. I wanted to explain to everyone up there how hatred and prejudice were so much stronger than love and acceptance. Of course I knew better than that, but if I could not convince myself, how could

I ever explain to the others. Everyone deserved an explanation, but no one more I suppose than my-self.

Brownie, I guess you have no idea what I am talking about but Grandma here, I know you do. I always had depression bouts but perhaps none worse than those few days.

'You have to get out man, and face up to things.'

It was Gladstone again. He was a good man who had gone out of his way to support me and the mission, but tact and patience were not among his strongest points I have to tell you. Still, perhaps I needed his prodding.

'You have to get out and figure things out for yourself. Clark leaves for Harpers next week and he has offered to take you along with him for a visit. You can rest up and then catch a train to Providence from there you know. I think it would do you good. There's no more to do here, you know that.'

Mr. Clark had made this offer, explaining that there were quite a few people in Harpers Ferry who felt the same way as I did about education and the slaves. He suggested that a few days there with these folk would help me prepare myself for returning to New England and in making new plans. It made sense to me and I agreed to leave with them the following week.

But Brownie, first I had something to take care of and maybe you can guess what that was. I had to see Franklin Smith.

Let me tell you both that it was not an easy decision. At first I told myself to forget him and just get on down to Harpers and home to Rhode Island. But I knew that if I did that I would blame myself for years to come, and I did not need that. I was a bit scared of him to be honest Brownie, but listen up here boy, this is important. There are times when you have to stand up for what you know to be right.

I went to Smith's place.

'Hey, that looks like a nasty gash on the face preacher man'

Franklin Smith stood outside his shed with his short legs stretched apart and with a self-pleasing and indulgent grin on his face.

'Looks like you might have been playing with fire somewhere and gotten the wrong end of something'

I don't think that Smith was usually a man of words, but he was decidedly amused at his own choice of words that day, and he cleared his mouth of tobacco spit with a satisfied and well-aimed shot between the two of us.

I had dismounted from the horse I had borrowed, and I was staring at the plantation owner. I can tell you that my feelings had taken a bitter turn many times on the ride over, but now I had no thoughts of violence. Not only were they against my nature, but also I was not stupid. If things turned that way then I would most certainly have come out the worst for it.

'Cat caught your tongue preacher? Well there is something new, a preacher who's lost for words!'

Again I could see that Smith felt good about his words.

'Maybe you was pretty lucky to come away with just a thump to the face. Maybe if you had been alone instead of with others, you might have gotten more than that. You know that I suppose. Of course that's just a thought on my side, not that I know what happened.'

He was taunting me just like bullies always do, and he had taken a few steps closer to me as if to add some physical threat to his words. But I was determined and ready and I spoke back at him.

'Mr. Smith, on Sunday afternoon no one saw you spread all of that lamp oil and set fire to the school. No one saw you come up and wait your chance and no one saw you leave. No one heard your laughter and no one felt your pleasure. You were too smart for that. Or rather you were too cowardly to risk being seen by a bunch of God fearing, loving folk and their children. Yes, I suppose that you would think that you were just too smart for that'

Smith took another step towards me, and he was no longer grinning. Had I gone too far I wondered?

'You can't prove a thing preacher. And anyway what would you do? You gonna take me to the law and tell how you was planning to open an illegal school to teach black children how to break the laws of Virginia?'

I was ready for him.

'Mr. Smith, you did not destroy a school on Sunday. You just burned a building. The school will be continued. Not this year I grant you, but sometime in the coming years this school and others will open. Children will learn, and children will learn what is wrong and what is right. You stand for hatred and oppression, and I am sorry for you because those things are all you understand and perhaps all you have ever known. But those ways are not all there is in life. In life there is far more than hatred. Children will be taught that and children will come to understand that. What you are trying to stop is the very thing that you need. And I feel so very sorry for you. All you have really done is to convince me of the need for this work, and what's more you have convinced others living close by. No flood of hatred will extinguish a single spark of love.'

And I bid him good day and turned away towards the horse.

Oh my Lord Brownie, as I walked away and back to the horse, I could feel his eyes glaring at me and I confess to wondering if he might come after me. But he did not. I'd like to think that my words had an effect, but I regret to say that I doubt that."

We had not noticed that the Reverend's daughter Jenny had come into the parlor. She had closed the door and quietly sat on the piano stool as she listened to the end of her father's dialog. She had heard him speak countless times at gatherings and of course during his sermon-time in church. She had always admired how he could convey the gist of a point with eloquence and a spot of drama.

With a little hand of mock applause, she broke into the talk.

'Well said father, well said, and knowing the impact of your words, I have a feeling that they may well have reached that horrid man. But be that as it may, I need to remind you that we have visitors tomorrow and I do not want you over tiring yourself.

Brownie and Annie, I think you should leave Reverend Hart now and let him rest.'

It seems that the Reverend had indeed forgotten that a couple of friends of the family from Hartford were to pay a visit. He motioned me to lean closer.

"Brownie, I had forgotten, so we have to take a break from all this story telling. Go out and get some fresh air tomorrow and play some. Maybe we can pick this up is a couple of days. Off you go now."

15.
Dec 13th 1941,
Dartford, West Virginia

———∞∞∞———

I have not written a word for a few days now. I needed a break after that long section. But I know that I need to get going again. The last outing quite wore me out with all that Big Lick violence. Of course we don't call it by that name any more. Nowadays we call it Roanoke and I visited there some years ago but I could not find any trace of what the Reverend knew. It is a nice city as I recall.

But I did tire myself with the last entry. Perhaps this whole exercise might have been better if I could have gotten someone to type as I dictated. But then maybe I would have missed something. There is something about typing out a feeling and then looking back at it.

Yesterday, as I was looking over my old notes and journals and my Uncle Elijah's notes and piecing them all together, I realized that I was probably feeling something like the Reverend felt as he tried to tell me so much history all at once. He used to get very tired.

Of course I am older now than he was then. Is age suddenly a virtue I wonder? I digress.

The papers have had no more about stopping school segregation. Except, that is, for a note that there is to be a meeting next week. I will have to see where that leads.

At least we do have a good elementary and high school for colored children. It is just at the edge of town and is fairly new. But it makes me so sad to realize that even as I piece together all of these old stories about the struggles we had, that school children are still separated by the color of their skin. Reverend Hart would be very happy to know that they all are getting an education, but I do believe that he would be very disappointed at the continued segregation.

I wonder if I could attend that meeting next week. Will have to see how I feel then. After the meeting over in the next town last week and what happened then, maybe I should not.

These past couple of days, I have been reading about how my family and Willard crossed paths for the first time and that is what I need to cover now. With all of my notes in place, it is back to 1876 once again.

16.

Dec 13th 1876,
Westhill, New Jersey

———✄———

The visit of the family friends from Connecticut had been
agreeable and Reverend Hart had enjoyed catching up
on the various happenings in their two families. Grandma
told me though that it had not started in such an agreeable
manner. It seems that the visitors had immediately begun
speaking in the tone of voice and with the choice of words
that are usually reserved for final goodbyes. Not a man to
mince words, Hart had put that straight by pointing out
that even though he was in bed, he was drinking coffee,
holding a conversation and was very much alive, thank you
very much.

Having straightened that out, they had an enjoyable
couple of hours. But that was enough. Apparently Mrs.
Hart had noticed the tiredness in his voice and she had very
diplomatically wound up the visit. By the time she had bid
farewell to the friends and returned to the parlor, I heard that
the Reverend was fast asleep.

But the next day, after a very good night's sleep, I was told by Grandma that he was itching to get back to the story of Willard and me. When Grandma took his breakfast tray into the parlor he had asked her to give him just half an hour or so and to then bring me back in.

Grandma told me that she had protested, thinking that he would tire himself too much. But the Reverend pressed the point saying that he felt good and that the pains were under control anyway.

And so the story resumed.

"Brownie, I think I had finished telling you about how I had gone to Big Lick full of ambition and then how badly it all turned out thanks to that man Smith and his like. Gladstone kept on about what I was planning next and I figured out that even if he could not bring himself to say it, he wanted me gone and out of their town. And I can't say I blamed him for that.

I decided that although I wanted to be with Mrs. Hart, it might be good for me to rest up for a while first, and so I took Mr. Clark's offer of a spell at Harpers Ferry. I figured that would indeed give me time to recover and to figure out what I was going to report back to the Society up in Rhode Island. Then I figured to take the train from there back to my family in Glocester.

I am glad that I made that decision Brownie, because it was during those few days in Harpers that I met Willard for myself. Let me tell you about that now."

17.
March 1860,
Harpers Ferry, Virginia

———

"The wagon ride to Harpers Ferry was good for me. As much as I had admired the Virginia scenery during the railway journey to Big Lick, I found myself just completely captivated by the beauty of the valley area, as we made the slow journey along the Shenandoah Valley, with the snow-capped mountains looking so beautiful.

Some stops were made along the way with Clark renewing acquaintances with old friends and colleagues, and conducting a little business. The weather down in the valley was reasonably moderate allowing us to make good time most days, and there was ample opportunity for Clark to tell me about Harpers Ferry. I can tell you now that I could feel my spirit returning and Clark told me that my change of heart was evident to them all. I was glad to hear that, but to be honest my boy, some pretty bad feelings would return at night and they caused me much sleeplessness.

By the time we arrived at Harpers Ferry, I knew a great deal about both the history of the area and current situation. Clark's retelling of the John Brown affair was illuminating for me as he filled in detail that had not been widely known up north. I had known nothing about the town connections with George Washington, or about how important the town's geographic position was. More importantly though, I remember getting all excited at the idea of spending time with more Virginian people who shared my opposition to slavery.

Clark's store was an imposing emporium, with the construction of the expansion well in progress. It was outside of town and it served not only Harpers but the surrounding farms and communities. Grandpa John and Grandma Annie and the children were given a four-room shack next to the old store and told to make it their home. The arrangement that Clark and John had made involved the provision of board and food, plus some small amount of money, in exchange for the family taking up employment in various kinds of work around the business. And Elijah and Beth were to receive some schooling from Mrs. Clark. Now that was exciting for them - and for me as well!

Although Clark had described the town quite well on the way over, I was still surprised at the activity of the community. As I strolled around the town on my first morning there, I counted a number of clothing stores, a shoemaker, a butcher and a couple of competing hardware stores as well as a number of taverns and no less than six churches. The town had expanded rapidly over recent years. There was a busy little kind of market place, where the farmers traded their wares and fish merchants sold the fresh seafood that was brought in daily by train.

Down at the river and adjacent to the railroad, stood the town's main employer – the U.S. Armory. It consisted of the factory and some twenty or more other brick and wood buildings. I learned that the Armory employed upwards of four hundred and fifty men, some of whom lived in neighboring towns and villages. The rifle factory was housed a short distance away on an island in the river. Brownie, can you believe that I was told that altogether these premises produced some ten thousand weapons each year? I thought that was horrible.

The railroad facilities were located along the riverbank and a covered railroad bridge across the Potomac River permitted rail service to Washington and Baltimore and beyond. It was there that I stopped and made arrangements to leave Harpers Ferry on March 17th and to return to New England.

After a couple of days relaxing and exploring the town, Clark had arranged for me to meet some of his friends who were supportive of the education mission. I learned that among the town and its neighbors, there were a number slaves and a similar number of free black people. And I learned that there was even some limited opportunities for these folk – both slave and free, to get some education here and there, though that fact was generally kept quiet. I was gratified to have this new information for the society back home and perhaps to have located a site for another mission attempt. I was very excited when Clark invited me to lead worship at his local church during the time I was in the town. They had been without a pastor for some time and he and another elder had been doing their best to lead services.

Clark arranged for me to visit the site of the John Brown raid and to have one of the munitions men give me a descriptive walk around. Well, as much as I appreciated the arrangement, and as informative as it all was, I was not sorry to give him my thanks and to be able to walk alone to the river to rest a little.

All the talk about John Brown brought me too strong a reminder of Franklin Smith and his bigotry and his violence, and of the burned schoolhouse and the effect that had upon the local people. And as much as I tried not to think too much about my own escape from the violence, my close call was just lodged firmly in my mind. I needed to get home to Rhode Island and to my family. I felt for my railway ticket in my pocket and felt a little better.

But my thoughts of going home were suddenly interrupted and I became aware of more trouble around me. Hearing angry swearing on my right I turned just in time to see a young boy of maybe thirteen or fourteen, land a heavy punch to the nose of your uncle Elijah. Elijah reeled backwards and fell into the river, blood gushing from his nose. He made a sorry sight splashing around and trying to hold his nose at the same time! Of course I ran to the river and waded out into the shallow water and hauled the boy to his feet and out of the water.

'Why do you want to help a no good runaway slave like that? He got no right to be here under this bridge where me and my daddy used to fish all the time'

Now Brownie, believe it or not, that was my introduction to young Willard Beauchamp.

The intensity of Willard's anger shook me, and it was clear that the boy was about to throw himself at Elijah again. Elijah for his part had recovered from the surprise and he was equally determined to hit back.

'I'm not a run-away and I'm not a slave at all. I just want to walk along the river. Why you hit me like that?'

Pulling a handkerchief from my pocket, I gave it to Elijah and told him to get on back to the store so that his mother could take care of him. The boy started to argue but then stormed off without another look at Willard.

Not knowing who he was, I tried to speak gently to the boy asking what that was all about. I sensed that there was more than plain rivalry at work. Willard just threw himself down and sat with his back against a large rock, as though he owned the place.

I started to walk away but thought better of it and turning around I sat down next to him, and we just sat there in silence as I tried to wring out the legs of my pants as best I could. The water was cold and I was determined not to hang around too long. So it was me who broke the silence.

'That was a nasty punch my boy, and I think that you may have broken his nose. He is a good young man, and by the way he is a friend of mine and he is free and not a runaway. Now just tell me, why did you do that?'

'As far as I'm concerned they are all the same to me. My Daddy died trying to help them when all they did was run away and hide somewhere. This here is my spot of the river and he had no right being here. I see you earlier up at the Armory today. You're not from around here, I can tell that. Suppose you are one of Brown's men from up north. Don't know what you want with us anyway.'

As he was talking, Willard got to his feet and began to climb up to the road. I got up and followed him and began to explain a little as to why I was in Harpers Ferry and as to how I was most certainly not one of John Brown's men.

But Willard just became quiet and more and more morose. Finally he went on his way.

And so Brownie, like I said, that's how I met Willard.

I suggest you run off now and go up to your room and play. All this John Brown stuff is a bit too much for you all at once

I reckon. I am more tired than I thought. We can carry on tomorrow a bit."

It seemed as though we had just started and I protested a little but one look from Grandma who had come in to the parlor sent me on upstairs to my room in the attic. That little room was mine and mine alone. No one ever bothered me up there so I could lie down and think about what the Reverend had been telling me.

Grandma told me years later that after I left the room, she got up to go into the kitchen but the Reverend beckoned her to stay.

"No Annie, stay awhile. There was more conversation between Willard and me that day and may God forgive me, but something happened the next day that I have always regretted not stopping. I should have gone to the Beauchamp farm and stopped the boy's plans. But I did not. I can't tell Brownie about it now, he is just too young and innocent, but you have to know this part so that you can fill him in a few years from now. He will need to know this and how it played a part in Willard becoming how he was."

So Grandma told me that she sat down again at the bedside.

'I have an idea of what went on that day Reverend. I recall how people talked about it, but go ahead now 'cuz you knows the details.'

The Reverend sat up a little before going on.

"Willard did not just walk away as I told Brownie. He turned on me with a vengeance and gave me an earful I can tell you Annie.

'Well you do what you want. Me, I'm going over to Charles Town tomorrow to see a man hang, in fact I'm going to see two men hang. They was two of Brown's men and they is going to hang them tomorrow and I am going to see them go, and be glad for it too. I hope that they suffer like my poor Daddy did.'

Oh Annie, I had not heard such anger and bitterness from one so young, and I just stood there and watched Willard walk up the hill. And then I went back to Clark's place.

It turned out that Elijah's nose was not broken, and he was off fetching some empty crates from the fish stall for Clark to use out back when I arrived. I sat down with Clark and described what I had just seen and heard. Clark filled me in a little about Willard and how he behaved after the John Brown affair.

'Willard is a very troubled young man Roger. He used to be such a friendly boy and was always coming into town to help me at the store. He used to say how much he enjoyed that instead of working with his brothers and his daddy on the farm all the time. I liked him. But after his father died, we never saw him at the store. We don't see much of him anymore now, or his mother for that matter. These days she spends all of her time up on the farm.

Roger, as far as I can tell, Willard just seems to be constantly making trouble both for him and for others. As far as he is concerned, black or white, we are all to blame for his father's death. I fear that these past few months have changed him for life and I don't know what can be done for him.

So he's off to Charles Town tomorrow is he? I am surprised his mother's letting him go, but you see that's part of the problem – she is grieving so badly that half the time I don't think she knows what the boy is going through. I suppose one of his brothers will go over there too.

You need to know that they are hanging Albert Hazlett and Aaron Stevens tomorrow. Hazlett escaped the fighting but they caught up with him pretty soon. I reckon that it is probably Stevens that Willard wants to see die. I guess that we should try to understand how Willard sees things Roger.

Stevens was shot during the raid but recovered. Frank Beauchamp was shot and died. No mercy there and no justice there for Willard. Stevens and Hazlett both hang at noon tomorrow. May God rest their souls, and maybe that will bring justice for our boy. But I doubt it.'"

Grandma told me how she could tell that the Reverend was searching for words as he told her all of this. I guess that it could be that he found it easier talking to a child like me. After a while he found the words.

"That exchange with Willard and then Clark's explanation caused me a restless night Annie. Ever since I had been a boy on my father's farm, I had been an early riser. As a child, the early morning had been a time for helping with the chores. Then in later years, it had been a time for study, and most recently for my prayers and sermon preparation. That Friday morning was no exception and by breakfast I had already been up and about for some hours. It had certainly been a restless and troubled night as my thoughts kept harping back to Franklin Smith and then on to Willard and the John Brown killings of last October. They all combined and I turned them all over and over in my mind. Long before dawn, I just gave up hope of sleep and I dressed and walked down to the bridge. I remember how beautiful it was.

A light mist sat over the river and an almost imperceptible breeze created strange shadow patterns over the water as the day began to break. The far side of the river came into view first and looking up stream I could see some big old trees leaning out over the water. Our rivers up in Glocester were nothing like this, just streams in comparison. But that morning I remembered a tree that grew over the river near my old home. As a boy I had strung up a swing and in the summer I would swing two or three times and then jump off into the water. Sometimes I was lucky not to hit a rock because it was quite shallow. I thought of home, and as the light opened up the valley, the sight of a locomotive parked on a siding reminded me that tomorrow I would be on a train and on my way back to my dear Mary. But first, I acknowledged a persistent nudging inside me telling me that I needed to try to do something for young Willard.

After some early morning coffee and bread with Clark, I borrowed one of the horses and rode out to the Beauchamp farm. I met up with Willard and his brother Frank as they were just turning onto the road to Charles Town.

It was then that I made the mistake of not stopping them. Instead, I stammered out some stupid remark about joining them.

'I thought that I would just ride over to Charleston to see the executions. Mind if I tag along with you two boys?'

What a useless thing for me to say Annie. Anyway, Frank was sharp and came right back at me

'Well, first of all, we are not going to Charleston. We are going to the county seat at Charles Town, where the courthouse is and we are going to take two of the men that helped kill our daddy and we are going to take them out to a field and hang them. People not from around here always mix up these two towns, but I know you from the Clark place and we might be glad of some new company. But I thought that you were headed back up north already?'

Frank's correction about the town and the invitation to join the brothers was given in a friendly enough way and so I came up alongside and introduced myself more fully. Willard scowled at me but said nothing.

'Yes, I'm taking a train out tomorrow and must admit to being more than a little anxious to see my wife and daughter again. It's been a couple of months since I left them. May I say how sorry I am about your father's death last year? By all accounts he was quite a man of principle who took a stand for what he believed in. I happen to be of the same mind about slavery and non-violence but I fear that we are in the minority. There is a solid movement towards conflict over this and it's coming to a head. You mark my words young man.'

We had plenty of time for conversation on the ride, but I decided not to press Willard for talk. Frank was genuinely interested in what had brought me to Virginia and for my part I was glad to relate the details, including the incident at the schoolhouse outside Big Lick.

'You should meet my Momma. I think that you would enjoy talking with her Reverend and that she would agree with your ideas. Quite a few folk around here would feel the same way too. My daddy always used to say that everyone deserved to learn how to read and write. Good God almighty, I loved him so much.'

Frank apologized for bringing God into it and said how his mother would have threatened to lick him for saying that, but I told him I was accustomed to it and made nothing of it. We rode in silence for a while until Willard began to ask his brother about Stevens and his part in the rebellion. I recall looking at the boy and realizing that for all of his show of feelings and his violent talk, Willard was still just a young boy who really knew very little about what was behind his father's death. I felt so bad for him Annie.

Frank, on the other hand, had read a lot about Stevens, and he took some time to explain to both Willard and me how things had gone wrong for the young soldier after the Mexican war.

I knew nothing about the man, so it was all very informative to me.

'Fact is he was born near your place Reverend, but over in Connecticut. He ran away from home and joined the army in Massachusetts to join in the Mexican War. Apparently he was an unpredictable man who, like many of our soldiers out west, sometimes drank too much. Anyway, after the war, and out in Taos, New Mexico, he somehow got caught up in a struggle against an officer and he was accused of attacking the man. He was court-marshaled and sentenced to death. For some reason President Pierce commuted the sentence and he was sent to Leavenworth for three years hard labor. That did not suit him of course, so he escaped and eventually joined up with Brown in Kansas. Daddy tried to tell me how Stevens was better than most of Brown's men, and how he tried to put Brown straight a few times when he got really wild. On that October day down at the firehouse in Harpers, he got shot under a white flag. Can you believe that? I read how he took at least four musket balls and was in fearful pain after the fighting. I suppose that he's recovered and is well enough to die now!'

The three of us let the irony of Frank's last remark sit for a while. I remember that it was Willard who spoke first. And although he still spoke with a bitter touch, the words were expressed more softly than before. But still they were spoken with a determination that brought a whole lot more concern to me.

'When I was under the bridge, I heard Daddy try to talk Brown out of it all, and I think that Stevens was with them. But he didn't side with Daddy then. He was as bad as any of them. I hope that he hurts some more as he dies.'

Charles Town was crowded that day with visitors by the time we arrived, although I heard that there was not as many as when John Brown was hanged. On that occasion, martial law had been declared for fear of an attempted rescue, and members of the general public were prevented from viewing the execution. We made our way to the field where the executions were to take place, and chose a place near the scaffold. I saw a fellow clergyman standing alone and to the side, and so I made my way over and introduced myself. In fact I enquired as to whether this man was to officiate at the execution.

The clergyman, Ira Jackson, was in fact retired and living out towards the town of Bolivar, quite close to Harpers Ferry. He greeted me warmly and expressed relief at finding someone with whom to share these terrible minutes.

'No. I am not involved. It is their specific request that no prayers or religious actions take place today. I am told that they are both spiritualists and that they deny any of our Christian attention. Hazlett's brother and Steven's sister and his fiancée came to town over the past few days, and I understand that the five of them had a farewell meal together this morning. The visitors have already left for Harpers Ferry where they will wait for the bodies to be delivered later today. I suppose they will catch either a late train or maybe wait until the morning.'

Frank and Willard came over and the four of us waited for the prisoners to arrive.

By eleven thirty, soldiers had taken up position around the scaffold and more spectators had begun to congregate. Word passed around that the condemned were now on their way by wagon, and I was struck with the differences of behavior among the crowd. Earlier in the day while contemplating this trip, I had almost decided to not come for fear of becoming part of a carnival like occasion. But now I became aware that only a relative few were making a party of it. Most were simply curious, perhaps more than a little anxious that this day's action would finally put an end to what had been a terrible five months for this part of Virginia.

There were a few strident antagonists who called out to defend their view on any number of issues from abolitionism to continued support for slavery, and to rally various political factions. Some were using boxes to stand on and call out their views. For the most part people either ignored them or ridiculed them. It was clear that my own feelings of apprehension and deep regret at the prospect of two men dying so needlessly were shared by many others. These people just wanted it over and done with.

'I don't believe that these were particularly bad men, especially young Stevens. Some folk say that he was a good soldier before the fuss in Kansas.'

It was as though Jackson had read my thoughts.

'They were just headstrong, all of them and especially Brown himself. Imagine if they had just worked along with those of us looking to resolve this peacefully.'

I shared that I agreed whole-heartedly with the remark, but unspoken was my growing awareness that politicians were failing to make any progress, and that the Union was slipping toward division and violence. There were too many Franklin Smiths and John Browns on both sides of the issue.

At ten minutes to noon, a hush fell on the crowd as the military guard accompanying the prisoner's wagon marched onto the field. Coming to a halt at the edge of the field, the guard ordered the two men to come down from the wagon and to walk to the scaffold. I was struck by the calm resignation that both men clearly felt. There was no anger and no fear, at least as far as could be seen. I silently prayed for those inner feelings that none of us could discern.

Led by Hazlett, the two men mounted the steps of the scaffold and walked to the ropes. During the last-minute official remarks and actions, Stevens calmly looked around the crowd of spectators and for a moment his eyes caught those of Willard. If Stevens saw the smile on Willard's face, he made no sign of it.

The officiating attendant quickly took charge of the moment, by placing the noose around each man's neck, and by checking the knot action and the mechanics of the drop. During these actions, I was again surprised by the ease of the two men, as both spoke kindly to the jailer and the guard with no expressions of animosity. Finally the two men shook each other by the hand. A hood was pulled over their heads and after a moment, the trap was released.

Hazlett died instantly, but some malfunction of the rope caused Stevens to suffer for quite some time before eventually ceasing the struggle.

I grasped Jackson by the hand and we prayed together that eternity would hold something for these two men that would be far better than the violence of the past months. Annie, I cannot tell you how much I regretted the decision to come with the two brothers.

Frank told me later how he thought about his father and how much he would have hated the scene that had just played out. He also wished that they had not come this morning.

Willard seemed to feel nothing. If he had expected some kind of relief then he was very disappointed. I could tell he was bewildered and that he clearly felt no sense of justice and no easing of the tension and pain that had gripped him since his father's death.

Turning away from Frank, Willard vomited.

Like most boys of his age he did not have, and indeed could not have, the fortitude necessary to support him through the violent act we had just witnessed.

The ride back to the farm was mostly taken in silence. It was clear that neither brother had any desire for talk. As much as I wanted to help Willard, I found myself unable to break into the boy's feelings. I just could not find the words and all attempts at talking the event through or of sharing how they felt were ignored. The depression that I felt at Big Lick, and the sense of failure that had brought me, came over me again.

As we approached the farm, Willard pushed his horse into a gallop towards home while Frank stayed back with me until we reached the turn into the farm. Frank suggested that I come down to the farm house and meet their mother but I decided against it. As I began to turn away for the short ride into town I stopped and spoke once more with Frank.

'I know that your young brother is hurt, and I am afraid that he is more disturbed by all of this than we can possibly know. I came along this morning with the hope and indeed the intent of helping him, but I failed him. Frank, look out for him now and try to help him back to something of a normal life. Try to keep him busy. Let him know that you care about him, and see if he can let go of John Brown and at the same time honor your father. I have the feeling that I may return to Harpers Ferry quite soon and I will make your acquaintance again at that time.'"

Grandma told me how by that point of the story she was holding the Reverend's hand and she was trying to help him as he relived that awful day.

'That was a terrible thing to have seen Reverend and I am glad that you sent Brownie away to his room. But you were right when you said that if the boy is to ever know Willard he must know all of that bad stuff. This is just somethin' else for me to tell the boy a few years from now. You get some rest now.'

18.

Dec 14th 1876,

Westhill, New Jersey

⊶⊷

I remember how the old house was still and very quiet the day after Reverend Hart had told Grandma about the hangings. Of course I did not know then what they had talked about, but I do remember now how Grandma had been very quiet that night at supper.

A light snow had fallen overnight and I had been busy clearing the paths up to the house. Having learned not to upset Grandma by traipsing water into the kitchen, I had left my boots and my coat out in the back porch. Although it was cold outside, I was hot from the work - but I still he enjoyed the stove as Grandma ran her hand through my hair.

'Good job Brownie. You did a real nice job clearin' all that snow away, not that we is expectin' visitors today, not after all of yesterday's comin's and goin's.'

The previous day had certainly been busy. After the morning talk with Grandma and me, Reverend Hart had refused his lunch. Then the doctor came visiting twice in the afternoon. That had me more than a little scared I can tell you! We were not at the end of the story and I knew that. But there was more to it than that because I hated to see the Reverend look and sound so weak.

Two other men who were dressed in what I considered to be very fancy clothes had called and spent some time with the Reverend and his son-in-law. When I asked Grandma who they were she took a while to answer. I knew that Grandma was worried.

'They, young man, were lawyers. Wealthy people put a lot of stock in gettin' all their papers and the like just right, especially when someone might just die soon. Not that the Reverend is wealthy 'cause they don't pay preachers much. But his son-in-law sure is. You just have to look around this house to see that. As far as I knows, they was just clearin' up some details about Reverend Hart's matters up in Rhode Island.

Now Brownie, the good news is that the doctor was pretty pleased with the Reverend's condition when he came again yesterday afternoon for the second time. Say it myself my boy, but I knows how to care for him, although I am worried somewhat. He wants so much to tell you all about Willard and I just hope it is not too much for him. Any way he wants to talk some more with you now Brownie, so get yourself together and go on in now. And mind my words about respect.'

Grandma had the habit of running her fingers through my hair and shaking my head when she talked about showing respect and I had a pretty thorough shake that morning!

It did not matter to me as I just wanted to hear more, so I made my way into the parlor. The smell of medicine was even stronger than a few days earlier so guessed that they were giving him more of whatever it was.

I fancied that he was feeling much stronger though, just as Grandma had said.

"Come on in Brownie and sit yourself down here. Those visitors yesterday and the doctor kind of interrupted our talk didn't they? The doctor said that I was doing better and he gave me some more of this tonic drink. Between you and me, I think it is your Grandma who is doing me the most good. Now don't tell her that for goodness sake or it will go to her head!"

Once again he gave me one of his winks as I sat down at the bed-side.

"Now I am not about to fool myself about my situation Brownie, but I am content that it is all pretty well in God's hands now. And I am certainly thankful for the time to talk with you my boy.

Where were we? I hope that I was able to show you how angry and worked up young Willard was when he was not much older than you are now. It was just terrible how his father had gotten all mixed up like that with John Brown.

The next day I took the train out of Harpers and rode up to Providence. My goodness Brownie, everybody on the train, and back home, were talking about the elections to be held later that year. Abraham Lincoln had just finished a tour through New England trying to get himself put up as the Republican candidate for President.

Oh Brownie, what days they were. The southern states wanted to hang on to their way of life and even to allow slavery to go on into the new western territories and states. They said that it was a matter for each territory and state to decide. And they made noise about separating from the Union and if necessary, that they would be ready to fight for what they believed in.

For our part we were split and some of us wanted nothing less than the total end to slavery everywhere. Others were for leaving the south alone but declaring all new territories to be free and any new state to be admitted to the Union only as a free state. Still others wanted to drop the whole matter and just get on with things. If it all seems too complicated for you now, well don't worry because a lot of folk felt that way then and I can see that this is all too much for you to follow now!

Let me just tell you that Mr. Lincoln made two speeches in Rhode Island and some friends told me that they came away thinking that there was a good chance for him to be elected as president, and that then there would be an opportunity for things to be worked out. So I decided to try to find a way to carry on with my work as a minister and to let the politicians work at the elections.

There was only one problem with that intention, and that was that I no longer had a job! I had to decide what to do next. Of course I had to give my report to the Society and after that I guessed that they would not want to try starting a school again anytime soon. I certainly would not be going back to Big Lick. Of that I was absolutely certain.

I remember how the roads in Glocester were in a poor state following the spring thaw and some torrential rainstorms. As often happens, this rain had also caused severe flooding both of the rivers and the canals that had been constructed to power the many textile mills that had sprung up in the Glocester region over the past decades. You see Brownie, the mills had extended up from Pawtucket and out to just about anywhere there was a running stream. A result of this was that the high water had flooded the lower level of many of these mills so work there was impossible.

Conditions were no better on the farms, and so there was not much work to be done there either. Out on the back roads, wagons frequently became mired down in the mud so that extra teams had to be fetched to haul them out. On the turnpike and other main roads things were not much better, and so most folk just stayed home waiting for conditions to dry out. Life was different out in the country Brownie, compared to in a town like this.

Anyway on that particular day, with heavy rain still continuing to beat down, I did the same thing and enjoyed another day shut in at home with Mrs. Hart and Jenny. There had been more than a few days like this since the return from Harpers Ferry, and I was feeling decidedly better for having the family around me.

But, my goodness, those first couple of days had been very difficult for me as I met my obligation to report to the church society. As I expected, there was a great deal of disappointment as to how things had worked out in Big Lick. On the other hand it was clear that they put no blame on to me. The elders told me that they had no doubt that I had tried my best in the situation there, and that in fact they believed that no one was at fault. The only ill feeling really, was directed at all of us for perhaps ignoring the facts and for getting somewhat carried away with enthusiasm. They now realized that the society had acted without really understanding all of the risks.

I confess Brownie that I had to bite my lip a few times and just shut up when they talked about risks! What did they know about facing a burning beam coming at me, or about that terrible man's threats to my face? I just let it all go though.

Since the congregation in Big Lick had provided most of the materials and all of the labor, use of society funds had been limited to travel and some of my very basic living expenses along with some of the preliminary school materials. A good portion of the money gathered for the project was still available and was in a secure account. I was very pleasantly surprised when the elders voted to send some of that money to Gladstone to cover the cost of rebuilding the meetinghouse, and I was asked to write a letter of appreciation. You see how people can be very good sometimes Brownie? The meeting ended with a unanimous vote to put any plans for the education of black children on hold until the political situation become clear. No surprise there.

But that raised the question as to what was I to do?

Mrs. Hart and I vowed to never be separated again as we had been for the past ten weeks. She had told me pretty clearly how she felt about that.

'It was not just the length of time Roger, as bad as that was, but it was more the feelings of how scared I was for your safety. I just could not shake that terrible feeling, almost a premonition that you were in some danger. And when I heard about what happened at the schoolhouse, well I almost looked into taking a train to join you straight away. But then your letter came telling me that you were going to Harpers Ferry of all places. At first I was so angry with you for not coming home right away. But now, after listening to you, I understand how you needed some time like that. I am grateful for Mr. Clark and the rest of them for helping you through.'

Our daughter Jenny had also been overjoyed at my return. She was thirteen and enjoying school with an eye on becoming a teacher after college. She was trying to understand the political battle that was being waged prior to the coming elections. Unlike most of her friends, Jenny had a genuine interest in those matters, so that beyond the great love that I knew she felt for me as a daughter, I know that Jenny also valued me as mentor and teacher. While I was away she had missed my advice and encouragement during evening discussions.

So maybe you can imagine how Jenny had been enthralled by my telling of the events of last October in Harpers, and by all of the little details that I was now able to provide. The information in the newspapers had been very limited and just recently she had read reports as to how Mr. Lincoln had mentioned the raid in his speech. Now, it all began to make some sense for her and she told me how she was beginning to understand John Brown and his argument.

The rain had eased off by lunch, and after a meal together Jenny had cleared up and gone to her room to read, leaving Mrs. Hart and me at the table. She came straight to the point.

'What are we to do with ourselves Roger? Should we take John Davidson's offer? And if we do, then what next?'

I had been expecting her questions.

'The church expected you to be away for at least two years and they have called young Tucker as minister. He and his new wife are very much liked already. That means that we can't go on living in the parsonage here. They need it.'

I acknowledged all of that. In fact I had already had a number of talks with Tucker and had assured him that I had no intention of trying to have him removed. But one consequence of this was that the church deacons had been forced to point out that Tucker needed the parsonage. So our family needed somewhere to live and I needed a job.

I had written to my old friend John Davidson – you remember me telling you about him and the mill Brownie – and he had immediately written back to me with an invitation for the three of us to stay with him while we decided what direction to take. And so I was able to answer Mrs. Hart.

I told her that I would like for us to settle in Harpers Ferry for a few years, adding just how much I liked those folk and that I knew that she would too. My plan was to write to Jason Clark about it and in the mean time to take John Davidson's offer and move in with him and Joan for a while. They had a good size house right on the river next to the mill and I knew that we would be welcome there for a few weeks. Now Brownie, you see the value of good friends? That's important in life, and you just mark my words about that. Whatever else you do, also try to make good friends.

Our daughter Jenny fit in with that plan alright, and she immediately began to get excited about the idea of travelling.

And so over the course of the coming week, we packed our possessions and moved just a few miles across the state to Pawtucket.

One day we were going through the mail when I came across a response from Clark. It was more than I expected Brownie. Not only were we welcome to come back, but he had held a meeting with his church elders and they were pleased to offer me the calling of pastor! I tell you my boy that I was so very thrilled at that. They couldn't pay me very much, but there a small house attached to the church and they thought that everything would work well for all of us. They also said how much they had enjoyed the couple of services I had led when I stayed with Clark.

Like I said Brownie, it was more than I had expected and so we wrote back and accepted the offer.

You know I am really feeling stronger with all this recollection and retelling the story Brownie and I do believe that it is as good for me as it is for you my boy. So now, let's get back to Harpers and pick up our story."

19.

July 1860,
Harpers Ferry, Virginia

———⊗⊗⊗———

"Harpers Ferry certainly had its fair share of churches in those days, in fact one more than now I think Brownie. The relationship between those churches was pretty open and cordial. It had to be in a small town like that. Some of the churches more than others of course, but all of them were generally tolerant of each other's views. The church that had called me was an independent congregation leaning towards the Baptist view of things when it came to matters of baptism and communion and the like, but I felt real warmth from all of my new colleagues in town.

My church had been without a regular pastor for more than a year, and so we immediately found ourselves accepted into the church family. Quite a few members had drifted away during that past year, but after a month, the Sunday service was attended by upwards of fifty folk – as many as had ever attended there in the past I think.

The church and the adjacent house were on the outskirts of town and up the hill in the direction of the Beauchamp farm.

That first month was wonderful for both Mrs. Hart and myself as we introduced ourselves around town and as I renewed acquaintances. The summer weather was warm without the higher temperatures and humidity that would follow in August, and we two New Englanders enjoyed each other and our new township. Jenny also settled in really well. She had plans move back to New England in the fall, to stay with an Aunt and to attend school.

I had told Mrs. Hart back in Rhode Island, that there was some teaching of young black children going on. In fact, under Clark's leadership this had been in practice for a few years and this was one of the reasons that I had felt drawn to the town. Mrs. Hart immediately offered to help expand the teaching – just a little you understand. So after engaging the help of three other women church members, a room at the back of the church was cleared out and some small tables and chairs set up for the purpose. All of the folk involved were determined to keep it at a quiet and low level and to avoid drawing attention to the work. Most of the town was of the opinion that no harm was being done and the few that frowned on it were hard pressed to make an issue out of things. With the events at Big Lick still playing hard upon my mind, let me tell you that I certainly saw the sense of keeping it all a bit quiet.

Around the town there was much talk of the political scene in Washington and of the coming elections and possible consequences, but I separated myself from all of that. I had had my fill of it all and at least for the time being, I was able to put all the talk aside and concentrate on becoming a part of the community.

But I have to tell you something now Brownie and here is another lesson for you. It is that it does not do to shut things out like that. Before long, like a lot of other people, I found myself looking back at that summer of 1860 with a real longing for better times again. It is better to face up to things, even bad things, and try to work them out.

On one of my early rounds of the town, I introduced myself to the Catholic priest and I asked about the Beauchamp family. I learned that Betsy had stopped attending the church. The priest told me that during visits to the farm, he had been unable to break into Betsy's depression and he admitted to a feeling of inadequacy about the matter. The older boys, like their father, had not been involved with the church for many years and so he could not reach their mother through them. Willard had been in the habit of going to church with his mother, but now he had also stopped attending.

I described my experience with Willard and how I had felt drawn to help the lad, and I asked the priest if he would be comfortable with me visiting the family and trying to help them. Well, there was no objection from him, and in fact Brownie I think I sensed some relief on his part that perhaps I could be of help.

Clark had given the us some hens to provide a steady supply of eggs, and so part of my morning routine was to clean the hen house, feed the hens, or 'the biddies' as I called them, and to collect the eggs. Far from being a chore, such times provided me with the opportunity to think on all I had to be thankful for and to offer prayers of thanks. It was during one of these times, just a few days after the meeting with the priest that Willard came into my mind again, and after delivering the eggs to the kitchen, I decided to visit the farm.

It was a fairly easy walk to the top of the hill to Hill Crest farm, and on that particular July morning it was a pleasure to walk that old beaten path between verges of high grass and wild flowers. The scent of the flowers filled the air with a fragrance that took me back to my boyhood in Rhode Island. Stopping at the flat rock where I later learned that Frank and his father before him had rested many times, I sat down and admired the view of the farm.

Off to one side of the farm it was quite wooded and I could just see some small clearings with ponds. I had no doubt that Willard had spent time exploring those.

In spite of everything, the boys had maintained the farm well over the past months and there were signs of a good summer to come. Seeing Sean and Frank junior working on the far meadow, I decided to go straight to the house.

Willard's mother Betsy was sitting on an old rocker on the porch as I approached the house. She was reading and seemed to be unaware of her visitor until on removing my hat, I introduced myself. She seemed to be not surprised to see me and did not even look up when she spoke.

'Well, well now Mr. Hart, I saw you coming down the hill and I know who you are. We heard that you were back in town. Frank has told me all about the trip to Charles Town and how upset you all were at the hanging. I must say that I have wondered many times what in the blazes could have allowed you to let my young boy go to a thing like that instead of bringing him and his brother straight home to their mother! What were you thinking of now?'

It was with those words that Mrs. Beauchamp had looked up from her book, and had looked me straight in the eye.

'Now what on earth were you thinking that morning? Oh for that matter I suppose, what the devil was I thinking not to have stopped it! And Sean and Frank, what were they all about? And now here you are back in town and set up as a preacher and on my front porch.

Sit your self down now while I get us some tea.'

I can tell you Brownie that I was relieved. After the initial sting, Betsy's voice had become lighter and just a touch more friendly I fancied. I think that her Irish brogue even softened the criticism for the Charles Town visit. I had expected such criticism anyway, although not with such an openness. But the soft Irish lilt had offset her anger, an anger that was clearly not directed to me alone anyway.

The tea was very welcome, and we sat there side by side in the morning sun with neither of us in any particular hurry to speak. Finally it was me who broke the awkward silence. Putting my cup down, and declining a refill, I told her why I had visited that morning.

'First Mrs. Beauchamp, my sincere condolence on the death of your beloved husband last year. Of course I was not here at that time but I have become aware of his bravery in trying to stop John Brown's foolish and ill-conceived plan. Also, I am very aware of the effect it had on young Willard. It was for that reason I joined them that morning in Charles Town. I wanted to help. I wanted so much to help, but I failed. Please forgive me. I suppose that I felt drawn to come out here this morning to see if there is any way, anything at all that I can do to help now.'

Brownie, I confess that it had all come out in too formal a manner for my liking. You see it was my coldness once more, that something that always came between me and my efforts to comfort those who were hurting - even those closest to me sometimes. After so many years in the ministry I still suffered with this. I was about to try to add some more comforting and soothing words, but she cut me off pretty sharply.

'Well now, so you are worried about Willard are you? And how about Sean and Frank then I might ask you, how about them now? They have kept their grief and anger bottled up inside them something terrible, and sometimes I can see how they are in awful pain. I just can't seem to help them. And then there's me-self who has also just been shutting everything out. It was all so stupid and unnecessary that day. Can't you see that?

Willard became so morose and he just cut himself off from all of us. I can't seem to help him any more than I can help the other two. I keep asking why it all had to happen, that's what I keep on wanting to know. And why did Frank have to get involved anyway?'

Betsy tossed her red hair to one side and her face flushed as so many painful thoughts came rushing back. And then she started to cry.

'These past few weeks I have begun to see how Frank only meant for the best. But he was so headstrong Reverend, and he so much wanted to do what he thought was right. I know that he felt the pain of others more than his own and I know that he honestly believed that the time had come to end slavery. But he also knew that violence was not the way, and yet he got all caught up in it. How he ever got involved with Brown I will never know, or how he ever thought that he could change things. I have thought on it and thought on it and now I see myself at the end of the rope and at a total loss as to what to do.

I will never be able to understand it all, but I know that I have to come out of my being down in the dumps all of the time. I know that. I can honestly say that I will be glad for any help that you or anyone else can give to our family. And you are so right about one thing Reverend, although we are all still suffering it is Willard that needs help the most.'

Betsy was crying and shaking inconsolably as words that had been unspoken for too long came pouring out. Putting aside both my New England reserve and my own usual remoteness, I leant over and gently put my arms around Betsy, holding onto her and telling her that I understood how she felt and that along with Mrs. Hart we would do whatever we could to help. I recall telling her that everyone understood how hard the past few months had been for her family, and how they could all begin to start over now.

She had begun to talk about things and that was good, and so I asked her to tell me about how her husband and son had gotten mixed up with John Brown in the first place. It was then that I heard how they fit into the story that I had heard from Mr. Clark and the others.

Oh Brownie, she was so upset and I was so thankful that I had made the visit just at the time that she was recognizing the need for help. One day I know that you will understand things like that Brownie. You are a sensitive boy.

Anyway, I know that Betsy appreciated both the warmth of my embrace, and of my genuine compassion and sympathy. After she told me about Frank Beauchamp's part in the raid we sat in silence for a few minutes partially because words were not necessary but also because I found myself searching for some appropriate words. It was at times like that Brownie that I envied some of my colleagues who always seemed to be able to say the right thing. I had to remind myself that sometimes it is not words that matter, and so I just tightened my hold around Betsy as she continued to cry.

I knew that by just being there I was helping Betsy - probably more than I realized, but as had happened so many times to me at moments like that, I just began to feel uncomfortable with this level of closeness. So I relaxed my hold a little and tried to move the conversation along by returning to Willard and I remarked that maybe we should talk about Willard and how we might be able to help him since we agreed that he needed it the most. I did not see him approach us.

'So Willard needs some help does he, even the most help? I heard that you were back in town Mr. Hart but what are you doing here hugging my mother like this? Shouldn't you be back down the hill teaching the black kids? And Mother, just what are you doing?'

Looking over Betsy's shoulder, I saw Willard leaning against the porch. Clearly he had been standing there for a few minutes and had heard the latter part of our conversation.

Betsy got to her feet, and drying her eyes, she walked to her son.

'Willard, mind your words now. These past days I have been seeing the need for me and you and your brothers to pull out of our sadness. Your father would not have wanted us to carry on like this. And the true fact is that we can't go on like this. Reverend Hart here just came up to visit us and to see how he can help us. Willard, I need help. No don't turn away like that. I really do need help. And so do you and your brothers. And listen boy, I need your help as much as you need mine. We have to work this out together Willard. And we have to start now. Can't you see that my love?'

I could see that the words were lost on Willard as he ran from the porch, out to a small herb garden and an old oak tree that had probably been a favorite climbing spot just a year ago. Leaning into the tree and pressing his head against the bark, I could see Willard fighting the anger and trying to hold back the grief and cursing under his breath all that had happened. I think that he felt very much alone at that moment and that he honestly believed that no one understood and perhaps even that no one cared. I walked over to the tree.

'Willard, I think that I know how you feel, and although you may not believe this, I think that I understand a little. And by the way, I really do care.'

I had approached the boy as gently as I could before speaking. He straightened up and turned to me.

'No one understands. How could you know anything about how I feel? You have never been through what I have and all of your preacher talk can't help me. Just go back to where ever it is that you came from. I heard that you nearly got killed down near Lynchburg or somewhere, so why don't you just go back there. '

Willard's voice was edged in bitterness, but Brownie I had cared for enough people to know and to recognize a call for help when I heard it. I tried to bring him to talk a little with me. So I began to talk about something that happened to me when I was a boy. You don't know about that yet Brownie, but let me just tell you now that it shook me up as much as the John Brown affair had shaken Willard. So I went on and told him a little about it.

'When I was just a bit younger than you are now Willard, something happened to me that caused me and my family much pain and confusion. Everything had been going so well for me and I was so happy. Then one day I saw something terrible happen. There was so much violence that day with blood and a killing, and then so many lies and so much grief. I blamed myself and I thought that I had caused it all. I may not have known your Daddy boy, but I think that I know something about how you feel. Believe me. Won't you let me help you?'

I had caught his attention, and Willard looked at me with more than a little curiosity about this turn in the conversation.

'What happened to you then?'

I remember closing my eyes, and I think that I probably clenched my fists a little. Other than Mrs. Hart this talk with Willard was the closest I had ever come to telling anyone about what had happened to me many years earlier on a Rhode Island beach. Brownie, I told your Grandma the story too, and she will tell you about it when you are a little older. But for now just try to understand what I told Willard that day.

'Willard, when I was twelve years old, I spent a few days on the shore back in Rhode Island. And I saw a man murder a young woman in a sand dune. I saw him beat her to death. I was so scared that I turned and ran as fast as I could to get away from them. People came and questioned everybody and I lied. I lied to them, I lied to my mother and I lied to my father. I lied to them and I lied to myself by trying to shut it all out of my thinking. But I never could. In the end I blamed myself for so much.

If I had shouted out, perhaps the man would have stopped beating her. I have told myself over and over again that he would not have attacked a young boy like me. I blamed myself for not telling my mother as soon as I got to the house. Maybe if I had, she would have run back to the dune and just maybe the girl might have been still alive and could have been saved. I blamed myself for some hurt that I brought between my mother and my father and for all the times after that when perhaps they wondered if I was telling the truth or lying about something or another. That's a problem with lies. Once you start telling them, people never know for sure when you are being truthful.

Willard you say that I don't know how you feel. Well, just maybe I do. I don't think that you told a pack of lies like I did, but I reckon you blame yourself for what happened to your daddy. You think that if you had told your mother, she might have talked him out of going into town that day. But inside, I think that you know that he would have still gone. So you feel that you have to share the blame with someone and you choose to blame the black people, especially the slaves and anyone like me who's trying to help them. Am I right?

Willard, your father was a good man. He would have stood against Brown whatever happened and whatever you might have said or done. Your father hated slavery and today he would be with me and the others who are trying to do something. I can understand that for you to try and see him like that seems to put him right back with John Brown. And that's something you can't bear to think about. But he wasn't like that, and you have to know that. It's a mess alright, that's the truth of it, but if you will start to understand what I am saying you can start to put it behind you. I was never able to do that Willard and...'

I stopped as Willard turned and pushed me aside and walked away from me and up towards the road. I knew Brownie that I had lost him again. He stopped half way up and called back to me.

'It's no good preacher. Can't you see that it's just no good? You got your problems and I guess that I got mine. Please do whatever you can to help my mother, but leave me alone. You got that?'

I went back to the porch and sat down again with Mrs. Beauchamp and we talked some more. I knew that this was helping her some and that I had timed my visit just as she was looking to find something that we call closure. That means putting stuff behind you and moving on with your life Brownie. I just told you a little about what happened to me when I was a boy and I wish that I had talked to someone then. But that's all in the past now.

Anyway, I watched Willard walk to the top of the hill where I was surprised to see him turn and wave to his mother.

I learned later from Elijah that Willard had walked down through the town to the spot on the river bank to the place where he punched Elijah when they first met. You remember? It turned out that Elijah and your Momma where already sitting on the bank and Elijah was fishing. When Elijah saw Willard approaching he became scared that that there was going to be a repeat of what happened before. Elijah was a big boy and last time he had been surprised by Willard. So he told me that he was not scared for himself, but because did not want your Momma to see trouble. Of course he had to get that in."

The Reverend gave me that familiar wink again and then quickly returned to his story.

"Elijah wedged his fishing pole between a couple of rocks and stood up and walked towards Willard ready to face whatever happened.

'OK Willard, if you want trouble, lets you and me go off on our own now.'

'Just sit down Elijah. I only want to talk a little.'

Elijah was surprised, and feeling off guard, he just stood there. Eventually he sat down next to Beth and shoved his feet out in front of himself and stared at them and at the water. Willard stood there for a while and then sat down on the other side of Beth. The three of them sat there, probably not knowing what to say. In the end Elijah told me that it was Beth who spoke first.

'Willard Beauchamp, just what do you want with us? You scowl around town so, and you punched my brother on the nose when we first come here and you ain't spoken a kind word with us since. So now, what you want with us?'

Still Willard said nothing for a while, seeming to gather his thoughts. Eventually he stammered a few words.

'I'm sorry I punched you that day Elijah. But you looked so happy – you always do – both of you, and I was feeling so bad about what happened to my daddy. Sometimes I still think that this place just belongs to my daddy and me. Do you know all about what happened to my father with that John Brown?'

Elijah told him that they had heard all about it from Mr. Clark and others and how it was that the black folk thought highly of Willard's father, much more so than that nasty John Brown. Elijah had to add that his Momma didn't feel exactly that way, but that most folk did.

They just sat there a while longer without saying anything. And then Beth put her hand on Willard's knee and began gently stroking it. She had learned this from her mother and she would do it to Elijah when he got angry at something and it usually made him feel better. It seemed to help Willard too, and they continued to sit there.

Finally Willard stood up and walked away without another word.

'Can we be friends then?'

Beth had stood and called after Willard. He stopped and turned and walked part way back.

'No, we can't!'

Now Willard was shouting.

'You two still make me sick. You act out like you are so happy and smarty like as though nothing ever happened. It makes me sick I tell you. You think you are free? Well, just try leaving Clark. Where would you go then? He is still your boss-man and he still controls you. You are nothing and you never will be anything. My Daddy was out there trying to help you folk and he got killed for it. I heard that even Reverend Hart nearly got himself killed trying to help your folk.

I don't know why I came over here today. I guess that I was looking to work things out, but you are murderers, all of you. And I hate you still.'

Beth was crying and Elijah was holding back his anger as he held on to his sister. Willard for his part was striding up the hill, trying to control his feelings but also at the same time I reckon that he was feeling some regrets at his words."

20.

Dec 14th 1876,
Westhill, New Jersey

—⦿—

"**B**rownie, now that is how between me and your family, we tried to start to turn things around for Willard.

I suppose that he became a little less lonesome and miserable. He even began helping out Mr. Clark at the store again. Mrs. Beauchamp started back attending her church and used to always have a kind word for me when we met. But poor Beth and Elijah seemed to never get over the harsh words, and they avoided Willard like the black plague. Of course that was particularly difficult on those few days that Willard helped Clark. It seemed like he always had some hard words for those two in particular as though deliberately trying to get them all riled up.

Although Elijah denied it, I am pretty sure that he and Willard exchanged punches a few times after that.

There was a time when I was visiting Clark and I came across Willard and Beth in the feed shed and he was making

fun of her and her family and calling them all kind of names –
very bad names Brownie. You need to know that he did have a
pretty nasty side to him, and that's for sure.

I noticed that Beth stood her ground and did not respond
to his unkind words. Seeing me, Willard stopped yelling and
he turned away from her. Beth started to tell him that no
matter how often he yelled at them, she was not going to get
all riled up like him. I was surprised when Beth added that she
liked Willard and felt sorry for him and his family. He did not
say another word, but turned around and walked away."

For a couple of minutes the Reverend and I sat quietly in
the parlor. Beth was my mother and so the fact that Willard
was nasty to her upset me, and it kind of made sense of how
Grandma avoided talking about him. But I remember that as
interesting as it all was, I failed to see what it had to do with
me and I had to ask the Reverend why he was going over this.

"I have been wondering when you would ask that Brownie.
I know it's a lot to take in but you are old enough to remember
most of what I am telling you and that's what I am hoping will
happen. I need to tell you a little about the war.

You have to know Brownie that Harpers Ferry was a part
of Virginia in those days before the war. The Armory and the
rivers and the railroad and the nearness to Richmond and
to Maryland and Washington all put the town on the list of
important places for both sides.

After the war started, the town changed hands so many
times Brownie, back and fro, back and fro as the two sides
fought. It seems that it was always on either one general's path
of advance or another's path of retreat. Or it was one army's
store and gathering point or the other's means of blocking the
enemy's progress. We had to keep leaving town and then try
to get back to some kind of normal until the next action. A lot

of town people left and did not return until near the end of the war. Some never came back.

Of course both sides wanted the Armory and the rifle factory. When Virginia seceded, one of the first acts of the war was for the Union force to destroy as much of it as they could before the Confederates could take it over. It was a fearful sight to see the fires and the destruction. That day also showed how sympathies lay around the town with either one side or the other.

Clark pretty well shut up shop and just kept to selling basic stuff to the town and to the communities further out. Grandma and her family stayed on with him. Like many of the farmers, Willard's family kept going, though it was very hard on them.

I am not going to give you a history story of the war my boy because that can come later when you really start school. Let's just say that life was pretty bad for most of us. Like I said, some families gave up and left town but many of us just stayed on, hoping that the end would come soon. We kept hoping that. Year after year we hoped that!

When the fighting got too close and too bad, we would go out of town or sometimes kind of hole up in the churches because we had the feeling that the soldiers would try to avoid the churches. At least that was what we prayed.

There was one really bad battle in September of '62 across the river at Antietam, you must have heard about that. There were twenty-three thousand casualties that day Brownie and more than thirty-six hundred men died. Just think about that a moment. And at the end of it all most people said it was a tie. Imagine that – a tie! Ah, but one important thing for you my boy is to know that it was just after that, that President Lincoln made his famous statement about the freedom of slaves. Emancipation he called it.

And that was a real milestone for your people Brownie.

Anyway, I had my first taste of it all just a couple of days after that battle. It was just a mess in Harpers. Jackson had been in control and the area around town was full of confederate soldiers pulling back. I was really scared that the Union men would come pouring in after them, but that never happened. We all fell into a kind of lull.

I was reading in the church one morning just a couple of days after the big battle, and Beth came running in.

'Rev Hart, we found a soldier in the old hog shed at Mr. Clark's place and he is really hurt bad. The soldier I mean, not Mr. Clark but the soldier. He is bleeding and moaning so. You just have to come now.'

Poor Beth could hardly get the words out straight she was so excited.

'Of course there's no hogs there anymore but we heard him and found him under the straw. He is hurtin' and is mighty 'fraid too. There is blood everywhere. You got to come help him.'

So I followed your Momma back to Clark's and into the hog shed. They used to smoke meat in there before the war and it still smelt kind of funny. Elijah was standing over a confederate soldier who had tried to hide under some straw that Clark was storing there. There was some blood on the straw, but not as much as your Momma had led me to believe. I guessed that the man had been there for the past day and night. He was certainly hurting pretty bad Brownie, I could see that right away, and he was moaning so loud. That was what had led your Momma and Elijah to find him.

Well, I tried to talk to him but he was not making much sense. It seems he ran away from the fight after being shot in the side. He kept saying how he was tired of seeing men die and was just going to find somewhere to go. I don't know how he made it across the river to our town, I guess his legs were OK and probably he was so frightened that he found the strength to keep going. It's not that far I suppose and his wound did not look that bad. But he had lost an awful lot of blood since the shot had hit him, and the real problem was that it was dirty and I guessed that a bad infection was probably setting in.

I did not want to frighten Elijah and your Momma, but to help a deserter was pretty serious and we were surrounded by Confederate people so we might be found out quickly. They would have had no mercy on your family on account of their color. So I just told them that we had to get some of his own people to help him. I knew that would probably mean that they would shoot the man, but it was obvious that without help, he was going to die anyway. I didn't say that part out loud Brownie.

Well, the poor man heard me say that we had to get him help, and he began hollering about us keeping him safe. He was getting all confused and was pretty soon in and out of sleep even as he tried to speak. Elijah got all excited about how we just had to take care of him and I was getting pulled one way and another. I knew we could not keep him and yet the idea of giving him over to be shot just stuck in my craw Brownie.

It was your Momma, Beth, who took over. She got down on her knees in the straw and cradled the man in her arms. She began to quietly sing an old song she had learned from your Grandma, and she just rocked him back and fro as he slept.

Elijah and I just stood there watching for a while. Then Elijah got down beside Beth and began to pray.

I just stood there. The preacher man wondering about how safe we were while they took care of this man. Yes, that's the truth Brownie and I am not proud of it.

Just then Willard came in and saw what was going on. I was afraid that he would go off running and hollering for help. But he surprised me by going over and kneeling next to Beth and Elijah. Pretty soon Beth stopped her singing and her rocking and laid the man back in the straw. Elijah stood up and came over to me.

'He's died Reverend. He just died there with Beth and me and Willard. What shall we do now?'

'What we do now is that Reverend Hart here, goes into town and fetches a soldier to come up and take this man away. You can say that you found him in the shed and that's true anyway. Elijah, you and me go home and forget this ever happened. We tried to help and in a way we did. Now it's over. Willard, if you know what's good for all of us you do the same.'

That's why I tell you this story Brownie. You see it was your Momma just what, fifteen years old, who took over that day. I want you to know that she was a very strong and a very loving young lady. You can be very proud of her my boy.

We all left the shed together and before they split up, Beth gave Willard a hug and told him again to be quiet. I was surprised that he held on to her for a moment before heading to the farm.

Like I said, I am not going to give you a history lesson my boy, so let's just say that the war dragged on and on year after year. Our part of Virginia never did embrace the idea of a break in the country, and in 1863 it became a state in its own right - West Virginia. That was the big milestone for all of us then.

Meanwhile so many of our men went off to fight and too many never came back. Willard's brother Frank went off with the Union army early in 1862 and it was months before we heard from him. Everybody kind of mixed in and helped out families that had men off to war. Willard took over the farm work with his brother Sean and his mother.

The whole thing dragged on until in 1864 when Willard just disappeared. He left a note for his mother telling her that he was off to join the Confederate army. He had the feeling that Frank would be home soon and with Sean would take over the farm again. He loved her. And that was that. It was just a short note from son to mother. I thought that it was very cruel of him Brownie.

A month later your uncle Elijah announced to his mother that he was joining the United States Colored Troops and would hear no protests. In his mind it was a done thing.

So there I was Brownie, consoling two mothers whose boys had gone off to join the opposing armies. It was worse for Willard's mother of course, at least until Frank came home from Atlanta late in August of '64. He was alive but he was completely worn out. He looked years older than his age and it was a while before he could do much around the farm.

Your Grandpappy and your Grandma actually became quite proud of Elijah. Grandma Annie told me that the fact that a son of hers could fight in the United States army was something special. She told me how she often thought of her father who had been sold and murdered just eleven years earlier and now here was her son fighting so that kind of thing would never happen again.

What neither lady knew was that in July of that year, their sons were facing each other in battle. When it was all over,

I was able to put that part of the story together from what I heard, and I will tell you about that tomorrow.

Right now I can hear Jenny coming and she wants to talk to me about more Rhode Island stuff. It doesn't mean anything to me anymore but it's important to them, so run off now my boy and come back tomorrow. But think on what I have been telling you."

21.
December 14th 1941,
Dartford, West Virginia

I had been busy writing that last section for a few days. I did take some time off for a short walk around the park one day, and I have kept my habit of walking to the corner each morning to buy the daily paper. I do that, not just to keep in touch with the news, but also to visit with the others there. It's the only time I get to talk with other people now as nobody visits me since I moved into this room. I have a good friend at the store by the name of Stan and it is always good to talk with him.

The news about school segregation continues to irritate me no end. As usual we have two active camps. The one is for the status quo and leaving the school system as it is while the other is all about pushing for an end to segregation.

Seems there are militant and peaceful folk in both groups. With war declared now, I suppose that people will turn their attention away from this issue for a while.

I reckon that what irritates me the most is that I can so clearly see the parallels with the past. As a retired educator who's family struggled first with slavery and then with the Civil War and the aftermath I want to be out there protesting and pushing for reform at all costs. I went to the meeting over in the next town last week and maybe I will go to this next meeting to see first-hand what is going on there. Or maybe not after the way I acted last week. I will have to see about that later.

The ghost of my namesake John Brown hovers over me and demands to know if I would really follow the violent path. Most of the time, I come to the conclusion that I would not be violent. And then the memory of my dear friend Roger Hart jolts me and tells me that I should do something.

I am seventy-five years old for goodness sake! What could I possibly get up to now that would border anywhere near the violent? Although I suppose that I was not exactly peaceful last week.

This all bothers me so much and I guess that is why I am spending these hours banging away on my old typewriter. It is why I am reading and re-reading all of the old notes and putting them into some kind of order. Oh, and I admit to filling in some gaps in the notes but only to round out the story and try to make it interesting enough to be read one day.

When it's finished there will be time to decide what to do next.

But I am still in the thick of it for now. The pile of discarded notes is still smaller than the heap of yet-to-be used notes.

The Reverend was good to his word about not teaching me a history lesson about the Civil War. I would not have understood it back then, and in any case it is in itself such a huge issue that I do believe that every American should take the time to have a close look at it.

But he did spend time talking about one of the battles. It turned out that although it could have been a decisive battle, it fell short because of ineptitude and the fear of political failure. What was important to me was that it involved two of the men the Reverend had been talking about – Willard and my Uncle Elijah.

When I was teaching about the Civil War, Elijah took the time to write me a long description of that battle. I used to use those notes in class to get the students thinking about what happened and to talk about how they felt. Today I can use Elijah's notes along with my own notes of what Reverend Hart told me.

So with fresh paper in the typewriter, I return to those days.

22.

December 15 and 16th 1876, Westhill, New Jersey

———❦———

Although I was as eager as ever to pick up the story the next morning, I had been told that the Reverend had taken a turn in the night and was not to be disturbed. Just what 'taken a turn' meant had to be explained by Grandma who seemed to me to be more upset than before. She explained that perhaps she just had to believe that the Reverend really was dying and that I should start to accept it, too. For my part, I became very nervous that I might not hear the rest of the story and so I recall that I spent the day helping out in the kitchen and day-dreaming about the war and Willard.

The next morning finally came and once again I could not wait to get downstairs to find how the Reverend was feeling. Grandma had his breakfast ready and smiled that the Reverend was feeling his old self again and would probably talk to me later. I was very relieved and I attacked my breakfast eggs and biscuits with renewed enthusiasm. After clearing up from the meal, I quietly made my way to the Reverend's bedside in the parlor. I say quietly because I most definitely wanted to be on my best and most respectful behavior. The Reverend looked up at me as I sat down.

"People worry too much about me Brownie and that's the truth. But they mean the best and I know that. The fact of the matter is that I have been looking forward to picking up our account again. I later learned enough of this part of the story to piece it together and you will be pleased to know that it starts with Willard.

When I say 'the fact of the matter' Brownie, I mean that I have learned more than enough about the war experiences and I am determined to spare you most of the detail. It was all too horrible and it would be just too much for you my boy. I have heard stories that made my own difficult times seem inconsequential. I am going to paraphrase it for you Brownie and that means that I am going to skip some detail but give you the facts.

Yesterday when they all tried to keep me quiet, I spent some time going over this in my mind so I pretty well know what I want to say now. Mind you, all of the detail that I am going to skip over is also fresh in my mind. It's all too fresh, because as much as I have tried to wipe Elijah and Willard's accounts of the battle out of my memory, they just will not ease. They will not go away. And last night I relived their stories.

Sit back boy and listen now."

23.

June – July 1864,
Confederate Lines, Petersburg, Virginia

—◦◦◦—

"Willard was surprised by what he saw as a lack of organization in the army. Prior to enlisting, he had heard about glorious battles and successes, and in his mind he was convinced that the confederation of southern states was valid and that the war should be ended as soon as possible in favor of separation. He had also heard some terrible accounts of troop losses so he was not under any illusions about an easy conclusion to the conflict. But the general tone of the division he was attached to concerned him. Some of the men clearly thought that the cause was lost and that the war would soon end in defeat. Others were just plain indifferent and went through the motions only for fear of disciplinary action. Willard was not encouraged.

Many of the men who had served for some time were fatigued and some even spoke about deserting. The food was awful and a common discussion at meal time centered on recollections of home cooking. And mind you Brownie, Willard's mother could cook pretty well.

And yet, Willard found a deliberation about the job to be done. For most of the men, all of the problems could be set aside when they were called to fight. Most of the officers were able to drum up renewed determination in the ranks and raise morale. Willard saw something of his father in some of the more effective officers.

In his mind, Willard had seen the army as a band of cavalier like soldiers, in neat grey uniforms working together in a disciplined organization. He quickly found out that even the uniforms were not uniform. It looked as though some men had brought their own hats and there was a variety of jacket styles and fabrics. But the army had been moving towards a new standard of grey tunic, pants and cap, and Willard became one the recent recruits to be issued the new outfit. The rifles needed so much continued attention to keep them in good operational form, that cleaning and oiling became a regular pastime. Men who appeared to know what they were talking about urged him to keep his bayonet sharp.

Training consisted mostly of learning the signals that might be a matter of life or death on the battlefield, and of course how to engage in conflict. He learned how to dig earth formations and how to hide behind them and yet be ready to go over the top and charge the enemy on command. Straw filled dummies were charged and dispatched with bayonets. Willard wondered if he could ever do that to another man.

And he ran mile after mile in the heat and the rain until his body was tighter and tougher than it had ever been.

Some of the recruits gave all of that token service, but Willard threw himself into it with all he had. He reckoned that if this was necessary then he might as well be the best he could be.

Eventually in July of 1864, he was dispatched to Petersburg, Virginia with the Confederate Army of Northern Virginia under the overall command of General Robert E. Lee and the immediate command of Brigadier Major General William Mahone.

It came as a bit of a shock to Willard when he heard that he was assigned to Lee's Northern Virginians. He could never forget the events of the day when his father was so badly injured and when this same man, then Colonel Lee, stormed Brown's holdout. And he vividly recalled Lee striding around the firehouse area and then up to the makeshift hospital to visit the wounded. To Willard's eye there had been a kind of a mixture of arrogance and relief to Lee's attitude, but he had been too young to make much sense of his feelings. He remembered though, that he had not cared much for Lee.

But now things were different and Lee had accepted the call to the Confederate force and had distinguished himself over the past few years. Willard felt that he probably was a good leader. Still it had been a shock.

William Mahone on the other hand was different. He was not a professional soldier at all but a railroad man who had made a fortune laying down tracks. He had become the president of the Norfolk and Petersburg Railroad before the war. When the war began, he immediately joined the army because he believed in the cause.

Willard soon heard that Mahone had a temper and was a strict disciplinarian, and that Willard should take care not to fall foul of him.

But the man stood just five foot five inches tall and weighed, maybe, one hundred and twenty pounds. He had gained the nickname of Little Billy and Willard had trouble seeing this little man as a threat. On voicing that thought to some of his buddies however, Willard was again warned about getting on the wrong side. As the weeks passed Willard came to admire Mahone and he settled into the encampment determined to follow out orders and to do his best.

Willard's mother, had she been present, would have immediately noticed that her boy had changed for the better. He was now more like his father with a determination to carry out a job whatever others might say or do.

At first, Willard had been amazed to learn that he was one of upwards of over fifty thousand men that Lee had posted around the Petersburg and Richmond area. In Willard's company alone, there were some six thousand men, and he wondered why so many men since the area appeared to have little importance other than being close to the capital in Richmond. Willard quickly learned that Petersburg was in fact a vital location for the confederates. A number of railroad lines came together in that area and then continued on into Richmond. For Lee, this town was potentially a main entry into Richmond and so it had to be defended and protected at all costs.

In June, just before Willard's arrival, Grant had unsuccessfully attacked the town and had retreated to form a line of entrenched Union troops around over one half of the town's perimeter and had settled into a quasi-siege mode. The intent appeared to be to attempt the blockage of supplies and people in and out of Richmond, and to make periodic attacks on the railroad lines.

Lee had countered by settling his men into trenches to defend against Grant. It was into this mixture of siege and stalemate that Willard had entered. He quickly realized why trench digging and trench defense and attack had figured so heavily in his training.

Prior to dawn on July 30th he was positioned in a small hollow with a dozen other men. The hollow was joined to other positions by a series of trenches with men spread along them. This was a familiar pattern of behavior that had been repeated day after day, with the men changing positions now and again seemingly waiting for an order to either attack or defend. Many of the men were bored by it all. Willard was alert.

On that day he leaned on the earth works and looked towards the Union lines some distance off. It was too dark to make out any detail and he wondered if some Yankee was looking towards him. Willard had no idea of what was planned for that day."

24.

June – July 1864,
Union Lines, Petersburg, Virginia

"Elijah was amazed. Life in Harpers Ferry had been so quiet until the attacks on the town that had begun right after the war started. It seemed to Elijah that before that, he had come to know just about everyone in the town and that they all knew him. Everybody had worked together and gotten along with each other and life was so good and so quiet. Life had been simple and easy.

After joining the United States Colored Troops, Elijah was surprised at the complexities of army life. He had learned that there were at that time well over one hundred thousand black troops in the army. Most of the early recruits had been free men from the northern states but by the time Elijah enlisted, the majority of black soldiers were from the southern states. And most of those were slaves who had run away at great risk for their lives.

Annie may have been proud of her son and how he was helping the nation in the struggle for freedom, but Elijah quickly found out that in the Union army there was no sense of equality. All the men may have been fighting for the same reasons, but the color of their skin still made a huge difference. He learned for example that until recently there had been a big difference in the pay levels and how after much political struggle this was in the process of being corrected. And as a colored man, he had little or no prospect for advancement in ranks. The colored troops were separate and they had to know their limits in that regard. All of their officers were white.

Elijah found that most of the officers in his group were fair and that they treated the colored troops with respect. But some were far from behaving like that. Some of them drank too much and many were bitter at the length of the war and especially at the stalemate in the campaign around Petersburg. These men tended to take out their feelings on the men under their command and showed little patience with any man who had trouble understanding and following orders. But still it seems that Elijah had some understanding of the situation, and he just became determined to do his best.

Brownie, I was glad that Grandma Annie and Mr. Clark, and then myself, had made sure that Elijah had received a good basic level of education. Elijah could read and write and he could understand and interpret instructions. The majority of the other colored troops could do little of that. Many of them were illiterate for the simple reason that no one had ever taken the time to help them. Most of them were good men who wanted to do all they could in the struggle, but simply lacked the skills. And so Elijah could understand why the officers sometimes became impatient. He felt for his brothers and he tried to help them whenever he could. And that was quickly noticed, and as a consequence Elijah's immediate officer began to give him more responsibility.

Basic training on both side of the conflict in Petersburg was similar, and so Elijah also became knowledgeable about digging trenches and in the skills of hand to hand fighting. Thrusting a bayonet into a bag of straw sickened him, but he understood the need and so he threw everything into the learning. Still, just like Willard, he wondered if he would ever be able to do to another man what he did to a straw sack.

His immediate officer was a young man from Washington named William, and William persuaded Elijah that when the time came, he could not afford to have any thoughts like that. Self-defense was self-defense and Elijah would just have to automatically do what he had been trained to do. Eventually this fact sank in and Elijah accepted that that was how it had to be.

At night Brownie, your Uncle still had doubts about his being able to kill.

After the training, Elijah and the men were assigned to a region and they settled into a routine of physical exercise, weapon cleaning and preparation and all of the actions necessary to be prepared for conflict. There were some minor skirmishes but as the weeks dragged out, he became as impatient as any one of the thousands of other men around him.

One evening, when William met him at an evening post on the front line, they talked together about the number of men and weapons lined up and facing each other. Elijah wondered out loud if the lull meant that the war might suddenly end and that everyone could just go home. William did not respond immediately but just looked out across the fields towards the confederate line. For a moment Elijah's perhaps naïve remark sounded good, but William knew better. Eventually William stood up and told Elijah that there was no chance of that. He added that action was planned very soon, and that the next morning Elijah would be hearing more about it, and he would learn that William had a special job in mind for him.

The watch changed at midnight and Elijah went to his cot and settled and tried to sleep. But William had gotten his curiosity up and sleep that night was scarce.

The next morning Elijah was called to William's tent. He found a couple of other officers there along with some enlisted men. Elijah was the only colored man present. William had a map spread out on a table and asked the men to gather around it. What followed held Elijah spellbound. He had never heard anything like it before. And the thought of him being a part of the plan enthralled him. He wished his mother and father could see him now and he wished that his Grand-pappy could see him now. William was pointing to a section of the confederate line on the map.

'We reckon that this area is a key point of defense for the confederates. It is near the town and it is near to a main railroad track into Richmond. If we could break through their line there we would be in a good position to just keep on going and start to turn the situation around here and maybe bring this whole mess to a close. This is our nearest line, maybe one hundred and fifty yards or so away from the confederate line. The generals have been mulling this over for weeks trying to figure out how to once and for all break through.'

At that point William hesitated and then stood back for effect.

'It turns out that we have an officer who is an engineer, by the name of Lt. Col. Pleasants and he has come up with what I first thought was a pretty wild idea. But now I see that it could just work.'

William turned back to the chart and pointed at the space between the two army lines.

'He suggested digging a tunnel right under this space, from our line here to under the confederate line there.'

William punctuated his dialogue by jabbing his finger onto the map with each here and there.

'Then he proposed digging two tunnels sideways like a kind of crooked letter T and filling each end with explosives and eventually blowing up the defenses above. Pleasants reckoned that the massive explosion would destroy hundreds of yards of the defense. At the time of the explosion our troops are to be on the move to storm around the crater and through the confederate line. At first I thought it a crazy idea since the enemy would surely see what was going on as we dug the tunnel and in any case, I wondered how men could breathe and work that far along the tunnel.'

Again the sense of drama was played out by William as he stood back and scratched his head as if puzzling over this great issue. Eventually he returned to the chart as though an epiphany had occurred.

'But by golly I was sure wrong about that! This man Pleasants had it all worked out with what is to me a somewhat complicated series of fires and bellows and shafts to move the air and keep it somewhat fresh. And he has found a pretty deep hollow where he would begin the tunnel entrance so it could not be seen by the enemy. And all of the earth can be hauled out of the dig and gotten rid of without any one from the other side ever knowing about it.'

William's sense of drama was beginning to wear on one or two of the men as he once again stood away from the chart and paused in his message. For his part though, Elijah continued to be spellbound with this talk and was wondering why on earth he had been called to be there. The other men were also quizzical as to why a colored man was present. William eventually took up his narrative again.

'Gentlemen, the facts are that Pleasants, commanded by Major General Burnside, sold the plan to the command and digging began this morning! And we have a part to play in this. Pleasants reckons it will take about four to five weeks to complete the dig and that gives plenty of time for our troops to plan and prepare for the assault. And gentlemen, we are to be among those troops! We are going to get busy and do something instead of just lying out around here.

Now, Grant has put us under the general command of Major General George Meade and Burnside and I have been assigned to lead this group. You will all get your individual assignments later but I wanted you know right up front that two brigades of Brigadier General Ferrero's USCT are to lead the assault. And that of course is why you are here Elijah. You have some smarts about you, I've noticed that, and I think that you can help us in training the colored troops for this action. Most of them have not seen much real action and they may not understand the importance of the job being given to them now. You can help with this.'

After weeks of little or no action, the men in the tent immediately became excited by the prospect of playing a key role in an action that might speed up the end of the war. One even slapped Elijah on the back, congratulating him and his like for being at the front. Elijah felt a mixture of pride and doubts. His mother and father and Beth and Harpers Ferry suddenly seemed so far away.

Training began immediately. William and some sergeants drilled the colored troops day after day, going over the plan again and again, and leading dummy offenses way behind the line and well out of sight of the enemy. Whenever a troop had difficulties with the strategy or the action, or whenever doubts or fears came into play, Elijah was called upon to explain and encourage and when necessary to lead the others. As a result, some of the men put Elijah down pointing out that a colored man would never be a leader far less an officer and that he was just being used. Elijah did not care about that. He was just thrilled at being at the center of it all and he honestly put everything he had into his job.

Weeks passed as the digging went ahead and the assault teams continued training. At one point, word began to spread that Meade had no intention of using the tunnel but was just allowing the work to go on as a deterrent to boredom and fatigue. William assured his team that this was just a malicious story and that all of the work of preparation would be used and would pay off. Elijah was told to stress this to the colored troops as the last thing the army needed was any hesitation or confusion once the order to breach the confederate line was given.

By July 17th the tunnel was almost finished. The assault teams were almost ready. The colored troops had already spent much time in preparation and on that day they began more intense training. Day after day they were drilled back and fro. Time and time again they gathered, charged and broke though simulated enemy lines, with one brigade skirting a mock crater to the left and another brigade to the right, while others took care of the enemy troops to the sides and down in the crater. Immediately behind the colored troops, brigades of white troops were to charge from the rear and press on through the enemy line to the railroad and into town to stage a commanding position for subsequent action. It was a good plan and everyone was wound up and itching to go into action. William and Elijah were especially proud of the level of preparation and discipline in the colored troops. All of the men felt that a decisive victory was at hand.

Training was complete by July 26th and the final phase of the dig was completed on the same day. The explosives were positioned and fuse wires were run the length of each of the side arms and along the main tunnel. Thirty or so feet of earth was packed into the side tunnels behind the explosives to contain the explosions, and on July 28th the charges were prepared. Burnside advised Meade that all was now ready, and the exercise was to go ahead early in the morning of July 30th. The excitement in Elijah's brigade was intense as William strode through the ranks encouraging the men.

And so the announcement of July 29 came to the men as a shock of similar proportions to that of the planned detonation!

'Gentlemen I have a really bad and surprising announcement to make this morning.'

William showed none of his normal dramatic pose as he addressed his core team that morning. He was angry and more than a little fearful for the consequences of the announcement he was making.

'General Meade has ordered Burnside to not use Ferreo's USCT brigades. He fears that if something goes wrong and things turn out bad for the brigades, then there will be huge criticism up north for exposing colored men to the risk. The political fallout would be bad for the army and I suppose would no doubt hurt certain careers.'

The latter point was made with undisguised bitterness.

'This has become a mess of major proportions. Meade asked for volunteer brigades to take over the initial advance planned for the USCT men. No volunteers came forth! So guess what? This morning they drew lots and men under a Brigadier General Ledlie's command were chosen. They have had no training for this assault and are now beginning to form up without, in my opinion, even adequate briefing. We are relegated to a secondary role behind Ledlie's men. I am sorry, but let us now do the best we can.'

As you can now imagine Brownie, your uncle Elijah was shattered. After all of the hard work they had gone through, some of the men began to taunt him. Some claimed that it was true after all that the whole thing had been a sham just to keep them busy. Others said that it was just to make them feel that they had a role to play. He did not hear most of the complaints and jibes simply because he was so disappointed at his leaders.

On the morning of July 30th at the planned time of 3:45am the fuse was lit. Ledlie's men were in position but lacking the necessary training, were not completely aware of when to move. They waited for the order.

Ledlie himself had remained behind the lines and had reportedly been drinking heavily during the night.

Elijah's brigade was in position behind the front leaders and they were straining and ready to move at the command. The level of preparation and determination of these men was a direct contrast to the confusion in Ledlie's ranks. And so they were all taken aback by the continued silence of the early morning. No explosion occurred and no orders were given and that was the last thing they had expected.

An engineer was sent into the tunnel and he discovered a failed fuse. He quickly spliced in a new section and returned to the command point for the tunnel.

At 4:40am the fuse was lit for the second time.

25.

July 30th 1864,
Confederate Lines, Petersburg, Virginia

Willard hated the early watch. Knowing that he would have to be up and about and alert early in the morning, always prevented him from getting any decent sleep. And then he did not like the darkness of the pre-dawn either. It always seemed to him to be a dreary time, frequently with mist in the air and dampness on the ground. Even back on the farm, it was the time of day he liked the least. In the trenches, the dawn was even worse and this morning was no exception.

On these mornings, it was not hard to imagine enemy soldiers storming out of the shadows, and so Willard had discovered that it was not good to just stare into the darkness that separated the two armies. He had learned that it was best to keep somewhat on the move in the little area of his hollow or trench or fort to keep the circulation going and to prevent his mind from getting ahead of itself. He had learned to use his ears in the darkness until the sun came up enough to separate reality from imagination.

But that morning he looked out across the expanse.

Rumors had spread that the Yankees were planning something big. There had even been talk of a tunnel being dug towards the confederate line and Lee had ordered some test shafts to be dug. Nothing had been confirmed and no big alert had been raised. His officer had simply told Willard to keep his eyes open and his wits about him. As the dawn broke Willard was on the alert, and he looked out across the line and then down the trench to his left at the men in position there.

The explosion was like nothing Willard had ever experienced or even imagined.

It seemed to Willard that two explosions had occurred together. One was just over two hundred feet to his left and the second perhaps another hundred feet or so further along, and he had been looking directly in that direction at the moment of the explosion.

The noise was deafening, and the ears that just moments ago had been straining to pick up any sounds from the Union side were now useless. The pain was intense. But far worse was the pain of what he was seeing.

Two columns of flame and smoke had shot a hundred feet into the air. The force of the explosion had destroyed the earthworks a hundred feet around each center and so hundreds of yards of earth and rock defenses were carried up with the flame and smoke. It was not the earth and rocks that distressed Willard the most.

Willard himself had been thrown backwards some twenty feet or so. As he lay on his back, he looked up into the chaos. He saw men and parts of men flying through the air. Some were going up with the main force and others were being thrown out to the left or right. Cannon and mortar were flung like a child's wooden toys. The smoke and the earth should have clouded out the early dawn light and they did obliterate what was happening further down the line, but in his immediate vicinity Willard saw everything only too clearly.

And then just for a moment it seemed as though everything was suspended in the air. The noise of the explosion quieted and was replaced by the sound of falling earth, rocks, timbers and munitions as Willard gazed up and saw everything go into reverse and fall back to earth. As his hearing began to recover, it was the sounds from the men that overpowered everything else for Willard.

Some were screaming at the top of their lungs and others were barely moaning as life left them. Some were shouting out trying to take measure of what was happening and trying to find some order in the chaos. Most were silent. In the first moment of the explosion nearly three hundred confederate men had died.

Men began to appear around him. Dazed and confused, they tried to look around them and down into the crater through the smoke and dust but no one took action. They simply did not know what to do. Willard got up, relieved to find that he had no injuries. He saw a man lying to the side who was in terrible pain. He went down on his knees to console the badly wounded man, knowing that there was nothing he could really do for him.

The shock and surprise took the confederate officers completely off guard and for a full fifteen to twenty minutes there was no leadership or direction. This lull was what the union officers had banked on and it should have given Ledlie's men the opportunity to take charge. The opposite took place with tragic consequences.

The men who had received no preparation and who at this critical point had no real leadership did not move. When they were finally goaded into action many of them forgot to pick up some boards that were intended to help them cross the trenches that separated the two lines. Consequently they had to crawl in and out of each trench as they left their own lines to approach the crater. It took them a deadly fifteen minutes to reach what was left of the confederate line.

Once there, the mistakes continued. Instead of taking the carefully worked out and intensively trained plan of the USCT to divide around the crater and advance, Ledlie's men made a fatal error by plunging headlong down into the crater looking to take shelter and to re-group. Ledlie himself had apparently stayed behind in the safety of the rear.

Meanwhile Mahone had begun to create some order in the Confederate line and had quickly organized his men around the rim of the crater. These men began the terrible act of retribution as they fired round after round of rifle fire into the Union men who were now unable to escape from the crater. Soon artillery joined the rifle fire as the massacre continued.

At the rear of the Union advance, Elijah and his brigade crossed the open space and reached the crater. As planned, they split into two groups with the intent of crossing the Confederate line each side of the crater and continuing on into Petersburg. They made very little progress before realizing that the Confederate men were in control of the battle and were blocking any move through their lines. To his horror, Elijah saw many of his colleagues break rank and fall back into the crater to join the melee down there. He continued on the planned route to the sides.

Willard had meanwhile joined the troops at the crater edge and was firing down into the mass of men. In the confusion some of the Union soldiers had managed to climb out of the crater and others were trying to force a passage through the lines to the sides. Willard and the men with him were quickly engaged in hand to hand combat.

The lessons from his basic training took over for Willard, with automatic actions as one bayonet thrust after another answered his earlier question as to whether he would ever be able to run a man through like the straw bags in training. During a moments lull, he fell back hoping to find perhaps some rest and perspective.

Stumbling over the body of a fallen man he went down on his knees just as a black Union troop came up to him. Quickly rising to his feet Willard lunged forward, but slipping again on the loose soil, he just cut through the tunic of his opponent. As Willard withdrew his bayonet, the other man took his opportunity and raised his rifle with both hands and drove the bayonet into Willard's bicep. But in the sheer fury of the moment, Willard did not feel the pain and he was simultaneously driving his bayonet into the man's chest. Both men fell to the ground. Willard remembered seeing the blood but never did figure out whether it was his or his enemy's. The struggle was over for both of them.

The battle continued for a couple of hours with some Union troops managing to break through the Confederate line. A counter attack drove them back and Burnside finally ordered the call to retreat. As the men fell back and returned to their line, some pursuit from the Confederates took place but this was also quickly called off and both sides tried to recover.

Elijah joined in the retreat.

The usual action of gathering the dead and wounded was honored and Burnside took measure of the disaster.

He had suffered nearly four thousand casualties with over five hundred dead and fourteen hundred missing or captured. So many men had been terribly injured. There had been no progress and the siege was destined to continue for months. Ferraro was devastated at the losses experienced by his colored troops and especially at the reports that some captured or injured colored men had been murdered by troops of both sides. These murders were mostly blamed on the fear of reprisal and the confusion of the battle, but Ferraro and many others smelled simple old-standing prejudice.

A few days after the battle, William came over to speak with Elijah.

"You and your men were all badly let down Elijah. I will never forget the lack of fortitude and courage that caused this catastrophe. We had the action so well planned and I am convinced that you and your men would have led us to victory. You all fought so bravely when you reached the line but that last minute change destroyed any chance of success. I am so sorry – I truly mean that. I am afraid that we are stuck with each other for many months now as I see little sign of the war coming to an end."

26.

August 1864,

Petersburg, Virginia

———⊛⊛⊛———

'"Young man, come on now! You are through the worst of it!'

Willard forced his eyes open and saw a bearded man leaning over him. For a moment he said that he thought it was me but in that moment the memory of the battle returned to him.

The man stood up straight and Willard saw the exhaustion on his face and the blood stained apron he was wearing. But the man was smiling now as he looked down at Willard and the edge came off of his voice.

'Alright now, that's better soldier. You lost a lot of blood on the edge of that damned crater but I reckon that you put up a good fight. All of our boys did.'

There was a sense of bitterness in that last remark but then again there came a change in the tone. Perhaps there was even a touch of tenderness.

'But my boy, blood is not all you lost out there. You had a nasty gash from that Yankee bayonet - and I had to take your arm. It took too long for them to bring you in and a bad infection set in. I had no choice boy. We saved your life, but you will never fight again.'

The surgeon's words carried on and he explained some of the detail but Willard heard none of that, a deep sleep having mercifully returned."

27.

December 17th 1941,
Dartford, West Virginia

‹—⸎—›

Once again I stopped writing for a few days. The battle notes quite wore me out I suppose.

As an educator, I was always determined that my pupils would pick up an appreciation of the issues surrounding the Civil War, and like I said, I used to use my account of the Battle of the Crater to challenge them to write comments about the management of the war. What I never did was to personalize the account by mentioning Willard and Uncle Elijah by name. In my curriculum, they just became soldiers north and south, representatives of the thousands who fought through the bloody battles. But they were personal to me of course, and that is especially true of Willard as I came to understand how the experience of war just pushed him further down a bad road.

The Reverend Hart was able to tell me a little about what happened after the war and how Willard acted. But it was Elijah who later added the real details that the Reverend did not want to share with me when I was a boy. Elijah included all of that in the notes he made for me and I can tell you now that Willard himself filled in some gaps. I am so very appreciative that they did this for me all of those years ago.

Yesterday I tried to put it all into some order. I found my anger rising just like it did the last time I read these notes.

I will have to come back to that later and explain my anger, but for now I need to break into the Reverends narrative and add what I learned from Elijah and Willard about the aftermath of the war. And then I will return to the Reverend's account of things.

28.

April 1866,

Harpers Ferry, West Virginia

——✸✸✸——

Willard sat on the rock, looking down over the confluence of the two big rivers. The sun had just set beyond the far hills and the shadows and the colors were changing. From as far back as he could remember this view had fascinated him. This rock was a much bigger than the one at the entrance to the farm. His father Frank used to tell him how the rock was named after Thomas Jefferson who had once stopped here on his way to Philadelphia, and like Willard now, he had been captivated by the view. From a boyhood perspective, the rock had seemed much larger to Willard and the hill had seemed more like a mountain, but now it was just an elevated rock with some fine views of the valley.

The rock was still warm from the late April afternoon sun and Willard lay back and remembered those days with his father. Frank had told Willard many times about his own adventures on this rock, and how it was that years ago the rock could be made to sway with just a push. Frank had once been chased up here by an imaginary bear and had hidden under the rock after giving it a quick nudge. For his part, Willard had fought his own imaginary enemies up here in many a game. The boyhood that had been cruelly cut-off from Willard seven years ago, returned for just a few moments, and the innocence of those years eased back. The rock was perhaps once again just a little larger, and his father was spinning a tale once again. The boy in Willard that once had been so easily pleased was suddenly glad to be back close to home again.

He had questioned his decision to make a brief return to Harpers Ferry a number of times. There was really little to bring him back except a desire to see his mother and to assure her that he was well, and to renew some old relationships. He had not expected the memories of his boyhood to break through so strongly. Perhaps, he hoped, it had been the right decision after all.

It had taken a few weeks for his army discharge to go through and he had needed some additional work done on his wound. He and a buddy named Brady, who had been discharged at the same time, had then spent the best part of six months just hanging around Richmond and getting themselves in and out of trouble until it became clear that the end was in sight. He had then made his way to the coast and it was there that word eventually came of Lee's surrender, and Willard had decided that maybe he should pay his mother a visit. But even then his bitterness held him back.

Months were spent just drifting around the coastal towns with no opportunity to work. The few jobs open needed men with two good arms and obviously that disqualified Willard. He fell in with a group of other men who were unable to find work. Any money that he did manage to earn was quickly lost in gambling which was just one of a number of bad habits picked up from Brady. Willard was simply a bad card player, and with his physical difficulty in handling cards, he was an easy target for other gamblers. But they did provide company of sorts and in a sense they were all in the same situation anyway. They kept together in a group just moving from town to town. They slept were ever they could find shelter and they ate very little and that was mostly food that was stolen or scrounged. Months dragged on and winter set in.

The winter months intensified the problems for Willard and his buddies and they became desperate as cold and hunger wore them down. Eventually they took the rash move to attempt to rob a general store.

That was not only rash but also stupid as any takings would have not gone very far among them. In any event the store personnel easily got the upper hand and very soon most of the group found themselves on the run. Not Willard. He simply tripped on the way out of the rear door and became the scapegoat for the rest of them.

Months in a local jail did nothing for Willard's health or demeanor. All that experience provided was time to think on how badly everything had turned out. Anger and a sense of worthlessness took over for most his jail sentence.

But day after day of self-pity and anger and hunger eventually gave way to some reasoning. One morning as he looked out over the courtyard he suddenly thought about how good it would be to return to the farm. That thought led to him thinking back on the people he had known and loved there. And the decision was made to go home as soon he was released.

And so on this April evening, perhaps with the setting of the sun and the consequent cooling of the air and fading of the light, the bitterness of the man once again began to push aside the child. He glanced at the stump of his left arm and felt useless. Years ago four small rocks had been placed underneath the main rock to prevent movement and on this evening the rock was steady. There was no moving it now to hide from an imaginary bear and there was no hiding from what had happened. There could be no turning back of time and events - not those pleasures of his boyhood or the horrors of John Brown or of the war. He would see his mother and then be on his way again, perhaps to Boston to meet up with Pete Brady.

Heavy rains and a late run off of snow from the hills way up the rivers had put them into mild flood conditions and had also turned the path from the rock down into the valley into a muddy track. More than once Willard slipped. The road through town was dry though and he made good time crossing through town and in beginning the climb up the hill towards the farm.

He stopped more than once as he crossed town. So much had changed in the years of warfare. All around was evidence of armies on the move. Some buildings were destroyed and damage was everywhere. He could see what was left of the Armory and the complex by the river. Willard wondered if the town would ever recover. He wondered if the farm was alright. That thought caused him to speed-up a little.

It was almost dark by the time he approached the door of the farm house but the lamps inside told Willard that his mother was likely still up and about. A movement inside the house confirmed this. He wondered for a moment if he should knock or just go in. He did not want to startle his mother any more than he could. The decision was made for him however as the door opened and Frank stepped out almost knocking Willard over.

Frank quickly stepped back, not knowing if a welcome or a defense was needed and began to speak into the darkness asking who was there.

Aware of his mother standing in the middle of the room, and not wanting to scare her, Willard quickly cut Frank off.

"Easy there Frank, it's me, Willard."

In no time the three of them were embracing in the near darkness of the front porch. Betsy was crying and Frank was saying how good it was to see Willard again after all this time of not seeing or hearing from him. Willard thought he caught a suggestion of cynicism in Frank's tone and he remained silent at first. But as Betsy held him tight, he did return the embrace with genuine warmth and eventually he began to join in the chatter. After a few moments of this, and realizing that all three of them were speaking at the same time, Betsy resumed her old role of being in control and ushered the boys into the house.

Betsy quickly produced a spread of very welcome hot food and some of her best coffee, apologizing for the lack of preparation and chastising Willard for not sending some notice. Willard ate slowly and listened to Frank tell about how things were at the farm and how Sean had decided to visit the grandparents in Norfolk as soon as the war looked like it was finished. He had been gone for nearly a year. Betsy ran through a list of updates concerning neighbors and the town in general. Willard pretty well knew how hard things had been for the town but he let the two of them go on. The food was better than he had had for many a month. Eventually it was his turn and he spoke a little about the war but without too much detail. A brief mention of hand to hand fighting in the heat of battle served to explain the severed arm. He had learned that people generally did not like to hear the details and certainly his mother was not up to hearing it. The jail was not mentioned.

Frank, for his part, had had his share of it all and remained silent during this turn of the conversation. No enquiry was made as to Willard's plans. Frank and his mother without a spoken word between them, agreed to put off such talk until the next morning.

As Betsy cleared up after the late supper, Willard and Frank sat in the corner and continued the reminiscing. Betsy looked across at them. She had not mentioned Willard's appearance to him but she was very disturbed at the weight loss, the filthy ragged clothes and his overall demeanor. This was another subject for another day as far as she was concerned. Tomorrow he could put on some of Franks stuff and go into town for some new clothes.

Frank was not so reserved and quietly questioned why Willard had made this sudden appearance.

"You look awful and you stink! How come you didn't write or at least clean yourself up some before coming here?"

But Willard was too tired for this now. He would not deny the feeling of being glad to be home, and along with Betsy's food and the rigors of the recent weeks, he was just too plain tired for more talk. How he got to bed that night he never did recall, but that night's sleep in his old bedroom was something that he had not enjoyed so much for many a long time.

The next morning Willard was wakened by his mother. Betsy had brought in some hot coffee and biscuits and put them on the bedside table. Frank had dragged the old tin bath tub into Willard's room and had filled it with a number of kettles of hot water. Closing the door, Frank instructed Willard in no uncertain manner that he was to get into the tub and have a really good scrub and then soak some while enjoying his coffee.

As Willard stripped off his underwear and stepped into the tub, Frank did hear a little more detail about the crater fight and the loss of the arm. It sounded to him as though on the one hand Willard needed to share more detail, and on the other he just needed to forget it all.

Leaving Willard to soak, Frank left the room saying that he would be back shortly with some of his clothes and that he would take Willard's stuff out to the refuse pile ready for the next trash fire. Then Willard and Frank could go into town to Clark's place and pick up some new clothes.

Willard was not up to admitting the fact, but the long soak in the tub while enjoying the coffee had been very pleasant. Stepping out of the old tin tub he toweled himself as best he could with the one arm. It was always the right arm and side that were tricky to dry, but he had learned how to make do. Frank had returned just then and had offered to help but Willard brushed that aside.

He put on the clothes that Frank had left on the side table and they walked out to see Betsy in the kitchen.

"My lord, you have lost weight Willard, and you looked a fearful sight last night just walking up with no notice. And now Frank's stuff is looking a bit silly on you, but that's that so get on down to town now, the both of you."

Willard smiled. He knew that had not really been a scolding, just Betsy showing her authority again.

The walk down to Clark's store was accomplished in short order since Willard was very conscious as to how peculiar he looked in Frank's oversize clothes, and with the folded sleeve where his arm should have been. He wondered if he would ever get over that feeling. Reaching the store, the two brothers walked in.

Willard started to introduce him-self but Clark cut him off assuring him that he remembered him well and was glad to see him home again. Willard fielded the inevitable questions about the war and what had happened to him. Clark for his part filled Willard in on how he thought that these days both Frank and Betsy were so much better, and of course how Willard's return could only help that. Looking through the clothing stock they found some new stuff that fitted Willard pretty well, even allowing for some weight gain that they knew would happen with Betsy's cooking. Jason Clark had wisely suggested that Willard keep on some of the new clothes and had packed Frank's things into a sack.

The walk back to the farm was made at a slower pace as the brothers tried to catch up some more. They stopped at the large flat rock overlooking the farm.

"Tell me about Shiloh Frank."

"No Willard, I heard about that crater mess in Petersburg but never dreamt that you were in the middle of it all. Elijah told me some as well. He doesn't know that you were in the same fight on the other side. I am glad that you two never met there.

And you have had your share of the blood dear brother and you don't need to hear more. Let me just say that I fought at Shiloh and now I fight to forget it. For me there was no glory, and you know just exactly what I mean by that."

Frank never expanded on his war experience.

"But like I said, you was on the other side little brother and I'm sure you heard a different story about things back there anyway."

Frank had added the comment without bitterness. He had long ago come to see how his brother felt about things and for the sake of their mother had decided to not make too big a deal out of it all. At least they had both survived the damned war.

Willard did not answer immediately but thought about a boyhood friend Jonah who, he had just heard from Frank, had been killed at Shiloh. And he thought about the others. He thought about so many others.

"No Frank, we pretty well knew what had happened. The officers and all tried to make it out as not so bad but the word got out and we knew better. My god Frank what I will never forget is them officers shouting out the orders for us to keep going, to keep running into the rifle fire and the explosions and the balls coming down all around and just tearing up men like they was oversized stuffed toys. But toys don't bleed and toys don't yell out do they."

Frank muttered something about how he felt the same. And then finding his words, added that as far as he was concerned, there had been no real right or wrong. It had all been a waste and should have been avoided by the political men. The brothers spoke of how some people would never get over it all. Frank wondered about his brother.

And leaning on a fence looking across town, all of the old resentments came back for both of them. Frank was the stronger of the two brothers, and he had already realized the need to move on with their lives.

"But we can get over it Willard. We came though the worst of it. What do you say but that we buckle down with Mother and get this farm back on track and give no more talk of the war? I think that Sean will be back soon although he has been talking about getting out of Harpers and maybe settling on the coast. We will have to see about that."

Frank had sensed that Willard would not agree to this but felt that he had to at least give it a try.

"No, I am going to New England Frank. Don't ask me why because I know that them Yankees may not welcome the likes of me. But they won the war and I hear tell that things are going well up there. Reverend Hart down in the town here told me some years ago how anyone could get a good job in the mills and I reckon that things must be a darn sight better now after the war. And I see you looking at what's left of my arm Frank! The other one will have to make up for it, that's all. Please do not mention this to Mother yet."

And so in Willard's mind, a longing for something better and a need to move on from the horrors of the past along with a blind determination to start over, clouded over any caution or real planning for his future. Anything must be better than what Willard was experiencing at that moment - and the farther away he could get the better it would be.

Back at the house, Betsy had prepared a good lunch of chicken and black-eye peas and biscuits. The daily routine of a light lunch gave way to the plan to fatten Willard up.

After they had cleared up from the meal, Frank went down to work in the sheds and Willard walked back into town. His first stop was at Reverend Hart's home. Mary met him at the door.

"Well Willard, come and sit down while I get us some cookies. The Reverend is just on his way home and will be so pleased to see you."

Willard kindly declined the cookies, explaining that he had just had a big plate full of food, and went on to tell about his mother's plans to fatten him up. For her part, Mary thought how glad she was to hear that since he had lost so much weight. Avoiding being too pointed, Mary simply said how she understood. Small talk about the town had hardly begun when Roger Hart stepped in and took Willard up in a warm embrace.

It was a genuine welcome. So many young men from the town would never return. So many families were grieving. And

Betsy had been so worried about both of her sons. Hart now felt her relief and held on to Willard for a few moments.

"It is so good to see you Willard. I have prayed for you and the others day after day, and I feel God's great mercy now as I see you here in our home. It's good to have you and your brother back home. Your mother must be over the hill with joy!"

Willard for his part genuinely appreciated the welcome, but declined to remark about the men he had heard screaming for God's mercy and apparently did not find it. It was not a time to be cynical. Maybe he would ask the Reverend about all of that later. Or maybe he would not. Some feelings were better left alone to eventually die off. That was Willard's hope anyway.

"Yes Reverend, mother is as you say 'over the hill."

The next thirty minutes or so were spent with Willard trying to answer some of Hart's questions. The crater was briefly described, along with the loss of his arm, and some talk about other battle field experiences. Hart caught the reluctance of Willard to go into any detail and held back from probing too deeply. He also hoped that there would be time for that later.

And so both men put aside the matters from the past for now, with a loose and unspoken intent to pick them up again later. Both sensed though, that with the passing of time that might never happen.

Instead, that afternoon the talk turned to the future and whether Willard had any plans. And that opened the door for Willard to ask about New England, with the request that Hart not mention this to Betsy just yet, as he was still undecided. He explained that Frank could run the farm along with Sean if he stayed around, and if not then Frank could certainly manage on his own with the hired help. He added that for his part he just had to get away. There were too many reminders around Harpers of the John Brown thing and the death of his father, and far too many reminders of the war and its consequences.

Hart, although surprised, could see the reasoning. He agreed to give Willard an introduction to Davidson who, Hart said, was sure to give Willard a job and would not hold the war against him.

The conversation continued around the affairs of the town again until Willard stood to leave. At the door he turned to Hart and stood and said nothing for a moment or so, searching for words.

"I am very sorry about my behavior a few years back Reverend. That whole business with John Brown and my daddy just about knocked me out as you know. But I have just learned the hard way that bitterness and revenge and violence and the like won't solve anything. I was very hard on mother and my brothers, and I know on you also. I really am sorry."

"I know Willard. I felt so bad – we all felt so bad for you. I have told myself a thousand times that I should have done more to help you. I certainly should have stopped you going to Charles Town that day."

But Hart stopped there. The mention of that visit was out of place and he could see Willard blanch at the memory. He returned to Willard's apology.

"Thank you for saying that Willard, it takes a lot for a man to say something like that. But if I may mention this, there are others who would feel better to hear you say that to them. And I reckon that you would feel a lot better too. It's Elijah and Beth that I have in mind, and their mother. Although Elijah has been through the pain of battle like you, I reckon that they are both still hurt by what you said to them and the way that you treated them. They simply do not understand why you took things out on them. When you feel up to it, please just take some time with them."

Walking home, Willard recalled what Hart had been referring to and thought about going to see them the next day.

The next day was a little warmer, with a slight breeze coming down the valley. He stopped at the brow of the hill and looked back at the farm and then turning again he looked down the lane towards the town. The farm looked like it always had for as long as he could remember, but the damage to the town was already evident from where he stood. Down the hill towards the edge of town, and close to Hart's church, the cottage of a friend of his mother was just a burnt out shell. He would have to ask someone what had happened there so close to the farm.

Willard walked on into town and up to Clark's store. There he watched as a local farmer tried his hand at bartering some early spring produce for some cattle feed. He smiled as he saw Clark come out the better on the deal. That was evident from Clark's smile and the farmers frown. Both men seemed reasonably content at the end though.

After some idle talk, Willard asked about Beth and Elijah.

Clark thought a moment or two on that before answering.

"They are both alright Willard, thank you for asking. Of course Beth grieved badly after her father John was murdered. Oh, you did not know about that? It was just months after you and Elijah left and it was a nasty business, because we never did find out who killed him. Everyone assumed that it was either some rogue confederate soldier or some sympathizer who had it in for all colored people. We had all gotten out of town as the fighting broke out again, and had just returned home after being away for some weeks when it happened. The very first morning that we were back, John went down to the bridge and he never returned. They found him later that day in the river. He had been stabbed to death.

You can imagine that poor Annie and Beth were grief-stricken, and Elijah being away in the fighting just made it worse for them. You know how confusing those days were and it took too long to get the word to Elijah.

Elijah is a big man now of course. And he is just safely home from the war too. He is down at the station waiting on some supplies coming in. Beth is your age and quite the young woman. I must say that their mother keeps them pretty well in line."

Clark did not add that he believed that Elijah would leave town and move on as soon as he could. Elijah had confided as much to Clark, explaining how he thought a larger town would suit him better. Clark also did not tell Willard how moody Beth had become since the death of her father, or how she would go off on her own some days to just wonder around the hills, and how she could not mix in with other folk but kept mostly to herself. Elijah was a good worker though and they both seemed happy enough with their mother. He turned back to Willard who had been idly looking at some hardware. Putting caution aside, Clark picked up the conversation.

"You, know they were both hurt by your behavior Willard. I think Beth really wanted to be a friend to you, and she certainly tried a few times to sort things out, but you would never have any of it. Willard, do us all a big favor and please try to patch things up as best you can. Maybe you could go down to the railroad depot now and help Elijah. Beth is off somewhere on her own taking the morning off, she has some favorite places where she goes to sit, but you could see her later too."

Taking his leave, Willard started down towards the depot. Passing a small meadow he felt the valley breeze again, with that old drift of spring time meadow flowers. He realized that Elijah and Beth could wait a day. This morning was so good that he decided to change his plans and to make his way to one of his favorite childhood places. It was a clearing in the forest up and over one of the hills to the east of town and near to the farm. It had wild flowers everywhere and a small pond. Years ago he had fished there until he realized that it was too small to hold any decent size fish. But he loved its quietness.

On the days after his father died, Willard had alternated between this place and his fishing spot down by the bridge at the river. He thought of both places as his own.

Much of the open ground around the town had been flattened and stripped by the two armies as they approached it time and time again over the past few years. Hauling men and equipment in and out had taken a toll that would take years to make up. But up on the farm side Willard felt at home again. This small part of Harpers remained relatively undisturbed and it looked pretty well as it did when he was a boy. In fact he noticed that as it had become even more overgrown. It had become perfect.

The new foliage caused Willard to slow down and figure out the old path into the clearing. He soon found it again and came out into the open area. It was just as he remembered it with the pond very still except for some ripples from the light breeze, and it was surrounded by grass and wild flowers.

But what took him completely off balance was Beth.

Beth was standing at the water edge, her head thrown back and staring into the sky and with both arms outstretched to the side as though about to take flight. She was obviously lost in her thoughts and the last thing Willard wanted to do at that moment was to break into them and startle her.

But there was something else too. He was completely taken back by her appearance. He remembered skinny young Beth but now he was looking at Beth the young woman. She was now tall and slender with a beautiful slim body. The breeze was just sufficient to press the printed frock against her body as she began to reach up to the sun and the clouds.

He realized that he was feeling some guilt. All of a sudden this did not feel right.

Just for a moment he wondered if it was because of the memories of their childhood fights, and then he wondered if it was because he had felt attracted to her for so long. He had put those thoughts out of his mind many a time, but this time he could not. He certainly was attracted right then, and just like in the past he became very conscious of the color of her skin. Either way, it did not feel right. Those thoughts only lasted a few seconds.

'Willard! Oh my lord how you scared me. Here I am just enjoyin' the sun and the pond and I turn around and there you is starin' at me! Where you spring from anyway?'

Beth was running up the slope towards Willard as she called out. She gave him a hug and then stepped back a few feet away from him.

"We heard that you was back from the fightin'. We got Elijah back you know. He was pretty well in charge of some things you know and we was mighty proud of him. Oh Willard I am real sorry about your arm. Does it hurt now? Was it just terrible to have been in all of that shootin'?"

There was a mixture of genuine curiosity and concern in Beth's words, but there was also a formality, at least as close to being formal as Beth could get. The bad memories seemed to just stand there between them.

For his part, Willard was confused by his feeling towards Beth, as though undecided as to whether to take her in his arms or to run back and away from the clearing. Such feelings might be common for adolescents, but both Willard and Beth were beyond that.

He shrugged his shoulders and sat down on the grass. Beth came up and joined him.

For a while the two just sat and stared down into the water. Willard spoke first.

"Well Beth, the arm is OK and it doesn't hurt too much anymore. I must say that I am glad to be out of that mess and back home again. Oh, and Beth I am really sorry to hear about your Daddy John. My God Beth it seems like killing was going on everywhere."

He turned and looked at the young woman.

"I just left Clarks place. He told me that Elijah is at the depot. I wanted to see both of you and I sure did not expect to bump into you here. You know this is a special place for me. I used to spend hours here after my daddy died and I bet I could describe every part of it. The thing is that I want to say how sorry I am about how we left things. I was so damned mixed up and full of nasty stuff, but I should never have spoken to you two like that, or treated you like I did. That was wrong and I am really sorry. My daddy brought me up better than that and that's for sure. None of that mess was your fault and I need you to forgive me Beth. And I need Elijah to forgive me too. Especially Elijah I guess since I nearly broke his nose a few times."

Beth laughed, and then was silent as she realized that Willard was collecting his thoughts. He stood and walked to the edge of the pond and kicked a small rock out into the water. After a moment he came back and sat down again, this time facing Beth.

"Being in the fighting, especially the last time over in Petersburg there, taught me that we can never make things right by hating and fighting. My God Beth, there was a time at that crater when I was actually walking over dead men as I fought for my life. I hope that someone took care of them later and showed them the respect they deserved. They were fighting for something that they believed in. Just for a moment there I felt that I was behaving like old man John Brown. I wanted to cry and I wanted to be sick and I wanted my Daddy to be there to take me out of it all. But instead I was fighting for my life. I am pretty sure I killed the man who took my arm. It was all too horrible Beth."

Willard was crying inconsolably as years of unexpressed emotions, going all the way back from that day he saw his father in the army cot, right through to the crater, just broke out of him. Perhaps it was the two of them sitting in this perfect spot or perhaps it was just the right time, but Willard wanted to be free of all the bitter thoughts and the anger and the confusion in his mind.

Beth had moved around to be next to him, and she came close to him and put her arms around him and gently rocked him.

"Now, now, Willard, this is somethin' I have never seen in you before. My Momma would say to me to just let it out. You know, Elijah and me never really held any of that stuff against you anyway."

Those words were not exactly true, but Beth sensed that this was some kind of a turning point for Willard and she was not up to breaking that moment for him, and so she let him cry as they sat together and she hugged him tight.

"You know Willard, after my daddy John was murdered and with Elijah away and all the war stuff goin' on, I got all moody just like you did. My Momma was so upset and cryin' so that I just didn't know what to do. They was bad times Willard and so I think that I do have some idea now of what you went through. I miss my daddy so much too."

They cried together.

The tears eventually stopped and both of them felt a little awkward at the embrace. But neither wanted it to end, and they lay back on the grass. And the embrace continued. Willard tightened his hold on Beth, but she pushed him back. They were both confused by their feelings for each other.

It was more than an hour before they were both on the path out of the clearing, with Willard on his way to the farm and Beth to Clark's place. Not a word was spoken as they separated at the clearing.

Back at the farm Betsy immediately noticed a change in Willard. He started to speak warmly about Mr. Clark and Reverend Hart but then brushed off any talk about Elijah or Beth or anyone else. Over the coming couple of days he ate like each meal was to be his last and Betsy even began to fancy that he was putting on some weight. But Willard avoided going back into town, and he began to spend hours off by himself again. Betsy sensed a feeling of guilt about something in her son's behavior.

One morning he was gone again.

He had given some more hints to Frank about New England but had not given any firm intentions. Once again a simple note to his mother was all he managed. It simply said that he was sorry to leave again without talking with her and sorry for any hurt he might cause her, but he just had to get away and start over somewhere else. She should not worry too much because thanks to Reverend Hart, Willard would be alright. The note ended with love and a hope to see her sometime soon.

After all, there was little else to say.

29.

July 1866,

Harpers Ferry, West Virginia

—⚬⚬⚬—

"Well no wonder that boy Willard done run off just like that and no one don't know rightly where he is. That Willard!

This was such a lovely day until now and you was lookin' so beautiful as you spun around in the sunlight. And now you just up and tell me that you is going to have a child! Oh Beth, you are little more than a child still yourself."

But there was no bitterness for Beth in Annie's voice. That was reserved for someone else.

Annie had been sitting on the back porch watching Beth enjoying the sunlight, and she had been thinking how beautiful Beth had become and how blessed she was with her two children. She missed John so much and she could hardly bring herself to think about what had happened to him by the river. So much had changed in Harpers since the start of the war, but at least Elijah had come home safely and all of her people had been declared free with a final end of slavery. No woman would ever see her father and brother taken away and sold like she had. Perhaps things were now really going to get better for her and the family and for all of her kin. Annie was just simply happy in that moment. Everything was beginning to feel good again along with the promise to get even better.

And then Beth had seen her and had come over and sat next to her.

"Momma, you look so lovely and happy this morning. Isn't this just a perfect day?"

With those words Beth had put her head on her mother's shoulder and had put her arm around her mother's waist with a gentle squeeze. For some minutes the two women sat without speaking, soaking up the morning sun. Beth was trying to find the right words, trying to find a way to turn her problem into some kind of good thing. In the end, the words just spilled out.

"Momma, I got something to tell you. You know how you always talk about one day being a grandma? How you used to love carin' for us when we was babies and how you want to do that again sometime? Well, Momma, I am goin' to have a baby."

The words were out. There was no way to take them back and at that moment Beth realized that her life would never be the same as it had been for so many years. What had happened to her could never be changed and neither could the consequence. Now her mother knew, and pretty soon so would everyone else. Some people would be all excited, some would be angry and some would think badly of her. Beth knew all of that and she had been thinking it over for a few weeks. She had gone over it all time and time again. The first sign of what was to come would become obvious in how her mother reacted now.

Annie did not react well.

She was suddenly so very angry and without knowing why she was absolutely sure that Willard was the father of Beth's child.

"One minute that boy is back home lookin' like death itself and then he is gone again leavin' his mother in such a sorry and sad state not knowin' where he is. The boy just upped and left his mother in a state like he did before with just a note. And now I see that he left you with this! I knew that somethin' had happened between the two of you and I seen you actin' up this last month, but I never dreamed you would be this stupid girl."

And there Annie had stopped, suddenly wishing that she had thought before speaking out like that. Beth was in tears. The beauty of that sunny morning was far off in the past.

"Now, come on Beth you can stop that. How did you think I would be after tellin' me that? How do you think you is goin' to raise a child? Mr. Clark is pushed as it is just to pay us, without you bein' off and then havin' another mouth to fill. And then, O lord, there is the matter of what everyone is goin' to say. We may have been slaves and maybe we don't got any money and such, but we have our pride Beth, we have our pride. And with Willard bein' a white boy, how is your child goin' to look? You ever stop to think about that? Tell me now, who knows about this? Willard? Elijah? Tell me now who knows?"

Beth had stopped crying and had stood up as Annie's questions poured out.

"I never said that Willard had anything to do with this, and I am never goin' to talk about that. And there is just the two of us that know just you and me Momma. Whatever happened and whoever it was, it's done and we's stuck with it Momma. We just have to see it through and make the best of it. Just think for a minute Momma, I is goin' to have a baby. A baby, just think about it and how wonderful that's goin' to be. We will get by, you'll see."

Beth sat down and once again the two of them sat awhile and thought on what to do and say next. Annie did feel some excitement at the thought of a baby but she was not yet up to acknowledging it to Beth.

Eventually Annie decided that they should talk with Reverend Hart and get his advice. But first they agreed that they should tell Elijah, and Annie just knew that he would be furious with his sister.

And so both were surprised that after hearing the news, Elijah just took Beth in his arms and hugged her and told her how he loved her and would do whatever he could to help. Elijah felt no anger against Beth and did not consider her stupid or careless. His tenderness towards his sister was offset by his anger at someone else though, but he held that in until he and Annie were alone.

"Momma, I know what happened. Don't go asking me how but I just know that Willard raped Beth. She would never have let him take her and there is nobody else she has been seeing. Those days after he came back he was awful moody again and then suddenly he was gone. He's guilty alright. I just know that but please don't ask me how. But I tell you this Momma, I tell you that I will find him and make him stand up to this. I will make sure that he helps take care of Beth and her baby."

Annie pondered for a while on what Elijah had said and decided for the most part to trust either in his intuition or in the fact that he knew something that she did not know. Either way, Beth was right. Whatever had happened, no amount of anger or recrimination now would change things.

With that thought, she went out into the back yard and caught up with Beth again and held her tight and assured her that everything was going to be alright. The love between the mother and her daughter had perhaps never been stronger than at that moment of uncertainty.

The next day the three of them paid a visit to Reverend Hart at the church. He was polishing the plain oak pulpit in the center of the platform up at the front of the pews. The furniture and the overall appearance of the church interior were quite bare, almost austere. The pulpit on the other hand, being central to the worship, was just a little fancier and Hart liked to see it shine.

"Well hello Annie and family, do come on in. I have just about finished my housekeeping for the day anyhow. It's one of the perks of being pastor to small church you know - that I am allowed to take care of some of the chores."

With a wink, Hart put down the polish and rag and gave Annie and Beth a hug and shook hands with Elijah.

"Sit yourselves down now. Elijah, each time I see you I give thanks for your safe return my boy. And I think about how well you did in the service. From what I hear you and others say, you made quite a name for yourself among the officers. Good job my boy. Good job. So what brings the entire family to church this morning?"

There was an awkward moment as no one spoke out. Elijah began to speak but Annie squeezed his leg and indicated towards Beth. Roger Hart was puzzled, but he remained quiet as Beth first stood up and then sat down again. He could tell that something was up.

"The fact is Reverend that we need your advice."

Beth's voice was strong. She had thought long and hard about this during the night.

"To put it as plain as I can Reverend, I am going to have a baby and I am not goin' to have a man to stand by me. Now, don't ask me about it because I won't speak to it. All of that is as I explained to Momma and Elijah. What is done is done. But what should I do? That is what I need to know now. That is what we all need to know."

Some of the strength had left her voice towards the end and Beth wondered if this was how it would be each time she told someone else about her baby.

Hart did not speak for a few moments.

Years of counseling had trained him to watch his words at moments like this. But that was not the only reason for his hesitation. His mind had leaped back many years to the sand dune in Rhode Island and the young woman he had seen there. And he had also immediately thought of his daughter Jenny and how he would react if she was in Beth's position. Over the years, as much as he had tried to suppress that thought, it had come to him from time to time. He supposed that all fathers with daughters went through that. Eventually he reached across the front pew to where the family was sitting, and took Beth and Annie's hands.

"My dear, I am not going to pry into what has happened. I can see that the three of you have begun to come to terms with the situation and I am glad about that. I could say that I will pray for you in this, and I certainly will do that, but I know that you are looking for some advice that is perhaps more immediate than that.

You say that the man responsible for this is not going to stand by you and... now do not get uppity with me Beth. I told you that I am not going to pry and I will not pass judgment or anything like that."

The last words had been a reaction to Beth letting out a gasp and starting to stand up. They had been given softly.

"Just relax a little Beth and believe me when I say that I think that I really do have some feeling for what you are going through. Now as I was saying, since the man is not going to stand by you, then the three of you are going to have to stick together. Does Mr. Clark know of this yet? No, I thought not. Then just keep it between the four of us for now and allow me to talk with him and with Mrs. Hart. We will work out something. Don't worry, if that is possible for you."

Hart had smiled at his casual 'don't worry' knowing that worry was what Annie would be doing the most in the days to come.

The four of them stood and took each other's hands to form a small circle at the front of the church, and in the silence of that place Hart prayed for them. He prayed for guidance and for understanding. He even slipped in a prayer for whoever the man was who was responsible, but feeling Elijah's hand tighten he had then closed the prayer with thanks for being given the opportunity for knowing Annie and her small family. It was a genuine prayer as Roger had come to love them ever since that awful night at Big Lick.

Roger was surprised at Clark's reaction. He knew that things had become more difficult for the general store with all of the changes that the war years had brought to Harpers. But still he was surprised that Clark's immediate response was so harsh. Apparently he was already having trouble keeping the family since it was really only Elijah who contributed to the work. And he confided to Roger that Elijah had mentioned possibly moving to Washington. Apparently he had received an offer from an ex-officer who now ran a successful building business in Washington. Building was booming in the nation's capital and it seemed that Elijah had made an impression on the builder as being a man who could be relied upon.

It became very clear to Roger that Beth could not expect a lot of sympathy from Clark and certainly not much in the way of material support.

Mary Hart on the other hand was as compassionate as always. She accepted the news without any sense of judgment, showing only concern for Beth. Later that day Mary even had the answer to the difficulty.

"Roger, now that Jenny has decided to marry Fred Craven and move to New Jersey, I do believe that we have the answer that Beth and Annie are looking for. Jenny has told us that Fred has a large house in Westhill where his law firm is to be based. They will need help in running the house and I think that Annie would be the perfect housekeeper along with Beth assisting."

Jenny had broken the news to her parents a few months earlier while visiting Harpers. Through mutual friends she had met Fred Craven while visiting New Haven. Jenny explained to her parents that Fred was a new graduate from the law school and that he was planning to set up practice with an uncle in Westhill, New Jersey. He had asked her to marry him and she had agreed. Any thoughts of teaching were now put aside. Just a couple of weeks ago Fred had paid a visit to Roger and Mary to introduce himself. They had both taken an instant liking to him and felt very good about the prospects of the marriage.

"Roger, it is the perfect way out for everyone. Jenny and Fred will have the trustworthy staff they need. Annie and Beth will be able to start over in a new town and will have good employment. Beth will be well looked after and after the baby is born she can stay on to assist in the running of the house. Mr. Clark will no longer have to worry about asking Annie and the family to leave, while Elijah can go off to Washington and put together a life for himself without worrying about Annie. Don't you see that it is simple and just perfect?"

Roger smiled and then laughed loudly at how Mary was talking as though she had just fixed the problems of the world!

And so it was all arranged. Roger and Mary travelled to Westhill where Roger helped officiate at a fairly large wedding ceremony. Jenny had asked him to conduct the service but he had pointed out the she was his only daughter, and that he had always looked forward to one day walking her down the aisle and giving her away. And that is what he did. After the lifting of her veil and exchanging one last kiss before she became Mrs. Craven, Roger had walked up onto the platform to assist the local minister in the service. It was one of the happiest days of Roger's life.

Annie and Beth had joined them on the journey to Westhill and had immediately settled into their new home and into their new responsibilities.

The return to Harpers was a bit of an anticlimax for Hart. Elijah had already left for Washington and Roger simply missed having the three of them around. John Clark began to make more comments about how bad business was becoming and shared with Roger that he even feared the possibility of having to close the business down. Apparently Clark thought that it would be many years before Harpers would recover from the war years.

Even the little church had lost attendance and Clark worried that the ministry might not be able to continue. Once again it was at the church one morning that matters took another unexpected turn for Roger.

Just over a month after the visit to New Jersey, he had been visiting a couple who lived out towards neighboring

Bolivar and who were still grieving over the loss of their son. The young man had been an early casualty of the war and even after a number of years the mother was unable to put it behind her. This was putting an enormous stress on the marriage and it was her husband who had asked Roger to spend time with them. He willingly did this and he tried his best at counseling. But these people were not the only ones that Roger was trying to help. Other families had lost loved ones, and among those who had escaped that torment, many were like Clark and were grieving the changes to the town and were worried about their future. This grief and anger and general confusion of his congregation had taken its toll on Roger.

The bouts of depression had begun to return, and he took to spending more time in the little church, either sitting in a pew and pondering what to do next with someone's problems, or down on his knees looking for divine guidance. He wondered if perhaps he and Mary should also make a break from Harpers and return to New England. When he had mentioned that possibility to Mary she had been inclined to agree, but Roger felt torn two ways. He was looking for guidance.

He was kneeling off to the side of the pulpit area, letting his uncertainties about his situation run through his mind. John Brown's words concerning the crimes of a guilty land needing to be repaid with blood kept coming back to him.

"How much trouble and how much blood, how much blood will it take? And how much grief and anger Lord, how much will it take until we can move on from John Brown and his like?"

Without realizing it, he had prayed the words out loud.

"Well Reverend, I hope that God can give you an answer to that question because he alone knows how many times I have asked that very same question of Him. And to this day still I don't know."

Betsy Beauchamp had slipped into the church and had quietly joined Roger. She had taken a seat in the front pew.

"You know, after all these years, this is the first time I have sat in this church. Some of my friends from the catholic church will tell me that I am risking eternity by being here, but I reckon that God is greater than that don't you think so now?"

Roger opened his mouth to respond but immediately closed it. This was not the time to discuss the relationships between Christian denominations. Instead he remained silent, looking straight ahead with his hands still clasped together. After a while he stood up and walked to the pew where Betsy was sitting and he joined her there as she continued speaking.

"I can't tell you how many times I have thought back to the summer of 1859. Just what – seven years ago? Everything seemed to be perfect and we had our lives to look forward to. And then Brown slipped into our little town and everything changed. My dear Frank was killed along with some of the town's people. And that poor black railway man who probably never hurt a soul in his whole life. Then the war and my Willard losing his arm and then running off like that twice. I can tell you that I also pray how much and how long?"

And so they sat there, side by side. The country preacher now approaching late middle age with his black hair and beard streaked with grey, and the widow with the flaming red hair. They sat in silence gazing at the communion table in front of them as though expecting a revelation. But they did not really expect that and indeed none came. It was Roger who broke into their thoughts.

"You have not heard from Willard then?"

"No, I've heard not a word since he left us. I know that you gave him an introduction to someone up north and on the one hand I am thankful to you for that. But on the other hand I have wondered many times why you did not share that with me before he left. If you had told me, then we might have handled things better. But there is no use crying over that now. I have done enough of that anyway. I was just wondering if you had heard anything from that quarter."

Roger shared that he had not and immediately felt guilty. He knew that he should have written to Davidson long ago enquiring as to Willard, but the business with Beth and Annie and the wedding and all of his work around town had taken up his time. Still he felt bad about it all and again they sat in silence with just the ticking of the Seth Thomas wall clock marking the minutes.

The old clock was hung at the rear of the church and to the side of the main door. He had always seen it as a not too subtle pointer to the preacher to not preach for too long. This morning it simply seemed to mark out the time as though to emphasize the uncertainty they both felt. It was Betsy who spoke next.

"That was all a bad business about young Beth. She is so young to have gone and got herself into that state. And now I hear that there is a nasty story going around that my Willard is the father of her child. That is so absurd Reverend don't you agree."

Roger immediately sensed that Betsy was not asking so much for his opinion but for his confirmation that Willard had not been involved with Beth. Clearly this was the real reason for her visit.

The truth of the matter was that Roger did not know. Obviously he had his thoughts about it all, and he knew what

Elijah was saying. But Beth had not confirmed it and so other than Beth and whoever the man was, no one knew the truth. The problem was that people expected him to know those things. And even if he did know, then he would have been held to confidentiality. He had learned long ago that when it came to town gossip he was in an untenable position. And so it was now with Betsy. He could not deny it and he could not confirm it because he simply did not know.

"Mrs. Beauchamp, Betsy, I wish that I knew, but please believe me when I say that I do not know the facts any more than you. If Willard had stayed around town we might have had his side of it all, but as it is, we just have to accept things as they are. When I gave him the letter of introduction I did not know about Beth's condition and I most certainly did not know that he would just run off again like that. If I had known then I would have held off, but there it is now I am afraid."

Betsy was on her feet, tossing her head and the red hair in obvious contempt.

"Oh so you don't know do you! If you ask me, I would say that you know a deal sake more than you are letting on, and as for me I think Willard is the man. There now I have said it! And in my mind I am disgusted to think of the two of them together like that. Her being, well you know what. I am of the mind to go to New England and find the boy and bring him back to face up to things. And don't go telling me to keep out of it all, and that Beth is better off without him. You tell me now, where did you send him?"

There had hardly been a single pause as the words came from Betsy. Obviously she had been holding all of this back for weeks. The idea of Betsy Beauchamp just taking off for Rhode Island in the hope of finding her son was ridiculous but at that moment Roger realized that she had made up his mind for him. As he stood, he quietly thanked God for coming through for him.

"Mrs. Beauchamp, I realize that I have not handled this well. The truth is that I feel very delinquent in my actions and for that I offer you my apologies, even though I did not and still do not know any details about Willard or Beth. What you do not know is that Mrs. Hart and I have pretty well decided to return to Rhode Island ourselves. When we do so, I will set out to find young Willard and see what the best direction to be taken is. And I will of course immediately send you word about all of it. Now, try not to worry too much. And as a matter of course, may I ask you to keep this between the two of us for now as I have not yet shared our plans with Mr. Clark or the church people."

Mary Hart was delighted and immediately began to make plans for packing and for stopping off in Westhill on the way, and then settling back in Glocester, Rhode Island. They had heard some time ago that Hart's old church was without a minister again as the young man who had replaced him had taken a calling in the city of Providence. There was no doubt in Roger's mind that the church would take him back.

Jason Clark understood perfectly, seeing Roger's decision as just an extension of what was happening all over the town. So many people had either left town or were planning to do so. Some had the intention to return and others were vowing to make a fresh start somewhere else. His business was suffering more and the church was having yet more difficulty. He remarked to Roger that most likely the few remaining congregants in the church would take an affiliation with one of the other churches in town. Their little church would close as it had done before and wait for better times to return. And, he assured Roger that they would return.

"Harpers Ferry will, one day, be a vibrant center again Roger, just you wait and see."

Clark's biggest concern was whether his business would survive until that day.

30.

December 18th 1941,
Dartford, West Virginia

The first time that I heard those details about my Momma, I recall that I had a rough time.

I am glad that I have now finished getting all of them out and on to paper in just two sessions. Having completed the typing, I looked through Elijah's and Willard's notes one more time and then read through these pages of mine, and I think that I have put all of the detail into the right sequence.

All of that information had been the first inkling as to why my family felt so badly about Willard. And I saw then why Grandma had always turned my questions away when I was a child. I also remember feeling very angry at Willard.

But at that time my feelings were mostly about my mother. After Elijah had finally told me what had happened, I remembered all those visits to Momma's grave when I was a boy and how I had wondered how she had died. I just felt so bad for Momma.

Now I want to return to Reverend Hart's narrative because I have always appreciated so much how he spent his last days telling me about the first few years of my story. The next part explained how I was born, and that was all too much for a ten year old to understand. And so the dear Reverend kind of skirted around a lot of the detail. Grandma filled in the gaps for me years later, and so in the next section I am again faced with working those details of Grandma's into the Reverends words.

It won't be hard for me, and I think that it will be pretty obvious where I add Grandma's details to the Reverend's talk.

31.

December 18th 1876,
Westhill, New Jersey

———◦◦◦———

It was a couple of days after hearing about the crater battle that I was called back into the parlor. Grandma told me that the Reverend had been feeling tired again but now he wanted to talk to me. I was starting to see that this was a kind of a pattern and I told her that I would be very quiet just so that I could hear all that he had to say.

It was just after mid-day and the Reverend was sitting up in the bed with I don't know how many cushions and pillows behind him. He was reading his Bible, but he put it down as I sat in the chair.

"It's good to see you Brownie. I want to get on with our story and what happened after Willard and Elijah came back from the war. Elijah can fill in some more of that when you are older but one thing you need to know is that your mother Beth suddenly found out that she was going to have a baby, and so it was arranged for her and your Grandma to come to live here in New Jersey.

Mrs. Hart and I had made plans to return to Rhode Island and it took me more than a month to make all of the arrangements for that.

The Baptist church in Glocester had immediately and enthusiastically written to say that they would love to have me return. They told me that most of the members there had wonderful memories of my ministry there back in late 50s. As you can imagine, that made me feel very good.

Neighboring ministers had been filling in after the young man who had replaced me had left. But that had become a strain for all concerned and the church had begun to meet just once a week. So I wrote back and promised them that I would return the church to the full meeting schedule and that Mrs. Hart and I would most likely stay with them until my retirement. I knew that they would be looking for some kind of a commitment like that.

So an agreement was reached that we would spend most of the month of December with Jenny and Fred in New Jersey, and then we would commence the new calling on the first Sunday in 1867. The thought of spending some weeks including Christmas with Jenny was exciting for both of us. And then there was the reunion with Annie and Beth to look forward to, and perhaps even the birth of the child; you my boy.

I had also written to Mr. Davidson in Pawtucket about our planned return, and since I had promised Betsy Beauchamp that I would enquire after Willard, I asked Davidson some questions about him. It was a big disappointment when my letter was answered and Davidson told me that Willard was not working in the mill. He remarked that it was a little complicated and that he had better explain when the two of us got together in January. Well, I decided not to tell Betsy

Beauchamp just yet but to wait until I had more information. After all, I had simply promised her that I would look into things following my arrival in Rhode Island and would send her a report as soon as possible. And that is what I planned to do.

As you might imagine Brownie, the farewells to the Clark family and to the church folk at Harpers were difficult. I knew how big a debt of gratitude I owed these people, but then, while they had all helped me recover from the Big Lick debacle, Mrs. Hart and I had in turn given all that we could to the ministry and caring of our neighbors.

So much had happened and so much had changed over the few years that we had lived in the town. The difficulties after the John Brown raid and then the trauma of the war years, had all taken their toll. But on my last afternoon in Harpers, Mr. Clark walked with me around the town and I noticed that he had taken on a much more optimistic tone.

'Roger, I have a growing feeling that we may make it here after all. That blasted war just about finished us off I know, with all the fighting and destruction and changing of hands. I don't think that your friends up north have any idea of the hell we have been through here. You know only too well how I have despaired these past six months or so, but today I start to feel just a bit better for some reason. It will take years I know, but look around. Some of the farms are doing better already, and the railways may be able to maintain a regular schedule again soon. People are starting to travel more. Perhaps a few will come and settle here in some of our empty houses.

And Roger, you must be very happy with the school that has opened up in the old quartermaster's building. These Free Will Baptist people are already teaching a whole bunch of freed slave children. And I am told that they have very ambitious plans about building up quite a college for colored students here. It is the dream that you had years ago come to fruition my friend!'

Brownie, I have to tell you that I was indeed thrilled with that development and was so glad that it came into existence while I still lived in the town. I had arranged a couple of meetings with the leader of the movement and had encouraged him in this venture. Although we were both from Baptist groups in New England, we had not met before this development in Harpers. The Free Will Society was much larger than the association that I was involved with and they had perhaps the sense to wait until the end of the war before commencing this huge undertaking.

Anyway, with our few personal belongings packed in three trunks, Mrs. Hart and I travelled by train and trap to our daughter's house here in Westhill. We arrived late in the day on December 5th."

32.

December 5th 1866,
Westhill, New Jersey

———— ✦ ————

"I remember that reunion so well. It was a great time for all of our family and of course for your Grandma Annie and your mother Beth as well. Grandma Annie had somehow wrinkled out of Jenny just what my favorite food was and she cooked that for us that evening. I was so happy.

Brownie, this next part is going to be very painful for you but it has to be told. It is why you and I are going through all of this after all. So keep up with me as I talk. Grandma has told me that you know how babies are born and all that, and I will try to keep this as easy as I can for you.

The day after our arrival, Mrs. Hart noticed that all was not right with Beth and she shared her concern with Grandma Annie a few days later.

'Annie, are you satisfied that Beth is well? I have noticed that she looks very weak, and now and again I have caught her holding her stomach and obviously feeling pain.'

Grandma seemed relieved that someone else had noticed.

'Well now Mrs. Hart, now you come to mention it I have been a bit worried, but just over these last few days. Beth has been just fine until now. But since you also notice things then I am really some worried for her now. I will talk to her later.'

And so since both of the ladies sensed that something was wrong with your Momma, Grandma asked her that evening if she wanted to share anything with her. Beth replied that she was a little scared now that her time was coming and that she had been having some pains but that she just assumed that was normal, adding that perhaps the excitement of the visitors arriving had something to do with it.

Your Grandma knew just about everything about babies being born and she did not go along with Beth's thinking. When Mrs. Hart heard about how Beth felt she immediately sent for the family doctor who had been seeing Beth through her pregnancy.

He spent some time examining Beth in her room with Annie by her side, and eventually after settling Beth comfortably on the bed, he indicated Annie to sit down.

'Beth, Annie, things are moving along a little faster than usual. I do believe that you are going to have the baby some weeks early and that you may have even been feeling some early labor pains. But there is something else that I have found and you need to know about it.'

Beth gave out a little cry and took Grandma Annie's hand. The doctor smiled at them and continued with his description.

'Now, now Beth what going on is not that unusual but we need to be aware and take some precautions. The baby is upside down, we call it breech, and it wants to come into the world bottom first instead of headfirst. There has been some work done in trying to turn a baby like that around before birth, but it is probably too late for that, and Beth you are so small that I am not recommending even trying. It's just too easy to harm the child by maneuvering it around. Your hips are really very narrow. I know that you probably felt good about that before but I am afraid that it is a little bit of a hindrance for having this baby.

Now, I do not want you to start worrying. I reckon that you should remain in bed now until the birth – which is going to be in the next week. Keep still, eat normally and get some good sleep. Your Momma here and Mrs. Hart will take good care of you and will call me at the first signs of real labor. OK, you got that?'

With his closing words he had looked at Annie to make sure that she understood. Leaving Beth to get some rest, Annie and the doctor stepped outside the room.

'Well Annie, I think that everything will be alright. As I said, I do not want to risk trying to turn the baby now, but I am somewhat familiar with methods of turning the baby a little during delivery and that is what I plan on doing if you agree. My only concern is that Beth is so small, but we will do all we can. Are you alright now? Call me when the labor starts and that will be in the next couple of days most likely. And then boil plenty of water because I will need to keep washing myself and everything we use since infection is going to be one our main enemies.'

His timing estimate was accurate and two days later the doctor and Grandma Annie were in Beth's room tending her delivery. Mrs. Hart and I waited in the parlor with more than a little degree of concern. Prayers had been offered and Beth's room had been prepared with the requested hot water and towels. Now we all waited.

Although neither Mrs. Hart nor I had any experience of a breech birth, the wait took even longer than we had expected. We had all hoped for a speedy birth even though the doctor had warned us that that was very unlikely. In fact it took longer even than the doctor had mentioned. And so there was a great feeling of relief when the baby was heard making his presence known very, very vocally.

And of course, that was you Brownie. You know how Grandma is often times telling you to be quiet? Well I can tell you that you came into the world making a lot of noise!

Mrs. Hart went to the door anticipating Grandma bringing the baby down to us, but the door to Beth's room remained closed after you had stopped crying. I joined her in the hallway not sure of what to do next. After a few minutes we just returned to the parlor and sat down to wait for the doctor. I said a prayer but I had a bad feeling about what was going on upstairs.

It was a good fifteen minutes later when the parlor door opened and the doctor came in to talk to us."

At that point in his narrative, I remember the Reverend asking me to fetch Grandma.

When she came in, the Reverend asked me to sit on the edge of the bed as Grandma took the chair. He squeezed my hand, and then he held on to it as he asked me to be brave as he told me the next part. I recall that Grandma began to cry even before the Reverend began again. He had some special words for her and then went on with his story.

"The doctor came into the parlor and stood over us.

'I am so sorry for all of you and for poor Beth. She tried so hard and I really thought that we had been successful when the child was finally delivered and in my hands. I had performed a partial movement of the child and succeeded in making the delivery possible without harming him. Oh yes, it is a little boy and he is perfect.

But there was too much bleeding, and I just could not contain it.

Annie is sitting with her daughter now, and the child is sleeping in its little cot. Reverend, give Annie a little more time and then go up to her. I have cleaned everything up as much as possible but as you can imagine, Annie is distraught.'

Oh Annie, you remember it like yesterday I know, and I also know that you remember how distressed we all were. In fact there was no consoling you. The love between you and Beth was so deep that I believe that you honestly felt that you yourself had died with Beth and that if not, then there was little left to live for. Beth had been just six years old when your father and brother were taken away from you, and it was Beth more than Elijah who helped you live through that nightmare. And when John was killed during the war and Elijah was away, it was Beth again who helped you come through.

When I went up to the room, I found you crying, with your head on Beth's breast. Looking back it is all a haze now, but I recall that I helped you to your feet and held you in my arms as we both cried together. Eventually I helped you away from the bed and you sat in a small chair in the corner of Beth' room. I went back to the bedside and said a quiet prayer for Beth and I pulled the sheet up over her face. You had stopped crying Annie.

'Oh Reverend what am I to do now? Beth was the center of my life, especially now with Elijah gone and settin' up on his own. She was all I had left. Who is goin' to take Beth's place and get me through this now?'

And then your crying began again. Annie I was so taken aback by the depth of your grief. There was nothing that I could do to console you and so I let you cry for the longest time. I admit that I was lost for words. I did not know how to answer your questions.

And then the baby gave a quiet murmur and I saw the next step quite clearly.

I walked to cot and picked up the boy, who was sleeping soundly. Walking across the room, I held the baby out to you and tried to help you through the moment. I was trying to help myself as well as I spoke.

I told you that this little boy was the one who was going to get you through your grief. That this little boy had a part of Beth in him and that he needed you just as much as you needed him. I told you to look at him and to take him in your arms.

And with that Annie, your tears began to come to an end as you sat rocking the baby in your arms. I can hear you now as you looked first at the boy and then at me and then began to talk to him.

'Oh just look at you my little boy. The Reverend here is right as usual and you and me are goin' to get through this together.'

Brownie, Annie, I am not for this world much longer - no don't wave that off Annie because I know it to be the case. But I have seen the two of you relive that moment so many times. Brownie you know how much Grandma here loves you and I want you to know that that love began when you were just a few minutes old.

But I need us to go back to that day.

Mrs. Hart had entered the room just then, and so I left the two of you together with the child. There were plans to be made and Elijah to be picked up in the morning. We had sent word to him some days ago when it was learned that Beth was to have the baby early. Now I was faced with giving him the tragic news.

A funeral service was held in the house and Beth was laid to rest in the field on the edge of town. Brownie, you know that place so well.

A light and unusually early snow had fallen, and I recollect how I was struck by the unexpected beauty of the scene as the mourners left the grave. Make no mistake now, I am a man of true faith and there was no doubt in my mind that Beth was in a better place. The quietness of the burial field, and the snow covering somehow framed everything for me in perfect peace. In some way it was a confirmation of the peace that Beth had found.

Brownie, I want you to know that I truly felt that your Momma was at peace that morning, and I know from how you have described your visits to her grave that you can understand that. But I must also tell you that all was not peaceful a few hours later in the kitchen of Jenny's house. Grandma, you will surely recall it.

Jenny and her husband were in the parlor and you were asleep in your downstairs cot. Annie had already given you your name Brownie.

I remember Annie, how you begged my forgiveness for dragging up the old stuff again. You apologized but said how you just felt strongly that John Brown had been part of the release of your people. You let it be known that you were naming the boy Brownie no matter what anyone said. And so it was done. By the way Annie, no one argued with you.

And now you know Brownie just how that happened. How you came to be given your name.

But I must go back again to that day to finish of this part of the story.

Later we were all sitting near the stove enjoying a pot of Grandma's best coffee when Elijah spoke out.

'So we have done right by Beth. I will say again that that was a beautiful service Reverend. But since I arrived here no one has mentioned Willard. He is behind this tragedy and we all know it. The question now is what are we going to do about him? I for one am not going to let him get away with this.'

I sensed the level of Elijah's anger rising, and so I chipped in that there was no real evidence that Willard had been involved. I did not believe my own words so I was not surprised when Elijah scoffed.

'Not involved! Now come on Reverend you know as well as I do that it had to be him.'

'Yes, I am afraid that there is little doubt about that now.'

You had spoken so quietly Annie that Elijah was about to rush on with his next point but checked himself.

'What do you mean Momma?'

'Towards the end, just as the doctor was at the last point of delivery and he was all tied up trying to get the baby's shoulders out of the way and ease its head through was when Beth cried out for Willard. Just that once but it made me bite my tongue seeing her go through all of that because of him. Oh no Reverend, there is no doubt that it was Willard alright.'

And that was all Elijah needed to hear. He was immediately on his feet and shouting about how he was going to get Willard to face up this.

'I know that he is up in New England and I know that you know where he is Reverend. I will go and fetch him and see that he pays for what happened to Beth and make sure that he takes care of her boy. When I think of what he did and then how he just ran off like that!'

I had to explain again that I did not know where Willard was. I explained how Willard had not stayed at the job in Rhode Island and I promised again to do my best to find the man and bring him to Grandma and to see the boy. I also promised to keep Elijah in the picture as to what was going on.

Of course I realized that I was taking on an impossible task. Willard could be anywhere and to be honest, I had a bad feeling that I would not be able to deliver on the promises.

A few days after the funeral, Elijah returned to Washington. He took some time to explain to you Annie as to how the business was coming along in a very satisfactory way and that he was doing pretty well at it. He wanted so much for you to be proud of him. I could see that.

Mrs. Hart and I stayed on as planned and had a pleasant enough Christmas with Jenny and Fred in spite of the tragedy.

Grandma took care of you Brownie and managed to keep up with her work, and so Jenny voiced that things would work out well, and that Annie and you Brownie should stay on as long as Grandma wanted. That was a big relief for me I can tell you.

And now you know that your father is Willard. Yes it was him."

33.

December 19th 1941,
Dartford, West Virginia

—❈—

Back 1876 in the front parlor of Miss Jenny's house, although I had only heard a little fraction of that account, I could not stop crying. I was after all only ten years old. And when Grandma told me the rest of it when I was about eighteen year old I remember crying all over again. And as I put it all together on paper yesterday, once again I found myself in tears.

I do come from an unusually emotional family, I know that, but I also believe that anyone in my position would have behaved like that.

My tears back in 1876 were because of the affirmation that Momma had indeed died giving me birth. And they were because I felt Grandma's pain. I had been hearing from the Reverend how much she had suffered over the years and to hear how Momma died right there in front of her just made me cry out for Grandma.

Then years later when I heard all of the detail I cried because of how Momma had been let down, in fact almost betrayed by this man Willard. It seemed that I still knew very little about him but to say that I did not care much for him then would have been an understatement.

But yesterday I cried for a different reason. Now I know the full story and my tears now are for more than Momma's death or Grandma's loss or Willard's betrayal.

But here I am again ahead of myself again. I must go back again to the front parlor and to the Reverends talk. I remember feeling that there was not much more he could tell me, and I began to worry about him.

34.

December 18th 1876,
Westhill, New Jersey

———∞———

"Brownie, the first few weeks were very busy and very enjoyable for me as I settled back into the ministry in the countryside of northern Rhode Island. Regular services in the meeting house were resumed and I visited as many families as I could in order to get to know them again.

I even attended an association meeting at the end of the month and was thrilled to be able to give them a report on the school that had been started in Harpers Ferry to teach colored children. It had not been the result of our endeavor but it was exactly what we had all hoped for.

Eventually I made the journey to Pawtucket to visit Davidson.

I learned that Willard had introduced himself and had impressed Davidson enough to be offered a job in the mill working at the dispatching end of the business.

'Roger, what with him only having the one arm, I figured that kind of work would suit him best. He struck me as an honest young man who really wanted to settle down and so I gave him the chance. At first he mixed in pretty well with the other workers. Most of them are immigrants you know, so they did not hold being a southerner against him.

But then he got all moody and such, and became belligerent with the other men. He mentioned a man named Brady who was working up in Boston in the rail yards and as to how he might just go and join him. Although goodness knows what he thought he could do there for work.

And then Roger, he was gone. Just like that. No by your leave or thank you very much. Took his wages one day and we never saw him again. I have no idea how you will set about finding him. What's so important about finding him any-ways? You and I gave him the chance and he just let it go.'

I had not shared about Beth and you Brownie before that and I did not go into it then. I simply told Davidson that I had promised Willard's mother to try and find the man, and left it that.

Some months later I was invited up to Boston to join a service of remembrance for the casualties of the war, and I took a ride down to the main rail yard and enquired about a Brady and a Beauchamp, but no one had any knowledge of either man. Or at least so I was told. I never could decide whether that was the truth or if the men were hiding something from me. Either way, I had to accept that it was a near hopeless task to find Willard. He might not even have been in New England anymore.

I sent the disappointing news to Betsy and to Elijah and I promised to keep my eyes and ears open for any news.

I was busy, and Willard gradually receded into the back of my mind as the ministry in Glocester grew and took up all of my time. Regular word from Jenny kept Mrs. Hart and me up to date on Grandma and your progress, and of course our occasional visit to Westhill confirmed those reports.

My word Brownie, the reports told as to how you were growing to be a very sensible boy who responded well to your Grandma's and Miss Jenny's teaching. She told me as how you just took up reading, and that very soon you would read everything you could lay your hands on. It was your Grandma's dream that you would one day attend a school and Mrs. Hart and I became determined to do whatever we could to make that possible. We all love you, you know that.

Right after Jenny moved to Westhill, I became aware of a school for black children just close by, and on Grandma's behalf I had made contact with the group running the school. This school had been started by a group of local Quakers who up until the start of the war had aided runaway slaves by providing food and shelter on their run north. Remember me telling you about Mr. Davidson in Pawtucket and how he helped runaways? Well those Quakers were another step in that journey for some. They had had a number of standoffs with slave catchers over the years but had successfully thwarted each attempt and had continued the help until their work was so well known that they deemed it prudent to back-off.

With the start of the war, the little group changed their emphasis and opened the school for colored children of local families. It was this school that I had set my sights on for you Brownie. After a few years I was able to make arrangements for you to be able to join the school after your tenth birthday providing that you could demonstrate some basic knowledge and ability. I just knew that would not be a problem for you.

And so that is how you are starting there in January! Grandma told me how much you are looking forward to that."

Reverend Hart did not share this next part with me on that day, but later I learned just how much he did love me and what lengths he took to arrange a good education for me. I learned that he had a bigger opportunity in mind for me but like I said, he did not share this with me or with Grandma at the time.

It was his hope that I would be able to enroll in the new school in Harpers Ferry to reach a higher level of education and if all went according the school's plans, to be trained as a teacher myself. To this end the Reverend had contacted the folk whom he personally knew and he made all of the arrangements. I was to be admitted on my seventeenth birthday – again providing that I met the necessary standards. All of that came out when I was around fourteen or so.

But before getting to that, there was more to be told by the Reverend that day.

"Brownie, with the arrangements made for you and with the knowledge that all was well with Jenny and with your Grandma, I quickly settled into the yearly routine of being a country pastor out in Henryville, Rhode Island.

Sermons were preached, children were taught and church members were baptized, married or buried as necessary.

My word, I remember now one February when one of our young men decided on baptism. Snow had fallen and the pond that we used for baptizing was frozen solid. But he was insistent and I was never one for talking anyone out of that decision. That afternoon the congregation went down to the pond and the deacons went ahead of us, and armed with shovels they cleared a path to the pond. There they broke up the ice with axes and I went down into the water with the young man. To his credit, I do not believe that he had any second thoughts, but my goodness Brownie, as I dunked him under the water and lifted him up again his expression was priceless! I said something to the effect that the Holy Spirit would bring warmth, and then the two of us hightailed out of there I can tell you!

I had so many wonderful times like that. The satisfying times far outweighed the disappointments, and my old enemy of depression became less of a familiar visitor.

That is until this past summer when everything changed again."

35.

July 4th 1876,
Henryville, Rhode Island

———✺———

"You know all about July 4th Brownie and maybe you have seen some of the parades here in town. The July 4th celebrations out in the village where I lived were very special. They were the highlight of the village life each summer and the people prepared for the day with much excitement. For the centennial celebrations this year, there was a special interest in as much as I had persuaded a visitor from England to come out from Providence and speak about how much the British people now admired the American experiment with freedom. He was of a mind to encourage all of us to continue with the work. I had explained all of this to my congregation and had told them that the speaker planned to warn us all about the consequences of not keeping to the faith and not maintaining civil responsibility and diligence. In fact I preached a number of sermons on what had happened to the people of Israel over the centuries when they neglected their faith and their responsibilities. I did that as a kind of warm up to the visitor's July 4th talk.

July 4th was hot and sunny. The village was decorated with ribbons and flags. And well before noon the open area was filling with farmers coming in to join the village people.

As was custom, there were two services planned for the day in addition to the visiting speaker's talk. The local churches joined together in the services and it fell to me to lead the noon time service. The congregation joined in a most stirring singing of the Star Spangled Banner during which the children ran up and down the Meeting House aisles with flags. Prayers were offered and I delivered a sermon. The service concluded with the singing of America! And then all the people joined in the cool shade of a number of large elm trees where the ladies served generous portions of clam chowder followed by peaches and bananas with ice cream. Endless jugs of lemonade provided the liquid refreshment, so much of it in fact that I wondered where it was all coming from. Oh Brownie, you would have loved it!

The afternoon was very warm and although various games had been organized, it was mostly the children who joined in while the older folk retreated to the meeting house again, this time to listen to the visitor. The doors to the meeting house and the windows were all wide open and just about everyone had some kind of fan to wave in front of their faces.

His words were well received, although a few folk complained that they could not understand his English accent. I had to smile at that as I remembered a similar problem that I had faced with some of the people in the south. It was all very pleasant.

After the talk, more than a few villagers dozed in the late afternoon sun while others took the opportunity to socialize.

More fruit along with various cakes was then served along with even more of the lemonade. Finally the evening service was enjoyed including more of the stirring patriotic music. My contribution to that service was to give the benediction and send the folk home.

It had been a most pleasing day and as the sun began to set, Mrs. Hart and I sat in some garden chairs outside the Meeting House reflecting on how much we had to be thankful for. Big Lick and Harpers Ferry were far from our minds and the sudden interruption to our quiet evening talk shook us both.

'Good evening Reverend. Good evening Mrs. Hart. May I join you on this lovely July evening?'

Mrs. Hart started, and I wheeled around to look at the new comer. It took a minute of two for me to recognize him. All I could think of was that I was more than surprised to hear his voice and so I know that my response was more than a little abrupt.

'Good grief Willard Beauchamp, now where did you spring from on this festive evening? No one has heard a word about you for what it must be ten years or more? What on earth are you doing just showing up like this?'

Mrs. Hart got to her feet and paid a cool welcome to Willard and excused herself as she walked towards the house. She knew that the two of us needed to be alone and I knew that she had some pretty bad feelings towards him.

Willard took the now vacant chair as I repeated the question.

'Well Reverend, your friend Davidson was good to me but all of them at that mill were just so damn patronizing that I couldn't stay on there. So I took off for Boston to meet up with a buddy from the army of the name of Pete Brady, but nobody would hire me around the rail yards with the arm gone and all. Back home that was kind of a badge of honor but obviously not so in Boston. So I just drifted for a while with Brady and then he got into trouble with the law. So I went back down to Providence with the idea of going to see Davidson again. But when I got there, I couldn't do it. I guess that I felt guilty about how I just took off on him. So I got myself a job in a restaurant working around the kitchen. I thought about going home to Harpers but figured that would not have worked out. I put that thought away and I stuck to the job for a year or more - and I did pretty well at it, even if I say so myself. The owner told me that he appreciated my work.

So when one of the main food suppliers said that he was looking for someone to help out in the office and warehouse with scheduling and the like, the boss put in a good word for me and I got that job. It paid a bit more and was easier for me. I have to tell you Reverend that it did all work out pretty well.

And that is where I have been all this time - just down the road as it were. I made some good friends and I have been able to put a little money away.

A few days ago I went to see Davidson to find out if he knew where you were. To be honest Reverend, I didn't know how you would take to me again. You saw how Mrs. Hart just walked out on me and left us. That is what I expected from you both. Anyhow, Davidson told me that you had returned some years back, and so I decided to take a chance and come out to talk to you.

You see, I am thinking about going back to Harpers to see how Mom and Frank are. And I want to see some of the old folk like Mr. Clark and Annie and of course Elijah and Beth. I want to catch up and find out how they are all doing.

Elijah might have moved away because I know he was thinking of it. And of course I suppose that Beth is married and settled by now. She probably has half a dozen little ones!'

Willard had laughed at the last remark. But on that warm summer evening, I felt suddenly very cold.

'So I thought Reverend, that I would take a risk and come out and pay you this visit, to see if you know how things are back there, because I figure that you will have been in contact with them all at different times. What do you think now, will they be pleased to see me or should I just keep away? Be honest with me now Reverend.'

Brownie I was startled to realize that Willard knew nothing about your Momma. Obviously he had not had contact with anyone back home and of course his folk had never learned where he was working and so had been unable to contact him. He did not know about Beth. And he did not know about you Brownie.

I remember getting up and taking a good swing at an unusually big black-fly. I was also searching for words. Eventually I just had to get it all out.

'Willard, first let me say that it is good to see you. I knew from your mother that you were an honest hard working young man back in Harpers when you put your mind to it, so I am not surprised to hear that you have held a steady job.

But you have been so wrong in not keeping up with your family. Your mother has been desperate to know how you were and where you have been all this time. And you have shirked another responsibility, one that I can clearly see you know nothing about.'

I knew that it was all coming out pretty hard and too quickly and that what I was about to say would badly shake

Willard, but it had to be done. It had to be said. I sat down again next to him.

'And what you did to Beth can never be excused. Nothing you can say now can justify that.'

I was back on my feet and pacing around him.

'You just took off without a word and left Beth alone with the shame of what you did. She was such a young and innocent young girl for you to have forced yourself on her like that.

Oh it's no good looking like that. Beth never spoke to anyone about what you did and she never told anyone about it, but everyone knew when you ran off like that. And it's no good protesting Willard so stop it now.

Beth had a baby.

You are a father!

Sit down man. There is worse to come.'

I threw myself back into the chair and we both sat there in our wooden lawn chairs and I tried to soften my voice even if only a little.

'Beth and Annie were so ashamed that they moved to New Jersey to work for my daughter Jenny and her husband, and for Beth to have her baby there.

Willard, Beth died in childbirth. There was a complication with the birth and the poor girl died.

You have a beautiful son Willard. He is ten years old and he is becoming quite the scholar. His name is Brownie. Annie named him after John Brown'

I had gotten carried away, and as the words came from my mouth, I regretted giving that detail just then. I immediately sensed that this was going to be another traumatic moment for Willard.

'Beth is dead? And you tell me that her mother Annie named the boy Brownie! That she named him after John Brown?'

My premonition was accurate. Willard was on his feet in a moment with his fists clenched. It seemed for a moment that your name Brownie, caused him more concern that all of the other details I had just told him.

'John Brown! He's the man responsible for my Daddy's death. You calmly tell me that they named my boy after him! And I never knew anything about all of this.'

Brownie, I was lost and just gave a quiet sigh. I had half expected Willard to deny any involvement but his response just confirmed what everyone believed. He had forced himself on your Momma Beth, and then run away. I tried to explain some more.

'Willard, first of all you can only blame yourself for not knowing any of this. What would you expect after disappearing like that? And do not blame Annie. You know nothing about how she suffered and what she went through as a slave. She just sees John Brown's action as the start of something that led to freedom for her people. It's as simple as that. And for what it's worth, Beth never said a bad word about you. You had better come back to the house and stay the night. Let's talk more in the morning.'

You see, I knew that he had just heard too much and that he needed time to let it all sink in. And so the walk to the house was done without any conversation. I knew that Willard was in shock and was trying to make some sense of all that he had just heard. When we entered the house, Mrs. Hart was still very cold towards him and she left me to show Willard where to sleep. I did offer him some food but he ignored me.

I know that sleep must have been hard to come for Willard that night and on more than one occasion I am sure that he must have been moved to dress and just run off again. That had been his pattern after all. But something must have told him that now was the time to stop running and face up to the situation. I guess that he realized that he needed advice and help, and that I was the nearest source of that.

The next morning, I think that as soon as Willard heard us in the kitchen, he got up and dressed and came in to join us. Mrs. Hart had a mug of coffee ready for him. She had given the matter a lot of thought and had decided what Willard needed now was help and not bitterness. I bid him good morning as though it was just like any other morning. That was a little silly I know, but I had figured out what needed to be done. But I was more than a little hesitant as to how to tell him what our advice was.

'Good morning Willard, I trust that you had some sleep last night. Mrs. Hart and I talked a little earlier this morning and we have a suggestion to give you. If you agree, I will contact your mother and let her know that you are alright. I will contact Annie and tell her that we have spoken and that for the first time, you now know all about Beth and Brownie.

Mrs. Hart and I plan to visit our daughter Jenny at the beginning of August and we suggest that you travel with us. Its far better I think to give everyone some warning, and for the three of us to arrive together than for you to just show up after all this time and confront them. Think about your son Willard. Think about Brownie. Later you can continue on to Harpers and I know that your mother will be so pleased and relieved to see you. What do you say?'

Willard took some time to think about that suggestion. His first inclination had indeed been to get Jenny's address and go there right away. But he could see the sense of giving some notice and of taking some of the drama and shock out the situation.

So it was agreed as I had suggested Brownie. I would do the writing. I would first write to Jenny and ask her to tell Annie about the development and what was to happen. And then I would write to Betsy Beauchamp.

After breakfast, Willard returned to Providence to arrange for some time off for a visit to his family in West Virginia. He did not mention you to his employer. I made the contacts as agreed and preparations were made for the August visit. We arranged to meet up at the Providence train station and to journey together."

36.

August 1876,
Westhill, New Jersey

———⊗⊗⊗———

"So Brownie that is what we agreed as far as arranging for Willard to meet your Grandma and to see you – just a few months ago. I can tell you now that I felt a strange feeling of apprehension mixed with some relief that perhaps some closure could be made.

As we rode down on the train to New Jersey, I talked with Willard about what he might expect when we arrived. Neither of us knew how it would all work out and so we had agreed that the best thing would be for him to stay at a nearby rooming house and not with Jenny and the family.

I was open in telling Willard that Jenny's response to my first letter had not been promising. Apparently Annie, you had sworn that Willard would never see his son. Not after all of these years. But Jenny had added that she expected you to maybe soften a little. After all Brownie, she pointed out that you needed to know about your father.

Because of all of the uncertainty, you were told nothing of what was going on Brownie. And so after arriving in Westhill, Willard was dropped off at the rooming house and then Mrs. Hart and I continued on to Jenny's house here.

It had been eighteen months since the Hart family had been together and so our reunion was wonderful. Jenny was looking remarkably well and was obviously enjoying the life as a quite wealthy lawyer's wife. She and Mrs. Hart immediately started to talk about all of the functions and events that Jenny was involved with. But I could tell immediately that something was worrying Jenny. When she nodded towards the kitchen area I made my excuses and went to the kitchen.

Annie, you embraced me very warmly and then it became very clear as to what was on Jenny's mind. Elijah was waiting in the kitchen.

'Well Reverend, this is a shake up and no mistake. Mr. Willard Beauchamp just turning up like this after all these years. Momma here wrote to me and I come up right away to be here before you bring him into this house. Brownie is fine. You know that he is starting school soon thanks to you. He is going to be a good scholar for sure, we all know that. He don't need to be all messed up now with Willard. So we ask you to just keep him away from here please. There is no good to be done by him now.'

You were not so sure Annie and you asked me if I agreed with Elijah. I thought for a moment or two before answering you.

'I can certainly see Elijah's point as far as Brownie is concerned. But Elijah, don't you think that the boy deserves to know who his father is? And then there is Willard. Say what we might about him, he deserves to see his son. I know it's all confusing and hurtful, but I think we should bring them together. I do believe that it will be the best move going forward.'

The three of us went back and forth, largely just repeating our original opinions. Finally Annie brought it to a stop by saying that she agreed with Elijah but that she believed he should go and meet up with Willard before they made a decision. And in the mean-time nothing should be said to you Brownie about all of this. And so it was agreed. Elijah was given the address of the rooming house and he set out alone to meet with Willard.

The rooming house was an old three story wooden structure set in some quite spacious grounds near the center of town. Most of the occupants were full time residents who worked in town. Just a couple of rooms were kept for short term visitors and Willard was in one of these on the top floor.

The custodian had enquired as to whether Willard would see his visitor who had been described simply as Elijah from Harpers. With quite some misgivings Willard had agreed and Elijah was brought up to his room. He entered and closed the door behind him. I heard later that there were no niceties in the greeting.

'Willard Beauchamp, you have one hell of a nerve showing up here now! Momma and Brownie have settled so well into this place and even though she will never forget what happened to Beth, she is making the most of everything here for the boy's sake. My God man, she was in the room when Beth died because of what you did to her - and where was you? Nobody knew! All we knew was that you didn't care.'

Willard opened his mouth to defend himself and to point out that he had not known about Beth, but Elijah went right on.

'No, you just keep your mouth closed for a minute or two and hear me out.

How could you have done that to my sister? Just forcing yourself on her and then running off. You know what? She never had a bad word to say about you and never accused you but we know what happened and she never denied it.

Brownie is a good boy and a good learner. The Harts have been so good to us all and the Reverend has made all kind of arrangement for Brownie's schooling. He is going to be alright and he doesn't need to know you now. No good will come of that. You just get to hell back where you come from and forget all about us. Because we plan to forget you and make sure that Brownie never knows about you and what you did to his mother, my sister. So Willard, I am telling you to just clear out of here now.'

The anger had been building as Elijah had unloaded his feelings and at the last word he had walked across the room and punched Willard square in the face. This was followed up with a hard blow to the stomach.

Willard fell to the floor, his nose bleeding profusely. On the way down he had pulled over a table which crashed to the floor alongside him. A lamp smashed on the wooden floor making a noise that echoed through the house.

Willard eased himself into a sitting position with Elijah standing over him. As boys, the two men had been of similar build with Elijah having a slight lead, but now Willard was at a disadvantage. Sitting on the floor and bleeding, he must have made a pitiful sight especially with the shirt sleeve neatly folded where the arm should have been. But Elijah felt no pity and was preparing to lift Willard and deliver another blow when the door burst open.

'What in damnation is going on in here?'

The custodian had raced up the two flights of stairs from the second floor landing he had been cleaning.

'I had almost not allowed you up here. I had a bad feeling about you and now I know I was right. What a mess and just look at you man you need to stop that bleeding.'

Elijah stood back as the custodian helped Willard to his feet and place a handkerchief over his nose.

'Now here is what we are going to do. The two of you are leaving this house now. You can pack your stuff right away and go. I am keeping the rent you paid up front to pay for the lamp and the cleaning. You got ten minutes before I call the officials.'

Elijah went downstairs and sat on a bench in the garden. Willard stuffed his few clothes into the bag and followed him down. They sat in silence for a couple of minutes until Willard spoke up.

'Well that was stupid Elijah and it did no good at all. I come here to make up for my actions; that was all. But if everyone feels as strongly as you do then maybe I should just clear off as you put it. If the boy don't know about me now then maybe we should just leave him alone. I suppose that you might be right about that.'

Conscious of the custodian standing at the front door, the two men stood and walked down the street. Willard was still feeling shaky and thought about sitting down again on a bench at the corner of the town green. A number of horse traps stood in line at the corner and the pungent smell of the horses put him off. The whole matter was a stink anyway and he did not really know what to do for the best. Elijah took Willard's case from him and they walked on.

Eventually they came to the train station and sat on a bench there.

'Willard, now you know how strong I feel about this. But let's put that to one side for a minute. Think of Brownie. He don't know who his father is and he don't even rightly know what happened to his mother. All of that can come later when he is older. Just let it be for now I say. Just let it be. You can't help by suddenly coming into his life.

How about you and me just getting on a train right now. You got everything with you and I only got one change o' clothes back at the house and I won't miss that. We can go south, me to Washington and you on to Harpers to see your folks. What you do then is up to you but just don't come back here. What you say now?'

So it was agreed. Whether it was for good or bad Willard did not know. He was just too confused and wishing he had never come out from Providence that July 4th. The last thing he wanted to do was to add to the hurt he had caused, especially to you my boy.

Elijah took a trap back to the rooming house to apologize to the custodian and to leave a note addressed to The Reverend Hart. I guess that he knew that eventually I would come by to check up on what had happened.

Our family enjoyed a good dinner that evening and managed to catch up on most of the happenings since we had last been together. We all agreed that Annie had prepared a most delicious meal for us. As the ladies retired to the drawing room and Fred went to his study to do some work, I went to the kitchen.

You and your grandmother were just finishing up your meal and so I sat at the table with you and started to catch up on what you were up to Brownie.

'So Brownie, I hear that your reading and arithmetic are coming along well. That's good my boy because I know that you are going to enjoy school very much. Your Grandma here is as good a teacher as she is a cook I think!'

I winked at Annie and looked around with a passing a glance that clearly asked where Elijah was.

Brownie, you were sent off to the dining room to pile the dishes there ready to be brought to the kitchen.

'Reverend, Elijah never came back.'

Annie spoke in a hushed voice.

'I is real worried and I just hope that those two have not gotten themselves into trouble. Somebody should go down to that house and see where they is.'

I had to agree, and so I excused myself to Mrs. Hart and Jenny explaining that I needed to check up on Willard.

At the rooming house the custodian described what had taken place and he gave me Elijah's note. I was disgusted and I apologized for the younger men's behavior and went back to Jenny's house.

In the drawing room, I read the note to the family. Elijah was quite brief but also very clear:

'Reverend, I made a mess of this but I guess I got Willard to see some sense. I am on my way back to Washington and he is with me. I wanted to be sure that he left town without visiting the house. He is going on to see his mother and then I don't know what he will do. My guess is he will go back to Providence. He promised me that he will not try to see Brownie. Give Momma my love and tell her I will write soon.'

'My goodness me, after all of that we accomplished nothing!'

Mrs. Hart expressed all of our feelings.

Our visit continued for the planned ten days and then we returned to Rhode Island. We were thoroughly refreshed and only mildly disappointed with the Willard outcome.

Brownie, it seemed to me that I was the only one who felt any sympathy for Willard, and I vowed to see him in Providence if he should return to that city."

37.

December 20th 1941,
Dartford, West Virginia

I finished writing that section yesterday morning. Elijah had obviously told the Reverend about some of it and of course I remembered the Hart's visit to Miss Jenny's house that summer.

At that time I knew that something had happened, but I had no idea that my father had been so close to me. That he had been literally just down the road.

Years ago when I first learned about it all, I told Elijah that he had been wrong to stop Willard from seeing me. Yesterday I felt even more that way.

As I have been putting all of these things into sequence I have been feeling like I was living those days all over again. I felt cheated then. I still feel cheated now out of not knowing my father while I was still a child. I told Elijah that in no uncertain a way, and in time he apologized but to the end maintained that he acted for my good. I am sure he did. That did not help then and it still does not help now.

Most of the earlier parts of these reminiscences have been based on what the Reverend told me back in 1876 and I need to pull myself together and finish this section. It will be hard for me. After the visit to Westhill, the Harts returned to Rhode Island and on one of my last visits to the front parlor the Reverend told me what happened there.

38.

November 1876,
Glocester, Rhode Island

———

"**B**rownie, I did not succeed in finding Willard in Providence. I must admit now that I did not try very hard. I am so sorry but I had grown tired of it all and my only hope was that you would turn out alright. I did make a trip into Providence last month to pay a visit to the restaurant where Willard had worked years ago to see if I could find out the address of the food distributor. But nobody there knew what I was talking about and I let the matter drop.

A quick visit to Davidson's place brought no assistance either. He confirmed that the man had come to see him back in July, but he knew nothing about where he might be.

I think you know that I have always had a certain soft spot for you my boy and I was already looking forward to the next time we could visit Westhill and I would be able to hear about your schooling.

But like I said, I was tired and on top of everything else, I was not feeling at all well.

My periods of depression over the years, and the stress from my tendency to worry over the slightest thing, had caused me numerous stomach problems. I had learned to come to live with that. But recently they had become much worse and I increasingly found myself tired after even a slight exertion. Also I realized that I was losing weight. Finally at Mrs. Hart's pressing I solicited the doctor's opinion.

After a review of all of my symptoms and after a number of examinations, the doctor had delivered the bad news that there was growth in my stomach. It was far advanced and, to the doctor's opinion, there was nothing that could be done. He reckoned that I had perhaps a month or so to live, certainly no longer. I cannot tell you Brownie how I felt."

The Reverend and I just sat there for a while. He had his eyes closed but I could see a tear. I knew that we were coming to the end of the Reverend's story and that we were just about up to date.

After a few minutes, he continued.

"Mrs. Hart and I had already started discussing my retirement from the church at some time in the future, but we both had decided that I would continue to work for a number of years. Both of us enjoyed living in the village and things at the church were going so well. Unfortunately we had just communicated that to the church elders and congregation and everyone had been overjoyed at the decision. We were all so happy.

And so it was a terrible moment when I told Mrs. Hart what the doctor had just told me. We just hung onto each other for the longest time with her crying and me trying to console her. I knew that this would be the ultimate test of our faith, and in my mind there was no doubt but that we would continue to put our trust in God and in each other.

The congregation was overwhelmingly supportive, but it was a difficult and tearful time when, on the weekend after I had received the news, I told them the situation. It was right after the Sunday service.

A letter was immediately sent off to Jenny who responded that Mrs. Hart and I should come to Westhill as soon as possible. Jenny and Fred would hear of no arrangement other than of them taking care of me.

The church was wonderfully accommodating and they told me that they would be making temporary arrangements. I was to understand that they considered me to be their pastor and that they would be praying for my return.

My last service with them was a very emotional evening service on a cold Sunday evening. Afterwards we returned to our Glocester home for the last time. Everything had been packed ready for the journey the next day, and so we settled in for the night.

Brownie, please leave me now and come back in the morning."

39.

December 1876,
Westhill, New Jersey

———⁊⁊⁊———

My memory pretty well now serves as sufficient to conclude the Reverend's part in my story.

I remember hearing how the journey was very tiring for him and as soon as they arrived at Miss Jenny's house he retired for the night. Mrs. Hart and Fred and Jenny had a quiet meal and then settled in the drawing room for a talk. I was not there of course, but towards the end the Reverend told me about some of what he heard had been discussed that evening.

"You see Brownie, Mrs. Hart explained to them that although we both considered a miracle quite possible, there was no other hope of my recovering. I had already expressed my wish to be buried in the Westhill graveyard and I had even prepared notes for my service. We preachers like to do things like that Brownie. I planned to take the notes to the church as soon as I felt up to it, and to talk them over with the pastor there. Mrs. Hart was surprised to find that she was able to discuss all of this. When she told me that, I just remarked that

I wasn't surprised because to me it was simply indicative of the strength of her faith.

Fred said that he would write to a local lawyer in Glocester and make all of the arrangements to close out our affairs up there. As far as he and Jenny were concerned, Mary's home would be in Westhill with them for as long as she wanted. Mary hugged them both and said how blessed she was to have them be so understanding.

Over the next week, as you know Brownie, I alternately felt strong or weak. When Fred's doctor visited on the second day he prescribed some medication for the pain and to provide what he called a tonic to boost me up a little.

It was in the third week after we arrived that I felt strong enough to pay that visit to the church down in the town. Jenny had tried to talk me into not going, saying that the pastor would visit us, but I can be stubborn Brownie and so I insisted. The visit to the church had in fact become a kind of become a marker for me as an indicator of my strength. It was on that Saturday that Mrs. Hart and I visited the church, and I did feel decidedly well. Both the trip and the discussions were very agreeable. Or at least as agreeable as such discussions can be.

Partly out of respect, and I suppose partly to make me feel better about myself, the pastor invited me to preach one Sunday. Well, neither he nor Mrs. Hart expected me to accept the invitation and so they were both very surprised when I not only accepted but suggested the next morning. Preachers don't turn away offers like that Brownie!

Anyway, I pointed out that we all knew that I did not have much time and I told them that I would really like to preach an Advent service one last time.

And so it was agreed.

I probably should have known better Brownie because much to the families chagrin, the Sunday morning was cold and wet. Being unable to talk me out of my commitment, they bundled me up and got me to church without too much exposure to the weather.

The congregation was surprised to be introduced to the visiting preacher that morning. Most of them knew me from past visits with Jenny and Fred and they certainly made me feel very welcome. I preached a sermon contrasting the expectancy of birth for the Virgin Mary with the probability of my own death. I do believe that my frankness surprised everyone except of course my dear wife. I had given it a lot of thought and my closing point was that both occasions were rooted in hope and in faith and that they should all take heart and keep to the faith. I most certainly was doing both.

When it came time to leave the church, the sky opened with torrential rain and I got myself soaked as they settled me in the trap. But I felt good as I leaned against Mrs. Hart sitting there next to me.

I just don't think that the rain made a scrap of difference to my condition Brownie. Back home here at the house I made a complete change of clothes and I came down to settle next to the fire and enjoy some food and drink that your Grandma Annie had prepared. Once again I felt good and remarked to Grandma how strong I felt. You came in and sat awhile that evening and we talked about how you would be starting school soon, and you told me how you planned to visit your Momma's grave the next day, and that of course was your birthday.

By that night however, I was very tired and I fell into a deep sleep. It was then that they made up a bed for me here in the front parlor.

The following morning I felt pretty well again but they all decided to make the parlor my permanent room. It was warm and very convenient for the family and for Grandma.

And Brownie, it was on that day in the parlor, right here that I began to explain all of your family history to you. It has taken us the best part of two weeks to cover it all and I confess that I have a bit of a problem knowing how to close it all out for you. I can't bring myself to fully explain what had happened between Willard and Beth. You would not understand and so that will have to come later and someone else will have to be the bearer of that information.

I tell you what my boy, go and fetch your Grandma if she is not too busy. Ask her to bring some coffee at the same time."

Grandma was finishing peeling some apples and she was about to take a break she said, so with the requested coffee in hand we went into the parlor and we both sat next to the bed.

I remember Grandma nodding her head to the Reverend and at the same time shaking it as if to say that, perhaps against her better judgment, she understood what he was about to say. The Reverend took a sip of coffee and then leaning back he began to carefully speak to me again.

"Brownie, I have told you an awful lot about that John Brown mess and about my early life and how I met up with your grandmother and her family. I told you about the Beauchamp family and a little about Willard. Now there is a lot more that you don't need to know just yet, and your Grandma and Elijah will explain all of that one day when you are older. You know how sick I am and to be honest my boy, I have a feeling that God is making up a room for me right now. So let me just finish off the story now. Sit back now and try not to interrupt me, because I want to try to tie it all together for you.

You now know that during the war, both Willard and Elijah went off to fight and that we were all so thankful when they both came home safely at the end of it all. Elijah was none the worse but of course poor Willard lost an arm in the fighting. They both tried to settle down in Harpers but neither of them could. Elijah went off to Washington as you know and has done quite well working for a successful builder there.

And now you know how Willard just disappeared for the longest time and we had no idea where he was. We don't even know where he is now. But I don't want you to think too badly of him Brownie. I know that Your Grandma does not speak well of him and I know that your Uncle Elijah never mentions him, but I want you to try to see him differently."

The Reverend closed his eyes and I could see that he was thinking through what he was about to say next. I just sat quietly, perhaps sensing that something important was coming next.

"I have told you all of that stuff from the past hoping that one day you will be able to piece it all together and see how all of those things affected your family and their friends.

Brownie, Willard made a lot of mistakes that's for sure, and now you know that he is your father.

All of the whys and the hows will have to come later when Grandma thinks you are up to it. Things were terrible for this country ten to fifteen years ago and everything got all mixed up. Maybe John Brown was not the only one who took wrong actions, but things went wrong for Willard because of John Brown. All of that stuff had a terrible effect on Willard's life and I have come to understanding that and I do not hold things against him. I want you to feel the same way.

It seems that John Brown was right about one thing. Remember how I told you what he wrote just before he died? It was something about how the crimes of this guilty land could only be overcome with blood.

Brownie my dear boy, and please listen carefully now - there has been too much blood and too much hatred over the years and it is still going on. It ruined your father's life. Please do not let it ruin your life. I want you to one day find your father and to meet him. I am sure that he loves you boy but he is just too confused and maybe too scared to come here. Promise me Brownie that you will one day make the effort to find him and get to know him.

Now, I need to get some rest. You can go and talk some more with your Grandma but I must say that I am really tired just now."

I did not know what to say. I could hear that the Reverend was very tired and I could see that the pain had been nagging him for some time.

Grandma Annie became busy with the meal preparations, and I became quiet trying to take in all that I had been hearing. Finally I announced that I would like my Uncle Elijah to find Willard and to bring him to the house. Grandma said that she did not think that was possible just now. Only years later did I realize that with the memory of the meeting of Willard and Elijah just a few months earlier, she was probably not optimistic of that happening any time soon. In any case she reminded me that nobody knew where Willard was.

That night the Reverend had a peaceful sleep, but in the morning he was unable to take any food or to sit up in bed. He lay on the bed with Mrs. Hart holding his hand and reading one of his favorite passages from the book of Isaiah. Miss

Jenny and Fred came into the room and sat with them. I guess that they all sensed that the end was near. Grandma and I were asked to join them.

As Mrs. Hart finished the reading and closed the Reverend's old well-worn Bible, he gave a deep sigh and looked up at her.

"My dear Mary, I do believe that I am about to rise up on those very wings, just like those eagles that Isaiah wrote about. I have loved you so much. I have loved you all, and now I want you all to be at peace and not fret about me and not cry – at least not too much!"

It was one of those moments when I would have expected the Reverend to give one of his winks. I don't think that he managed that. His final thoughts and his last words were concern for his family.

Mrs. Hart and Miss Jenny were crying so hard and Grandma began to steer me out of the room. But Fred stopped her and told her to let me say my goodbyes.

'Brownie has been a source of strength these past weeks and I have a feeling that the Reverend loved him like a son. You should know that Brownie.'

I went back to the little bed that had been the center of my world those past couple of weeks and I thanked the Reverend for all that he had done for me. I was not crying. I was just so grateful and at the same time so disappointed that he had gone. I did kiss his forehead and I whispered a promise that I would one day find Willard. In a way, I suppose that I did feel that Roger Hart was my father, but I also now knew that my real father was out there somewhere.

The following day, guests came to pay their last respects to the Reverend. Although he had not spent a lot of time in

Westhill, he had touched a lot of people there. Of course the folk at the local church had come to know him somewhat, but I think that what surprised Mrs. Hart the most was the number of people she had never met. Some came from the school and they told her how much her husband had encouraged them and helped them with advice. Many of Grandma Annie's friends came by and politely asked if they might say goodbye. One elderly man who was a servant at a big house just down the road explained how the Reverend had helped him through the grief of losing his eldest son.

'Oh Mrs. Hart we is Baptist folk you know and we don't have saints and the like, but to us your husband was a saint. No mistakin' that. He was a true friend to us and I know from the stories he told us that folk like me up here and from Virginia to Harpers Ferry and clear up to Rhode Island are all better for knowin' him. He was a very special man.'

The funeral was held two mornings later, and I looked around the cemetery and thought back just a few weeks to the last time I had visited my Momma's grave. I had been right about one thing and that was for sure. Compared to where Momma lay, this graveyard was a grand sight with marble crosses and hearts and angels.

I stood with the family at the grave and I thought about my friend the Reverend, and I just knew that he would have been just as happy lying where my Momma was as much as in this place. I smiled to myself at that thought, and the smile turned into a chuckle which was abruptly cut off by a withering look from Grandma.

40.

December 22nd 1941,
Dartford, West Virginia

———— ⦿⦿⦿ ————

A nd that is how my dear friend Roger Hart died.

  I had to take a break yesterday from all of this remembering and writing. Next to Grandma, the Reverend was the closest person in my younger life. He was such a gentle man and he truly loved people. I imagine that he was everything that a pastor should be.

When I was at the teaching college and maybe nineteen years old, I almost made a career change with the intention to become a minister. The college was run by the Baptist folk and religious instruction and regular chapel attendance were both important parts of our lives. But I came to see that being a minister was a calling not a career decision and so I dropped the idea.

Going back to my account, I realize that it is time to close out the part that I owe to Reverend Hart's talks.

A week or so after the funeral, Elijah came to visit his mother and pay his respects to Mrs. Hart. Grandma told him how the Reverend had told me much about our history and that I now knew who my father was.

Elijah sat me down and tried his best to answer at least some of my questions about the past. After a while, Elijah even told me that he had to admit that the Reverend had been right about feeling better by being able to talk about things.

Elijah explained that some things would have to wait until I was older and now of course I understand that. But whenever I asked about Willard and my mother I got a strong feeling that Elijah was feeling uncomfortable and maybe guilty about something. But he promised to try and find Willard one day and bring him to meet me. He also explained that it might not be possible if Willard had moved on again.

Over the next few years, letters from Elijah seemed to confirm that situation and I was asked to accept that I might not ever see my father. But I promised myself that one day I would find him.

Life settled back into the way it was before and I enjoyed going to the Quaker school. Studying seemed to come easier to me than to most of the other boys at the school and I guess that I did pretty well with my tests and the like.

After a couple of years Miss Jenny and Fred had a little boy and they named him Roger. That was no surprise. A young lady was hired to help Miss Jenny with the baby and with some general work. Grandma told me that was fine providing the new woman did not try to interfere in the kitchen. I was learning how territorial people can become.

Of course I frequently thought about my mother and the Reverend, and every Christmas I would make a visit to both of the graves. I kept up my habit of speaking out aloud when I spoke with them there and did not care a bit when sometimes somebody would give me a look.

I had a good and a happy boyhood.

41.

January 1883,
Harpers Ferry, West Virginia

———⊗⊗⊗———

On my seventeenth birthday Elijah came to Westhill to pick me up and to take me to Harpers and to the school down there. Roger Hart had done all of us well and all of the details of my education had been settled before he died. The arrangements included for me to start school in Harpers Ferry as soon as I turned seventeen. The teachers were pleased to meet me and seemed to be impressed with my knowledge and my ability to learn. I suppose that I was the kind of pupil that they all dreamed of having. I have had a few pupils like that myself. I immediately settled into the school routine.

On the first weekend of the New Year, I excused myself and I made my way across town and up a hill to a farm that Elijah had described to me. At the hilltop, I sat on a low rock and looked down and across at the well-run farm.

I sat there for the longest time and I thought to myself that this had been Willard's home. I wondered how many times Willard might have sat on this very rock, perhaps with his mother Betsy. I knew now more about how Willard had run away and left my mother pregnant with me. On the way to Harpers, Elijah had given me all of the details that I wrote about earlier. He told me how Willard had forced himself on my mother.

"I am so sorry Brownie, but your mother told me herself and I know that there was no other way that it could have happened. Your mother was so good and would never have gone with a man like Willard."

Elijah had not used the word rape but I was old enough to not put too fine a point on the painful truth.

Sitting on the rock, I put those thoughts away and looked at the farmhouse. Outside and on the porch I could see a woman putting some boxes on the steps of the porch. The flaming red hair immediately identified her as Betsy. Since hearing that Willard was my father, I had often studied my own hair searching for any trace of red. I never found any. Now of course it is a uniform gray.

So this was my other Grandmother, and I had never met her. I felt a mixture of emotions. On one hand I wanted so much to meet Betsy and hug her and yet I was very aware that she might just turn me away. When it came to people of mixed color, I had already learned that some folk, even black folk, could be very uncomfortable. I wanted to be the one to introduce myself and that is why I had asked Elijah not to see Betsy and tell her that I was in town.

Putting caution aside, I got up and strode down the hill and up to the farmhouse. Grandmother Betsy looked up and came to the edge of the porch.

"Good morning young man, can I help you?"

After all these years Betsy still had that rich Irish brogue that the Reverend had first told me about. I found myself to be fascinated by it.

"Good morning ma'am, I do not want to disturb you."

I knew that I was stumbling and unable to find the words. I could hardly just call her Grandmother without any build-up or warning. And yet perhaps that was the only way.

"I mean, I am sorry for just walking in on you like this, but I just arrived at the school down in the town and up beyond the cemetery. I am a new student there and I just had to come and see you right away. Ma'am, my name is Brownie, and I am your grandson."

I braced myself for what might come next, perhaps anger and denial.

But instead Betsy walked up and looked me straight in the eye.

"Are you the son of Beth?"

"Yes ma'am, to be precise I am the son of Beth and Willard."

I regretted the words wondering if she would take them as sarcasm when in fact they were just part of my stumbling. I need not have worried.

Betsy took me in her arms and hugged me so tight that I had to push back for air. I can tell you now that it felt so good.

"Oh my boy, I have wanted to meet you for so long. I heard when you were born, but after that no one ever wrote to me again. Except the dear Reverend Hart that is, of course. I had asked him to find Willard but he could not and he wrote a few times about that and to tell me a little about you. But that was all I ever heard. Until a few years ago when Willard turned up out of the blue just like that and spent a few days with us here. But he told me that he had never seen you and had only just heard about you. Oh my dear he was so confused and mixed up again. Come up onto the porch and I will fetch us a cold drink."

The cold grape juice was delicious and I savored the moments sitting on the porch seat with my grandmother. There was so much that we needed to ask each other and to say to each other. There was almost a sense of urgency to catch up.

After a while Frank came up from the shed and joined us. After introductions he was initially cool towards me but soon took to me and joined in the talk. He knew that his father Frank would never have held the mistakes of Willard against me and would not have allowed any thought of color to come between the family bloodline, and neither would Frank Jr. let that happen.

A midday lunch was very pleasant and it gave the three of us more time to catch up. Betsy was agreeably surprised at how well educated I was and how I could speak on matters. She told me so and said as to how she just knew that was Reverend Hart's doing. I excitedly confirmed that and explained how Roger had arranged first my home schooling with Annie and then the little school in Westhill and now the big one here in Harpers.

Of course I did not say as much, but I sensed that for all her acceptance of me, what she really meant was that I was so well schooled for a colored boy. I knew only too well that was just the way of things. I was used to it anyway and would not hold it against her.

Betsy told me that when Willard had last visited he had told her about the job in Providence and that he was planning on returning to that after leaving Harpers. I guess that Willard had also told her about how Elijah had acted towards him. She did not mention it to me anyway, probably not knowing if I knew and not wanting to cause any conflict between me and my uncle.

"But then after Willard left us again, I never heard from him so I do not know if he is still in Providence. He became so distant, removed even from us again. I did hear once from Elijah saying that he had no success in finding my son."

Over the years, I confess that I had wondered just how much Elijah had tried to find Willard and now I realized that perhaps he really had tried. After all if Willard's mother did not know where he was, then who did? Perhaps he was dead.

During those school years I regularly visited the Beauchamp farm and came to feel that I had truly become a part of their family. I also took a part-time job in Clark's emporium which had recovered quite well after the war years, although not completely up to the pre-war level. Since the end of the war, serious flooding had occurred on a number of occasions, but enough people kept coming back and rebuilding to enable Clark to keep going. Mr. Clark liked to point out the irony of me working where my grandparents and my mother and my father and my uncle had also worked.

Financially, Roger Hart had arranged everything between some grants from the Baptist society and the generosity of Jenny and Fred. This meant that I was able to put most of the money from the job away for the future.

While I was at school, Betsy received just two letters from Willard. Both were post marked Providence but he never gave any information about where he lived or worked so no return correspondence was possible. But they proved that he was alive and I became ever more resolved to do nothing until I graduated, but then to visit Rhode Island and do whatever I could to find my father.

The years in Harpers Ferry passed quickly with me enjoying every moment and achieving very high scholastic levels in my subjects. My teachers all predicted a very successful and effective teaching career for me.

During the summer vacations I worked at the farm and at the emporium and got to know folk around town very well. I learned that people thought highly of Frank Beauchamp and of his efforts to stop Brown. I also learned that people had divided views about my mother and father. I was not accepted at all by some of them.

Each year I did take a week or two up in Westhill with Grandma. She was always pleased to hear how I was doing at school.

42.

Summer 1887,
Harpers Ferry

—◆◆◆—

I suppose that every student looks forward to graduation. I know that to have been true of most of my own pupils. Only later did I realize how the teacher also looked forward to seeing the job completed for a class.

My graduation time came and I was thrilled that Fred and Jenny were able to attend the ceremony and that they brought Mrs. Hart and Grandma Annie with them. Of course Elijah came up from Washington. Betsy and Frank sat with them and I felt good about my mixed family and friends sitting together. Naturally they were all so very proud of me and in turn I was very grateful to all of them.

Grandma told me that to her, the ceremony was like a dream. She could not understand some of what was going on but she knew that it was all very special and that her grandson was right there in the middle of it all. She told me what she could not get out of her mind, was that there I was up on the stage, the grandson of a slave – no, the son of a slave because my mother had been owned prior to Clark coming along. And there I was now, all dressed in my fine new clothes, receiving my diploma and applause, and facing a life that she could never have imagined. Grandma cried tears of joy that day.

Just three people were missing that afternoon.

I knew that Reverend Hart would have been very emotional at the ceremony, and at seeing his long-standing dream of education for the colored children become not just a reality but even a reality for one that he had come to love. I still missed the Reverend and I knew how much I owed to him and his colleagues.

Having never known my mother, I could only imagine how she would have felt. From Grandma and Reverend Hart's descriptions, I could just about imagine her as an elegant woman sitting and applauding along with the others. She would be crying, of course. I had missed knowing my mother on so many occasions, but perhaps none as keenly as on that graduation afternoon. If only she had not died. And then the thought came to me that if she had not died, things might have worked out very differently, and that maybe I would not be where I was that afternoon. It was a sobering moment, and I made a mental note to keep that thought for future analysis and to perhaps write about what the consequences might have been. I was always thinking like that back then. But on that day it was enough to just think on how proud my mother Beth would have been.

But it was Willard who was really missing.

He was the only one of the three who could have attended, and it was that that made his absence so hurtful. But I had to accept that he knew nothing about the occasion or about how well his son had done. This had to be put right, and that afternoon I began to lay out plans for finding my father. First though, I was determined to enjoy the day and to enjoy having my family and closest friends all together.

The evening of graduation day was spent at the farm. Frank and Elijah cooked a mix of steaks and ribs and boiled two large pots of corn. Betsy had prepared what appeared to be an endless supply of potato salad to go with the main meal and two large apple pies for desert. Everyone ate their fill and expressed feelings of deep satisfaction. Fred stood up and delivered a little speech and gave a toast to my future.

It had been a good day, and as darkness came down, Grandma Annie left to go and spend the night with the Clark family while Mrs. Hart, Fred and Jenny returned to the guest house where they were staying. Elijah and I stayed on at the farm where we shared Willard's old room. Oh my goodness, but I slept well that night.

The next day was busy with helping the out-of-town guests get packed and on board the northbound train. It had been such an exciting few days that I hated to see them come to a close. I kept back a special hug for my Grandma Annie.

"Grandma, I can never thank you enough. You have been both my mother and my grandmother. You have given me everything I ever needed as I grew up. I owe an awful lot to the Harts I know, but without you none of this would have happened."

Grandma cried the tears of a deep level of satisfaction. Everything had come out better than she had ever hoped. But it seemed there was just one thing that still needed to be taken care of.

"Oh, Brownie don't go on so. You have been the pride of my life boy and I would not have missed a moment of it all."

There was a brief pause and Grandma broke the hug, pushing me back but still holding on to my shoulders.

"I know that I have been critical of your father and that I should have told you about him earlier. I truly thank God for Reverend Hart being able to tell you the stories. But Brownie, I remember what the Reverend asked you to do, and I ask you now to try to find your father and put things right for all of us. Do it for your mother and do it for yourself. What he did was terrible wrong, but enough is enough."

I acknowledged that that was my plan for the summer and that I intended to pick up some loose ends from Elijah that very day and then travel north myself.

Elijah and I lingered on the station platform long after we had waved the train out of the station. Elijah had decided to stay on a few days to visit some old friends before returning to Washington where he had a new project about to start. Yet another bridge was to be built across the Potomac, and William's company had received part of the construction contract.

I took the opportunity to share my plans to visit Rhode Island to find Willard and I asked Elijah to go over what he knew one more time so that I could make some notes.

Elijah gave me the details of the Providence restaurant that had denied knowing Willard. Mary Hart had already given me the details for Davidson's mill in Pawtucket. It was not much to go on, but it was all that I had.

While Elijah was going over the Providence information, I once again had the distinct impression that my uncle was not comfortable, as though hiding something. The information that I had was just too slim to risk missing anything and so I decided to take a direct approach with Elijah.

"The last time we spoke about Willard I had the feeling that you were holding back Elijah, and now I get that same feeling all over again. What are you hiding? I know there is something."

Elijah got to his feet and strode along the entire length of the platform before returning and sitting next to me again.

"Yes, I have been hiding something Brownie. That is not why I am uncomfortable though. In fact uncomfortable is the wrong word completely. What I am feeling is guilt and I reckon that I need to come clean right now and just hope that you will find it in yourself to forgive me Brownie."

Elijah had looked down at his feet as he spoke, as though looking for the right words. I was thinking that I would forgive just about anything if it yielded any new information.

"I lied about Willard and your Momma. I knew that they were together just before he ran off. Right before we found out that she was expecting you.

I just could not believe that she would have willingly gone with a man like Willard. There is no doubt that he is your father Brownie, but I lied when I said that Willard raped her. I guess that I just wanted that to be the case. No, don't interrupt me now, there is more to tell you.

The last time I saw your Momma up in Westhill, we sat and talked and I told her that I knew that she was raped by Willard and asked why she was not telling everyone, because she was still not saying anything at all and that was confusing for all of us. I told her that there was no shame in her not being able to defend herself against him. And it was then that she told me about that day down by the pond.

She said as to how they had met unexpectedly and they had got carried away in the sun and in the feelings of being together. She said that she had always loved Willard but knew that any chance of them being together was impossible.

On that afternoon she felt that Willard was attracted to her and that they both had feelings for each other, as impossible as it was. And then they made love, without second thoughts, and at the moment with no regrets.

She told me that she had made no attempt to put him off and in fact that she had gotten completely carried away with him. That it was all such a wonderful feeling to be able to hold on to him after all those years. In the sun and by the pond the color of their skin made no difference. They were in love and they did not care about anything else.

Afterwards she told me that they both became embarrassed and felt just a little stupid since there was no chance of having a real relationship. They did not talk about it, but both of them knew that they could not tell people about their love. That they just had to go on with life as it was.

And so they just parted that afternoon and went to their homes without another word. And then Willard was gone and no one knew where. And they never saw each other again.

That last time we were together, your Momma begged me to stop telling people that she was raped and that it was time to tell the truth. I promised that I would and that we would tell people the truth together when she was ready. But then things all happened so quickly Brownie and the next thing I knew was that my sister was dead. Everybody kept so much from you but I made it worse by continuing to tell people that it was a rape. I guess that I just could not accept that Beth had willingly gone like that with your father. I could not see how she could have been in love with him.

The worst thing for me is that I betrayed the promise that I made to your mother, and that has haunted me all of these years.

And then when Willard went out that July 4th to see the Reverend, he learned for the first time everything that had happened and that everyone believed that he had raped Beth. I never understood why Willard had not immediately denied it after Hart told him about Beth. Not until that day in Westhill at the railroad station after I had punched him out. He told me then that since he was such a loner and not liked by anybody, he had decided to let the rape story go on rather than risk people feeling bad about Beth. In a way I suppose that took guts Brownie, but I don't know.

Then Willard told me Brownie that he loved your Mother and that if he had known that she was pregnant and if he been anything of a man, he would have taken the consequences and stayed with her even if marriage was impossible. But it was easier, he said, to just let people go on thinking the worst of him then after ten years had passed.

So Brownie, it seems that between me and Willard himself, we have made more of a mess of your Daddies life than it should have been. I failed to follow my promise to your Momma. Reverend Hart has gone to his grave thinking the worst of Willard. Worst of all, I have led you into first knowing nothing, and then to thinking the worst about your Father.

I have been struggling with this for so long but didn't know how to tell you. The facts are that, as impossible as it was, Beth and Willard loved each other and they would have loved you Brownie. We might argue that they got carried away with passion that afternoon, but I knew from Beth that it was love. If they had both been white or both been black things would have worked out fine. Instead it became a mess that just got worse and worse thanks to me.

Try not to think badly about me Brownie. I never meant to hurt no one. Now you had better go and try to find your father and tell him all of this. He deserves to know what I should have told him years ago."

43.
December 24th 1941
Dartford, West Virginia

———— ✦ ————

That was all so long ago. My word it does not seem like that, but it was a long time ago that I found out that my mother and father loved each other. I discovered that I was not the result of a violent moment of lust and I was not the result of a few moments of careless passion. I was, no I am, the son of a couple who loved each other but who felt that they had no chance to openly show that love.

Traditions, social moirés, prejudice, narrow-mindedness and that old curse of bigotry- they all came together to make an outward expression of their love impossible.

The Reverend told me once that love conquers everything. Perhaps he should have said that love conquers almost everything. Back in 1866, for love to conquer anything it had to be acceptable. And the relationship of my mother and father would not have been that. It still would not be today.

And then Grandma Annie used to tell me that as bad as things were for us colored folk, they used to be a whole lot worse. I suppose that she was right about that. It is easy for us to narrow the view and complain about this and that and forget just how bad it was for her and her family. Slavery was wicked and no other word is acceptable to me when it comes to describing that. My mother was a slave.

Today in 1941 the relationship between my mother and father would still not be acceptable and life is still too hard for us colored people. And that is especially true the further south you might go. That is why I started to write all of this stuff down. But right now I need to pick up again about my search for Willard.

All of these years later, I cannot satisfactorily write about my emotions and feelings towards Willard at that time. They were too confused.

I remember how I experienced mixed feelings. I felt relieved to finally know the truth but I also had strong feelings of disgust towards my uncle. I was relieved to know that my mother and father had good feelings for each other - even love. But I loathed the idea of my father not standing up for himself and her, in spite of what others thought.

Over the next day, as often happens, the emotions softened and I told Elijah that I would let him know what happened that summer. We parted on reasonable terms. Mostly I began to feel very sorry for my father.

As I pieced together again all that Roger Hart had told me, I began to see my father as a victim of continual bad circumstances and I became more determined than ever to find him.

But first I had to call on Grandma Betsy and Frank.

At the farm I got them together and told them what Elijah had told me. It was not an easy talk and I recall feeling very embarrassed telling Grandma Betsy the details, but I could not accept the thought of anyone unnecessarily going on thinking so bad about my father - especially his mother and his brother.

Frank did not have much in the way of a reaction but Grandmother Betsy did. She told me the old story again of how she and her husband Frank had almost not been allowed to marry because of the religion difference. And she wondered if my mother and father might have been able to work out their differences. We sat quietly in the farmhouse kitchen as she voiced that thought.

But I was twenty one years old, and I had already felt the suspicions and the bad feelings against me and my people too many times. I knew that such a relationship would never have been accepted.

"Grandmother, it's just no good thinking along those lines. I have done that many times since I heard the truth, but it is all so much wishful thinking. A Catholic and Protestant difference does not carry any outward difference in appearance. Beth and Willard would have stood out like two sore thumbs – or worse. And then there is me. I am not black and I am not white and that would have reminded people about how things were all of the time.

If Willard had stayed around, he and Beth would have probably tried to keep their little secret. Most likely I would have been born here and people would have slowly put one and one together and made a hundred and one. It would have been terrible for all of us. As hard as this maybe to accept, the way things worked out may have been for the best. I don't mean my mother's death of course, but most everything else."

I did not feel as certain as I may have sounded.

Grandmother Betsy nodded her head in agreement and the three of us fell silent again.

After a few more days in Harpers, I boarded the train that would eventually take me to Providence. It was a good journey and I found myself glued to the train window like a young school boy. Washington, Baltimore, and New York were all experienced either in a blur through the window or from platforms whilst changing trains. Parts of Connecticut reminded me of the little town in New Jersey and I was enthralled by my first sight of the sea.

But now I have to stop writing. My fingers are aching from typing away and I need a few days away from my memories. It is almost Christmas and I plan to attend the Episcopal Church on Christmas Eve because I always love the singing. Then I will go along to the little Baptist chapel on Christmas morning. I still miss going to the two graves at Christmas. But I will just close my eyes and go there anyway.

I see that I need to get myself a Christmas gift – some more typing paper!

44.

December 27th 1941,
Dartford, West Virginia

———⚬✲⚬———

The two Christmas services were just wonderful. I say one thing about the Episcopalians – they know how to make a joyful noise unto the Lord! The organ and the choir shook me to the very bone as we celebrated Christmas Eve. The incense made me cough a little but the grandeur and what I can best describe as theatrics did move me very deeply. As the hour turned at midnight, Christmas Day came in with much joy.

And then I just loved the simplicity of the Baptist chapel service on the day itself. As I listened to the lady play the piano and then the little choir sing about the manger, I thought about the Reverend Hart and I wondered how many Christmas services he had led. His eyes would have sparkled and I do believe that he would have turned to me with one of his famous winks. Perhaps he did.

My Christmas dinner was a plate of cold beef that I had saved up from a couple of days earlier. No one came to visit but I had a good time. I really put my memory to the test and found myself re-living past celebrations, especially those in Westhill. Miss Jenny certainly knew how to put on a Christmas celebration back in those days!

And that brings me back to my notes and back to 1887 and my search for my father. It is time to finish off my narrative.

45.

Summer 1887,
Providence, Rhode Island

———— ⚬⚬⚬ ————

Providence was reached early on the evening of the second day and I checked into a rooming house that Elijah had told me about. Not every establishment took kindly to colored people and I was relieved to escape that embarrassment by using Elijah's past experience.

The very next morning, my first call was to the restaurant where Willard had worked for some years and had apparently earned a good reputation. Against reason I suppose, I hoped that Willard might have kept in contact with them. So when I discovered that the restaurant had gone out of business and closed, it just seemed to be in keeping with all that had gone on. Why should I have expected things to start going right then?

My next stop was to the food distributor who had hired Willard away from the restaurant. I had made a list of distributors and on the second stop my luck changed for the better. The ownership had changed but a clerk overheard my question and remembered the one armed man. He told me that some years ago the man had taken some time off to visit family in West Virginia or somewhere down there. Shortly after coming back though, he had decided to move on again. He had no idea where Willard might be now.

I realized that I was pretty well treading in the same footsteps as the Reverend and Elijah before me. The only two possible connections with Willard turned out to be unsuccessful. I really did have no idea where to turn next. That night I had trouble sleeping which was very unusual for me at that time.

The next day I took some time off to tour the city to take my mind off of the task for a while. Everyone was very proud of the new city hall that had been completed just a few years earlier. I could see why. It was a magnificent baroque style building with a kind of four sided dome feature at the top. Inside it was beautifully finished with marble, stone and polished wood. I had never seen anything like it before and my mind went back to my studies of Europe. I realized how much I was looking forward to going back to Harpers and starting to teach.

When Mrs. Hart had learned about my plans to try to find Willard, she had asked me to go and see Mr. Davidson at the mill and to pass on her very best regards. She had added that since I was determined to go up there, then I might as well meet a friendly and charitable person. I also thought as to how this man had once hired my father and that there just might be a clue there.

The next morning, I made my way out of the city to neighboring Pawtucket. It was no distance at all and in fact I found myself in Pawtucket without knowing I had left Providence. I wondered to myself how city people managed to keep their minds. Everything seemed to blur together and everyone was in such a hurry. Non-the-less I enjoyed the views as the hansom cab carried me across the bridge and up to the mill where my father had once worked.

At the front office I introduced myself as a friend of the late Reverend Hart and asked if Mr. Davidson was available. After fifteen minutes or so, Davidson came out to meet his visitor. Within minutes Davidson had grasped who I was and he ushered me back to his office.

"My word young man, it is good to see you. From time to time over the years Roger Hart kept me aware of you and your Grandmother, and the entire goings on down there. He was really very attached to you. I think that it had something to do with the terrible happenings at Big Lick. The trader Clark and your family saw him through the worst of all of that and I think he was always grateful to them. He was a remarkable man you know. I never knew a more loving person or one who sincerely had the welfare of everyone at heart so much. I was so sorry when Mary's letter arrived telling me that he had died. You were there of course. So tell me about it and tell me what you have been up to because Roger told me that you were to be a scholar and most of all tell me why you are here."

I almost took a breath for the man. He had been talking like these city people lived - fast and moving from one point to another without a pause!

I filled in the details for Davidson and how Mrs. Hart had asked me to visit and pass on her very best wishes. I mentioned that I was trying to find Willard Beauchamp but did not go into any details as to why. I also told Davidson about the two blind alleys that I had just encountered and that I really had no idea what to do next.

"My goodness young man, this Willard must be quite the man. Hart asked me to take him on and I did for a while until he disappeared. Then Hart was out here looking for him and then a colored man from Washington came out to see me and all because of this Willard man. What is so special about him anyway?

I knew then that Elijah had indeed made an effort to find Willard and I was pleased at that. So I explained that the man from Washington was my Uncle Elijah, the son of the Grandma Annie that Davidson had heard about. And after a moment's hesitation I plunged in with the fact that Willard was my father and that I needed to find him. No details were necessary and none were asked for. That was a relief as I had no desire to go into any details just then.

Davidson stood up and gave a little cry as if he had made a momentous discovery.

"Well now, and wait a moment young man, here is an extraordinary turn of events! An Elder from Roger's church takes a ride over to see me whenever he is in Providence. We just chat for a while. It all started when he and Roger stopped in together one day years and years ago. Anyway, some months after Roger died the Elder came in and gave me an update on the church. It seems that when Roger left for New Jersey and then passed away, they called a retired minister to serve the church while they searched for a permanent man. It took longer than expected and when he came to see me they had just made the call so he stopped by and filled me in on it all.

But then he told me that one day a young man had stopped by the church asking for Reverend Roger Hart. He was told that Roger had died and apparently the stranger became quite distraught. He kept saying that meant that he was too late, but he would not go into details. But here's the thing! I remember

Willard coming to see me just a while before all of that happened and just before the Reverend died, asking if I knew where Roger Hart was living.

Anyway, I heard that he left the church that day and stopped in town to get a bite to eat. In the tavern he learned that the owner was looking for someone to run the place for him. The stranger, who said that his name was Will, asked for the job and he gave the names of a restaurant and some food distributor in Providence as references. That must have worked out OK because he got the job. No mention was made of whether this man Will had just the one arm so I cannot comment on that.

Now see here Brownie, I never made the association, but that man looking for Roger – he might be the man you are looking for. Yes he must be. He must be your father."

It had all come out with Davidson's usual rush of words. At first I had been impatient but as the gist of Davidson's tale became apparent I became more and more excited. I did not go into details about why Willard might have thought it too late for something or another but I just knew that this Will was my father. I simply told Davidson that I had to get to Henryville as soon as possible. Davidson sensed the urgency.

"Well, I can tell that I have hit a nerve or something. One of my men will take you back to the station if you like and with luck you can get the afternoon train and trap to Henryville and be there before sundown."

46.

Summer 1887,
Henryville, Rhode Island

———∞———

I remember pausing and looking across Main Street at Henry's Hotel, as the old tap house had come to be called sometime a few years earlier. Henry's was hardly a hotel in the real sense of the word but more a lodging place that sold food and liquor. It was one of those typical New England wooden structures, built a hundred years earlier. Over the years it had become a maze of rooms and corridors built with over-size timbers and planks that had long since dried out. The exterior was covered with equally dry clapboards. Inside the tavern, open fires and oil lamps were distributed throughout the rooms.

In that respect, it was little different to most of the village dwellings. One difference, however, was that people generally took care of their homes and watched out for their safety.

At Henry's on the other hand, the occupants were more often than not simply on their way to somewhere else and not infrequently were befuddled with strong ale or more. It was only a few years earlier that the tavern, the church and most of the village had been fortunate to escape destruction when a porch fire at a neighboring store had rapidly spread, destroying several buildings before being brought under control. All of the small New England villages were very vulnerable like that.

To the west of Providence and a few miles off the Putnam Pike, Henryville village was a secondary stage stop, and Henry's stood a block east of the village center. Just up from Henry's was a branch of a river, and the divided waters provided power for a number of mills, both in the village and up and down stream. In a sense the river was the life flow of the village, its artery if you like, and Henry's was known locally to be the spot to check its pulse.

After a while I walked across Main and looked into the tavern. The sun had just set, and inside the tavern it was dark, in-spite of the oil lamps. I had often heard from the Reverend about the frugal Yankees, but this was ridiculous! Glancing around, I could see quite a few patrons sitting at tables enjoying food and beverage. A server was carrying a tray and making his way through the array of tables. Six or seven men were leaning on the bar. And as my eyes began to adjust to the dark, I saw him. The man stood at the corner of the bar, rinsing glasses. There was no need to pull out the old photograph that Grandmother Betsy had given me. This was Willard.

The square jaw, high bushy eyebrows and the red hair, all confirmed that against all odds, I had found my man. And then of course the man was adeptly rinsing glasses with just one hand. Davidson's report had been correct. Here was Willard, in Henryville, and running the tavern.

For some reason an image of a dog chasing a rabbit came into my mind. The image of a dog running faster and faster

- sometimes in a straight line and when necessary in circles, but not stopping until the rabbit was caught. I had never seen a dog back off or sit and watch the rabbit. Smiling to myself, I backed off and took a seat in a corner of the taproom. The man remained in sight, and I ordered a beer.

This dog could wait for his rabbit. I had rehearsed the introduction and subsequent run of words and probable actions many times. I had worked out what was to be said and done. All the way out on the train from Providence and then even in the trap to Henryville, I had played this scene out. And yet now, somewhat to my amusement, I was in no hurry to complete the mission. It could wait a few minutes for goodness sake, and I could enjoy the completion of my search.

These pleasant reflections were broken in an instant as a door to the stables, just to the side of the bar crashed open and a man came running through it shouting that there was a fire – a big fire, in the stables. Smoke came pouring through the open door behind him and it became obvious that the fire had been active for a while. Pandemonium broke out in the tavern. There was just one door from the bar area out into the road and half a dozen men reached it at the same time. With fear being the main obstacle in their flight, each one refused to give way. One man slipped and fell to the floor right in the doorway, adding to the confusion. More men reached the door and fought to climb over the others. Meanwhile, flames were issuing from the stable and the cellar door as well as smoke, and because of the smoke, it was no longer possible to see across the bar area. Ignoring the chaos at the door I ran to the bar. Willard was no longer there.

Was he at the main door perhaps? That seemed the obvious place as he would certainly have been one of the first to see the stable door open and to hear the shout. Then he would have been the first on his way to the front door. Turning to the door, I could no longer make out any details through the smoke, other than to note that it looked as though men were now getting through and outside of the tavern. I began coughing badly from the smoke and I quickly got down to floor level where the air was a little clearer. Glancing back at the bar one last time, I saw a foot jutting out at the corner of the bar opening.

Crawling on my knees, I reached the man and saw that he was unconscious and that he was bleeding badly from the head. There was a tray and some broken dishes and glasses on the floor. Clearly the man had simply dropped a fresh tray of glasses and in his flight had slipped, catching his head on the brass corner of the bar. I could just see that it was a pretty nasty head wound.

Suddenly, a loud crash came from across the room and there was a fresh outburst of flames. The stable door and a portion of the floor around it had given way as flames began to come from both the stables and the cellar. The additional opening in the floor aided the airflow, feeding the inferno below and turning the open cellar door into a raging blaze. Drapes at the side of the bar immediately ignited and set off further blazes in the windows. The smoke became heavier.

There was no question of lifting the man and carrying him out. The smoke was too heavy for that. The only likely option was to try to drag him to the main door. That might just be possible I thought as I grasped him by the ankles. I began the difficult task only to immediately find progress blocked as the man's shoulders caught and wedged at the bar corner. Crawling to the corner I tried to twist the man around the edge, but the smoke had become overpowering even at floor level. Now I was coughing continually and my eyes were streaming. I could hear the destruction all around me as the walls began to blaze. I no longer had any idea of where the door out of the tavern was, but the reality of the situation was disturbingly clear to me.

My head was pounding as I collapsed to the floor and lay there next to Willard. My thoughts began to form around the apprehension that after all of these years, I had failed. I had failed so miserably and so stupidly. I suppose that I passed out before the thought was complete.

"Come on boy. Come on now and don't give up on me now. You can make it."

I became aware of an overpowering stench of smoke and burnt materials that had been dowsed with water. It was a horrible smell. My head was thumping and my throat felt as though it was on fire. Slowly I grasped that I was sitting half upright on some wet grass. A number of men were standing over me and just for the moment I felt totally confused as to where I was. And then the recollection of Willard, unconscious and collapsed in the fire, returned to me.

I had come so close, and now because of my vain moment of satisfaction I had lost the opportunity of ever knowing my father.

"Come on now. That's better. I knew you would come around but it was a mighty close thing. Drink some water now and sit right up."

I saw that we were on the other side of Main and I could just make out the crowd of men in the distance, furiously working a hand pump drawing water from the river and still trying to control the fire.

"Yes, my word that was close for you. When they finally got the pump down here and hooked up into the stream, somebody yelled out to aim the water at the bar. He said that just as he reached the door he had looked back an' he reckoned that he had seen someone get down behind the counter, and that the men should try to reach it before it was too late. And so in they went, spraying water ahead of them and then dowsing down the counter. They found you there alongside poor Will.

We figure you saved Will's life because a part of the roof come down right there just after they dragged you two out."

Saved Will's life!

The words sunk in and established themselves into my senses. No words had ever sounded sweeter than those just uttered – 'saved Will's life'

There was terrific crash as across the road another portion of the tavern's roof collapsed, but I was re-running those words over and over again through my head.

I tried to focus on the man who had been speaking. The feeling of hope overcame the pounding and the pain I was feeling.

"You mean that Willard is still alive?"

"Well, if you mean Will, then yes. You both barely made it. He is inside the house here having his head cleaned up and bound. He had a really bad gash. He's probably still unconscious. We was just about to move you in when you started to come around. Come on now and let me help you up and let's get you inside."

Inside the house, a man I judged to be a doctor was tending to someone with what looked like a broken wrist. I could see others sitting up and wrapped in blankets. Lying on a sofa was Willard and as the rescuer had guessed, he was still unconscious. I managed to walk and crossed the room to the doctor.

"Excuse me sir, but the red headed man there, is he going to be alright?"

"I think so. He had a bad knock but I don't reckon there is concussion or the like. He came around a bit and coughed like crazy and yes, I would say that he will be alright as you put it.

Now I understand that you are the stranger who tried to help him and who George saw go down at the bar and so was able to tell the others where to look first. Are you OK? You sure look a whole lot better than half an hour ago young man."

I acknowledged that I was indeed feeling a lot better, and thought to myself how I felt a whole lot better now I knew that Willard was alive.

Some of the casualties began to leave for their homes. Before the man George left he called out that he would be back shortly with some clothes. Everyone was relieved that no one had been killed and that the injuries were limited to a broken wrist and a lot of bruises, burns, gashes and the results of smoke inhalation. The most serious burns were to the man who had called out the first alarm. He had run back into the stables and released four horses that were being stabled for the night.

Pretty soon Willard and I were the only two casualties left in the house. We must have made a sorry sight, sitting there wrapped in towels since our clothes had been soaked with river water from the pump. Willard had come around and was able to sit up and listen to me explain to him what had happened in the tavern. Willard told me that he was pleased to note that he could remember most of it himself. He had a mighty bad headache and he reckoned that a loss of memory might have been a possibility.

The house owner filled in some of the details of what had happened after the two of us had lost consciousness, and Willard expressed his gratitude towards me.

"Well, thank you young man for coming after me like that. You most certainly would have been excused for running to the door with the rest of them and leaving me behind since we are strangers. I'd be interested to know who you are and what brought you to our little town. But for now I just want to say thank you again, because I have some other problems occupying my mind.

My biggest problem is that I have no idea what to do next! I don't think they will rebuild the tavern so I don't have a job. I don't even have a place to live anymore because I lived in rooms over the main level of the tavern. Everything's lost now. Where are you staying anyway?"

I had to explain that I was staying in Providence but I did not go into why I had come to Henryville. In fact I realized that I had given no thought as to where I would have spent this night. I suppose that I just had some vague notion that I would have stayed with Willard after explanations. And I was not ready for those just now. I don't think that either of us would have been up to them.

Before I had to explain my plans, or more accurately my lack of plans, I was interrupted by George coming in off the street with a bundle of clothes.

"Listen Will, you two can't leave this house in towels and all of your clothes are still wet. We put together some fresh clothes for both of you so get out of those damp towels and into these now. These old rags may not be up to much, but at least you won't get a chill or worse. And you can stay the night with me and Florence. She is making up a couple of beds for you right now."

We were glad to discard the towels and to put on the clothes that had been provided. They certainly were ill fitting and they were torn in a couple of places, but they felt perfect.

Stepping out of the house we paused to look across at the remains of the tavern. It was cloudless night and what was left of Henry's looked decidedly spooky. The fire had been brought under control but we could still see some small fires burning and steady streams of smoke and steam rising up into the night. To the left of the tavern, Willard said that he could just about make out enough detail to see that the neighboring house was pretty damaged. He shrugged and remarked that the place and the people here in town had been good to him.

It was three in the morning before we settled into the temporary beds in Florence's front room. We were both exhausted and were asleep in no time. I believe that my last waking thought was concerned with how to introduce myself with this turn of events. The thought carried me over into sleep and my dreams were most likely a strange mixture with Willard and Elijah and even Grandma Annie all chiding me for allowing the fire to take place.

When I did eventually stir, Willard was apparently already up and about. I was alone in the front room. A mug of coffee was next to my bed, but it was quite cold. Picking it up, I walked to the kitchen.

"Well young man, you finally came back to us! Here, let me refill that mug. I brought it in a good hour ago. Then you can tell me what you are doing here"

George was obviously pleased that both of his unexpected night guests were functional.

I did enjoy that mug of hot coffee while George threw some pancakes onto the griddle. I wondered out loud where Willard was.

"I cannot thank you enough for your hospitality George - and your wife of course. It is so kind of you both. Do you remember Reverend Roger Hart? Good, I thought you might. Well let's just say that I am an old friend of his and had to stop while in the neighborhood. Where is my comrade from the fire? He and I are extremely fortunate to be alive this morning. Lying on the floor of the tavern and surrounded by fire and smoke I confess that I believed that we were both about to expire."

With those brief words of introduction I attacked the pancakes realizing that it had been a long time since my last meal. George picked up the conversation.

"Will took off to look at the tavern but I am afraid that he is going to find nothing of value there. I have lived in this town all of my life and I have seen my share of fires I can tell you. That one was going well and there will be nothing left. Mark my words now.

Don't get me wrong young man, but you sound mighty well educated for a colored man, especially one with a bit of a southern accent. My children don't speak as well as you do! You mentioned Roger Hart and I must say that I believe that he would have loved to have met you this morning.

You see, he had this thing about educating colored kids down south. He even raised money and left us for a time to open a school down in Virginia. We all contributed to that fund. He was a lovely man and we still miss him. Did you know him well?"

I realized that I had inadvertently opened the door to the whole story and I certainly did not want it to get to Willard in a piecemeal fashion. And so I diverted the account enough to avoid that happening.

"Yes sir, you could say that I am a result of his work and your charity. I just graduated from college and when I return home I have a very good teaching job waiting for me. Now, the coffee and pancakes were very good, but if you will excuse me, I think that I will stroll down and take a look at the source of last night's excitement. I will see you later then."

And I quickly left the house before more questions needed answers.

The remains of the tavern were still smoking. The large stone chimney that had formed the center of the structure looked gaunt, itself standing erect while the timber walls had collapsed all around it. It was obvious that there was still a danger of a fairly large portion of a back wall falling in. A group of men were keeping guard and were keeping some curious children back. I thought as to how these children would tell about the big fire years from now.

Feeling very self-conscious that I was still wearing the make-do clothes, I walked past the group and then saw Willard sitting on the stone wall of the bridge that led across the river. I walked over to him.

"So you come to. You were still sleeping when I left George's place. I just thought that something might have survived but there is nothing. Just look at it. My two rooms were right there, half way up and next to the chimney. Now it's just empty space. Tell me about yourself."

I decided then and there that the best thing now was to just plunge in.

"Will, I know you as Willard. Just last week I was with your mother, Betsy and your brother, Frank. Yes, I can imagine that you are surprised but I was in Harpers Ferry and graduating from the teaching college there. Willard there is no short way to explain this. I am Brownie, my mother was Beth and you are my father."

It was out.

After all this time it was there and it was out in the open. Father and son were together and all that remained was some kind of connection. I suppose that it was the uncertainty of that that had caused me to have some doubts and even some apprehension the previous night. I just had no idea how my father would react.

I had not expected silence.

Willard did not say a word for the longest time and I chose not to intrude.

Eventually Willard stood and walked away from the bridge and clamored down over the boulders that formed the base of the bridge there, and he sat down on one of them and gazed into the fast flowing water.

I was not about to let the moment pass and so I followed him down to the river and stood next to Willard. Willard spoke first.

"This takes me all the way back to Harpers Ferry in 1859, sitting by the bridge there with my daddy. I had been fishing and had just overheard him talking with John Brown about the attack. I had no idea that my life was about to change forever. Things went from bad to worse after that.

I suppose that you have heard all about me from your uncle Elijah. If you want to let into me, then just go on and be about it. Get it over with. He tried once. No, he tried more than once. The only thing that puzzles me though is if you hate me as you have a right to, then I wonder why you risked your life for me last night. Surely it was not just to have the pleasure of getting even with me now?

I know how Elijah feels and I suppose that he will have told you how I forced myself on your mother Beth and then took off and never came back."

I knelt down beside him and he winced, clearly expecting a blow.

"Why do you keep up this act? I don't hate you. I know that my mother loved you and that you loved her. So why wouldn't I love you? The thing that bothers me is why you keep this act up.

Willard, you need to know that Elijah finally told me the truth. It took him a long time to get around to it. It took him far too long because but he was all bottled up with guilt and bad feelings about himself. It took a lot for him to let it go.

He finally told me about his last conversation with my mother and how she told him the truth. She told him that she had loved you for the longest time and that that afternoon she knew that you felt the same way about her. The only thing standing between the two of you was the color of your skin, and she told Elijah that that afternoon you both stopped caring about that. Why did you let the rape story go on without speaking up?"

"I did it because your mother was right. I did love her. I still do. And since you know the whole story, you know that it was years before I even knew what had happened. I ran off because I was scared for both of us. If we had told everyone about how we felt about each other there would have been hell to pay. And I never dreamed that she would be with child after just that one time.

When I did hear about you, all I could think was how people were saying how young and innocent your mother was and that she would never have done such a thing. And how they were all saying how bad that Willard was. So I let the story go on just to kind of protect her. I let people think the worst of me since I did not feel a part of their world anymore. What did I care anyway?

347

But at first I did care. That was after Hart first told me and we went together to New Jersey to see everyone. I went to see you Brownie. But then your damned uncle talked me into not speaking up. He told me the same old story again about all I would do was to cause hurt to everybody, especially that I would hurt you.

He told me how Beth was gone and you were in good hands and all that stuff. So I ran off again. I came back to Providence for a few years until I thought again about coming to see you. So and I came out here to see Reverend Hart and tell him what I planned. They told me at the church that he was dead. I never told him properly, but he did a lot for me and he was always trying to help me. I liked him a lot. When I learned that he was dead, I just felt like another door was slammed in my face, and like it was the story of my life.

And so I decided not to come to New Jersey. By chance I found the job in the tavern and got on real well with the people here and had a good life. Maybe because of the Reverend, I felt a connection. Often I thought about how small this world is. Here I was in the very area where Reverend Hart first decided to travel south. I guess that no one here ever made the connection or bothered to tell Mrs. Hart in their letters. Why would they?

I told myself that I should wait until you were a man and we could face this together. I guess that this is that time!

You are a fine young man Brownie, I can tell that. I am right proud of you. I know that you won't want people to know about the past so I understand if you just move on. It was good for us to have finally met and for you to tell me the truth about how your mother had asked Elijah to tell folk how we felt for each other. That damned uncle of yours!"

I stood up, pulling my father up with me.

"Listen Willard, no listen father, the very last thing that I want is to lose you again. We both know that some people are going to have bad feelings about us being black and white. You want to know what? I say that that is their problem and not ours. Some people will never accept that you and mother were in love. They will always think that either you took advantage of her or that she cheapened herself with you. Some people will always look for the bad. They will always rule out love because in their narrow minds they just can't accept that happening between two people like you and mother. That's something they have to live with.

But here is the truth - if you can take that stuff, then so can I.

I just graduated from teaching college in Harpers and they have hired me to teach there. It's a good job with good pay and good prospects. It's more than my Grandmother and her family could ever have imagined. But it is just the start.

I look to the day when I can teach kids anywhere, just kids with no color adjective. I look to the day when two people in love can be free to share that love no matter their background.

I know that you hate John Brown, but did you know that when he was on his way to the gallows he wrote something about this country? He wrote that he was certain that the crimes of this guilty land would never be purged away except with blood.

I say that enough blood has been spilt and enough people have been hurt. Just in our family there is your father; my grandfather Frank, my grandfather John and his family, and my mother Beth. There is all of the hurt Reverend Hart went through and then all of the men that you and Elijah served with. And then just look what you yourself have gone through. It's enough. No, it's more than enough.

Your mother Betsy is beginning to ail somewhat and she is anxious to have you home again while she can still enjoy having you around. And I hate to have to tell you this, but your brother Sean is dead. He was lost aboard a ship off of the outer banks when a big storm suddenly came up. I know for a fact that Frank is struggling with running the farm on his own now even with some hired help. Half the farm is rightly yours although I can see you might find that hard to accept after all this time.

But why don't we go back now and start over, with me at the school and you at the farm with the beginnings of a new life as a family?"

The two of us climbed up the bank and back on to the bridge. Willard was very quiet. We looked across the town and he pointed out the meeting house up on the hill. We could not see it from the river but Willard told me that there was small plaque on the wall there honoring the memory of Roger Hart. After learning that he had been buried in Westhill, the church members decided to honor his memory here with that little plaque.

"He truly was a good man Brownie and that's no mistake. But I fancy that he was not much at being realistic. Just look how he didn't allow for how folk would react to his ideas of teaching slave children back then for example.

To be honest, you sound like him now. It's an idealistic hair brained idea that you have. I can't just turn up and start over like nothing happened. It's been too long and I have been too selfish. And say what you will, it would for sure not be fair on Frank. And how do you think that people are going think of us walking about town as father and son and looking like two... I don't know how to finish that but you know what I mean.

People would look at me and then at you and they would see your mother and what I did. There would always be the reminder of what Beth and me did together. That we were also unrealistic, and that for a just a part of an afternoon we lived in a dream and took no heed of common sense. Everyone would think badly of me all over again and because of that – they would think badly about you too.

Don't you see Brownie that I could never go through that? Tell me honestly now if you could ever be proud to point me out and call me your father."

I had no answer. I knew what I wanted to say but held back. Just then the meeting house bell began to ring in an un-orderly way with somebody probably either practicing or working at it. I think that the sound kind of knocked me out of my hesitation.

"So you think you have been too selfish in the past? How about now then? Don't you think that you are being just more than a little selfish right now? What you just said has been mostly about you and what people might think of you. Well, how about your mother and brother and how much they need you? How about me? And then there is my mother and her memory – can you just give up on that for the rest of your life?

I already said that if people have a problem with the way we look then that is something they have to work out. Of course it won't be easy but let's at least give it a try. My grandparents, your mother and father, refused to give in to prejudice. They married in spite of all the objections and barriers. Your father stood up in his own way for what he believed in when it came to slavery. And Roger Hart, a man who quite honestly was my father for ten years, put his life at risk for what he believed in.

It's time for you face reality and stop running. The past is just that. You and I have to do our part now in standing up in the coming years. You asked me if I could ever be proud to point you out and call you father..."

We had not heard George come up behind us, and we both turned as he asked how we were. I spoke first.

"Hello George, we are well thank you and as you can see, we found each other down here by the river. Again we both owe you a debt of gratitude for taking us in last night. My father here and I both thank you from the bottom of our hearts."

My father looked at me and smiled.

"Well George that was a real mess last night for sure. But it brought me and my son Brownie here together and so I say that it was a very good night."

47.

December 29th 1941,
Dartford, West Virginia

⸺✲⸺

I recall now how the two us grinned and then just hugged each other right there, and how we laughed at poor George's face. His expression was just beyond description.

That facial expression was one that we would experience many more times in the future and I regret to write now that the response was not always a grin or even a smile. I eventually came to see that it was me who had been selfish and unrealistic on that morning after the fire.

I came to realize that when we want something very badly it is very easy to transfer the want to another person and to be persuaded that what we want is the best for the other as well. I wanted so badly to be a part of a family that I honestly thought it would be the best for Willard. I wanted so much for at least a near completeness of my life. I wanted Willard's mother and brother to find satisfaction in having at least one of their lost family members back home for good. I wanted to fill a hole that I felt was in my life. And I wanted the satisfaction of seeing things put right between Willard and Grandma - because then I would feel better.

As a consequence I suppose that I put the pressure on to Willard to make all of those things happen. All I can say now is that I meant well.

What I did the other night before deciding to write these pages was a result of too many years of being called names and of being put down. Grandma would have reminded me that things used to be worse but still I was angry. Just about none of the hopes that I had held for Willard and myself really worked out.

So I can write now that I know that it was me who was selfish and unrealistic.

48.

Summer 1887,
Westhill, New Jersey

———— ✦ ————

We spent a couple of days staying with George and his wife while Willard settled his affairs in the village and at the bank and such. Most of the village people knew Willard from the hotel and they had a lot of trouble accepting that I was his son. For his part I could see that Willard had difficulty explaining about himself and my mother. It got so hard that he stopped trying to explain and when the issue was raised he began to just laugh it off with a 'you know how things happen' remark. I told him that I was not happy about that but since we were leaving soon, I didn't push the matter. I did not see how those moments were an indication of what was to come.

Eventually we took the train into Providence to pick up my stuff before heading south. The big question between us was where to stop first. Willard was all for going straight to Harpers but I wanted to visit Grandma on the way. I failed to see how hard that would be for Willard and we went head to head on the issue.

He finally came around to my view after saying that he would like to visit mother's grave. And so we stopped off the train and took a ride out to Westhill.

The afternoon was well along when we arrived in town. It was one of those hot summer days when the moisture in the air is so thick that you get wet just walking a hundred yards or so, and the coolness that might come in the evening was eagerly anticipated. We went straight to a rooming house and took a room for a couple of nights. There had not been time to send a letter to Grandma and so I realized that it would be helpful for me to visit the house and give everyone there some warning about Willard. I did not want to surprise the household by just turning up with my father. We agreed to go to Momma's grave that first evening and for me to go to see Grandma early the next morning.

After eating a light meal, we headed out of town along one of the main roads. I knew the way very well and as we walked I described some of my memories of my boyhood and the many times I had taken this little trip. And we were thankful for the dryer and cooler evening air.

The old grave yard looked just like it did when I was a boy and the old elm trees were in full foliage that day. There was one tree very close to the section where Momma is buried and we stopped under it to look around. I did not know whether to go to the grave with Willard or to let him go there alone for a few minutes to kind of say hello in some way or another. He answered that question.

"Come on now Brownie, I see these graves but which one is Beth's. Lead the way now."

So I took a turn down beside some of the older graves and stopped at Momma's. On one of my visits to Grandma and Miss Jenny during the school years, I had replaced the little wooden cross with a metal one that Mr. Clark had gotten for me. I remember how I had taken some time to mark Momma's name on it. That evening I could see that it was rusting pretty badly and that it was tipped over to one side and looking like it was ready to fall over completely. I got down on my knees and straightened it up and pushed it firmly back into the earth. I thought how my life was a little unsure at that moment but was under no illusion of being able to fix it so easily. Willard just stood there with his head bowed and his eyes closed. I stood up and decided to walk away a little to give him some time alone with Momma.

"No Brownie, I don't want you step away like that. I want us to be together right now and here, kind of like the three of us being together for the first time. I should have done this a long time ago. I know that now"

We stood there for a good half an hour and we spoke with Momma as if she could hear us, just like I used to do when I was a boy. We didn't feel bad about that, or kind of stupid or anything. It just came natural as Willard told her how he felt about things and how much he had loved her. And I told her how I found Willard. It was good for us and we walked back to the rooming house with good feelings.

Sitting by the window before heading for bed, Willard suddenly pointed at the other chair and told me to sit down.

"Brownie, there is something I need to tell you about that day when your Momma and I met at the pond. I want you to know that what happened was not just a moment's wild stupidity on my part. Elijah could not have told you all of it because I don't believe that he knew everything from Beth.

That day when I came into the clearing, she looked so beautiful standing and staring into the sky. Everything was peaceful and still and I felt something I had never felt before.

And then she saw me and came running up and just hugged me.

After a while we sat down and talked about what had been happening in our lives. It was small talk and I reckon that we both knew it. Your Momma was always the strongest of us and it was she who finally came out with it, and told me how she had loved me since as far back as we first met. Then I told her how I felt and how I had wanted to tell her before I went to the war.

She had some reservation because of our differences and she tried to tell me that we should wait and try to work something out. But then we talked about how that would never happen. We lay there in the grass and in the end we both gave in to our feelings. We made love, and I want you to know that that is the word, love.

And here's the thing Brownie, later on we sat and talked about the future. Beth was of the mind then to just tell folk how we felt about each other and she began to push me hard to just take a chance and for a while I agreed. It all sounded so good. But then I began to think about things. I told her how her mother and her colored friends would never just accept me and how we both knew how the town folk would react. We became very quiet and eventually we just got up and made our ways home. We never spoke again.

That was when I decided to take off and leave Harpers. And I now know that was wrong, even though neither of us knew then that she was pregnant. Your Momma and I really did love each other just as much as if we were both white or both black. I keep telling myself that somehow we could have worked things out. But I ran and let her down. And I let you down.

I just want you know that Brownie. To know that we were in love and that I would have done anything for her. But I did not, and I am so sorry."

So now I had heard the story directly from Willard along with how they felt afterwards.

The next morning Willard decided to take a stroll around the town while I visited the house. It was close to nine-thirty when I began the short walk up the hill towards the house. At the house I went around the back lane as I always had and I stepped up to the kitchen door, but I did not just burst in with a shout of 'hi Grandma - I am home' like I used to. My purpose after all was to give some warning and not to startle her.

So I just tapped on the door and pushed it open. There was no one in the kitchen. I stepped in and closed the door behind me. As I began to walk into the old familiar kitchen, the door to the dining room opened and Grandma walked into the kitchen with a breakfast tray in her hands. The tray was overloaded from clearing up the house breakfast dishes and food. I had a nasty feeling that any shock would cause Grandma to drop the tray and that would have made a terrible din. I had no time to prepare her.

"O my Lord Brownie, now where did you spring from, you do give an honest woman some awful frights at times."

At least Grandma did not drop the tray but managed to put it down on the sideboard before turning and giving me one of her hugs that near stifled me.

"It is so good to see you and just so soon after we was all in Harpers for your graduation. Now I recall tellin' you to go up north and try to find your father. Are you on your way now? Well God bless you my love for stoppin' off on the way."

Without knowing, Grandma had made it easier for me to tell her why I was there that morning. At least she remembered telling me to go and find Willard.

"Yes and no Grandma. I am not exactly on my way north. I already made that journey and now I have stopped off on my way back to Harpers."

Grandma's face fell and I saw the disappointment as she assumed that I had failed to find Willard.

"Don't worry yourself Brownie, it's been so long since anyone heard from him that it might take you quite some time to find him and then to..."

But I had walked to Grandma and put my finger gently against her lips.

"Now, now Grandma, you got this all wrong. I have been to Rhode Island and I found Willard. He is just down the road now and waiting for me to fetch him here. But I figured that it would be well to just tell you and Mrs. Hart and Miss Jenny first, so as not to give all of you too much of a shock.

Now tell me Grandma, after all you have said about him, are you sure that you are really ready to see Willard?"

Grandma had sat down in her own special kitchen chair, looking straight ahead. I suddenly had a remembrance of being a very young boy and sitting on her lap in that very chair listening to her tell some stories. It was a good moment for me.

"Yes Brownie, I reckon that I am ready. He caused us all so much hurt that I truly thought that I could never forgive him and I am not sure that I can now. But after hearin' that he and Beth were in love - yes I know all about that now - I have had to put some of the old stuff out of my mind. I still struggle with it all when I think of them but I can't go on with the hatred. There is already too much of that goin' around.

Sometimes I can see your Momma again upstairs here and havin' you. I can see her dyin' again right in front of me. I blamed Willard so many times but now I know that it was really not altogether his fault. Your Uncle Elijah wrote to me after the graduation and told me the truth and how he had also told you all about it too. I can tell you Brownie that I will have some words ready for Elijah the next time I see him and that's no idle threat!"

Grandma had got up from the chair as she spoke.

"Now you just go and fetch Willard so that we can at least start to get all of this behind us. When I heard from Elijah, I naturally told Mrs. Hart and Jenny what I had learned so I think that they will be alright. I tell you what, I will go and prepare them now and you go fetch the man. And thank you Brownie for considerin' us and of thinkin' to kind of soften us up before we would be seein' him. You were always a good considerate boy like that."

And so I went back to the rooming house and met Willard just as he was going to go inside.

"I am not sure that this is a good idea Brownie. I never met Miss Jenny but I can tell you that Mrs. Hart was not into welcoming me when I went out that July 4th and I reckon that she might not even want to see me now. As for your Grandma, well I get the feeling that she just might want to tan my backside."

Somehow I once again persuaded Willard that everything would be OK and so we set out towards the house.

When we reached the house I was about to go around the back as I always had done but Miss Jenny opened the front door and beckoned us to come in that way.

"Come on in now both of you. I saw you walking up the hill just a minute ago. As far as we are concerned Brownie, you can always visit us and come in by either door. And you must be the Willard Beauchamp that we have all heard so much about.

Come on into the parlor and sit yourselves down while I fetch your Grandma Brownie, and Mrs. Hart."

As Jenny left the room I looked around. This was where I had first heard all of the old stories about my mother and father, before everything was put together for me. The old clock was still ticking away but the little bed was gone now. And yet somehow I could still feel the presence of the Reverend. I realized the silence was unsettling for Willard and so I began to describe how things were when the Reverend told me the stories. We were quickly interrupted by Grandma and Miss Jenny coming into the room.

"Well now Willard, here you are finally come to face us."

Grandma had spoken first with quite a stern tone of voice and she did not look very happy to see my father.

"No, don't say a word now. I have thought and thought on this moment and on how I should behave. There was times I could have rung your neck like one of old man Clark's chickens. I have blamed you so many times for dear Beth's death. And look how you have treated your own mother. And Lordy now you come in to see us like nothin' even happened.

No, don't interrupt me Brownie, because I am not sure what to say as it is, so just let me go on a bit. Like I was sayin' just now, for years I had no feelin's except that I despised you Willard. But then when I heard from Elijah somethin' made me mind the times that I told Brownie here that Beth's death was no bodies fault. And then I remembered that you was the last person she cried out for Willard. You two was crazy and between you both you have caused so much grief - and you most of all for runnin' off like that and never tellin' the truth. Elijah says, and just you wait until I get my mind on him; he says that you loved each other. Loved. What did you two know about love and just what could that have meant to two people like you. How could a love like that ever be real? You must have minded how it could never have worked out.

Obviously Beth had some feelin's for you and so I know that I can't go on hatin' and blamin' like. But Willard, I have to tell you that I am not yet up to forgivin' you, but I want the best for Brownie and that may be just that he gets to know you now. In fact it was me who encouraged him to go find you. You is quite the smartest young man Brownie for trackin' him down like this!

No I am not up to forgivin' you Willard but I can say that it is good to see you together now. Maybe I will soften up some more as the time goes by and for now I will just say God bless you both. You two go on down to Harpers now and sort things out there."

Willard could only mumble a few words of thanks and was obviously most uncomfortable. He tried an apology but that never came out right either. I just tried to assure Grandma that things would all work out now. We all went very quiet with me wanting Grandma to give Willard a hug but knowing that was not going to happen just then.

Miss Jenny broke into the unhappy quietness.

"Don't fret Annie. I do believe that Brownie is correct and that it is just going to take time. Brownie, I am afraid that I have to tell you that Mrs. Hart is not coming down. She sends you her love but asked me tell you that she also needs more time. At least we are all being honest about how things stand.

I am glad that you both came here this morning. I do believe that this is the start of some healing and I know that my father would be so happy that the two of you have finally met up. Now I agree with Annie here, and I think that you should be on your way to Harpers Ferry and begin by fixing matters up down there.

Brownie, Willard, for my part I just want to say that you will both be welcome here at any time. Now I suggest that you take your leave."

Miss Jenny could be very direct just like her father but I really felt good that Willard had heard those words.

Grandma had a big hug stored up for me and that felt good as well. I do believe that she loved me more than anyone else in the world. She managed a pat on the shoulder for Willard and his look told me that that was more than he had hoped for. And then we were on our way again.

We didn't talk much on the way to the rooming house to pick up our stuff or on the way to the train station. Mostly we just had small talk about how the visit had not gone too badly, and how Grandma had been much more open to accepting Willard than we had both feared. I tried to explain to Willard why Mrs. Hart probably had not joined us but he seemed to understand that anyway. He told me all over again how she had been on the July 4th visit.

It was only when we were on the train headed south again that Willard opened up about something that was worrying him.

"Brownie I guess that you know all about the Klan. As a colored boy growing up you must have had a fear of them from time to time."

I acknowledged that of course we had all heard about them and their ways and I told him that our class at school had spent quite some time learning about the movement. I was about to go into some detail but then decided to let Willard talk because one of the things that bothered me about my father was his long periods of silence and how he could withdraw into himself. That was exactly how Reverend Hart had described Willard. So I simply said that in Harpers we had never had any real trouble and then let him go on.

"When the war ended there were so many Confederate soldiers who felt that they had been somehow cheated, and they could not accept that the changes that the federals wanted would be enacted. At first of course they were spread out and without any real organization but they were still real troublemakers for blacks and any white man who looked overly sympathetic.

Things changed in 1866 or there about, when some veterans of the southern army over in Tennessee formed an association that became the Klan. Branches of the organization quickly formed all over the south, or so it seemed. When I visited Harpers that time, Frank told me how somebody once tried to get him to join but he told them that he had already had more than a bellyful of that stuff. Besides, like you said Brownie, there never was much action around Harpers.

Anyway, they just did whatever they could to avoid the equality of the races becoming a reality. That was the way they spoke when they tried to enroll Frank. Hiding behind their robes and ugly masks they used threats, kidnapping and murder as their tools, and like I said they targeted anyone who disagreed with them, whether they were black or white. There were too many lynchings and murders and disappearances but it went on and on. Eventually the government took action and acts were passed to stop them in their ways.

By the time you were ten years old Brownie they had pretty well faded out. But make no mistake, their actions and those of other groups like them, played a part in making the world that you live in now in the south, what it is. There is not the freedom and the equality that so many people expected and fought for. You know that better than I do. And that is especially true when it comes to schools.

And here's my worry – there are still many down there who feel as strong as ever about the cause. They still come out at night and threaten and kill. There may not be as many as years ago and they don't wear robes and such, but they will be a real threat to you and me and our families Brownie. The fact is that you and I are just unacceptable to many of those people, and some of them may get dangerous."

Of course I was very much aware of what Willard was speaking about and I knew we were facing some danger. But I made some remarks again about how Harpers would not be such a problem to us.

"Oh, is that so Brownie! Well listen up now because once word gets out that you and me are set up together as white father and black son – a black son who is a fancy teacher even, I tell you that the word is going to spread and attract trouble from way beyond Harpers."

In the end we both had to agree that we faced some danger but we managed to keep changing the subject of conversation as the trip played out.

Once again I can see now how I was being unrealistic and that I was ignoring the situation. I should have known how violent some people would be when they learned about Willard and me.

Eventually we reached Harpers. We had already agreed to go straight to the farm. I knew that Mrs. Beauchamp had not been well recently and that Frank was worried about his mother. So I had sent word on ahead to let her know that I had found Willard up in Rhode Island and that she could expect us soon. That way I figured to avoid us being too much of a shock for her.

49.

Summer 1887,
Harpers Ferry, West Virginia

———— ✺ ————

We left our bags at the station and began the walk through town and up the hill towards the farm. The bags could be picked up later with the farm wagon. They were quite safe.

As we walked through the town, many people recognized me and some remembered Willard. Of course his red hair and the one arm gave him away to many of the town's folk. I could see how curious some of them were to see us walking side by side and I think that we both began to feel uncomfortable at the thought of having to explain everything over and over again. But we were determined. At least I was.

As we reached the familiar flat rock at the farm entrance, we saw Frank down in the near meadow and he spotted us at the same time. He waved and immediately put down the fork and strode towards the house. Clearly he was planning to give his mother some notice of our arrival. We took our time until we saw her come to the door and I was surprised that Willard broke into a run to meet her.

I continued to walk and by the time I arrived at the door they were in a loving embrace and both were crying. I had come to see how emotional my father could be. I envied him. Even back then I was starting to see how hard it was becoming for me to show how I felt about things.

Seeing me approach, Grandma Betsy opened one of her arms and pulled me into a three way embrace.

"Oh my Brownie, I am so glad that you found my boy here. When we received your letter I could hardly believe what I read. Just knowing that you had finally found each other and that you were both coming home made me so glad. Come on in now both of you. Frank is inside waiting. If only dear Sean could be here but there it is now. I must be grateful for what I have. Willard, I feared that I would die without ever seeing you again."

The afternoon was taken up with Grandmother Betsy and Frank and Willard catching up on what had been going on in their lives. For the most part I just sat and listened. I felt so good at seeing my father and his family together. Eventually Willard began to ask about Sean but Frank cut him off and suggested that the two of them take the horse and cart down to the station to pick up our bags. Frank added that he would drop my stuff off at the school residence.

Grandmother and I went out and sat on the front porch with a jug of her grape juice and a couple of glasses. As we watched the brothers drive up the hillside she sighed and gave me what I believe is called a 'knowing look'

"Dear Frank, he tries so hard to protect me. I caught Willard's question about Sean and I know that they will be talking about that now. As you know Brownie that was a terrible time for me, but if I learned just one thing after your Grandfather's death it was that we have to pick up and carry on after bad things happen. I vowed never to fall into a slump again.

But now, you tell me just what you plan to do. I know in your letter you said as to how you would stay living at the school and keep coming here now and again like you have been. And that you hoped that Willard would settle in here and work the farm with Frank. This afternoon it certainly sounded like that is what he plans to do. Or at least I gather that he is going to give it a try. I can see that he still gets terribly conscious about his injury.

The trouble as I see it Brownie is how people around here are going to react. Many people remember Beth from twenty years ago and many of them believed the nonsense that your uncle Elijah put around. It could be terribly hard for the both of you. Now don't give any mind about me and Frank because we will stand behind you both. But you must know what people are going to think and say.

Of course this kind of thing has happened before but always the child was put out somewhere or nothing was said and things were just hushed up and covered over. But you two seem to be determined to stand together, and I just wonder if you have thought it through."

I remember now how I gave her the same kind of answer I gave Willard back in Rhode Island, that if anybody had a problem then they were going to have to live with it. I was still so caught up in the pleasure of being part of the family that I avoided the plain truth of the matter. Like I wrote earlier, I know now that I was being selfish.

Even though it was summer vacation and I would normally have stayed at the farmhouse those few weeks, after supper I walked back to my room at the school. I wanted the brothers and Grandmother Betsy to have some time together. Also I believe that her questions had finally begun to register with me and I began to see how difficult I might be making things for Willard and his family. But I told myself that it was too late to back down and I went straight to bed and slept well.

Over the next few weeks Willard kind of settled into the farm picking up from Frank where he could be of help. I visited most days even though I was trying to put together a new course of teaching for the fall. We did not spend much time in town together, and maybe that was deliberate. I could tell that some of the old timers who remembered Beth from before the war held bad feelings against Willard. I guess that the story that Elijah had put around was just too easy to believe. They were making things hard for Willard. Those same people knew me from the school years and they were mostly very kind, treating me as a victim and that was causing me much grief.

But it was some of the people who had come into town since the war, and who had never known Willard or Beth or Grandma who were the source of our real trouble. They just knew that a local farm boy had gotten a black girl into trouble and that the child of that mistake was now teaching at the new school. What was worse for them was the father and the boy were openly acknowledging each other and living together some of the time. Letters were sent to the school asking if the authorities there knew that one of their teachers was the illegitimate son of a white father and an ex-slave girl. I learned how words could be skewed and emphasized to make a point.

If asked, I am sure that those people would have denied any prejudice or feelings of narrow-mindedness, but that is how they were. At least that is how I saw them. I realized later of course that it was just how they had been raised and that those feelings were natural to them. At the time I could not see that Willard and I were almost flaunting our relationship.

Since then I have had to acknowledge my selfishness many times.

It was all beginning to wear on me and I began to spend more time at the school. I began to wonder if we had made the wrong decision after all. The joy and excitement of those early days began to fade.

But they really began to come to an end one Saturday afternoon when a boy from Clark's store came running up to the school shouting that I should go to the farmhouse as quickly as possible. He told me that Mrs. Beauchamp was really sick.

When I arrived at the farm Grandmother Betsy had already died. The priest was just leaving and I fancied that he ignored me and that did not sit right. Willard and Frank took me into the bedroom and we stood together and looked down at our mother and grandmother. Once again Willard was in tears. I could see that Frank had been earlier. I was just upset that I had not been able to say goodbye. Willard spoke up.

"Her last words were for you Brownie. She said to me 'tell Brownie that I thank him from the bottom of my heart for bringing Willard home again. Tell him that he is loved as the grandson he truly is.' And then she just passed away."

Willard pulled me towards himself as he spoke those words.

There was a grand funeral service at the Catholic Church and the priest had some really kind words to say about Grandmother. I think that it might have been the first time that many of the newer congregants heard about our family's involvement in the John Brown affair.

Grandmother was laid to rest next to her husband over in the family grave plot at the farm. It was just by the side of a nice marker for Sean. Of course he was not there.

The priest walked around and talked kindly with the people and he had some nice words for Frank and Willard. He eventually came over to me and placed his hand on my shoulder.

"Brownie, you probably have no idea as to how proud your Grandmother Betsy was of you. She would come up to me at church and tell me all the latest things that you were up to at the school. She was a rare person you know and she once told me how she did not give a leprechaun's cuss about the color of your skin. And yes, those were her words. Things must be very hard for you young man but I want you to know that she loved you very much. God bless you now."

I felt bad and realized over again how easy it is and how wrong it is to jump to conclusions about someone.

A few weeks after the funeral, I walked over to the farm to have a meal with Frank and Willard and the two hired hands Pete and Ben. We talked about Grandmother and about the farm. Frank acknowledged how glad he was to have Willard working alongside of him. For the first time I heard Frank talk at length about his father. After we had cleared things away, Willard and I walked out across the farm to a clearing on the far side quite close to one of the old back roads to Bolivar. It was a quiet spot and Willard told me how it used to be one of his favorites.

We sat down on the grass and Willard began to tell me how he was having a real problem with how some folk were behaving towards us.

"Brownie, I know how badly you want this to work but I am having thoughts of moving on again. As long as I am here the issue of you and me and your mother is going to keep coming up and I fear that it might jeopardize your position at the school. If I stay on much longer, Frank is going to start relying on me more than on Pete and Ben, and that will make leaving even harder. So I figure that now the..."

Neither of us had heard the two men approaching through the trees between us and the old road. The first we knew was them jumping out into the clearing and one of them landing a considerable punch to my face. The other man grabbed Willard and pushed him to the ground.

"Well, well now look at what we have here. A one armed boy who goes with colored women and his little black boy who thinks he is good enough to be a teacher. We heard about you boys way down in Virginia and took it upon ourselves to come on out here and teach you a few things about how white men should behave and how black boys should know their place. And you know your place boy?"

With that he kicked me in the stomach with such a force that I thought I was going to lose my senses. I saw Willard try to move but he then got a vicious kick to the head.

"Now, now keep calm you two because we got a lot to cover yet. We are of a mind to kill you boy but to do that slowly. And you white boy we want you to see it all and then we plan to beat you up pretty badly and leave you to sort it all out. We are sure that you will never forget this evening and that you will think twice before talking about equality of peoples.

See now, I reckon that is something to look forward to before the sun goes down. Of course nobody around here knows us so we can be off and clear gone before you can get any help."

I could see blood running down Willard's face and I was retching something awful as the bigger of the two began to bend down to show me a knife.

"Let's see what we can do with this for a little while shall we. I figure a little cut here and there and to let your pappy here see good and proper how we treat no good coloreds who overstep their place in this here world. Then I see a good sturdy tree bough over there – just right for slipping a rope over and then stringing you up just like we used to do."

The blast was so close that it shook the clearing and set my ears ringing so badly that I thought for a moment that the other man had shot me. But I felt no new pain and so I looked up. My antagonist was on his feet and facing Frank who was holding a double barrel shot gun. It was smoking from one side. The man who had kicked Willard was on his knees and I could see some blood coming through his pants at the knee.

"I was looking for my brother and his son when I just happened to see you two boys jump out of the bushes. I heard how cowardly men like you still hold lynching events and the like and how you threaten good honest people. But I never thought I would see you come over this way. That firing was meant to be a warning although I see that some of the shot caught you in the knee and I don't feel sorry about that. A second shot will get one of you and that's for sure. Whichever one of you does not get shot will feel the barrels of this gun across the head. We can do it that way or you can just sit down here until my hired hands join us with some rope for your wrists. Or maybe we will use that rope that I see you brought with you.

The Klan is pretty well done these days but our local marshal still has jurisdiction against them and there is no doubt that you two are trying to keep the old ways going. He will take care of you and that is for sure."

Frank's voice was strong and left no doubt as to whether he meant the threat. Even I believed him. The two men were confused and clearly of two minds. The one who had taken buck-shot to the knee stood up and started to lurch towards

Frank but the other pulled him back. By then I had picked up the knife and was on my feet. I heard Pete and Ben shouting as they ran towards us.

After those couple of minutes of confusion the two men turned away to look across the clearing and for a moment I thought they were going to make a run for it, but the reality of the situation caused them to stop and just sit down.

Later that evening the three of us sat at the old kitchen table. We had taken the two men down to the railway depot and made a full report. They would be on their way to Charles Town the next morning and we knew we would not hear from them again.

Frank had taken down some of his father's old whiskey, and we each had a glass or two. Frank had been keeping this for a rainy day and we all agreed that it had just rained heavily. The old whiskey was smooth and it helped calm us down, because the ride into town and then all of the reporting, and then the ride home, had left us as unsettled as ever. We just could not believe that the two men had come so far to make trouble. As for me, I kept feeling that rope around my neck. Willard took a good swig and coughed.

"Frank, when those men jumped us I was just telling Brownie that I was of the mind to be moving on again. Now I am absolutely sure. Others may come after them, and next time you might not be around to save us dear brother. In any event I was telling Brownie that people are never going to accept us. This is just a pipe dream Brownie. You can surely see that now.

I am not going to just run off again but I reckon that I am going to head back to New England. You and the boys can run this place just fine Frank. And Brownie you need to just get fully involved in that school. Stay there and make it your life for a year or so until people start to forget about you and me and how we are. Pretty soon you will just be that fine teacher up on the hill."

50.

December 29th 1941,
Dartford, West Virginia

—⦅∞⦆—

A nd that indeed is how it all worked out after the attack.
A few days later Willard took the train out of Harpers
and headed for New England. We promised to keep in touch
and so we did. Over the years we exchanged regular letters
and we had occasional visits together. I am so glad that I put
in the effort that summer to find Willard. I felt as though some
emptiness in my life had been filled and that even though we
were separated, we somehow grew closer each subsequent
year.

My father never married. When I asked him once if he ever
had feelings for a woman he simply said no, he did not. I do
believe that his love for my mother was very deep but I also
think that there was more to it than that.

Willard had been betrayed by circumstances, but his own
actions had brought more than enough trouble on to himself
and to those around him. I know that he felt a continual guilt

for all of that and I reckon that for him to have taken up with another woman would have just added to that. It might have tipped him over some edge. I don't really know, but I cannot say that he was ever a happy man.

The happiest I ever saw him was when my son was born. Willard came to visit us for a couple of weeks then and, like I said, he was very happy. When he held Adam for the first time he looked at me and he smiled.

'Well Brownie, this is what I never got to do with you. Thank you for all you have done.'

Willard was taken ill in 1912 and came back to Harpers Ferry and to the farm. Frank and I took care of him as best we could but Frank was not well himself so it was mostly me that tended to Willard. And that was as it should have been.

Just a month after returning to Harpers, Father died. It was very peaceful and I was with him at the end.

Sitting by his bedside for two days, my mind wondered back to the bedside of Roger Hart, and I thought about all that our little family had been through. I think that Willard's last thoughts must have been along similar lines as he began to talk about the old days. He rambled a little, but he did manage to keep events more or less in order. He spoke very clearly about Mother and how much he missed growing old with her. With that remark he looked at me and grinned and then closed his eyes. A few hours later he died.

Of course we buried Willard in the family plot at the farm.

That summer I visited Westhill and Momma's grave. The old metal cross was still there but as usual it was leaning over to one side. I was determined to fix that once and for all and so I filled a tin bucket with some concrete mix that I had brought and I set the cross into that. I buried the bucket so that just the cross was standing up out of the ground. Before the concrete set however, I stuck another cross into it. In my mind Willard and Beth, Momma and Dad, were now together side by side.

But let me go back to 1887 for a moment. I took Willard's advice, and for the best part of two years I pretty well lived for the school and classes. I did well if I say so myself. I never had any trouble with the town folk, or any more unwelcome out-of-town visitors. Back in the twenties the Klan flared up again but they never came my way. By then I was here in Dartford and teaching at the local school for colored children.

Frank ran the farm until the end of his days.

One by one my folk all passed away, and so that today there is just Adam and myself left.

So am I finished? The facts are down on paper and I do believe they are in more or less the right order. I just spent a couple of days reading it all. I feel very good that after all these years I have finally written it all down. Whether anyone will ever read these pages I do not know. Maybe my grandson will as even he does not know all of the details of our story.

But now I think back just a few weeks to what happened down at the school, because it was that event that started me down this path of writing.

It all began with an entry in the newspaper about a group of citizens who were going to meet late in the afternoon of that day at the school over in the next town to protest segregation. The reporter said that they were law abiding people who just wanted to peacefully make their views known. Well of course I immediately decided to join them.

Stan from the corner store picked me up that afternoon and we drove the few miles to the town in his big old Buick. We parked around the corner from the school and we walked to where a small group of people were standing. They had brought a little box and one of them was standing on it and speaking about what a good school they had for the colored children and how fortunate they were. He quickly turned that around though by pointing out that it could be so much better if both white and black children could attend together.

His point seemed to be that if the children grew up together in school without separation and if they could learn from each other's experience, then their education would be rounded and they would be all the better for it. They would all get the same education opportunity and maybe their generation could begin to dismantle all forms of segregation. I thought it was a good position and that it was well stated. I applauded and called out my support.

A few people on the other hand began to heckle and call him names. I had heard most of that stuff many times before but still I blanched when one man yelled out that the speaker was a no good nigger lover. How I hate that word and I can hardly type it now but that is what was said and that is that.

Grandma used to tell me that I should hate nothing but hate itself and I guess that is what I am doing now as I type these words.

Anyway, most of the crowd shouted him down while another man got up to speak. He was well into talking about how some black children had grown up into responsible citizens in spite of segregation when he spotted me. I did not know him but it seems he knew about me.

"Well now, I see Mr. Brownie Beauchamp standing over there. Ladies and gentlemen, some of you probably know about him but for those who don't let me introduce him now. Mr. Beauchamp is a retired school teacher and from what I have heard he was a very well respected teacher who struggled to attain that position. Mr. Beauchamp sir, would you care to come up and say a few words?"

I was, as some of my students would say, flabbergasted! That was the last thing I had expected or wanted that afternoon. I shook my head and said something about how I would rather not do that. But the people around me pushed me forward and before I knew it I was standing on that box. What could I say to add to their meeting? What difference could an old man like me make to their cause – as much as I believed in it?

I started out by correcting my sponsor by saying that I had not struggled but had been fortunate to have had the love and support of some good people. Somebody yelled out that he could not hear me and so I reached in and found my teacher's voice again and spoke up.

I told them just a little about Reverend Hart and how much he would have cheered them on today. I talked a little about some of my students and finally I wished them well. That was as much as I felt I should interfere. And then that man at the back yelled out again and called me a name that I am not about to spell out here.

The crowd went very quiet and I felt them staring at me waiting for some outburst. Instead I just stood down and walked back to stand next to Stan. He is a good friend and he put his arm on my shoulder and said something about how ignoring people like that was sometimes the best. I did not feel that way and I truly wanted to have it out with that loudmouthed man. Instead I stood quietly as the man went on more and more about how he felt.

There were some other speakers and then gradually the crowd began to walk off as the darkness began to fall. It was by then early evening. On the whole I thought that it had been a good meeting and I know that some local newspaper people in the crowd would report on it all the next day. I felt that meetings and reports like that could only help the cause.

As Stan and I reached the car the man who had been so offensive stepped out in front of us and took a swing at poor Stan calling him a 'n....r lover' You see how it is, that I can't bring myself to type the word a second time? Now Stan is a good few years younger than I am and he is in much better shape. So as he took the punch on the nose he quickly gave back and before I knew it they were on the ground punching each other as hard and as fast as they could.

I soon realized that the man had been drinking, and pretty soon Stan had the upper hand and was able to stand up. The other man lay still and I could see that he was pretty well out of things. I suddenly felt sorry for him and for some reason at that moment I saw something about my father in him. Looking around I saw that no one had seen the altercation.

I told Stan to put him in the back of the car and take us back to my room. Of course Stan protested but I made a case that if something happened to the man then somebody might tie us to him, and in any case if he came to more harm it would weigh heavy on my conscience. That was not altogether true I confess, as I felt a deep loathing for the man and all that he stood for. I wanted to teach him a lesson and another idea was forming in my mind.

So very reluctantly, Stan put the man on the back seat and he drove me home. No sound came from the back of the car during the ten minute drive. Clearly the alcohol and Stan's fists had put the man out completely.

We carried him into my room and put him in one of my two wooden kitchen chairs. He stirred a little.

I asked Stan to tie the man's wrists behind his back and to tie his ankles together and to the chair and to make the knots good and tight. I just wanted the opportunity to have a good talking to with a literally captive audience was the reason I gave.

Poor Stan did not know what to do. He knew me as well as anyone in town knew me, and he knew me to be a man of quiet and pretty well submissive ways. But I could see he had his doubts about all of this. In the end he agreed when I told him to just do it and then to stand at the back of the room while I had it out with this nasty man.

By the time Stan had tied the last knot, the man was pretty well recovered and he immediately started straining at the ropes. I pushed a very reluctant Stan back into a corner near the door and then came back and sat opposite my captive.

Oh boy was he mad.

"What the hell is going on? Just what are you up to old man?"

He began to grin as I shouted back at him.

"Just shut up and for once in your life listen. I want to tell you a few things and then show you something."

I was surprised that my voice was strong and did not betray the concern that I felt inside. I knew only too well that if he did break free then I would be in real trouble. In fact I swear that I could feel that rope around my neck from so many years ago! I hoped that Stan would respond quickly if that should happen.

But much of my past was running through my mind just then. I could see men like Franklin Smith in Big Lick and the two men who had jumped my father and me that evening and I felt for Roger Hart and Willard and my mother. These thoughts had not come to me so strongly for years until that night, and then they began to overpower me. I felt such a feeling of revulsion for the man in front of me. He was sobering up fast and began grinning at me again.

I got up and went to my corner cupboard and pulled down a box from the top shelf and brought it over to the table. I sat down again and opened the box. Slowly I pushed aside some old papers and took out a long hunting knife and held it pointing at my guest. He was no longer grinning. He became silent.

For some reason I told him about my Grandfather John and how he was murdered with a knife like this one for no reason other than the color of his skin. I told him what a quiet and gentle man my Grandfather John had been and how it was that he would not have hurt anyone. I added that that was how folk would have described me until tonight.

My opponent said nothing and was no longer straining against Stan's fine rope work. His chair was a good four feet away from the table and I could see that his feet had stopped resisting. I could also tell that the alcohol had not worn off completely and that he was both confused and scared.

I told him about my Grandfather Frank and how he had tried to reason with John Brown and how for his efforts he was murdered. And yes I used that word because that is how both Willard and I felt about it. And I kept turning the knife over and over in my hand still pointing at the man. I was leaning across the table holding the knife closer and closer to his face. I was embarrassed to see a dark stain appear around his groin area.

I told him about my father and about the evening when the two men tried to kill me. And then I stood up and came up to him with the knife and held it directly in front of his face.

"Take a good look at this knife my friend. See how sharp it still is. I picked this up from the man who intended to kill me and I have kept it all of these years. Now I plan to use it."

Stan began to move forward but I motioned him back.

I made my way to the table and sat down again.

"But first I just want you to understand how things are in this great country of ours. There is a huge injustice that you and your like keep going. It is an injustice that is hundreds of years old. It has caused misery to untold millions of people including close to a million men, women and children in the Civil War and after.

All you can think of is violence and hatred to keep the injustice going and I for one have had enough of it. In a sense I feel very sorry for you because you obviously believe that somehow violence will improve things."

I know that I must have sounded like Roger Hart speaking with Franklin Smith. That was deliberate I suppose. Anyway, I stood up again and walked over to the man and stood behind him. He could feel the point of the knife in his back and he was motionless. So was Stan now.

"My namesake John Brown tried his way to put an end to it all but he made the mistake of using violence. Do you know my friend what he wrote just before his execution? He wrote that the crimes of this guilty land will never be purged away but with blood. And I guess he really believed that."

I was aware that Stan had started to move towards me again and that he was obviously unsure about what to do. I motioned him to be quiet.

"You my friend, and others like you, could make a difference but you have chosen to follow those before you who felt hatred. How I wish and pray that you and your like would take a different path, but I fear that in your minds there is still much blood to be shed before anything changes."

And I pushed the knife as hard as I could down his back and into the rope at his wrist as I continued to talk.

"But not your blood, and certainly not shed at these hands of mine."

Stan caught on as to what my intention was and he was quickly at my side. We also cut through the rope at the man's feet before he grasped what was going on. Stan pulled him to his feet as I quietly spoke up.

"Get out of here now and think about what I have said."

We shoved him out of the door and watched him stagger as fast he could down the road. I would like to think that I made a difference in this world that night, perhaps with just that one man. I don't know of course.

After awhile Stan left me and it was then that I sat down at this table and thought about my life, and it was then, at that very moment, that I decided to write it all down.

Now it is finished and I will put this manuscript in the old box with the knife and the other stuff. My guess is that Adam will be the one who discovers it. And to you my grandson, I ask you to please read it all and then do whatever you can to help change things in your generation.

If life is a journey, then my trip has been pretty easy. That has not been true of my two families however. As I have written here, they struggled so much with things that were unnecessary and that could have been avoided.

But this is such a wonderful country.

No matter what John Brown said, the nation itself is not guilty. As I write this, we are at war again and I just have to look at other nations to see how much hatred is spread around outside of our country. It is just that too many people here have made mistakes and caused too much hurt for too many years.

And now my words to you Adam are that it is time to turn that all around.

As I see it, people do not have to agree on everything, but I just look for the day when we can accept each other and make allowances for each other whether it is a difference in color or religion or political views or whatever.

I say that acceptance and forgiveness and even love, are the only ways to purge the crimes of this nation or any other nation, and then move on. I am not intending to preach, and I realize that I must sound like dear Roger Hart, but I mean it Adam.

I remember on one occasion when the Reverend was talking with me and Grandma.

"Just look at the three of us Brownie. I am an old preacher man who is the grandson of a man who came over from England. Your Grandma is a wonderful lady who had been a slave, as had her family for generations. And then there is you my boy. Your mother had also been a slave and your father is a white man. Even with those differences, we love each other and I want you to see that we are more alike than we are different. Try to live that Brownie, please promise me that you will try to live it."

And so I have Adam. I have tried as best I could. And yet there is still so much to be done. Perhaps your generation will be able to work at this and do what all of us so far have failed to do. Anyway, that is my dream and that is my hope for you Adam, and for anyone else who may read my story.

CPSIA information can be obtained at www.ICGtesting.com
Printed in the USA
LVOW121220210413

330162LV00001B/338/P